Lara Adrian lives with her h[...] England, surrounded by centuries-old graveyards, hip urban comforts, and the endless inspiration of the broody Atlantic Ocean.

'Evocative, enticing, erotic . . . Enter Lara Adrian's vampire world and be enchanted.'
                J.R. Ward, *New York Times* bestselling author

'A thrilling blend of dark passion and heart-pounding action. Lara Adrian always delivers a keeper!'
                Gena Showalter, *New York Times* bestselling author

'Adrian's newest heroine has a backbone of pure steel. Rapid-pace adventures deliver equal quantities of supernatural thrills and high-impact passion. This is one of the best vampire series on the market!'
                Romantic Times (4.5 stars)

'*Veil of Midnight* is yet another great instalment . . . With hot romance, sexy (yet realistically flawed) alpha-male heroes and a fast-paced fantasy action plotline that just keeps getting better.'
                Lovevampires.com (5 stars)

'I am dying to see that happens next in this paranormal, yet contemporary and believable world. *Veil of Midnight* will enthral you and leave you breathless for more.'
                WildOnBooks.com (5 stars)

VEIL
OF
MIDNIGHT

LARA ADRIAN

ROBINSON

Constable & Robinson Ltd
3 The Lanchesters
162 Fulham Palace Road
London W6 9ER
www.constablerobinson.com

First published in the US in 2008 by Bantam Dell,
1745 Broadway, New York, NY 10019

This edition published by Robinson,
an imprint of Constable & Robinson Ltd, 2010

A copy of the British Library Cataloguing in Publication
Data is available from the British Library.

ISBN: 978-1-84901-109-9

Printed and bound in the EU.

For Lindsey,
steel magnolia with a heart of solid gold.
This one is for you, in hope of better, brighter days.

ACKNOWLEDGMENTS

It bears repeating (again and again) that I am very grateful to so many for the privilege of being able to wake up each day and do something I genuinely love. A debt of thanks to: my fabulous agent, Karen Solem, and my wonderful editor, Shauna Summers, for getting me into print; to my awesome readers for keeping me there; to the booksellers, librarians, and bloggers who've so generously spread the word about my books; to my friends and family for all the love.

And to my husband, cherished friend, beloved partner, keeper of my heart. Thank you for every moment of this life together.

⇥ CHAPTER ONE ⇤

On stage in the cavernous jazz club below Montreal's street level, a crimson-lipped singer drawled into the microphone about the cruelty of love. Although her sultry voice was pleasant enough, the lyrics about blood and pain and pleasure clearly heartfelt, Nikolai wasn't listening. He wondered if she knew – if any of the dozens of humans packed into the intimate club knew – that they were sharing breathing space with vampires.

The two young females sucking down pink martinis in the dark corner banquette sure as hell didn't know it.

They were sandwiched between four such individuals, a group of slick, leather-clad males who were chatting them up – without much success – and trying to act like their blood-thirsty eyes hadn't been permanently fixed on the women's jugulars for the past fifteen minutes straight. Even though it was clear that the vampires were negotiating hard to get the humans out of the club with them, they weren't making much progress with their prospective blood Hosts.

Nikolai scoffed under his breath.

Amateurs.

He paid for the beer he'd left untouched on the bar and headed at an easy stroll toward the corner table. As he approached, he watched the two human females scoot out of the booth on unsteady legs. Giggling, they stumbled for the restrooms together, disappearing down a dim, crowded hallway off the main room.

Nikolai sat down at the table in a negligent sprawl.

'Evening, ladies.'

The four vampires stared at him in silence, instantly recognizing their own kind. Niko lifted one of the tall, lipstick-stained martini glasses to his nose and sniffed at the dregs of the fruity concoction. He winced, pushing the offending drink aside.

'Humans,' he drawled in a low voice. 'How can they stomach that shit?'

A wary silence fell over the table as Nikolai's glance traveled among the obviously young, obviously civilian Breed males. The largest of the four cleared his throat as he looked at Niko, his instincts no doubt picking up on the fact that Niko wasn't local, and he was a far cry from civilized.

The youth adopted something he probably thought was a hardass look and jerked his soul-patched chin toward the restroom corridor. 'We saw them first,' he murmured. 'The women. We saw them first.' He cleared his throat again, like he was waiting for his trio of wingmen to back him up. None did. 'We got here first, man. When the females come back to the table, they're gonna be leaving with us.'

Nikolai chuckled at the young male's shaky attempt to stake his territory. 'You really think there'd be any contest if I was here to poach your game? Relax. I'm not interested in that. I'm looking for information.'

He'd been through a similar song-and-dance twice already tonight at other clubs, seeking out the places where members of the Breed tended to gather and hunt for blood, looking for someone who could point him toward a vampire elder named Sergei Yakut.

It wasn't easy finding someone who didn't want to be found, especially a secretive, nomadic individual like Yakut. He was in Montreal, that much Nikolai was sure of. He'd spoken to the reclusive vampire by phone as recently as a couple of weeks earlier, when he'd tracked Yakut down to inform him of a threat that seemed aimed at the Breed's most powerful, rarest members – the twenty or so individuals still in existence who were born of the first generation.

Someone was targeting Gen Ones for extinction. Several had been slain within the past month, and for Niko and his brothers in arms back in Boston – a small cadre of highly trained, highly lethal warriors known as the Order – the business of rooting out and shutting down the elusive Gen One assassins was mission critical. For that, the Order had decided to contact all of the known Gen Ones remaining in the Breed population and enlist their cooperation.

Sergei Yakut had been less than enthusiastic to get involved. He feared no one, and he had his own personal clan to protect him. He'd declined the Order's invitation to come to Boston and talk, so Nikolai had been dispatched to Montreal to persuade him. Once Yakut was made aware of the scope of the current threat – the stunning truth of what the Order and all of the Breed were now up against – Nikolai was certain the Gen One would be willing to come on board.

First he had to find the cagey son of a bitch.

So far his inquiries around the city had turned up nothing. Patience wasn't exactly his strong suit, but he had all night, and he'd keep searching. Sooner or later, someone might give him the answer he was looking for. And if he kept coming up dry, maybe if he asked enough questions, Sergei Yakut would come looking for him instead.

'I need to find someone,' Nikolai told the four Breed youths. 'A vampire out of Russia. Siberia, to be exact.'

'That where you're from?' asked the soul-patched mouthpiece of the group. He'd evidently picked up on the slight tinge of an accent that Nikolai hadn't lost in the long years he'd been living in the States with the Order.

Niko let his glacial blue eyes speak to his own origins. 'Do you know this individual?'

'No, man. I don't know him.'

Two other heads shook in immediate denial, but the last of the four youths, the sullen one who was slouched low in the booth, shot an anxious look up at Nikolai from across the table.

Niko caught that telling gaze and held it. 'What about you? Any idea who I'm talking about?'

At first, he didn't think the vampire was going to answer. Hooded eyes held his in silence, then, finally, the kid lifted one shoulder in a shrug and exhaled a curse.

'Sergei Yakut,' he murmured.

The name was hardly audible, but Nikolai heard it. And from the periphery of his vision, he noticed that an ebony-haired woman seated at the bar nearby heard it too. He could tell she had from the sudden rigidity of her spine beneath her long-sleeved black top and from the way her head snapped briefly to the side as though pulled there by the power of that name alone.

'You know him?' Nikolai asked the Breed male, while keeping the brunette at the bar well within his sights.

'I know *of* him, that's all. He doesn't live in the Darkhavens,' said the youth, referring to the secured communities that housed most of the Breed civilian populations throughout North America and Europe. 'Dude's one nasty mofo from what I've heard.'

Yeah, he was, Nikolai acknowledged inwardly. 'Any idea where I might find him?'

'No.'

'You sure about that?' Niko asked, watching as the woman at the bar slid off her stool and prepared to leave. She still had more than half a cocktail in her glass, but at the mere mention of Yakut's name, she seemed suddenly in a big hurry to get out of the place.

The Breed youth shook his head. 'I don't know where to find the dude. Don't know why anyone would willingly look for him either, unless you got some kind of death wish.'

Nikolai glanced over his shoulder as the tall brunette started edging her way through the crowd gathered near the bar. On impulse, she turned to look at him then, her jade-green gaze piercing beneath the fringe of dark lashes and the glossy swing of her sleek, chin-length bob. There was a note of fear in her eyes as she stared back at him, a naked fear she didn't even attempt to hide.

'I'll be damned,' Niko muttered.

She knew something about Sergei Yakut.

Something more than just a passing knowledge, he was guessing. That startled, panicked look as she turned and broke for an escape said it all.

Nikolai took off after her. He weaved through the thicket of humans filling the club, his eyes trained on the silky black hair of his quarry. The female was quick, as fleet and agile as a gazelle, her dark clothes and hair letting her practically disappear into her surroundings.

But Niko was Breed, and there was no human in existence who could outrun one of his kind. She ducked out the club door and made a fast right onto the street outside. Nikolai followed. She must have sensed him hard on her heels because she pivoted her head around to gauge his pursuit and those pale green eyes locked on to him like lasers.

She ran faster now, turning the corner at the end of the block. Not two seconds later, Niko was there too. He grinned as he caught sight of her a few yards ahead of him. The alley she'd entered between two tall brick buildings was narrow and dark – a dead end sealed off by a dented metal Dumpster and a chain-link fence that climbed some ten feet up from the ground.

The woman spun around on the spiked heels of her black

boots, panting hard, eyes trained on him, watching his every move.

Nikolai took a few steps into the lightless alley, then paused, his hands held benevolently out to his sides. 'It's okay,' he told her. 'No need to run. I just want to talk to you.'

She stared in silence.

'I want to ask you about Sergei Yakut.'

She swallowed visibly, her smooth white throat flexing.

'You know him, don't you.'

The edge of her mouth quirked only a fraction, but enough to tell him that he was correct – she was familiar with the reclusive Gen One. Whether she could lead Niko to him was another matter. Right now, she was his best, possibly his only, hope.

'Tell me where he is. I need to find him.'

At her sides, her hands balled into fists. Her feet were braced slightly apart as if she were prepared to bolt. Niko saw her glance subtly toward a battered door to her left.

She lunged for it.

Niko hissed a curse and flew after her with all the speed he possessed. By the time she'd thrown the door open on its groaning hinges, Nikolai was standing in front of her at the threshold, blocking her path into the darkness on the other side. He chuckled at the ease of it.

'I said there's no need to run,' he said, shrugging lightly as she backed a step away from him. He let the door fall closed behind him as he followed her slow retreat into the alley.

Jesus, she was breathtaking. He'd only gotten a glimpse of her in the club, but now, standing just a couple of feet from her, he realized that she was absolutely stunning. Tall and lean, willowy beneath her fitted black clothing, with flawless milk-white skin and luminous almond-shaped eyes. Her heart-shaped face was a mesmerizing combination of strength and softness, her beauty equal parts light and dark. Nikolai knew he was gaping, but damn if he could help it.

'Talk to me,' he said. 'Tell me your name.'

He reached for her, an easy, nonthreatening move of his hand. He sensed the jolt of adrenaline that shot into her blood-stream – he could smell the citrusy tang of it in the air, in fact – but he didn't see the roundhouse kick coming at him until he took the sharp heel of her boot squarely in his chest.

Goddamn.

He rocked back, more surprised than unfooted.

It was all the break she needed. The woman leapt for the door again, this time managing to disappear into the dark-ened building before Niko could wheel around and stop her. He gave chase, thundering in behind her.

The place was empty, just a lot of naked concrete beneath his feet, bare bricks and exposed rafters all around him. Some fleeting sense of foreboding prickled at the back of his neck as he raced deeper into the darkness, but the bulk of his atten-tion was focused on the female standing in the center of the vacant space. She stared him down as he approached, every muscle in her slim body seeming tensed for attack.

Nikolai held that sharp stare as he drew up in front of her. 'I'm not going to hurt you.'

'I know.' She smiled, just a slight curve of her lips. 'You won't get that chance.'

Her voice was velvety smooth, but the glint in her eyes took on a cold edge. Without warning, Niko felt a sudden, shat-tering tightness in his head. A high-frequency sound cranked up in his ears, louder than he could bear. Then louder still. He felt his legs give out beneath him. He dropped to his knees, his vision swimming while his head felt on the verge of exploding.

Distantly, he registered the sound of booted feet coming toward him – several pairs, belonging to sizable males, vampires all of them. Muted voices buzzed above him as he suffered out the sudden, debilitating assault on his mind.

It was a trap.

The bitch had led him there deliberately, knowing he'd follow her.

'Enough, Renata,' said one of the Breed males who'd entered the room. 'You can release him now.'

Some of the pain in Nikolai's head subsided with the command. He glanced up in time to see the beautiful face of his attacker staring down at him where he lay near her feet.

'Strip him of his weapons,' she said to her companions. 'We need to get him out of here before his strength returns.'

Nikolai sputtered a few ripe curses at her, but his voice strangled in his throat, and she was already walking away, the thin spikes of her heels clicking over the field of cold concrete underneath him.

❧ CHAPTER TWO ❧

Renata couldn't get out of the warehouse fast enough. Her stomach roiled. A cold sweat popped out along her forehead and down the back of her neck. She craved the fresh night air like her last breath, but she kept her stride even and strong. Her fisted hands held rigidly at her sides were the only outward indicator that she was anything but calm and collected.

It was always like this for her – the aftermath of using her mind's crippling power.

Outside now, alone in the alley, she gulped in a few quick mouthfuls of air. The rush of oxygen cooled her burning throat, but it was all she could do not to double over from the rising pain that was coursing like a river of fire through her limbs and into the center of her being.

'Damn it,' she muttered into the empty darkness, rocking a bit on her tall heels. Taking a few more deep breaths, she stared at the black pavement under her feet and focused simply on holding herself together.

Behind her came the swift, heavy shuffle of booted feet from out of the warehouse. The sound drew her head up sharply. Forced a look of cool apathy over the hot tightness in her face.

'Careful with him,' she said, glancing at the slack bulk of the big, nearly unconscious male she'd disabled, and who was now being carried like felled game by the four guards working with her. 'Where are his weapons?'

'Catch.'

A black leather duffel bag came sailing at her with barely a warning, heaved toward her by Alexei, the appointed leader of tonight's detail. She didn't miss the smirk on his lean face as the heavy duffel full of metal crashed into her chest. The impact felt like the pounding of a thousand nails into her sensitive skin and muscles, but she caught the bag and swung the long strap up over her shoulder without so much as a grunt of discomfort.

But Lex knew. He knew her weakness, and he never let her forget it.

Unlike her, Alexei and her other companions were vampires – Breed, all of them. As was their captive, Renata had no doubt. She'd sensed as much when she'd first seen him in the club, a suspicion confirmed by the simple fact that she was able to take him down with her mind. Her pyschic ability was formidable, but not without its limitations. It only worked on the Breed; the more simplistic human brain cells were unaffected by the high-frequency blast she was able to mentally project with little more than a moment's concentration.

She herself was human, if born slightly different from basic *Homo sapiens* stock. To Lex and his kind, she was known as a Breedmate, one of a small number of human females born with unique extrasensory skills and the even rarer capability to successfully reproduce with those of the Breed. For women like Renata, ingesting Breed blood provided even greater strength. Longevity too. A Breedmate could live for some long centuries with regular feedings from a vampire's nourishing veins.

Until two years ago, Renata had no idea why she was different from everyone else she knew, or where she might belong. Crossing paths with Sergei Yakut had quickly brought her up to speed. He was the reason that she and Lex and the others were on guard tonight, prowling the city and looking for the individual who'd been asking around for the reclusive Yakut.

The Breed male Renata found at the jazz club had been so careless with his inquiries all night, she had to wonder if he was trying to provoke Sergei Yakut into coming to him. If so, the guy was either an idiot or suicidal, or some combination of both. She'd have her answer to that question soon enough.

Renata took her cell phone out of her pocket, flipped it open, and speed-dialed the first number on file. 'Subject retrieved,' she announced when the call connected. She gave their location, then snapped the phone closed and put it away. Glancing over to where Alexei and the other guards had paused with their limp captive, she said, 'The car's on the way. Should be here in about two minutes.'

'Drop this sack of shit,' Lex ordered his men. They all released their grasps on the Breed male, and his body hit the asphalt with a jarring thud. Hands on his hips, fists framing his holstered pistol and a large hunting knife sheathed on his belt, Lex peered down into the unconscious face of the vampire at his feet. He pulled in a sharp, disapproving breath, then spat, narrowly missing the blade-sharp cheek below. The foamy white glob of his saliva landed with a wet *splat* on the dark pavement not an inch away from the man's blond head.

When Alexei glanced up again, there was a hard glint in his dark eyes. 'Maybe we should kill him.'

One of the other guards chuckled, but Renata knew that Lex wasn't joking. 'Sergei said to bring him in.'

Alexei scoffed. 'And give his enemies another chance to take his head?'

'We don't know that this man had anything to do with the attack.'

'Can we be certain he didn't?' Alexei turned to stare

unblinkingly at Renata. 'From now on, I trust no one. I would think you'd be as unlikely to risk his safety as I am.'

'I follow orders,' she replied. 'Sergei said to find whoever was in town asking about him and bring him in for questioning. That's what I intend to do.'

Lex's eyes narrowed under the severe brown slashes of his brows. 'Fine,' he said, his voice too calm, too level. 'You're right, Renata. We have our orders. We'll bring him in, like you say. But what are we going to do while we wait out here for pickup?'

Renata stared at him, wondering where he was heading now. Lex strolled around to the side of the unconscious Breed male and gave an experimental jab of his boot into the unprotected ribs. There was no reaction at all. Only the soft rise and fall of the male's chest as he breathed.

Alexei peeled his lips back and grinned, jerking his chin toward the other men. 'My boots are dirty. Maybe this useless baggage will clean them off while we wait, ah?'

At the encouraging chortles of his companions, Lex lifted one of his feet and let it hover over the unresponsive face of their captive.

'Lex—' Renata began, knowing he would ignore her if she tried to persuade him to stop. But it was at that precise moment that she noticed something strange about the blond male lying on the ground. His breathing was steady and shallow, his limbs unmoving, but his face . . . he was holding himself too still, even if he truly was unconscious. He wasn't.

In a split second of clarity, Renata realized without a shred of doubt that he was very much awake. Very much aware of everything that was happening.

Oh, Christ.

Alexei chuckled now, lowering his leg as he started to bring the thick sole of his boot down onto the man's face.

'Lex, wait! He's not—'

Nothing she could have said would have changed the resulting explosion of chaos.

Lex was still in motion as the man brought his hands up and caught him at the ankle. He clamped down and twisted hard, sending Lex flying off him and howling in agony on the ground nearby. Not a second passed before the man rolled up onto his feet, fluid and strong, like nothing Renata had ever seen in a fighter before.

And holy shit – he had Lex's pistol.

Renata dropped the cumbersome duffel and grappled for her own gun, a .45 concealed in a holster at her back. Her fingers were still sluggish from her earlier mental exertion, and one of the other guards responded before she could free her weapon. He squeezed off a hasty round, missing his target by half a foot.

And faster than any of them could track him, the former captive returned fire, putting a bullet squarely in the front of the guard's skull. One of Sergei Yakut's hand-picked, longest-serving bodyguards went down on the pavement in a lifeless heap.

Oh, Jesus, Renata thought in mounting worry as the situation rapidly headed south. Could Alexei have been right? Was this Breed male the same assassin who had tried to strike here before?

'Who's next?' he asked, one foot planted on the center of Lex's spine while he coolly swung the pistol from the other two guards to Renata. 'What, no takers now?'

'Kill this son of a bitch!' Lex roared, writhing like a trapped bug under the heavy heel that held him down. His cheek mashed against the pavement, fangs emerging in his rage, Lex threw a slivered glare at Renata and his men. 'Blow his head off, goddamn it!'

Before the command was totally out of Alexei's mouth, he was yanked up onto his feet. He screamed as his weight shifted to his injured ankle, but it was the sudden presence of his own pistol nuzzled behind his ear that really made his amber eyes go wild with panic. His captor, on the other hand, was as calm and steady as could be.

Oh, sweet Mother Mary.

Just who the hell were they dealing with?

'You heard him,' Lex's captor said. His voice was low and unrushed, his gaze piercing even in the dark. He stared straight at Renata. 'Bring it on, if any of you are man enough. Then again, if you'd rather not see his brain splattered all over this building wall, then I suggest you drop your weapons. Down on the pavement, nice and easy.'

Beside her in the alley, Renata registered the low grunts and snuffles of transformed Breed males. Individually, any one of the vampires was physically far stronger than she was; as a pair, they might be stronger than Lex's attacker, although neither of them seemed willing to find out. A soft *clack* of metal sounded as a weapon was placed carefully on the asphalt. That left only one guard on backup with her. A second later, he surrendered his gun too. Both vampires retreated a couple of slow paces, surrendering in wary silence.

And now Renata stood alone against this unexpected threat.

He gave her a half smile in acknowledgment, baring his teeth and the tips of his emerging fangs. He was angry; those lengthening canines were evidence of that. As was the amber light that was beginning to fill his eyes as they too began to transform with his Breed features. His smile broadened, twin dimples appearing beneath his razor-sharp cheekbones. 'Looks like it's down to you and me, sweetheart. I'm not going to ask any more politely the longer you make me wait. Put your fucking gun down or I'll waste him.'

Renata quickly considered her options – what few she had at the moment. Her body was still as raw as an exposed nerve, the aftershocks of her mental exertion still battering her, beating her down. She could attempt another assault on his mind, but she knew she was operating on fumes. Even if she hit him with all she had, she wouldn't be able to take him down again, and once she was spent to that degree, she would be of no use to anyone.

Her only other option was an equally large risk. Ordinarily she was a crack shot, reflex fast and sniper accurate, but she couldn't count on either skill when it would take a great deal of her focus just to command her limbs and fingers to work. No matter what she did, right now it seemed pretty slim odds that Alexei might come out of this in one piece. Hell, the chances of her or anyone else walking away from this situation were looking nil.

This Breed male was holding all the cards, and the look in his eyes as he watched, waited for her to decide her fate, seemed to say that he was very comfortable in his power position. He had Renata, Lex, and the rest of them right where he wanted them.

But she'd be damned if she'd go down without a fight.

Renata inhaled to gather her resolve, then she brought her gun around and leveled it on him. Her arms screamed with the effort it took to hold them out and steady, but she sucked up the pain, pushed it aside.

She flipped off the gun's safety. 'Release him. Now.'

The muzzle of Lex's weapon remained jammed up tight behind his ear. 'You don't actually think we're negotiating here, do you? Drop. Your. Weapon.'

Renata had a clean shot, but so did he. And he had the added benefit of superhuman speed. He might be able to dodge her bullet since he'd easily see it coming. There was a fraction of a second delay between chambering rounds, even at her best time. That meant ample opportunity for him to open fire as well, whether he chose to shoot Lex first or after he took her out. In another second, they might all be eating lead. This man was Breed; with his accelerated metabolism and healing power, he stood a decent chance of surviving getting shot, but her? She was staring at certain death.

'You got a problem with me specifically, or is it him you really want to see dead tonight? Maybe you just hate anything with a dick. That it?'

Although he kept his aim locked, his tone was light, as if he were only toying with her. Not taking her seriously at all. The arrogant prick. She didn't answer, just cocked the pistol's hammer back and rested her index finger lightly on the trigger.

'Let him go. We don't want any trouble from you.'

'Too late for that, don't you think? All you're looking at is trouble now.'

Renata didn't flinch. She didn't dare so much as blink for fear that this man would sense it as weakness and decide to act.

Lex was shaking now, sweat pouring down his face. 'Renata,' he gasped, but whether he wanted to tell her to stand down or make her best move, she wasn't sure. 'Renata . . . for fuck's sake . . .'

She kept a steady aim on Alexei's captor, her elbows locked, both hands gripped on her gun. A light summer breeze kicked up, and the soft gust of air raked over her hypersensitive skin like jagged shards of glass. In the distance she could hear the pop of fireworks from the finale of the weekend's festival, the muted explosions vibrating like thunder in her aching bones. Traffic buzzed and braked on the street outside the alley, vehicle engines throwing off a sickening melange of exhaust fumes, heated rubber, and burning oil.

'How long do you want to drag this out, sweetheart? Because I gotta tell you, patience isn't one of my virtues.' His tone was casual, but the threat couldn't have been more dire. He brought the pistol's hammer back, prepared to bring the night to its bloody end. 'Give me one good reason why I shouldn't fill this asshole's brain with lead.'

'Because he is my son.' The low male voice came from halfway up the darkened alley. The words were devoid of emotion but ominous in their cadence and thickly accented with the cold rasp of Sergei Yakut's Siberian homeland.

CHAPTER THREE

Nikolai swung his head around and watched Sergei Yakut approach in the narrow alleyway. The Gen One vampire strode ahead of two anxious-looking bodyguards, his stark, unblinking gaze moving casually from Niko to the Breed male still being held at gunpoint. With a nod of acknowledgment, Niko clicked the pistol's safety back into place and slowly lowered the weapon. As soon as he loosened his grasp, Yakut's son threw him off with a growled curse and moved himself well out of reach.

'Insolent bastard,' he snarled, all venom and fury now that he was standing some safe distance away. 'I told Renata this cur was a threat, but she wouldn't listen. Let me kill him for you, Father. Let me give him pain.'

Yakut ignored both his son's plea and his presence, instead striding in silence up to where Nikolai stood waiting.

'Sergei Yakut,' Niko said, turning the disarmed gun around and offering it to him in a gesture of peace. 'Hell of a welcome wagon you've got here. My apologies for taking one of your men. He left me no choice.'

Yakut merely grunted as he took the pistol and handed it off to the guard standing nearest to him. Dressed in a cotton gauze tunic and worn leather pants that looked more like weathered hide, his light brown hair and beard wild and over-grown, Sergei Yakut had the look of a shrewd feudal warlord, centuries out of his time.

Then again, despite his unlined face and tall, muscular build, which aged him in the vicinity of his early forties at most, only the Breed male's thick pattern of swirling, interlocking *dermaglyphs* tracking down his bared forearms gave any indication that Yakut was an elder member of the Breed. As a Gen One, he could be a thousand years old or more.

'Warrior,' Yakut said darkly, his stare unwavering, twin lasers locked on target. 'I told you not to come. You and the rest of the Order are wasting your time.'

In his peripheral vision, Niko caught the exchanged looks of surprise that traveled between Yakut's son and the rest of his guards. The female especially – Renata, she was called – seemed completely taken aback to hear that he was a warrior, one of the Order. Yet as quickly as the surprise registered in her gaze, it vanished, gone as though she had forced all emotion from her features. She was placid calm now, cold even, as she stood a few feet behind Sergei Yakut and watched, her weapon still in hand, her stance tentative and ready for his any command.

'We need your help,' Nikolai said to Yakut. 'And based on what's been going down near us in Boston and elsewhere within the Breed population, you're going to need our help too. The danger is very real. It's lethal. Your life is at risk, even now.'

'What would you know about that?' Yakut's son scowled at Niko in accusation. 'How the fuck can you know anything about that? We've told no one about the attack last week—'

'Alexei.' The sound of his name on his sire's lips shut the younger Yakut up as if a hand had been clamped over his mouth. 'You do not speak for me, boy. Make yourself useful,' he said, gesturing toward the vampire Nikolai had shot dead. 'Take Urien up to the warehouse roof and leave him there for the sun. Then sweep this alleyway clean of evidence.'

Alexei glared for a second, as if the task were beneath him

but he didn't quite have the guts to say so. 'You heard my father,' he snapped to the other guards standing around idle with him. 'What are you all waiting for? Let's get rid of this worthless pile of rubbish.'

When they started to move off at Alexei's bidding, Yakut glanced toward the female. 'Not you, Renata. You can drive me back to the house. I am finished here.'

The message to Niko was clear: He was uninvited, unwelcome to stay in Yakut's domain. And, as of now, summarily dismissed.

Probably the smartest thing to do would be to check in with Lucan and the rest of the Order, tell them that he had given it his best shot with Sergei Yakut but came up empty, then leave Montreal before Yakut decided to hand him his balls on his way out. The short-tempered Gen One had done worse to others for far lesser sins.

Yeah, packing it in and heading out was definitely the wisest course of action at this point. Except Nikolai wasn't accustomed to taking no for an answer, and the situation facing both the Order and the whole of the Breed – hell, humankind as well – was not going away anytime soon. It was growing more volatile, more distastrous with every passing second.

And then there was Alexei's careless blurt about a recent attack . . .

'What happened here last week?' Nikolai asked, once it was just Yakut, Renata, and himself in the dark alley. He knew the answer but posed the question anyway. 'Someone tried to assassinate you . . . just as I warned would happen, isn't that right?'

The aged Breed male swung a glower on Niko, his shrewd eyes flinty. Niko held that challenging stare, seeing a long-lived, arrogant fool who believed himself beyond the reach of death, even though it had likely been knocking on his door only a few days ago.

'There was an attempt, yes.' Yakut's lip curled in a mild sneer, one thick shoulder lifting in a shrug. 'But I survived – just as I assured you I would. Go home, warrior. Fight the Order's battles back in Boston. Leave me to look after my own.'

He jerked his chin at Renata, and the wordless command put her in motion. As her long legs carried her out of earshot up the alleyway, Yakut drawled, 'My thanks for the warning. If this assassin is idiot enough to strike again, I will be ready for him.'

'He *will* strike again,' Niko replied with total certainty. 'This thing is worse than we first suspected. Two more Gen Ones have been killed since you and I last spoke. That brings the count to five now – out of less than twenty of your generation still in existence. Five of the oldest, most powerful members of the Breed nation, all dead in the space of a month. Each one apparently targeted and taken out by expert means. Someone wants all of you dead, and he has a plan already in play to make it happen.'

Yakut seemed to consider that, but only for a moment. Without another word, he pivoted and began stalking away.

'There is more,' Niko added grimly. 'Something I wasn't able to tell you when we spoke on the phone a couple of weeks ago. Something the Order discovered hidden in a mountain cave in the Czech Republic.'

As the elder vampire continued to ignore him, Niko exhaled a low curse.

'It was a hibernation chamber, a very old one. A crypt where one of the most powerful of our kind had been tucked away in secret for centuries. The chamber had been made to protect an Ancient.'

Finally Niko had his attention.

Yakut's steps slowed, then stopped altogether. 'The Ancients were all killed in the great war within the Breed,' he said, reciting the history that had until very recently been accepted by all the Breed as irrefutable fact.

Nikolai knew the story of the uprising as well as anyone else of his kind. Of the eight savage otherworlders who had fathered the first generation of the vampire race on Earth, none survived the battle with the small group of Gen One warriors who'd declared war against their own fathers for the protection of both Breed and humankind alike. Those courageous few warriors had been led by Lucan, who to this day retained his role as leader of what was to become the Order.

Yakut slowly turned to face Nikolai. 'All of the Ancients have been dead for some seven hundred years. My own sire was put to the sword back then – and rightly so. If he and his alien brethren had been left unchecked, they would have destroyed all life on this planet in their insatiable Bloodlust.'

Niko nodded grimly. 'But there was someone who disagreed with the edict that the Ancients should be destroyed: Dragos. The Order has uncovered proof that instead of taking out the creature who fathered him, Dragos instead helped to hide him. He made a sanctuary for the creature in a remote area of the Bohemian Mountains.'

'And the Order knows this to be true?'

'We found the chamber and saw the crypt for ourselves. Unfortunately, it was empty by the time we got there.'

Yakut grunted, considering. 'And what about Dragos?'

'He is dead – killed in the old war – but his line lives on. So does his treachery. We believe it was Dragos's son who located the chamber before we did and freed the Ancient from his sleep. We also suspect Dragos's son is the one behind the recent assassinations among the nation's Gen Ones.'

'To what gain?' Yakut asked, arms crossed over his chest.

'That's what we intend to find out. We've got some good intel on him, but it's not enough. He's gone to ground, and it's going to be harder than hell to flush him out. But we'll get him. In the meantime, we can't afford to let him make any progress with whatever plans he's got in motion. That's why the Order is reaching out to you and the rest of the Gen Ones. Anything you might hear, anything you may have seen—'

'There was a witness,' Yakut said, interrupting Niko with the abrupt admission. 'A young girl, a member of my household. She was there. She saw the individual who attacked me last week. In fact, she startled the bastard enough that I was able to break away and escape.'

Nikolai's head was spinning with this unexpected news. He doubted very much that a child could scare off a seasoned, skilled assassin, but he was interested enough to hear more. 'I need to talk to this girl.'

Yakut nodded vaguely, lips pressed flat as he glanced up at the dark sky overhead. 'It will be dawn in a few hours. You can wait out the daylight at my home. Ask your questions, do your business for the Order. Then, tomorrow night, you leave.'

As far as cooperation went, it wasn't much. But it was more than he'd had even a few minutes ago from the cocky Gen One vampire.

'Fair enough,' Niko replied, as he fell in beside Sergei Yakut and walked with him to the waiting black sedan that idled at the curb.

⇥ CHAPTER FOUR ⇤

Renata had no idea what the blond stranger might have said to persuade Sergei Yakut into inviting the outsider home to his private compound north of the city. In the two years since Renata had been introduced to life as a member of Yakut's personal guard, no one outside the vampire's small circle of servants and private security detail had ever been permitted on the secluded woodland grounds of the lodge.

Suspicious by nature and reclusive, cruel to the point of tyranny, Sergei Yakut's world was one of scrutiny and mistrust. God help you if you crossed him in any way, for when the fist of his rage came crashing down, it came down like an anvil. Sergei Yakut had few friends and even fewer enemies; neither seemed to survive long in the chill of his shadow.

Renata had come to know the male she served well enough to sense that he was not exactly amenable to the notion of uninvited company, but the fact that he hadn't killed this inter-loper – this warrior, as he'd referred to him back in the alleyway – seemed to indicate at least some small degree of respect. If not for the warrior himself, then for the group he belonged to, the Order.

As she swung the armored, custom Mercedes up to the entrance of the rough-timbered main house at the end of the long drive, Renata couldn't resist flicking a glance in the rearview mirror to the two vampires seated in silence behind her.

Ice-blue eyes met her gaze in the glass. He didn't blink away, not even as the seconds stretched beyond curiosity to that of bald challenge. He was pissed off, his ego no doubt still bruised by the fact that she had duped him in the alley and led him into a trap. Renata feigned polite ignorance as she broke the heavy hold of his stare and brought the car to a halt in front of the lodge.

One of the Breed males on guard at the entrance came down the wide plank steps to open the back door of the sedan. Behind him a few paces stood another guard, this one holding a pair of leashed Russian wolfhounds. Their bared teeth gnashing, the big watchdogs barked and growled like savages until the moment Sergei Yakut came out of the car. The animals were as well trained as the rest of the vampire's household: one look from their master and they fell into an instant, submissive silence, massive heads held low as he and the warrior stalked into the house.

The guard standing near the car closed the open back door and shot a questioning glance at Renata through the tinted glass of the window.

Who the hell is that? was the obvious look on his face, but before he could motion for her to roll down the window so he could ask it, she put the sedan into gear and tapped the gas.

As she eased the car off the gravel drive and took it around to the garage in back of the lodge, the pain and tension she'd been feeling earlier began to creep back into her body. She was tired from the whole confrontation tonight, her limbs and mind equally wrung out. All she wanted was her bed and a long, hot soak in the tub. She really didn't care which came first.

Renata had her own small quarters in the lodge, a luxury that Yakut did not afford any of the males who served him. Even Alexei bunked with the other guards in common quarters, sleeping on fur pallets spread out on the floor, like a garrison straight out of the Middle Ages. Renata's room was only fractionally better than that: a narrow space big enough only for the twin bed, nightstand, and the trunk that held her meager clothing. A bathroom with a footed tub was located down the hall and shared with the only other female in Sergei Yakut's charge.

The amenities were rustic at best, as was the rest of the hundred-year-old log compound, and the furnishings were sparse. Not to mention a bit revolting.

Although Yakut once told her he and his household had only been living there for the past decade, the old hunting lodge was filled with what seemed to be half a century's worth of animal pelts, stuffed game, and mounted antlers. She assumed the taxidermy decor had belonged to the previous owner, but Yakut didn't seem to mind sharing his home with all the morbidity. In fact, he seemed to relish the primitive-ness of the place. Renata knew the Siberian vampire was older than he appeared – much, much older, as those of his kind often were. But it didn't take a lot to imagine him clothed in skins and furs, armed with steel and iron, and wreaking bloody havoc on the defenseless villages of Russia's remote northern regions. Time hadn't smoothed away any of his edge, and Renata could testify firsthand to Yakut's deadly nature.

That she could serve someone like that made her gut twist with regret. That she was pledged to protect him, to be loyal to him, both in thought and action, made her feel herself a stranger in her own skin. She had her reasons for staying – especially now – but there was still so much she wished she could change. So much still to regret . . .

She pushed aside the thoughts that were too dangerous to even let form in her mind. If Sergei Yakut were to sense the slightest weakness in her allegiance to him, there would be swift, severe repercussions.

Renata closed her door after she entered her room. She

unfastened her weapon holsters and laid the guns and knives neatly on top of the old trunk at the foot of the bed. She ached all over, muscles and bones screaming from the earlier tax on her mind. Her neck was stiff, full of knots that made her wince as she tried to massage them away.

God, she needed some peace from the pain.

A gentle scratching noise started up on the other side of the wall. It grated in her ears like nails on a chalkboard, her head feeling as fragile as a glass bell.

'Rennie?' Mira's girlish voice was soft, just a meek little whisper coming through the gaps in the logs. 'Rennie . . . is that you?'

'Yes, mouse,' Renata answered. She moved up to the head of the bed and rested her cheek against the rounded timber of the wall. 'It's me. What are you doing still awake?'

'I don't know. Couldn't sleep.'

'More nightmares?'

'Uh-huh. I keep . . . seeing him. That bad man.'

Renata sighed, hearing the hesitation in the soft admission. She thought about the warm bath that was only a few minutes out of her reach. It was a welcome solitude she needed more than anything at times like this, when the aftermath of her psychic ability – the very thing that had spared her life two years ago on this plot of remote, wooded land – seemed determined to kick her ass.

'Rennie?' came Mira's quiet voice again. 'Are you still there?'

'I'm here.'

She pictured the innocent face through the knotted pine. She didn't have to see the child to know that Mira had probably been sitting there in the darkness all this time, waiting to hear Renata come back so she wouldn't feel so alone. She'd been pretty shaken up the past few days – understandably, given what she'd witnessed.

Oh, screw the damn bath, Renata thought harshly. Swallowing down the pain that ran over her skin as she stood up, she reached over and pulled a Harry Potter novel out of her night-stand drawer.

'Hey, mouse? I can't sleep right now either. How about if I come over and read to you for a little while?'

Mira's joyful shriek sounded muffled, as though she'd had to cover her mouth with her pillow to keep from alarming the entire household with her outburst.

Despite her pain and fatigue, Renata smiled. 'I'll take that as a yes.'

Sergei Yakut led Nikolai into a large, open room that might have been a banquet hall when the old hunting lodge was in its heyday. Now there were no rows of tables or benches, only a pair of big leather club chairs arranged in front of a towering stone fireplace at the far end of the room and a massive wooden desk crouched nearby.

The pelts of bears and wolves and other, more exotic pred-ators lay spread out as rugs on the wood plank floor. Mounted to the stone above the fireplace was the head of a bull moose with a huge rack of broad bone-white antlers, his dark glass eyes fixed on some distant point across the wide expanse of the hall. *His long-gone freedom?* Niko thought wryly as he followed Yakut to the leather chairs at the hearth and sat down at the Gen One's gestured invitation.

Nikolai idly glanced around, guessing the lodge to be at least a century old, and built for human residents originally, although the sparse windows were currently rigged with crucial UV-blocking shutters. It wasn't the sort of place you might expect a vampire to settle in as his home. The Breed tended to prefer more modern, luxurious surroundings, living in family groups or communities called Darkhavens for the most part, many such places equipped with perimeter alarms and secu-rity fences.

As civilian Breed domiciles went, Yakut's rustic camp, while remote enough for a good amount of privacy from curious humans, was anything but typical. Then again, neither was Sergei Yakut himself.

'How long have you been in Montreal?' Nikolai asked.

'Not long.' Yakut shrugged, his elbows braced on the arms of the chair he was slouched into. His posture may have been relaxed, but his eyes had not stopped studying Niko – assessing him – since the moment they sat down. 'I find it to my benefit to keep on the move and not get too comfortable in any one place. Trouble has a way of catching up to you when you overstay your welcome.'

Nikolai considered the comment, wondering if Yakut spoke from personal experience or if it was meant as some kind of warning to his unexpected guest.

'Tell me about the attack on you,' he said, unfazed by either the flat stare or the obvious suspicious nature of the Gen One. 'And I'll need to talk to that witness too.'

'Of course.' Yakut motioned over one of his Breed guards. 'Fetch the child.'

The tall male nodded in acknowledgment, then left to carry out the order. Yakut sat forward in his chair. 'The attack occurred here in this room. I had been sitting in this very chair, reviewing a few of my accounts when the guard on watch heard a noise outside the lodge. He went to investigate, and returned to tell me that it was only raccoons that had gotten into one of the sheds out back.' Yakut shrugged. 'This was hardly unusual, so I sent him out to drive the pests away. When several minutes passed and he did not come back, I knew there was trouble. By then, no doubt, the guard was already dead.'

Nikolai nodded. 'And the intruder was already inside the lodge.'

'Yes, he was.'

'What about the girl – the witness?'

'She had taken her evening meal and was resting in here with me. She'd fallen asleep on the floor near the fire, but she awoke just in time to see that my assailant was standing directly behind me. I hadn't even heard the bastard move, he was so stealthy and quick.'

'He was Breed,' Niko suggested.

Yakut inclined his head in agreement. 'No question, he was Breed. He was dressed like a thief, all in black, his head and face covered with a black nylon mask that left only his eyes visible, but there is no doubt in my mind that he was our kind. If I had to guess, I would say he might even have been Gen One himself based on his strength and speed. If not for the child opening her eyes and crying out a warning, I would have lost my head to him in that next instant. He brought a thin wire garrote down on me from behind the chair. Mira's scream drew his attention away for a crucial second, and I was able to bring up my hand to block the wire from slicing across my throat. I twisted out of his range, but before I could leap on him myself or call in my guards, he escaped.'

'Just like that, he turned tail and ran?' Nikolai asked.

'Just like that,' Yakut replied, a slow smile teasing at the corner of his mouth. 'One look at Mira, and the coward fled.'

Niko swore under his breath. 'You were damn lucky,' he said, finding it hard to reconcile that the sight of a mere child could cause such a distraction for what had to be a highly trained, expert assassin. It just didn't make sense.

Before he could point that out to Yakut, footsteps approached from the other end of the long room. Walking in ahead of the guard Yakut had dispatched was Renata and a delicate waif of a girl. Renata had shucked her weapons somewhere, but she strolled alongside the child protectively, her cool gaze wary as she brought Mira farther into the room.

Nikolai couldn't help staring at the girl's odd attire. The

pink pajamas and bunny slippers were unexpected, but it was the short black veil that covered the top of her face that he found most jarring.

'Renata was reading me a story,' Mira supplied, her soft voice chiming with a bright innocence that seemed so out of place in Yakut's crude domain.

'Is that so?' the Gen One asked, a slow reply that seemed directed more at Renata than the child. 'Come closer, Mira. There is someone who wants to meet you.'

The guard stepped back once Mira stood before Yakut, but Renata's booted feet held steady at the girl's side. At first Niko wondered if the child might be blind, but she moved without hesitation, walking the few remaining steps to where Yakut and Nikolai now stood.

The small head pivoted toward Nikolai without error. She definitely was sighted. 'Hello,' she said to him, and gave a polite little nod.

'Hello,' Nikolai replied. 'I heard what happened the other night. You must be very brave.'

She shrugged, but it was impossible to read her expression when just her small nose and mouth were visible beneath the hem of the head covering. Nikolai looked at the young girl – the impish, three-and-a-half-foot waif who had somehow driven away a Breed vampire on a mission to kill one of the most formidable members of their kind. It had to be a joke. Was Yakut jerking him around somehow? What could this child possibly have done to thwart the attack?

Nikolai looked to Yakut, ready to call him out for what had to be a line of pure bullshit. There was no way in hell the attack could have gone down the way he'd described.

'Remove your veil,' Yakut instructed the girl, as if he knew the line of Niko's thinking.

Her small hands reached up to grasp the edge of the short black strip of gauze. She swept the veil back off her face but seemed careful to keep her eyes downcast. Renata stood very still beside the child, her expression placid even while her fingers curled into fists at her sides. She seemed to be holding her breath, waiting with an air of wary anticipation.

'Lift your eyes, Mira,' Yakut commanded her, his mouth curving into a smile. 'Look at our guest, and show him what he wants to know.'

Slowly the fringe of dark brown lashes came up. The girl raised her chin, tipping her head up and meeting Niko's gaze.

'Jesus Christ,' he hissed, hardly aware that he was speaking at all as he got his first glimpse at Mira's eyes.

They were extraordinary. The irises were so white they were clear, as liquid and fathomless as a pool of colorless water. Or, rather, a mirror, he amended, looking deeper into them because he couldn't help it, drawn closer by the startling, unusual beauty of her gaze.

He didn't know how long he stared – couldn't have been more than a couple seconds at most – but now her pupils were getting smaller, shrinking down to tiny pinpricks of black within the endless circle of silvery white. The color shimmered, rippling as though a breeze had skated across the tranquil surface. Incredible. He'd never seen anything like it. He peered deeper, unable to resist the strange play of light in her eyes.

When it cleared, Nikolai saw himself reflected there.

He saw himself and someone else . . . a woman. They were naked, bodies pressed together, sheened with sweat. He was kissing her heatedly, burying his hands in the dark glossy strands of her hair. Pushing her down beneath him as he thrust deep inside her. He saw himself baring his fangs, lowering his head and placing his mouth to the tender curve of her neck.

Tasting the sweetness of her blood as he pierced her skin and vein and began to drink –

'Holy hell,' he ground out, tearing his gaze away from the startling, all-too-real reflection. His voice was rough, his tongue thick behind the sudden emergence of his fangs. His heart was racing, and farther down, his cock had gone stiff as stone. 'What just happened?'

Everyone was staring at him except for Renata, who seemed more concerned with helping Mira replace her veil. She whispered something in the girl's ear, soothing words, by the soft tone of them. Sergei Yakut's low, rumbling chuckle was echoed by a few amused chortles from the other men.

'What did she just do to me?' Niko demanded, not the least bit entertained. 'What the fuck was that?'

Yakut leaned back in his chair and grinned like a tsar making a public joke of one of his subjects. 'Tell me what you saw.'

'Myself,' Nikolai blurted, still trying to make sense of it. The vision was so real. As if all of it were truly happening just then, not the mirage it had to be. God knew his body was convinced it was real.

'What else did you see?' Yakut asked blithely. 'Tell me, please.'

Fuck that. Niko mutely shook his head. He'd be damned if he was going to lay the whole salacious thing out for everyone in the room. 'I saw myself . . . some vision of myself, reflected in the girl's eyes.'

'What you saw was a glimpse of your future,' Yakut informed him. He motioned for the girl to come to his side, where he wrapped his arm around her thin shoulders and pulled her close, like a prized possession. 'One look into Mira's eyes and you see a vision of events in your life that are destined to come.'

It didn't take much to conjure the image back into his head. Oh, hell no, not much at all. That picture was as good as permanently burned into his memory and all of his senses. Nikolai willed his thrumming pulse to calm. Called his raging hard-on to heel.

'What did Mira show your attacker last week?' he asked, desperate to turn the attention away from himself now.

Yakut shrugged. 'Only he can know. The girl has no knowledge of what her eyes reflect.'

Thank God for that. Niko hated to think of the education she might have just gotten otherwise.

'Whatever the bastard saw,' Yakut added, 'it was enough to make him hesitate and give me a chance to escape the death he came to deliver.' The Gen One smirked. 'The future can be startling, especially when you are not expecting it, yeah?'

'Yeah,' Nikolai murmured. 'I suppose it can be.'

He'd just gotten a decent dose of that knowledge firsthand.

Because the woman who'd been wrapped around him, naked and writhing so passionately in his arms? It was none other than cold, beautiful Renata.

≼ CHAPTER FIVE ≽

Those carnal, all-too-real images dogged Nikolai for the next couple of moonlit hours as he prowled the forested grounds of the lodge, looking for any evidence that might remain from the aborted attack on Sergei Yakut. He checked the perimeter of the main house but found nothing. Not even a single trace footprint in the loamy, muddy soil.

The trail, if the intruder had left one, was dead cold now. Still, it wasn't difficult to guess how the assailant might have gotten close to his target. This deep in the woods, without security fences, cameras, or motion detectors to alert the household of trespassers on the property, Yakut's attacker could have hidden out in the surrounding forest most of the night, waiting for the best chance to strike. Or he might have chosen a more brazen location, Nikolai thought, his gaze settling on a small barn that sat a few yards from the back of the lodge.

He strode over to it, figuring the outbuilding to be a recent addition to the property. The wood was dark, not from natural weathering like the rest of the place, but from a walnut stain that made it blend into its surroundings. There were no windows on any side of it, and the wide paneled door in front was reinforced with a Z of two-by-fours and outfitted with a large steel lock.

Through the oily stink of the varnished wood, Nikolai could have sworn he caught a vague whiff of copper.

Human blood?

He dragged in another breath, sifting the taste of it through his teeth, over the sensitive glands of his tongue. It was definitely blood, and definitely human. Not very much had been spilled on the other side of the door, and by the faint tickle it put in his nostrils, he judged it to be long dried and aging probably several months or more. He couldn't be certain unless he had a look inside.

Curious now, he palmed the big lock and was about to yank it loose when the snap of a twig behind him drew his attention. As he turned to meet the noise, he reached for one of his guns – and cursed to remember that Yakut was still holding all of his weapons.

He looked up to find Alexei glaring at him from where he stood at the corner of the barn. Judging by the contempt sparking in his eyes, it appeared his bruised pride hadn't yet recovered from their confronation in the city. Not that Niko cared. He had little use for strutting dickhead civilians, especially those with entitlement issues and delicate egos.

'You got a key for this lock?' he asked, his hand still curved around the cold lump of reinforced steel. If he wanted to, being Breed, he could tear the thing loose with a flex of his wrist. Cleaner still, he could flex his mind and open the lock with a mental command. But it was more interesting to piss in Alexei's direction for the time being. 'You mind opening this door, or maybe you need to get permission from your papa first.'

Alexei grunted at the barb, arms folded over his chest. 'Why should I open it for you? There's nothing of interest in there. It's just a storage barn. Empty besides.'

'Yeah?' Niko let the lock fall from his hand, the metal thumping heavily against the wood panels. 'Smells like you've been storing humans in there. Bloody ones. The stench of hemoglobin just about knocked me over the closer I got.'

An exaggeration, but he wanted to see Alexei's reaction.

The young vampire frowned and threw a cautious look at the barred door. He slowly shook his head. 'You don't know what you're talking about. The only humans who ever stepped foot in this barn were the local carpenters who built it a few years ago.'

'Then you won't mind if I have a look,' Nikolai prompted.

Alexei chuckled low under his breath. 'What are you really doing here, warrior?'

'Looking to figure out who tried to kill your father. I want to know how the intruder might have gotten close enough to strike and where he might have fled afterward.'

'Pardon my surprise,' Alexei said, no apology in his tone, 'but I find it hard to believe that one failed attack – even on a Breed elder like my father – is enough to bring out a member of the Order for a personal visit.'

'Your father was lucky. There've been five other Gen Ones within the population who weren't so fortunate.'

Alexei's smug look faded, replaced with a somber gravity. 'There have been other attacks? Other killings?'

Nikolai gave a grim nod. 'Two in Europe, the others in the States. Too many to be random, and too expert to be anything but the work of a professional. And it doesn't seem to be a solo effort either. For the past weeks, once we learned of the first couple of assassinations, the Order has been contacting all of the known Gen Ones to warn them of what's been going down. They need to understand the potential danger so they can take appropriate security measures. Your father didn't tell you?'

Alexei's scowl furrowed his dark brow. 'He said nothing of this. Damn it, I would have guarded him personally.'

That Sergei Yakut hadn't informed his son of Niko's recent contact, or of the current rash of Gen One slayings, was telling. No matter how Alexei tried to posture himself as his father's right arm, Yakut evidently held him at some distance when it came to trust. Not surprising, given Yakut's suspicious nature. Evidently that suspicion extended to his own blood kin as well.

Alexei cursed. 'He should have told me. I would have made certain he had proper protection in place at all times. Instead, the bastard who attacked him is still on the loose. How can we be sure he won't come back to try again?'

'We can't be sure of that. In fact, we're better to go on the assumption that there will be another attack. My guess would be sooner than later.'

'You need to keep me informed,' Alexei said, his tone taking on that irritating edge of entitlement again. 'I expect to be alerted immediately of anything you find, and anything you or the Order may know about these attacks. Anything at all. Understood?'

Nikolai let his answering smirk spread slowly over his face. 'I'll try to remember.'

'My father thinks he's untouchable, you see. He has his hand-picked bodyguards, all of them trained by him, loyal to him. And he has the counsel of his private oracle too.'

Niko gave an acknowledging nod. 'The child, Mira.'

'You've seen her?' Alexei's gaze narrowed, though whether with mistrust or basic curiosity Nikolai couldn't guess. 'So,' Yakut's son said, 'he let you meet her, then. He let you look into her witchy eyes.'

'He did.'

When Niko's jaw remained firm, probably rigid, Alexei grinned. His voice dripped with sarcasm. 'Pleasant glimpse she gave you of your fate, was it, warrior?'

An instant replay of the heated vision ran through his mind like a brush fire, searing him from the inside. He shrugged with a cool he damn well didn't feel. 'I've seen worse things.'

Alexei laughed. 'Well, I wouldn't worry if I were you. The little bitch's talent is far from perfect. She can't show you everything of your future, only brief flashes of what may come, based on the now. And she can't help you put anything of what you see into context either. Personally I don't find the brat nearly as amusing as my father seems to.' He grunted, lifted one shoulder along with the corner of his sneering mouth. 'The same could be said of the other female he insists on keeping around despite my doubts.'

There was no question who he meant. 'You're not fond of Renata, I take it?'

'Fond of her,' Alexei muttered, crossing his arms over his chest. 'She's an arrogant one. Thinks herself above everyone else because she's managed to impress my father a time or two with her mind skill. Since the night she arrived here, she's been far too bold for her own good. You'd be hard-pressed to find a man among all those in my father's employ who wouldn't like to see her taken down a notch. Put the cold, uppity bitch in her rightful place, eh? Maybe you feel the same way, after what she did to you tonight in the city?'

Nikolai shrugged. He'd be lying if he said it didn't irk him on some primal level that a female had laid him low in combat. As grating as it was to have been on the receiving end of her mental assault, Nikolai couldn't deny some amount of awe. Obviously she was a Breedmate, since nature was averse to wasting powerful extrasensory gifts on basic *Homo sapiens* stock.

'I've never seen anything like her,' he admitted to Alexei. 'Never even heard of a Breedmate with that level of ability. I can see why your father would sleep better knowing she was nearby.'

Alexei scoffed. 'Don't be too impressed with her, warrior. Renata's skill has its merits, I'll grant you. But she's too weak to control it.'

'How so?'

'She can send the mental wave out, but the power bounces

back at her, like an echo. Once the reverberation hits her, she's utterly useless until it passes.'

Nikolai recalled the debilitating blast of mental energy that Renata had unleashed on him in the warehouse. He was Breed – his alien genes giving him the strength and resilience of easily ten human men – and he had been unable to bear the pain of the incredible sensory assault. For Renata to go through that same anguish every time she used her skill?

'Christ,' Niko said. 'It must be pure torture for her.'

'Yes,' Alexei agreed, not bothering to conceal his light tone. 'I'm quite sure it is.'

Nikolai didn't miss the smile on the younger Yakut's lean face. 'You enjoy that she suffers?'

Alexei grunted. 'I couldn't care less. Renata is unsuitable for the role my father has given her. She's ineffective as his bodyguard – a risk I fear might yet get him killed one day. If I were in his place, I wouldn't hesitate to turn her out on her haughty ass.'

'But you're not in your father's place,' Niko reminded him, if only because Alexei seemed overly eager to imagine it.

The vampire stared at Niko in silence for a long, awkward time. Then he cleared his throat and spat on the ground. 'Finish your search, warrior. If you find anything at all of interest, you will inform me at once.'

Nikolai merely stared back at Yakut's son, wordlessly daring the civilian to command his promise. Alexei didn't press it, just pivoted slowly on his heel and marched back in the direction of the lodge.

❧ CHAPTER SIX ❧

Renata quietly opened the door to Mira's room and peered inside at the sleeping child who rested peacefully on the bed. Just a normal little girl in pink pajamas, her soft cheek lying against the thin pillow, breath puffing rhythmically out of her delicate cherub's mouth. On the rustic little table next to the bed lay the short black veil that shielded Mira's remarkable eyes at all times when she was awake.

'Sweet dreams, angel,' Renata whispered low under her breath, hopeful words.

She worried about Mira more and more lately. It wasn't just the nightmares that had set in after the attack she'd witnessed but Mira's overall health that concerned Renata the most. Even though the girl was strong, her mind quick and sharp, she wasn't well.

Mira was rapidly losing her sight.

Each time she was made to exercise her gift of precognitive reflection, some of her own eyesight deteriorated. It had been fading steadily for months before Mira had confided in Renata about what was happening to her. She was afraid, as any child would be. Perhaps more so, because Mira was wise beyond her eight years of age. She understood that her value to Sergei Yakut would evaporate the moment the vampire deemed her of no more use to him. He would cast her out, perhaps even put her to death if it pleased him.

So on that night, Renata and Mira had made a pact: They

would keep Mira's condition a secret between them – take it to the grave, if need be. Renata had taken the promise one step further, vowing to Mira that she would protect her with her life. She swore no harm would ever come to her, not from Yakut or from anyone else, human or Breed. Mira would be safe from the pain and darkness of life in a way that Renata herself had never known.

That the girl had been trotted out to entertain Sergei Yakut's uninvited guest tonight only added to Renata's current irritated state. The worst of her psychic reverb had passed, but a headache still lingered at the edges of her senses. Her stomach hadn't yet stopped pitching. Small waves of nausea lapped at her like a slowly receding tide.

Renata closed Mira's door, shivering a little with the roll of another body tremor. The long bath she'd just come from had helped ease some of her discomfort, but even beneath her loose-fitting graphite-colored yoga pants and soft white cotton jersey, her skin still tingled, raw with the crackling electricity that swam underneath her skin.

Renata rubbed her palms over the sleeves of her shirt, trying to chase away some of the fiery sensation still traveling along her arms. Too wired for sleep, she stopped by her own room only long enough to retrieve a small cache of blades from her weapons trunk. Training always proved a welcome outlet for her restlessness. She relished the hours of physical punishment she inflicted on herself, glad for the rigorous training exercises that wore her out, toughened her up.

Since the terrible night she found herself plunged into Sergei Yakut's dangerous world, Renata had honed every muscle in her body to its peak condition, worked slavishly to make sure that she was as sharp and lethal as the weapons she carried in the silk-and-velvet wrapper now clutched in her hand.

Survive.

That simple guiding thought had been her beacon from

the time she was a child – even younger than Mira. And so alone. An orphan abandoned in the chapel of a Montreal convent, Renata had no past, no family, no future. She existed; no more than that.

And for Renata, it had been enough. It was enough, even now. Especially now, navigating the treacherous underworld of Sergei Yakut's realm. There were enemies all around her in this place, both hidden and overt. Countless ways for her to misstep, to misspeak. Endless opportunities for her to displease the ruthless vampire who held her life in his hands and end up bleeding and dying. But never without a fight.

Her mantra from her early childhood days served her just as aptly here: Survive another day. Then another, and another.

There was no room for softness in that equation. No allowances for pity or shame or love. Especially not love, not in any form. Renata knew that her affection for Mira – the nurturing impulse that made her want to smooth the way for the child, to protect her like her own kin – was probably going to cost her dearly in the end.

Sergei Yakut had wasted little time exploiting that weakness in her; Renata had the scars to prove it.

But she was strong. She'd been dealt nothing in this life that she could not bear, physical or otherwise. She had survived it all. Sharp and strong, lethal when she had to be.

Renata stepped outside the lodge and strode through the darkness to one of the peripheral outbuildings in back. The hunter who'd originally built the woodland compound had evidently doted on his dogs. An old timber kennel stood behind the main residence, laid out like a stable, with a wide space cutting down the center and four gated pens lining each side. The open-beam roof overhead peaked some fifteen feet high.

Although small, it was an open, airy space. There was a larger, newer barn on the property that would allow for better movement, but Renata tended to avoid the other building.

One time inside that dark, dank place was plenty. If she had her way, she'd burn the damn thing down to cinders.

Renata flicked on the switch inside the kennel door and winced as the bare bulb overhead poured a wash of harsh yellow light into the space. She walked in, over the smooth, hard-packed earthen floor, past the dangling ends of two long, braided leather straps that were looped around the center rafter beam of the structure.

At the far end of the kennel interior stood a tall wooden post that used to be rigged with small iron hooks and loops for storing leashes and other gear. Renata had pried away the rigging months ago, and now the post functioned as a stationary target, dark wood scored with deep gashes, gouges, and nicks.

Renata placed her wrapped blades on a tight bale of straw that squatted nearby. She slipped out of her shoes, then padded barefoot to the center of the kennel and reached up to take the pair of long leather straps, one in each hand. She looped the leather around her wrists a couple of times, testing the slack. When it was comfortable, she flexed her arms and lifted herself up off the floor as smoothly as though she had wings.

Suspended, feeling weightless, temporarily transported, Renata began her warm-up with the straps. The leather creaked softly as she turned and shifted her body several feet off the ground. This was peace to her, the feel of her limbs burning, growing stronger and more agile with each controlled movement.

Renata let herself slide into a light meditation, eyes closed, all her senses trained inward, concentrating on her heartbeat and breathing, on the fluid concert of her muscles as she stretched from one long, taxing hold to another. It wasn't until she had pivoted into an upside-down pose, her ankles now caught securely in the straps to hold her aloft, that she felt a stirring in the air around her. It was sudden and subtle, but unmistakable.

As unmistakable as the heat of an exhaled breath that now warmed her cheek.

Her eyes snapped open. Struggled to focus on the inverted surroundings and the intruder who stood under her. It was the Breed warrior – Nikolai.

'Shit!' she hissed, her inattention making her sway a bit from the straps. 'What the hell do you think you're doing?'

'Easy now,' Nikolai said. He lifted his hand as if he meant to steady her. 'Wasn't trying to scare you.'

'You don't.' Flat words, spoken coldly. With a liquid flex of her body, she moved herself out of his reach. 'Do you mind? You're interrupting my training.'

'Ah.' His dark blond brows quirked upward as his gaze followed the line of her body to where she still hung by her ankles. 'What exactly is it you're training for up there, Cirque du Soleil?'

She didn't dignify the jab with a reply. Not that he waited for one. He pivoted away from her and walked over to the post at the far end of the kennel. He reached out, fingers tracing the deeper of the wood's many scars. Then he found her blades and lifted the cloth that contained them. Metal clinked together softly within the folded square of ribbon-tied silk and velvet.

'Don't touch those,' Renata said, freeing herself of the straps and swinging around to bring her feet onto the ground. She stalked forward. 'I said, don't touch them. They're mine.'

He didn't resist when she snatched the prized possession – the only things of value she could claim as her own – out of his hands. The spike in her emotions made her head spin a little, lingering aftereffects of the psychic reverberation that she'd hoped was past. She took a step backward. Had to work to steady her breath.

'You okay?'

She didn't like the look of concern in his blue eyes, as if

he could sense her weakness. As if he knew she wasn't as strong as she wanted to – needed to – appear.

'I'm fine.' Renata brought the blades over to one of the kennel pens and unwrapped them. One by one, she carefully set each of the four hand-tooled daggers down on the wooden ledge in front of her. She forced a smug lightness into her voice. 'Seems like I should be the one asking you that question, don't you think? I dropped you pretty hard back there in the city.'

She heard his low grunt somewhere behind her, almost a scoff.

'We can never be too cautious when it comes to outsiders,' she said. 'Especially now. I'm sure you understand.'

When she finally glanced over at him, she found him staring at her. 'Sweetheart, the only reason you had the chance to drop me was because you played dirty. Making sure I'd notice you, pretending you had something to hide and knowing I'd follow you out of that club. Right into your little trap.'

Renata lifted her shoulder, unapologetic. 'All's fair in love and war.'

He gave her a slow smile that hinted at twin dimples in his lean cheeks. 'War, is it?'

'It sure as hell isn't love.'

'No,' he said, all serious now. 'Never that.'

Well, at least they agreed on something.

'How long have you been working for Yakut?'

Renata shook her head as if unable to recall specifically, even though that night was etched in her mind as if it had been burned there. Blood-drenched. Horrific. The beginning of an end. 'I don't know,' she said lightly. 'A couple of years, I guess. Why?'

'Just wondering how a female – even a Breedmate with your powerful psychic ability – would end up in this line of work, particularly for a Gen One like him. It's unusual, that's all. Hell, it's unheard of. So, tell me. How was it you hooked up with Sergei Yakut?'

Renata stared at this warrior – this stranger, dangerous and cunning, suddenly intruding on her world. She wasn't sure how to answer. She certainly wasn't about to give him the truth. 'If you have questions, maybe you should ask him.'

'Yeah,' he said, studying her too closely now. 'Maybe I'll do that. What about the kid – Mira? Has she been here as long as you?'

'Not as long, no. Just six months.' Renata tried to sound casual, but a fierce protective instinct rose in her at the mention of Mira's name on this Breed male's lips. 'She's been through a lot in that short time. Things no child should have to witness.'

'Like the attack on Yakut last week?'

And other, darker, things, Renata acknowledged inwardly. 'Mira has nightmares just about every night now. She hardly sleeps more than a couple hours at a time.'

He nodded in sober acknowledgment. 'This is no damn place for a kid. Some might say it's no place for a female either.'

'Is that what you would say, warrior?'

His answering chuckle neither confirmed nor denied it.

Renata watched him, questions of her own bubbling into her mind. One in particular. 'What did you see in Mira's eyes earlier tonight?'

He grunted something low under his breath. 'Trust me, you wouldn't want to know.'

'I'm asking, aren't I? What did she show you?'

'Forget it.' Holding her gaze, he raked a hand through the golden strands of his hair, then exhaled a ripe curse and looked away from her. 'Anyway, it doesn't matter. The girl definitely got it wrong.'

'Mira is never wrong. She hasn't been wrong once, not in all the time I've known her.'

'Is that so?' His penetrating blue stare swung back to her, both hot and cold as it traveled the length of her body in a slow, assessing glance. 'Alexei tells me her skill is imperfect—'

'Lex.' Renata scoffed. 'Do yourself a favor and don't put your faith in anything Lex tells you. He says and does nothing without an ulterior motive.'

'Thanks for the tip.' He leaned back against the blade-scarred post. 'So, then, it's not true, what he said – that Mira's eyes only reflect events that *could* happen in the future, based on the now?'

'Lex may have his own personal reasons for wishing it wasn't so, but Mira's never wrong. Whatever she showed you tonight, it's fated to be.'

'Fated,' he said, sounding amused by that. 'Well, shit. Then I guess we're doomed.'

He looked pointedly at her as he said it, all but daring her to ask if he deliberately included her in that observation. Since he seemed to find the idea so damned entertaining, she wasn't about to give him the satisfaction of asking him to explain why.

Renata picked up one of her blades and tested the weight of it in her open palm. The cold steel felt good against her skin, solid and familiar. Her fingers itched to be working. Her muscles were limber from the warm-up, ready to be pushed with an hour or two of hard training.

She pivoted around with the blade in hand and motioned to the post Nikolai was leaning up against. 'Do you mind? I wouldn't want to misjudge my mark and accidentally hit you instead.'

He glanced at the post and shrugged. 'Wouldn't you rather make it interesting, spar with a real opponent – one that can strike back? Or maybe you operate best with the odds stacked unevenly in your favor.'

She knew he was baiting her, but the glint in his eye was playful, teasing. Was he actually flirting with her? His easy nature made her hackles raise with wariness. She ran her thumb along the edge of the blade as she stared at him, unsure what to make of him now. 'I prefer to work alone.'

'Okay.' He inclined his head but took only a fractional step out of the way. Challenging her with a look. 'Suit yourself.'

Renata frowned. 'If you're not going to move, how can you be sure I won't aim for you?'

He grinned, full of cocky amusement, his thick arms crossed over his chest. 'Aim all you want. You'll never hit me.'

She let the blade fly without the slightest warning.

Sharp steel bit into the wooden post with a solid *crack*, striking home exactly where she'd sent it. But Nikolai was gone. Just like that, vanished from her line of sight completely.

Shit.

He was Breed, far faster than any human and as agile as a jungle predator. She was no match for him with weapons or physical strength; she knew that even before she sent the dagger airborne. But she'd hoped to at least nick the cocky son of a bitch for goading her.

Her own reflexes honed to precision, Renata threw her arm out and reached for another one of her waiting blades. But just as her fingers closed around the tooled grip, she felt the air stir behind her, heat sifting through the swaying chin-length strands of her hair.

Razor-sharp metal came up under her jaw. A wall of hard muscle crowded her spine.

'You missed me.'

She swallowed carefully around the light press of the blade beneath her chin. As smoothly as she could manage, she relaxed her arms at her sides. Then brought the hand with the dagger in it from behind her to rest meaningfully between his parted thighs. 'Looks like I found you.'

Simply because she could, Renata hit him with a small jolt of her mind's power.

'Fuck,' he growled, and in the instant his hold on her eased up, she slipped out of his reach and whirled to face him. She expected anger from him, feared it a little, but he only lifted his head and gave her a small shrug. 'No worries, sweetheart. I'll just have to toy with you until the reverb kicks in and takes you down.'

When she stared at him, confused and stricken that he could know about the flaw in her ability, he said, 'Lex clued me in to a few things about you too. He told me what happens to you every time you fire off one of those psychic missiles. Powerful stuff. If I were you, I wouldn't waste it just because you feel you need to prove a point.'

'Screw Lex,' Renata muttered. 'And screw you too. I don't need your advice, and I sure as hell don't need either of you talking shit about me behind my back. This conversation is over.'

Angry now, she recoiled her arm and released the dagger in his direction, knowing he could easily step out of its path just like before. Only this time he didn't move. With a lightning-quick snap of his free hand, he reached out and caught the sailing blade in midair. His smug grin totally set her off.

Renata snatched the last dagger from its resting spot on the kennel ledge and let it fly at him. Like the other before it, this one too was plucked from the air and now caught in the Breed warrior's nimble hands.

He watched her, unblinking, and with a masculine heat that should have left her cold, but didn't. 'Now what will we do for fun, Renata?'

She glared at him. 'Entertain yourself. I'm out of here.'

She turned, ready to stalk out of the kennel. No sooner had she taken two steps than she heard a *whoosh*ing sound on either side of her head – so close it made a few errant strands of her hair blow forward into her face.

Then, ahead of her, a blur of flying, polished steel blasting toward the far wall.

Thunk-thunk.

The two daggers that had sailed past her head with unerring aim were now buried into the old wood halfway to their hilts.

Renata spun around, furious. 'You assho—'

He was right on top of her, his massive body forcing her backward, blue eyes flashing with something deeper than amusement or basic male arrogance. Renata retreated a pace, only far enough that she could brace her weight on one heel. She rocked back and pivoted, her other leg coming up in a roundhouse kick.

Fingers as unyielding as iron bands locked down around her ankle and twisted.

Renata went down onto the kennel floor, flat on her back. He followed her there, spreading himself over her and trapping her beneath him while she fought with flailing fists and pumping legs. It took him all of a minute to subdue her.

Renata panted from the exertion, chest heaving, pulse racing. 'Now who's the one with something to prove, warrior? You win. Happy now?'

He stared down at her in an odd sort of silence, neither gloating nor glowering. His gaze was steady and calm, too intimate. She could feel his heart hammering against her sternum. His thighs straddled hers, and he'd caught both her hands above her head in one of his. He held her firmly, his fingers trapping coiled fists in a loose, incredibly warm grasp. His gaze strayed up to their locked hands, fiery light crackling in his irises as he found the little crimson teardrop-and-crescent moon birthmark that rode on the inside of her right wrist. His thumb stroked over that very spot, a mesmerizing caress that sent heat coursing through her veins.

'You still wanna know what I saw in Mira's eyes?'

Renata ignored the question, certain it was the last thing

she needed to know right now. She struggled hard underneath the heavy muscular slab of his body weight, but he held her down with damn little effort. Bastard. 'Get off me.'

'Ask me again, Renata. What did I see?'

'I said, get off me,' she snarled, feeling panic rise within her chest. She took a calming breath, knowing she had to keep her head. She had to get the situation under control, and fast. The last thing she needed was Sergei Yakut coming out and finding her pinned and powerless beneath this other male. 'Let me up now.'

'What are you afraid of?'

'Nothing, goddamn you!'

She made the mistake of lifting her gaze to his. Amber heat sparked inside the blue of his eyes, flame devouring ice. His pupils were narrowing swiftly, and behind the peeled-back grimace of his lips, she saw the sharp points of his emerging fangs.

If he was angry now, that was only part of the cause of his physical transformation; where his pelvis bore down on hers she felt the hard ridge of his groin, the very obvious length of his cock pressing deliberately between her legs.

She shifted, trying to escape that hot, erotic grind of their bodies, but it only wedged him tighter against her. Renata's racing pulse jumped into a more urgent tempo, and an unwanted warmth began to bloom in her core.

Oh, God. Not good. This was so not good.

'Please,' she moaned, hating herself for the weak quaver of the word. Hating him too.

She wanted to close her eyes, refuse to see his searing, hungry gaze or his mouth so near her own. She wanted to refuse to feel everything illicit that he was stirring in her – the danger of this unexpected, deadly desire. But her eyes stayed rooted on his, unable to look away, her body's response to him stronger than even her iron will.

'Ask me what the child showed me tonight in her eyes,' he demanded, his voice as low as a purr. His lips were so close to hers, the soft skin brushed against her mouth as he spoke. 'Ask it, Renata. Or maybe you'd rather see for yourself.'

The kiss went through her blood like fire.

Lips pressing together hotly, warm breath rushing, mingling. His tongue tracing the seam of her mouth, thrusting inside on her wordless gasp of pleasure. She felt his fingers caressing her cheek, sliding into the hair at her temple, then around to her sensitive nape.

He lifted her to him, deeper into the kiss that was melting her, breaking down all her resistance.

No.

Oh, God. No, no, no.

Can't do this. Cannot feel this.

Renata tore herself away from the erotic torture of his mouth, turning her head aside. She was shaking, emotions spiked to a dangerous level. She risked so much here, with him now. Too much.

Mother Mary, but she had to extinguish this flame he'd lit within her. It was molten, deadly so. She had to snuff it out fast.

Warm fingers touched her chin, guided her gaze back to the source of her distress. 'Are you all right?'

She extracted her hands from his loose, one-fisted grasp above her head and shoved at him, incapable of speech.

He moved off at once. He took her hand and helped her up to her feet, assistance she didn't want but was too stricken to refuse. She stood there, unable to look at him, trying to collect herself.

Praying like hell she hadn't just signed her own death warrant.

'Renata?'

When she finally found her voice, it leaked out of her, quiet and cold with desperation. 'Come near me again,' she said, 'and I swear I will kill you.'

CHAPTER SEVEN

Alexei had been kept waiting more than ten minutes outside his father's private chambers, his request for an audience given no more consideration than any one of Yakut's other servant guards. The lack of respect – the flagrant disregard – no longer stung Lex as it had at one time. He'd moved past that useless bitterness ages ago, in favor of more productive things.

Oh, in the deepest pit of Lex's belly he still burned to know that his father – his only living kin – could think so little of him, but the heat of constant, blatant rejection had at some point become less painful. It was simply how things were. And Lex was stronger for it, in fact. He was his father's equal in ways the hard old bastard could never imagine, let alone stoop to acknowledge.

But Lex knew his own capabilities. He knew his own strengths. He knew without any doubt that he could be so much more than what he was now, and he yearned for the opportunity to prove it. To himself and, yes, to the son of a bitch who fathered him as well.

The *snick* of the metal latch as the door finally opened brought Lex's pacing feet to a halt. 'About fucking time,' he snarled at the guard who stepped aside to let him enter.

The room was dim, lit only by the glow of the logs that burned in the massive stone fireplace on the opposite wall. The lodge was wired for electricity, but it was seldom used –

no real need for lights when Sergei Yakut and the rest of the Breed had preternaturally acute vision, especially in the dark.

The Breed's other senses were also keenly sharp, but Lex suspected that even a human would be hard-pressed to miss the combined odors of blood and sex that mingled with the tang of woodsmoke.

'My apologies for the interruption,' Lex murmured as his father came out of an adjacent room.

Yakut was naked, his cock still partially erect, its ruddy length bobbing obscenely with his each swaggering stride. Revolted by the sight, Lex blinked, started to look away. He quickly thought better of it, refusing to give in to a weak impulse that was sure to be counted against him. Instead he watched his father enter the room, the old vampire's eyes glowing like amber coals set deep into his skull, pupils reduced to narrow vertical slits at their center. His fangs were huge in his mouth, points fully extended and sharp as blades.

A sheen of sweat coated Yakut's body, every inch of him livid with color from the pulsing hues of his *dermaglyphs*, the unique Breed skin markings that spread from the Gen One's throat to his ankles. Fresh blood – unmistakably human, yet weak-scented enough to indicate a Minion source – smeared across his torso and flanks.

Lex wasn't surprised by the evidence of his father's recent activity, nor by the fact that the trio of muffled voices in the other room were those of his current stock of human mind slaves. Creating and keeping Minions, something only the most powerful, purest bloodlines of the race were capable of doing, had long been an illegal practice among polite Breed society. However, that was among the least of Sergei Yakut's offenses. He made his own rules, dispensed his own justice, and here, in this remote place, he made it clear to all that he was king. Even Lex could appreciate that kind of freedom and power. Hell, he could practically taste it.

Yakut aimed a dismissive glance at him from across the wide space of the room. 'I look at you, and I see the dead standing before me.'

Lex frowned. 'Sir?'

'If not for the warrior's restraint and my intervention tonight, you would be lying beside Urien on that warehouse roof back in the city, both of your corpses awaiting sunrise.' Contempt edged every syllable. Yakut picked up an iron tool from hearth-side and stabbed at the logs on the grate. 'I spared your life tonight, Alexei. What more do you expect I owe you this evening?'

Lex bristled at the reminder of his earlier humiliation, but he knew anger wouldn't serve him well, particularly not when he was facing his father. He gave a deferential bow of his head, finding it a damned hard struggle to keep the edge out of his voice. 'I am your faithful servant, Father. You owe me nothing whatsoever. And I ask nothing of you but the honor of your continued trust and confidence in me.'

Yakut grunted. 'Spoken more like a politician than a soldier. I have no need for politicians in my ranks, Alexei.'

'I am a soldier,' Lex replied quickly, raising his head and watching as his father continued to jab the iron poker into the fire. The logs broke apart, sparks shooting upward, crackling in the long, deadly silence that fell over the room. 'I am a soldier,' Lex stated again. 'I want to serve you as best I can, Father.'

A scoff now, but Yakut swiveled his shaggy head to regard Lex from over his shoulder. 'You give me words, boy. I put neither trust nor confidence in words. Lately I can't see that you've offered me anything more.'

'How do you expect me to be effective if you don't keep me better informed?' When those amber-hued eyes with their slivered pupils narrowed sharply on him, Lex hurried to add 'I ran into the warrior on the grounds. He told me about the recent Gen One killings. He said the Order had contacted you personally to warn you of the potential danger. I should have been made aware of that, Father. As the captain of your guard, I deserve to be informed—'

'You *deserve*?' The question hissed from between Yakut's lips. 'Please, Alexei . . . tell me just what it is you feel that you deserve.'

Lex remained silent.

'Nothing to add, son?' Yakut cocked his head at an exaggerated angle, his mouth pulled into a tight sneer. 'A similar charge was hurled at me some years ago from the lips of a stupid female who thought she could appeal to my sense of obligation. My mercy, perhaps.' He chuckled, turning his attention back to the fire to stab again at the incinerating logs. 'No doubt you recall what that got her.'

'I recall,' Lex answered carefully, surprised by the dry catch in his throat as he spoke.

Memories swirled out of the undulating flames in the fireplace.

Northern Russia, the dead of winter. Lex was a boy, barely ten years old, but the man of his meager household for as long as he could remember. His mother was all he had. The only one who knew him for what he truly was, and loved him regardless.

He'd worried the night she told him she was taking him to meet his father for the first time. She said Lex had been a secret she'd been keeping – her little treasure. But the winter had been hard, and they were poor. The country was in turmoil, unsafe for a woman raising a child like Lex on her own. They needed shelter, someone to protect them. She prayed Lex's father would provide for them. She promised that he would open his arms to them in welcome once he met his son.

Sergei Yakut had welcomed them with cold fury and a terrible, unthinkable ultimatum.

Lex remembered his mother's pleas for Yakut to take them in . . . completely ignored. He remembered the proud, beautiful woman getting down on her knees before Yakut, begging that if he would not care for them both that he look to Alexei alone instead.

The words rang in Lex's ears, even now: *He is your son! Isn't he worth anything to you? Doesn't he deserve something more?*

How quickly the scene had spun out of control.

How easy it was for Sergei Yakut to draw his sword and slice that blade cleanly through the neck of Lex's defenseless mother.

How brutal his words, that he had room only for soldiers in his domain, and that Lex had a choice to make in that moment: serve his mother's killer, or die along with her.

How weak Lex's answer had been, hiccuped through his sobs.

I will serve you, he'd said, and felt a bit of his soul desert him as he stared down in horror at his mother's broken, bleeding body. *I will serve you, Father.*

How cold the silence that followed.

As cold as a grave.

'I am your servant,' Lex said aloud now, bowing his head more from the weight of old memories than out of deference to the tyrant who sired him. 'My allegiance has always been to you, Father. I serve at your pleasure only.'

A sudden heat, so intense it felt like open flame, pressed to the underside of Lex's chin. Startled, he lifted his head, flinching away from the pain with a hissed cry. He saw smoke curl up in front of his eyes, smelled the sweet, sickly stink of seared flesh – his own.

Sergei Yakut stood before him, holding the long iron poker in his hand. The glowing tip of the metal rod smoldered, red-hot except for the spot of ashy white skin that clung to it from where it had torn away from Lex's face.

Yakut grinned, baring the points of his fangs. 'Yes, Alexei, you serve at my pleasure only. Remember that. Just because my blood happens to run in your veins doesn't mean I am opposed to spilling it.'

'Of course not,' Lex murmured, jaw clenched for the blistering agony of his burns. Hatred seethed in him for the insult he could only swallow and for his own impotence when it came to the Breed male daring him with his glower to make a move against him now.

Yakut backed off at last. He dragged a brown linen tunic from off a chair and shrugged into it. His eyes were still lit with blood hunger and lust. He let his tongue skate across his teeth and fangs. 'As you are so eager to serve me, go and fetch Renata. I have need of her now.'

Lex gritted his teeth so hard they should have shattered in his mouth. Wordlessly he walked out of the room with his spine held rigid, his own eyes flashing with the amber light of his outrage. He didn't miss the confused look of the guard on post at the door, the uneasy drift of the other vampire's eyes as he took in the odor of scorched flesh and the likely heat of Lex's roiling fury.

His burn would heal – in fact, it already was, his accelerated Breed metabolism mending the seared skin as Lex's feet carried him into the main area of the lodge. Renata was just coming in from outside. She saw Lex and paused, turning around as if she meant to avoid him. Not fucking likely.

'He wants you,' Lex barked from across the lodge, not caring how many other guards heard him. All of them knew she was Yakut's whore, so there was no reason to pretend otherwise. 'He told me to send you in. He's waiting for you to service him.'

Cold jade-green eyes leveled on him. 'I've been training outdoors. I need to wash off the dirt and sweat.'

'He said now, Renata.' A clipped command, one he knew

would be obeyed. There was more than a little satisfaction in that small, rare triumph.

'Very well.' She shrugged, padded over on bare feet.

Her bland expression as she neared said she didn't care what anyone thought of her, least of all Lex, and that lack of suitable humiliation only made him want to degrade her further. He sniffed in her direction, more for effect than anything else. 'He won't mind your filth. Everyone knows the best whores are the dirty ones.'

Renata didn't so much as blink at the vulgar remark. She could cut him down with a blast of her mental power if she chose to – in fact, Lex almost hoped she would, if just to prove that he had wounded her. But the cool flick of her gaze told him she didn't feel he was worth the effort.

She strode past him with a dignity Lex couldn't even begin to fathom. He watched her – all of the guards in the immediate area watched her – as she walked toward Sergei Yakut's chambers as calmly as a noble queen on her way to the gallows.

It didn't take much for Lex to imagine a day when he might be the one in control of all who served this household, including haughty Renata. Of course, the bitch wouldn't be so haughty if her mind, will, and body belonged entirely to him. A Minion to serve his every base whim . . . and those of the other males at his command.

Yes, Lex mused darkly, it would be damned good indeed to be king.

⇥ CHAPTER EIGHT ⇤

Nikolai pulled one of Renata's daggers free from the thick wooden post where she'd thrown it. He had to give her credit; her aim was dead-on. If he'd been human, not Breed, cursed with a human's sluggish reflexes, Renata's strike would have surely skewered him.

He chuckled at that as he placed the blade on its elegant wrapper with the other three of the set. They were beautiful weapons, sleek and perfectly balanced, obviously handcrafted. Niko let his gaze stray over the tooling on the carved sterling silver hilts. The pattern appeared to be a flourish of vines and flowers, but as he looked closer he realized that each of the four blades also bore a single word engraved lovingly within its ornate design: Faith. Courage. Honor. Sacrifice.

A warrior's creed? he wondered. Or were they the tenets of Renata's personal discipline instead?

Nikolai thought about the kiss they'd shared. Well, to say they had shared it was a stretch, considering how he'd descended on her mouth with all the finesse of a freight train. He hadn't meant to kiss her. Yeah, and just who was he trying to kid? He couldn't have stopped himself from doing it if he'd tried. Not that it was any excuse. And not that Renata had given him any chance to fumble through excuses or apologies.

Niko could still see the horror in her eyes, the unexpected yet obvious revulsion for what he had done. He could still feel the sincerity of the threat she delivered just before she high-tailed it out of the building.

The dented part of his ego tried to soothe him with the possibility that maybe she really did despise males in general. Or that maybe she was just as cold as Lex seemed to think, a sexless, frigid soldier who just happened to have the face of an angel and a body that called to mind all manner of sins. Too many sins, each more tempting than the last.

Nikolai had an easy charm when it came to women; not a total boast, but a conclusion he'd reached based on years of experience. When it came to females, he enjoyed easy, uncomplicated conquests – the more temporary the better. Chases and struggles were amusing, but best saved for true combat, in bloody battles with Rogue vampires and other enemies of the Order. Those were the challenges he relished most.

So why was he fighting such a wicked urge to go after Renata now and see if he couldn't thaw some of the ice that encased her?

Because he was an idiot, that's why. An idiot with a raging hard-on and an apparent death wish.

Time to get his eye back on the damned ball. It didn't matter what his body was telling him – no more than it mattered what he saw in Mira's gaze. He had a job to do, a mission for the Order, and that was the only reason he was here.

Niko carefully wrapped Renata's daggers in their silk-and-velvet case and placed the small bundle on the bale of straw to await her return for them and her discarded shoes.

He left the kennel outbuilding and headed into the darkness to pick up his search of the lodge grounds. A crescent moon hung high in the night sky, veiled by a smattering of thin, coal-gray clouds. The midnight breeze was warm, sifting gently through the spiny firs and tall oaks of the surrounding woods. Scents mingled in that humid summer air: the tang of pine pitch, the musty stamp of shaded soil and moss, the mineral crispness of fresh, rolling water from a stream that evidently cut through the property not far from where Niko stood.

Nothing unexpected. Nothing out of place.

Until . . .

Nikolai lifted his chin and cocked his head slightly to the west. Something very unexpected drifted across his senses. Something that could not, should not, belong here.

It was death he smelled now.

Subtle, old . . . but certain.

He jogged in the direction his nose led him. Deeper into the forest. Some hundred yards away from the lodge, the thicket dipped sharply. Niko slowed as he reached the place where his nostrils began to burn with the stench of aging decay. At his feet, the leaf-strewn, vine-tangled ground dropped away into a steep ravine.

Nikolai glanced down into the cleft, sickened even before his eyes settled on the carnage.

'Holy hell,' he muttered, low under his breath.

A pit of death lay at the bottom of the ravine. Human skeletal remains. Dozens of bodies, unburied, forgotten, simply dumped one on top of another like rubbish. So many, it would take time to count them all. Adults. Children. A slaughter that showed no discrimination or mercy in its victims. A slaughter that might have taken years to accomplish.

The pile of bones glowed white under the scant moonlight, legs and arms tangled together wherever the dead had fallen, skulls staring up at him, mouths agape in ghoulish, silent screams.

Nikolai had seen enough. He stepped back from the edge of the ravine and hissed another curse into the darkness. 'What the fuck has been going on out here?'

In his gut, he knew.

Jesus Christ, there wasn't much room for doubt.

Blood club.

Fury and disgust rolled through him in a black wave. He had the instant, overwhelming urge to rip the limbs from every vampire involved in the outlawed, wholesale killings of these people. Not that he had that right, even as a warrior member of the Order. He and his brethren didn't have a lot of friends among the Breed's governing branches, least of all the Enforcement Agency, which acted as both police and policy-makers for the general vampire populations. They considered the Order and the warriors who served it to be on the far outer fringe of civilized society. Vigilantes and militants. Wild dogs just begging for an excuse to be put down.

Nikolai knew he was out of bounds on this one, but that didn't make the itch to dispense his own brand of justice any less tempting.

Even though he seethed with outrage, Niko willed himself to calm. His fury wouldn't help any of the lives that were scattered below. Too late for them. Nothing to be done, except show them some bit of respect – something they'd been denied even after death.

Solemn now, if only for a few needed moments, Nikolai knelt down at the sharp drop of the ravine. He spread his arms wide, calling upon a bright power within him, a Breed talent that was uniquely his and, in his line of work particu-larly, of little use to him. He felt that power kindle in his core as he summoned it. The power grew in force and in light, spreading through his shoulders and down into his arms, then into his hands, twin orbs that glowed beneath the skin at the centers of his palms.

Nikolai touched his fingers to the earth at either side of him.

Vines and bramble rustled around him in response, green

tendrils and small forest wildflowers waking up at his beckoning. All of it growing at accelerated speed. Niko sent the burgeoning shoots into the ravine, then stood to watch as the dead were soon draped by a blanket of soft new leaves and blossoms.

As a burial rite, it wasn't much, but it was all he had to offer the souls who'd been left there to rot in the open.

'Rest in peace,' he murmured.

When the last bone was covered over, he headed back toward the lodge at a hard clip. The storage barn where he'd smelled blood earlier now drew his eye.

Just to confirm his suspicions, Niko stalked over and willed the lock loose. He pushed open the door, looked inside. The barn was empty, just as Lex had told him. But then again, the steel cages built inside weren't constructed for any kind of permanent storage. They were tall pens, locked holding cells designed for one purpose – human prisoners of the temporary sort.

Live game to be released for illegal sport here in the remote woods of Sergei Yakut's domain.

With a growl, Nikolai left the barn and stalked into the main lodge.

'Where is he?' he demanded of the armed guard who leapt to attention the second he flew through the door. 'Where the fuck is he? Tell me now!'

He didn't wait for an answer. Not when two other guards, both posted outside a closed door off the great hall, took on a sudden battle stance. Behind them, Yakut's private quarters, obviously.

Nikolai stormed over and shoved one of the steakheads out of his way. The other brought a rifle around and started to level it on him. Niko smashed the weapon into the guard's face, then tossed the stunned vampire into the nearest wall.

He kicked in the door, splintering old wood jambs and breaking oiled iron hardware clean off their fixtures. Nikolai strode through the showering debris, ignoring the shouts of Yakut's men. He found the Gen One half dressed on a leather sofa, sprawled possessively over the bared throat of a dark-haired female who was caged within the vampire's arms.

At the disruption, Yakut lifted his head from his feeding and looked up. So did his blood Host . . .

Renata.

No fucking way.

She was blood-bonded? Could she possibly be a Breedmate to this monster?

All of the accusations Nikolai was prepared to hurl at Sergei Yakut died a sudden death in his throat. He stared, his already roiling Breed senses ratcheting tighter at the sight of the female's blood on Yakut's lips and dripping from his huge fangs. The scent of it carried across the room, slamming hard into Niko's brain. He wouldn't have expected such an odd contrast to her chilly demeanor, but her blood scent was a warm, heady mix of sandalwood and fresh spring rain. Soft, feminine. Arousing.

Hunger coiled in Nikolai's gut, a visceral reaction that he had to fight damn hard to hold back. He told himself it was simply his Breed nature rearing up. There were few among his kind that could resist the siren's call of an open vein, but when his eyes locked on to Renata's unblinking gaze across the distance, a new heat flared to life inside him. Even stronger than the primal thirst to feed.

He wanted her.

Even while she was lying beneath another male, allowing that male to drink from her, Nikolai hungered for her with a ferocity that staggered him. Bound by blood to another or not, Renata made Niko burn to have her.

Which, by even his own flexible code of honor, lowered him to something close to Yakut's despicable level.

Niko had to mentally shake himself loose of the disturbing realization, yanking his focus back to the trouble at hand.

'You've got a serious problem,' he told the Gen One vampire, hardly able to contain his contempt. 'Actually, I'm guessing you've got about three dozen of them, rotting out there in your woods.'

Yakut said nothing, but the glow of his transformed, amber gaze darkened to one of defiance. A low growl curled out of him before he turned his head back to his interrupted meal. Yakut's tongue slid from between his lips to lick at the punctures he'd put in Renata's neck, sealing the wounds closed.

Only then, as Yakut's tongue swept her skin, did she look away from Niko. He thought he saw something quiet, something resigned, pass across her face in the seconds before Yakut stood up and released her. Once free, Renata moved to the corner of the room, tugging her clingy shirt back to some semblance of order. She was still dressed in her clothes from before, still barefoot as she had been outside.

She must have come straight here after what happened between Niko and her.

Had she run to Yakut for protection? Or for simple comfort? *Jesus.*

Niko felt like even more of an ass when he thought about kissing her the way he had. If she was blood-bonded to Sergei Yakut, that bond was sacred, intimate . . . exclusive. No wonder she'd reacted as she had. Nikolai kissing her would have been insult and degradation both. But he wasn't there to apologize now – not to Renata or her apparent mate.

Nikolai turned a hard look on the vampire. 'How long have you been hunting humans, Yakut?'

The Gen One grunted, smiling.

'I found the holding pens in the barn. I found the bodies. Men, women . . . children.' Nikolai hissed a curse, unable to contain his disgust. 'You've been running a goddamn blood club out here. From the looks of it, I'd say you've been at this for years.'

'What of it?' Yakut asked blithely. He didn't even attempt a respectable show of denial.

And in the corner of the room, Renata remained silent, her eyes rooted on Niko but showing no shock at all.

Ah, Christ. So, she knew about it too.

'You sick fuck,' he said, looking back to Yakut now. 'All of you are sick. You won't be allowed to continue this. It stops right here, right now. There are laws—'

The Gen One laughed, his voice warped from the transformation to his more savage side. 'I am the law here, boy. No one, not the Darkhavens and their vaunted Enforcement Agency – not even the Order – has any say in my affairs. I invite anyone to come here and try to tell me otherwise.'

The threat was clear. Despite the fact that everything honorable and just screamed for Nikolai to launch at the smug son of a bitch with weapons flying, striking to kill, this was no ordinary vampire. Sergei Yakut was Gen One. Not only gifted with strength and powers exponentially greater than Niko's or any other later-generation Breed, but a member of a rare class of individual. There were only a few Gen Ones in existence – fewer still, following the rash of recent assassinations.

As abhorrent as the outlawed practice of blood clubs was among Breed society, attempting to kill a first-generation vampire was an even bigger offense. Nikolai couldn't raise a hand against the bastard, no matter how badly he wanted to.

And Yakut knew as much. He wiped his mouth with the hem of his dark tunic, dabbing at Renata's sweet-scented blood.

'Hunting is in our nature, boy.' Yakut's voice was deadly calm, utterly confident, as he strode toward Nikolai. 'You are young, born of weaker stock than some of us. Maybe your blood is so diluted with humanity, you simply cannot understand the need in its purest form. Maybe if you had a taste of the hunt, you'd be less sanctimonious of those of us who prefer to live as we were meant to be.'

Niko gave a slow shake of his head. 'Blood clubs aren't about hunting. They're about slaughter. You can shovel your bullshit however deep you want it, but in the end, it's still bullshit. You're an animal. What you really need is a muzzle and a choke collar. Someone needs to shut you down.'

'And you think that you or the Order is up for that task?'

'Do you think we're not?' Niko challenged, some reckless part of him hoping the Gen One would give him a reason to draw his weapons. He didn't expect he'd walk away from a confrontation with the elder vampire, but he sure as hell wouldn't go down without a damned vicious fight.

Instead, Yakut backed off, amber eyes blazing, their elliptical pupils tiny slivers of black. His bearded chin came up, head cocked severely to the side. His lips parted with his savage, fang-baring grin. Like this, it wasn't hard at all to see the alien part of him – the part that made him and all the rest of the Breed what they were: blood-drinking predators not quite belonging to this mortal, Earth-born world.

'I told you once that you were not welcome in my domain, warrior. I have no use for you, or for your proposed alliance with the Order. My patience is at its end, and so is your stay here.'

'Yeah,' Niko agreed. 'I'm fucking gone from this place, and gladly. But don't think this is the last you'll hear from me.'

He couldn't help glancing over at Renata as he said it. As contemptuous as he found Yakut to be, he couldn't muster the same kind of fury for her. He waited for her to tell him that she didn't know about the crimes taking place on this patch of blood-soaked land. He wanted her to say that – to say anything to convince him that she wasn't actually a knowing party to Yakut's sick practices.

She merely stared back at him, her arms crossed over her

chest. One hand reached up to idly finger the healing wound on her neck, but she remained silent.

Watching as Nikolai stalked out of the open door and past Yakut's befuddled guards.

'Return the warrior's personal effects and see that he leaves the property without incident,' Yakut instructed the pair of armed men outside his private chamber.

When the two set off to carry out the command, Renata started to follow after them. Some unbalanced part of her hoped she might be able to catch up to Nikolai privately and . . .

And what?

Explain the truth of how things were for her here? Try to justify the choices she'd been forced to make?

To what end?

Nikolai was leaving. He would never have to return to this place, while she would be here to her dying breath. What good would it do to explain any of this to him, a stranger who probably wouldn't understand, let alone care?

And still, Renata's feet kept moving.

She didn't even get as far as the door. Yakut's hand clamped down on her wrist, holding her back.

'Not you, Renata. You stay.'

She glanced at him with a look she hoped was devoid of the queasiness she was trying so hard to tamp down. 'I thought we had finished here. I thought maybe I should go along with the others, just to make sure the warrior doesn't decide to do anything stupid on his way off the property.'

'You will stay.' Yakut's smile chilled her to the bone. 'Tread carefully, Renata. I wouldn't want you doing anything stupid either.'

She swallowed the sudden lump of cold unease in her throat. 'I'm sorry?'

'You will be,' he answered, his grip tightening on her arm. 'Your emotions betray you, beauty. I can feel the rise in your heart rate, the spike of adrenaline that's running through your veins even now. I felt the change in you from the moment the warrior entered the room. I felt it earlier as well. Care to tell me where you were tonight?'

'Training,' she replied, quickly but firmly. Giving him no reason to doubt her, since it was essentially the truth. 'Before you sent Lex to call for me, I was outside, running through my training exercises in the old kennel. It was a taxing workout. If you felt anything from me, that's all it was.'

A long silence stretched, and still that hard grip stayed latched onto her wrist. 'You know how much I value loyalty, don't you, Renata?'

She managed a brief nod.

'I value it as much as you value the life of that child sleeping in the other room,' he said coldly. 'I think it would destroy you if she should end up in the boneyard.'

Renata's blood seemed to freeze in her veins at the threat. She stared up into the evil eyes of a monster – one who grinned at her now with sick pleasure.

'Like I said, dear Renata. Tread very carefully.'

⊰ CHAPTER NINE ⊱

The city of Montreal, named for the broad mount that afforded such a royal view of the Saint Lawrence River and the valley below, glittered like a bowl of gemstones under the crescent sliver of the moon. Elegant skyscrapers. Gothic church spires. Verdant parkways, and, in the distance, a shimmering ribbon of water that nestled the city in its protective embrace. It truly was a spectacular view.

No wonder the leader of the Montreal Darkhaven chose to settle his community near the summit of Mount Royal.

Standing on the baroque-style limestone balcony off the mansion's second-floor drawing room made the old hunting lodge outside the city seem a thousand miles away. A thousand years away from this polite, civilized manner of living. Which, of course, it was.

The wait to meet with Edgar Fabien, the Breed male who oversaw the Montreal vampire population, seemed to take forever. Fabien was well known around the city and rumored to be very well connected, both within the Darkhavens and their policing arm known as the Enforcement Agency. He was the natural choice for a delicate situation like this.

Still, it was a gamble that the Darkhaven leader would be willing to cooperate. This unannounced late-night visit had been a spontaneous thing, and a very risky one at that.

Just by coming here, he was declaring himself an enemy of Sergei Yakut.

But he'd seen enough.

Endured enough.

The prince was sick and tired of licking his father's boots. It was time for the tyrant king to fall.

Lex turned at the sound of footsteps approaching from within the drawing room. Fabien was a slim male, tall and meticulously dressed, as if he'd been born in his tailored suit and shiny leather loafers. His ash-blond hair was slicked back from his face with some kind of perfumed oil, and when he smiled at Lex in greeting, his thin lips and narrow birdlike facial features became even more severe.

'Alexei Yakut,' he said, coming out onto the balcony and offering Lex his hand. No fewer than three rings sparkled on his long fingers, gold and diamonds to rival the glitter of the city outside. 'I'm sorry to have kept you waiting so long. I'm afraid we're not accustomed to receiving unannounced guests here at my personal residence.'

Lex gave him a tight nod and took his hand out of Fabien's grasp. The Darkhaven leader's private home wasn't exactly going to turn up in any Montreal tour guides, but a few questions posed to the right people in town had led Lex there without too much trouble.

'Come in, please,' the Darkhaven male said, motioning for Lex to follow him back into the house. Fabien settled himself onto a fancy settee, leaving room for Lex on the other side. 'I must admit, I was surprised when my secretary told me who had come to see me. A shame we've not had the opportunity to meet until now.'

Lex took a seat beside the Darkhaven male, unable to keep his eyes from traveling over the endless luxury of his surroundings. 'But you know who I am?' he asked Fabien cautiously. 'Do you also know the Gen One who is my father, Sergei Yakut?'

Fabien gave a mild nod. 'Only by name, alas. I am remiss

in not having made formal introductions when you folks first arrived in my city. However, your father's bodyguards made it clear when my emissary inquired about a meeting that your father was something of a recluse. I understand he enjoys a quiet, rural life outside the city, communing with nature or some such.' Over the steeple of his bejeweled fingers, Fabien's smile did not quite reach his eyes. 'I suppose there is something to be said for living with that kind of . . . simplicity.'

Lex grunted. 'My father chooses such a life because he believes himself above the law.'

'Excuse me?'

'That's why I'm here,' Lex said. 'I have information. Critical information that needs to be acted on quickly. Covertly.'

Edgar Fabien leaned back against the cushions of the settee. 'Has something . . . happened out at the lodge?'

'It's been happening for a long time,' Lex admitted, feeling a queer sense of freedom as the words spilled out of his mouth.

He told Fabien everything about his father's illegal activities, from the blood club and the boneyard full of his victims' remains, to the keeping and frequent killing of his human Minions. Lex explained, not quite truthfully, how it had been eating him up to keep this secret for so long and how it was his own sense of morality – his sense of honor and respect for Breed law – that compelled him to seek out Fabien's help in putting a stop to Sergei Yakut's private reign of terror.

It was excitement – thrill at the depth of his courage – that put a quiver in Lex's voice, but if Fabien took it for regret, so much the better.

Fabien listened, his expression carefully schooled, sober. 'You understand, I'm sure, that this is no small matter. What you've described is . . . problematic. Disturbingly so. But there will be certain factors that will come into play on this type of investigation. Your father is Gen One. There will be questions for him to answer, protocols that will need to be observed—'

'Investigation? Protocol?' Lex scoffed. He shot to his feet, awash in both fear and fury. 'That could take days or even weeks. A fucking month!'

Fabien nodded apologetically. 'It could, yes.'

'There's no time for that now! Don't you get it? I am handing my father to you on a platter – all the evidence you would need for an immediate arrest is right there on his property. For fuck's sake, I am risking my goddamn life just by standing here!'

'I am sorry.' The Darkhaven leader held up his hands. 'If it's any comfort to you, we would be more than willing to offer you protection. The Agency could remove you once the investigation begins, take you someplace safe—'

Lex's sharp bark of laughter cut him off. 'Send me into exile? I'll be dead long before then. Besides, I'm not interested in going into hiding like a whipped dog. I want what I deserve. I want what I am due, after all these years of waiting for handouts from that bastard.' It was impossible to mask his true feelings now. Lex's rage was on a full boil. 'You want to know what I really want from Sergei Yakut? His death.'

Fabien's gaze narrowed shrewdly. 'That's very dangerous talk.'

'I'm not the only one to think it,' Lex replied. 'In fact, someone even had the balls enough to attempt it just last week.'

Narrower and narrower went those cunning little eyes. 'What do you mean?'

'He was attacked. An assailant stole into the lodge and tried to sever his head with a length of wire, but in the end he failed. Of all the damned luck,' Lex added under his breath. 'The Order feels it's the work of a professional.'

'The Order,' Fabien repeated airlessly. 'How are they involved in any of what you've described?'

'They sent a warrior here tonight to meet with my father.

Apparently they are trying to warn the Gen Ones about the recent slayings among the population.'

Fabien's mouth worked for a second without forming words, as if he wasn't sure what question to tackle first. He cleared his throat. 'There is a warrior here in Montreal? And what is this about recent slayings? Whatever are you talking about?'

'Five dead Gen Ones, between North America and Europe,' Lex said, recalling what Nikolai had told him. 'Someone seems hell-bent on picking off the whole remaining first generation, one by one.'

'My word.' Fabien's face was the picture of astonishment, but something about him was bothering Lex.

'You didn't know anything about the killings?'

Fabien rose slowly, shook his head. 'I am stunned, I assure you. I had no idea. What a terrible thing.'

'Maybe. Maybe not,' Lex remarked.

As he stared at the Darkhaven leader, Lex noticed a sudden stillness coming over the vampire – so still he had to wonder if Fabien was actually breathing. There was a subdued but rising panic in his raptorlike eyes. Edgar Fabien held his body in check with rigid precision, but from the look in his shifting gaze, he looked as though he wanted to bolt from the room. *How intriguing.*

'You know, I would have expected you to be better informed, Fabien. Your reputation around the city paints you as quite the player. With all your Enforcement Agency friends, are you trying to tell me that none of them clued you in? Maybe they don't trust you, eh? Maybe they have good cause.'

Now Fabien met Lex's gaze. Amber sparks flashed in his irises, a telltale sign of a pricked nerve. 'Just what kind of game are you trying to play here?'

'Yours,' Lex said, sensing an opportunity and pouncing on it. 'You know about the Gen One slayings. The question is, why would you lie about it?'

'I don't publicly discuss Agency issues.' Fabien all but spat his reply, puffing out his thin chest with self-righteous indignation. 'What I know or do not know is my own business.'

'You knew about the attack on my father before I mentioned it, didn't you? Were you the one who called for his death? What about the others who've been killed?'

'Good Christ, you are mad.'

'I want in,' Lex said. 'Whatever scheme you're involved with, Fabien, I want in.'

The Darkhaven leader expelled his breath sharply, then gave Lex his back as he casually walked over to one of the tall bookcases built into the silk-papered wall. He smoothed his hand along the polished wood, chuckling idly. 'As illuminating and entertaining as our conversation has been, Alexei, perhaps it should end here. I think it best if you go away and calm yourself before you say anything more foolish.'

Lex charged forward, determined to convince Fabien of his worth. 'If you want him dead, I am willing to help get it done.'

'Unwise' came the hissed reply. 'I can snap my fingers and have you held on suspicion of intent to commit murder. I may still, but right now you're going to leave and neither one of us will speak another word of this conversation.'

The drawing room door opened and four armed guards filed inside. At Fabien's nod, the group of them surrounded Lex. Given no choice, he started to leave.

'I'll be in touch,' he told Edgar Fabien with a light baring of his teeth. 'You can count on that.'

Fabien said nothing, but his shrewd gaze remained fixed on Lex with grim understanding as he walked to the drawing room doors and gently closed them tight.

Once Lex was out on the street alone, his mind began to churn over his options. Fabien was corrupt. What a surprising, and sure to be useful, bit of information. With any luck, it wouldn't be long before Fabien's connections were Lex's as well. He didn't particularly care how he had to acquire them.

He glanced up at the beautiful Darkhaven mansion and all its pristine luxury. This was what he wanted. This kind of life – lifted high above the filth and degradation he'd known under his father's boot heel. This was what he truly deserved.

But first he would need to get his hands dirty, if just one last time.

Lex strolled along the tree-lined, meandering road and headed back down into the city with renewed purpose.

⊰ CHAPTER TEN ⊱

Nikolai woke up in total darkness, his head resting against the coffin of an apparently well-to-do Montreal man who'd been dead for sixty-seven years. The private mausoleum's marble floor had made for a hard few hours of rest, but it served Niko well enough. The night had been creeping dangerously close to dawn when he'd left Yakut's place, and he'd sure as hell slept the daylight off in worse places than the cemetery he found at the city's northern edge.

With a groan, he sat up and flipped open his cell phone to check the display for the time. Shit, just after one P.M. He still had about seven or eight hours to wait in here before sundown, when it would be safe for him to be outside. Seven or eight more hours, and he was already feeling itchy from sitting idle for so long.

No doubt Boston was wondering about him by now. Niko hit the speed dial for the Order's headquarters. Halfway through the second ring, Gideon picked up.

'Niko, for fuck's sake. About time you reported in.' The warrior's vague English accent sounded a bit rough. Not surprising, considering that Niko was calling in the middle of the day. 'Talk to me. You good?'

'Yeah, I'm good. My objective here in Montreal is fucked ten ways to Sunday, but other than that, 'sall good.'

'No luck finding Sergei Yakut, I take it?'

Niko chuckled. 'Oh, I found the bastard all right. The Gen

One is alive and well and living north of the city like some kind of throwback to Ghengis Khan.'

He gave Gideon a quick rundown of everything that had happened since his arrival in Montreal – from the ass-kicking welcome he'd gotten from Renata and the other guards, to the strange handful of hours he'd spent at Yakut's lodge, culminating with his discovery of the dead humans discarded out back and his subsequent ejection from the property.

He described the recent failed attempt on the Gen One's life and the incredible role Mira played in thwarting that attack. Niko left out the part about what he'd personally seen in Mira's eyes. He saw no reason to share the details of a vision, which, despite Renata's insistence that Mira was never wrong, had roughly zero chance – no, scratch that; it had *exactly* zero chance – of happening now.

It should have come as a relief to him to know that. The last thing he needed was to get mixed up with a female, especially a piece of work like Renata. Yakut's blood-bonded mate. The thought still gnawed at him, far more than it should. And he wasn't feeling particularly chipper about the fact that even the slightest recollection of that kiss with her was enough to render him as hard as the granite tomb that surrounded him.

He wanted her, and there had been a split second as he was leaving the lodge that he thought she might come after him. He had no reason to think it, but it had been a nudge in his gut, a sense that maybe Renata might run up behind him and ask him to get her out of there.

And if she had? Christ, he might have been just stupid enough to consider it.

'So,' he told Gideon, mentally steering himself back to reality. 'The net of it is, we can't count on any cooperation out of Sergei Yakut. He basically told me to shove it, and that was before I called him a sick fuck in need of a muzzle and choke collar.'

'Jesus, Niko,' Gideon sighed, probably, on the other end of the line, scrubbing his hand through his spiky blond hair in frustration. 'You really said that to him – to a Gen One? You're damn lucky he didn't tear your tongue out before he sent you on your way.'

Probably true, Nikolai acknowledged to himself. And he'd have lost more than just his tongue if Yakut knew the kind of lust he had been feeling for Renata. 'You know I'm allergic to ass-kissing, even if the ass in question happens to be Gen One. If this was a total public relations mission, you picked the wrong guy.'

'No shit.' Gideon chuckled around another low curse. 'You coming back in to Boston, then?'

'I see no reason to linger. Unless you figure Lucan will look the other way if I decide to go back and put a torch to Yakut's house of horrors. Put him out of business, at least for a while.'

He was kidding . . . mostly. But Gideon's answering silence told him that his fellow warrior knew the wheels were turning inside Niko's head.

'You know you can't do anything of the sort, my man. Way out of bounds.'

'And doesn't that suck,' Nikolai muttered.

'Yeah, it does. But this kind of thing belongs to the Enforcement Agency, not us.'

'Tell me how Yakut is any different from the Rogues we take off the streets, Gid. Hell, from what I've seen of him, he's worse. At least the Rogues can blame their savagery on Bloodlust. Yakut can't even cling to blood addiction as his excuse for hunting those humans out there. He's a predator, a killer.'

'He is protected,' Gideon said, firmly now. 'Even if he wasn't Gen One, he's still a civilian, still a member of the Breed. We can't touch him, Niko. Not without a lot of serious shit hitting the fan. So, whatever you're thinking, don't.'

Nikolai exhaled sharply. 'Forget I said it. What time should I plan on catching a ride back to Boston tonight?'

'I'll have to make a couple of calls to get a flight plan filed on short notice, but the private jet's still waiting for you at the airport. I can text you the time once I have it firmed up.'

'Okay. I'll chill and wait for your go.'

'Where are you at, anyway?'

Nikolai glanced at the coffin behind him, the other one across from him, and the bronze urn gathering dust on a pedestal against the back wall of the dark mausoleum. 'I found a quiet little place to grab a rest in the north end of the city. Slept like the dead, in fact. Or with them, at any rate.'

'Speaking of dead,' Gideon said, 'we've got a report of another Gen One killing overseas.'

'Christ. Picking them off like flies, aren't they?'

'Or trying to, from the looks of it. Reichen's following up on the report from Berlin. Got an e-mail from him that he'll be calling in later today with an update.'

'Good to know we've got eyes and ears that we can trust over there,' Niko said. 'Shit, Gideon. Never would have thought I'd have any use for a Darkhaven civilian, but Andreas Reichen is proving to be a damn good ally. Maybe Lucan ought to officially recruit him into the Order?'

Gideon chuckled. 'Don't think he hasn't considered it. Alas, we're just a part-time gig for Reichen. He may have the soul of a warrior, but his heart belongs to his Berlin Darkhaven.'

And a certain human female, from what Nikolai understood. According to Tegan and Rio, the two warriors who'd spent the most time with Andreas Reichen at his Berlin headquarters, the German Darkhaven leader was romantically involved with a brothel owner named Helene.

It was unusual for a Breed male to have more than a casual, short-term relationship with a mortal woman, but Niko wasn't about to question it since Helene was also proving instrumental in the Order's intelligence-gathering efforts overseas.

'So, listen,' Gideon said. 'Cool your heels where you are, and I'll let you know once I have your departure info for tonight. Sound good?'

'Yeah. You know how to find me.'

The murmur of a velvety female voice, soft from sleep, carried vaguely through the receiver.

'Ah, hell, Gid. Don't tell me you're in bed with Savannah.'

'I was,' he replied, leaning hard on the past tense. 'Now that she's awake, she says she's tossing me over for a hot shower and a cup of strong coffee.'

Nikolai groaned. 'Shit. Tell her I'm sorry for the interruption.'

'Hey, babe,' Gideon called to his beloved, blood-bonded mate of some thirty-odd years. 'Niko says he's sorry for being such a rude bastard and waking you up at this ungodly hour.'

'Thanks,' Niko muttered.

'You're welcome.'

'I'll check in with you again from the plane heading home.'

'Sounds good,' Gideon said. Then, to Savannah on the side: 'Hey, love? Niko wants me to tell you that he's hanging up now. He says you ought to come back to bed and let me ravish you slowly from your clever and beautiful head to your delectable little toes.'

Nikolai chuckled. 'Sounds like fun. Put me on speaker so I can listen at least.'

Gideon snorted. 'Not a chance. She's all mine.'

'Selfish bastard,' Niko drawled wryly. 'I'll catch you later.'

'Right, later. And Niko – about the Yakut situation? Seriously. Don't even think about being a cowboy, yeah? We've got bigger issues to contend with than trying to corral one loose-cannon Gen One. It's not our area, especially not right now.'

When Niko didn't immediately agree, Gideon cleared his

throat. 'Your silence isn't exactly giving me the warm fuzzies, my man. I need to know you're hearing me on this.'

'Yeah,' Nikolai said. 'I'm hearing you. I'll see you in Boston later tonight.'

Niko closed his cell phone and slid it back into his pocket.

As much as it fried him to think of turning a blind eye to Yakut and his sick activities, he knew Gideon was right. What's more, he knew that the Order's leader, Lucan, as well as the rest of the warriors at the Boston compound would say the same thing to him.

Forget about Sergei Yakut, at least for the time being. That was the sensible, smartest thing to do.

And while he was at it, he would be wise to forget all about Renata too. She'd made her bed, after all. The fact that she'd evidently made it with sadistic scum like Sergei Yakut was none of Nikolai's business whatsoever. Beautiful, ice maiden Renata was not his problem, so good riddance to her.

Good riddance to the entire nest of vipers he'd uncovered in Yakut's domain.

Just a few more hours to kill before nightfall, and then he could put it all behind him.

She never had gotten used to sleeping through the daylight hours, not in the whole two years she'd been living in service to a vampire.

Renata lay in her bed, restless, unable to relax and close her eyes even for a few minutes. She tossed and turned, flipped onto her back and blew out a sigh, staring up at the timber rafters.

Thinking about the warrior . . . *Nikolai*.

He'd been gone for hours – nearly half an entire day – but she still felt the weight of his contempt pressing down on her. She hated that he'd seen Yakut feeding from her. It had been hard to pretend she wasn't ashamed when he caught her gaze from across the room. She'd tried to appear unaffected, defiant. Inside she'd been shaking, her pulse jackhammering almost out of control.

She hadn't wanted Nikolai to see her like that. Even worse that he had learned of Yakut's brutal crimes and clearly thought her to be a part of it as well. She couldn't get the withering, accusatory look he'd given her out of her head.

Which was ridiculous.

Nikolai was Breed, like Yakut. He was a vampire, the same as Yakut. Like Yakut, Nikolai had to feed on humans in order to survive. Even in her limited understanding of their kind, Renata knew that drinking from human beings was the only way the Breed could obtain nourishment. No convenient vampire-friendly blood banks where they could pick up a pint of O-Negative for the road. No animal predation as a substitute for the real thing.

Sergei Yakut and all the rest of the Breed shared the same driving thirst: the need for *Homo sapiens* red cells, taken directly from an open vein.

They were deadly savages who happened to look human most of the time, but who at their core – in their soul, if they even had one – lacked all humanity. Why she should think that Nikolai was any different was beyond her.

But he had seemed different, if only a little.

When she'd sparred with him in the kennel – when he'd kissed her, for God's sake – he had in fact seemed remarkably different from the others of his kind that she knew. Not like Yakut at all. Not like Lex either.

Which probably only proved that she was a fool.

And she was weak as well. How else could she explain the wrenching wish she'd had that Nikolai might have taken her out of this place when he'd left today? She didn't often indulge in futile hopes, or waste time imagining things that could never come to pass. But there had been a moment . . . a brief, selfish moment when she pictured herself torn away from Sergei Yakut's unbreakable hold.

For one unfettered instant, she wondered what it might feel like to be free of him, free of everything that held her there . . . and it had been glorious.

Shamed by her thoughts, Renata swung her legs over the side of the bed and sat up. She couldn't lie there for another minute, not as long as her head was spinning with thoughts that would do her no good at all.

The fact of the matter was, this was her life. Yakut's world was her world, the lodge and its many ugly secrets her unshakable reality. She didn't feel sorry for herself; she never had. Not at the convent orphanage all those years as a child, nor the day she was tossed out of her home with the Sisters of Benevolent Mercy at the age of fourteen and forced to leave for good.

Not even on the night, just two summers before, when she'd been plucked off the streets in Montreal and brought with a group of other frightened humans to the locked holding pens of the barn on Sergei Yakut's property.

She hadn't shed a single self-pitying tear in all this time. She sure as hell wasn't about to start now.

Renata got up and left her modest room. The main lodge was quiet at this hour, the few windows in the place shuttered tight to banish the sun's lethal rays. Renata took the thick iron bar off the exterior door and walked out into a gloriously warm and bright summer afternoon.

She headed straight for the kennel outbuilding.

Amid all the drama that had occurred last night, both alone with Nikolai and in the time afterward, she'd completely forgotten her blades outside. The careless oversight bothered her. She never let the daggers out of her possession. They were a part of her now, as they had been the day she'd received them.

'Stupid, stupid,' she whispered to herself as she entered the old kennel and looked to the post where she expected to find the embedded blade she'd thrown at Nikolai.

It wasn't there.

A cry slipped past her lips, disbelief and anguish.

Had the warrior taken her blades for himself? Had he fucking stolen them?

'Damn it. No.'

Renata stormed across the center aisle of the building . . . then came to an abrupt halt as she reached the back of the place and her eyes settled on the stout bale of straw near the scarred wooden post.

Carefully folded atop it and placed neatly beside the pair of shoes she'd left behind last night as well was the silk-and-velvet wrapper that contained her treasured daggers. She picked it up, just to reassure herself that the fabric sheath wasn't empty. Its familiar weight settled into her palm and she couldn't hold back her smile.

Nikolai.

He'd taken care of the blades for her. Collected them, wrapped them up, and left them here for her as if he knew how much they meant to her.

Why would he do that? What did he expect his kindness to buy him? Did he actually think her trust might come so cheaply, or was he just hoping for another chance to force himself on her the way he had with that kiss?

She really didn't want to think about kissing Nikolai. If she thought about his mouth on hers, then she would have to admit to herself that as unexpected and uninvited as his kiss had been, force was hardly to blame for it happening.

The truth was, she'd enjoyed it.

Mother Mary, but just thinking on him now lit a slow, liquid heat in her core.

She'd wanted more of him, despite that every survival

instinct in her body had been screaming for her to get away from him, and get away fast. She hungered for him – then and now. Burned for him, in a place she'd long thought to be frozen over and dead.

And that little admission made what he'd said about Mira – the implication that whatever he'd seen in the child's eyes might somehow involve Renata and him intimately together – all the more unsettling.

Thank God he was gone.

Thank God he would likely never return after what he'd discovered here.

It had been a long time since Renata had gone down on her knees to pray. She knelt before no one anymore, not even Yakut at his terrifying worst, but she bowed her head now and begged heaven to keep Nikolai away from this place.

Away from her.

No longer in the mood for training, especially when memories of what had taken place here last night were still ripe and swimming in her head, Renata grabbed her shoes and walked back to the lodge. She went inside, replaced the bar on the door, then walked the hallway leading to her room and what she hoped might be at least a few hours' sleep.

She sensed something out of place even before she noticed Mira's door was unlatched.

No lights were on in the child's room, but she was awake. Renata heard her soft voice in the dark, complaining that she was sleepy and didn't want to get up. More nightmares? Renata wondered, feeling a pang of sympathy for the child. But then another voice hissed over Mira's groggy protests, this one cold and harsh, clipped with impatience.

'Stop your sniveling and open your eyes, you little bitch.'

Renata pressed her hand to the paneled door and pushed it wide. 'What the hell do you think you're doing, Lex?'

He was bent over Mira's bed, the child's shoulders caught

in a bruising hold. His head swiveled around as Renata came into the room, but he didn't let go of Mira. 'I have need of my father's oracle. And I don't answer to you, so kindly get the fuck out of here.'

'Rennie, he's hurting my arms.' Mira's voice was tiny, pinched with pain.

'Open your eyes,' Lex snarled at her. 'Then maybe I'll stop hurting you.'

'Take your hands off her, Lex.' Renata stopped at the foot of the bed, her sheathed blades a tempting weight in her grasp. 'Do it. Now.'

Lex scoffed. 'Not until I'm through with her.'

When he gave Mira a hard shake, Renata let loose with a blast of mental fury.

It was just a spurt of power, only a fraction of what she could give him, but Lex howled, his body jerking as though he'd been hit with a few thousand volts of electricity. He reeled back, dropping Mira and falling away from the bed, ass-planted on the floor.

'You bitch!' His eyes bled amber fire, pupils tight slivers in their center. 'I should kill you for that. I should kill the brat and you both!'

Renata hit him again, another small taste of agony. He slumped, clutching his head and moaning from the debilitating second blast. She waited, watching as he worked to collect himself from his sprawl on the floor. He didn't pose much of a threat to her like this, but in a few hours he would be recovered and she would be the vulnerable one. Then she might have a bit of hell to pay.

But for the time being, Mira was no longer of interest to Lex, and that was all that mattered.

Lex glared up at her as he dragged himself to his feet. 'Get out of my . . . way . . . goddamn . . . whore.'

The words were choked, sputtered between his gasps for

breath as he clumsily moved toward the open door. When he was out of sight, his footsteps scuffing along the hallway outside, Renata went to Mira's bedside and hushed her softly.

'Are you all right, kiddo?'

Mira nodded. 'I don't like him, Rennie. He scares me.'

'I know, honey.' Renata pressed a kiss to the child's brow. 'I'm not going to let him hurt you. You're safe with me. That's a promise, right?'

Another nod, weaker this time as Mira settled her head back onto her pillow and exhaled a sleepy sigh. 'Rennie?' she asked quietly.

'Yes, mouse?'

'Don't ever leave me, okay?'

Renata stared down at the innocent little face in the dark, feeling her heart squeeze tightly in her breast. 'I'm not going to leave you, Mira. Not ever . . . just like we promised.'

CHAPTER ELEVEN

The moon rose high, casting dappled light over Lake Wannsee in an exclusive area outside Berlin. Andreas Reichen leaned back in his cushioned chaise on the rear lawn of his private Darkhaven estate, trying to absorb some of the peace and quiet of the evening. Despite the warm, pleasant breeze and the calm of the night-dark water, his thoughts were morose, turbulent.

The news of the latest Gen One killing, this time in France, weighed him down. It seemed to him that the world was going increasingly mad around him. Not only the world of the Breed – his world – but that of humankind as well. So much death and destruction. So much anguish everywhere one looked.

He had the terrible feeling, deep in his gut, that this was only the beginning. Darker days were coming. Perhaps they had been coming for a long time already and he'd been too ignorant – too caught up in his own personal pleasures – to notice.

One of those pleasures came up behind him now, her elegant stride unmistakable as she walked through the estate's manicured gardens and down onto the grass.

Helene's lithe arms wrapped around his shoulders. 'Hello, darling.'

Reichen reached up to caress her warm skin as she bent over him and kissed him. Her mouth was soft, lingering, her long dark hair fragrant with the lightest trace of rose oil.

'Your nephew told me when I arrived that you've been out here for the past couple of hours,' she murmured, lifting her head to gaze out at the lake. 'I can see why. It's a lovely view.'

'It just got lovelier,' Reichen said, as he tipped his chin up and looked at her.

She smiled without coyness, having long become accustomed to his flattery. 'Something is troubling you, Andreas. It's not like you to sit alone and brood.'

Could she know him so well? They had been lovers for the past year, a casual dalliance that had somehow turned into something deeper if not entirely exclusive. Reichen knew Helene had other men in her life – human men – as he also occasionally took his pleasure with other women. Theirs was not a relationship plagued by jealousies or possessiveness. But that didn't mean it was devoid of affection. They shared a mutual concern for each other, and a bond of trust that extended beyond the barriers that generally made human and Breed relationships impossible.

Helene had become a friend and, of late, an indispensable partner in Reichen's important remote work with the warriors back in Boston.

Helene came around to the front of the chair and seated herself on the broad arm. 'Have you relayed the news to the Order about the recent assassination in Paris?'

Reichen nodded. 'I did, yes. And they tell me there was also an attempted killing in Montreal a few nights ago. At least that one failed, by some miracle of fate. But there will be others. I fear there will be many more deaths to come before the smoke finally clears. The Order is convinced they will put a stop to the madness, but there are times when I wonder if the evil at work here isn't greater than any amount of good.'

'You're letting this consume you,' Helene said as she idly petted his hair off his brow. 'You know, if you were looking for something to do with your time, you could have come to me instead of the Order. I could have put you to work at the club as my personal assisant. It's not too late to change your mind. And I assure you, the fringe benefits alone would be worth it.'

Reichen chuckled. 'Tempting, indeed.'

Helene bent down and nibbled his earlobe, her breath tickling and heated on his skin. 'It would only be a temporary position, of course. Say twenty or thirty years – a blink of time to you. But by then I will be wrinkled and gray, and you will be eager for a new, more appealing plaything who can still keep up with your wicked demands.'

Reichen was surprised to hear the twinge of wistfulness in Helene's voice. She'd never talked about the future with him, nor he with her. It was more or less understood that there could never be a future, given that she was mortal with a finite life span and he – barring prolonged UV exposure or massive bodily harm – would continue living for something close to eternity.

'What are you doing wasting your time with me when you could have your pick of any man?' he asked her, running his fingers along the smooth line of her shoulder. 'You could be married to someone who adores you, raising a litter of clever, beautiful children.'

Helene arched a flawlessly manicured brow. 'I suppose I never was one to make the conventional choice.'

Neither was he, in fact. Reichen acknowledged that it would be very easy to ignore everything he and the Order had discovered a few months ago. He could forget about the evil they'd tracked to that mountain cave in the Bohemian hills. He could pretend none of that existed, renege on his offer to help the warriors in whatever way he could. It would be the simplest thing in the world to retreat to his role as head of his Darkhaven household and slide back into his carefree, libertine ways.

But the simple truth was, he'd grown tired of that lifestyle long ago. Someone years past had once accused him of being a perpetual child – selfish and irresponsible. She'd been right, even then. Especially then, when he'd been fool enough to let that woman and the love she'd given him slip through his fingers. After too many decades of self-indulgence, it felt good to be making a difference. Or trying to, as it were.

'I don't expect you came by tonight just to distract me with kisses and attractive offers of employment,' he said, sensing a seriousness had come over Helene.

'No, I didn't, unfortunately. I thought you should know that one of my girls at the club may be missing. You recall me mentioning that Gina, one of my newer girls, showed up with bite marks on her neck last week?'

Reichen nodded. 'The one who'd been talking about a rich new boyfriend she was dating.'

'That's right. Well, it's not the first time she's missed her shift at work, but her housemate told me this afternoon that Gina hasn't been home or telephoned for more than three days. It could be nothing, but I thought you'd want to know.'

'Yes,' he said. 'Do you have any information on the male she was seeing? A description, a name, anything at all?'

'No. The housemate had never met him, naturally, so she couldn't tell me anything.'

Reichen considered the numerous things that could happen to a young woman who found herself unwittingly mixed up with one of his kind. Although most of the Breed were law-abiding members of the vampire nation, there were others who reveled in their savage side. 'I need you to discreetly ask around at the club tonight, see if any of the other girls heard Gina mention this boyfriend of hers. I'm looking for names, places she might have gone with him, even the smallest detail could be important.'

Helene nodded, but there was a note of interest in her eyes. 'I rather like this serious side to you, Andreas. It's incredibly sexy.'

Her hand trailed down the open front of his silk shirt, her long painted nails playing over the ridges of his muscled abdomen. Although his thoughts were grim, his body responded to her expert touch. His *dermaglyphs* began to saturate with color, and his vision sharpened with the flood of amber that was swiftly filling his irises. Lower still, his cock stiffened, swelling where it now rested beneath her palm.

'I really shouldn't stay,' she murmured, her voice husky and teasing. 'I don't want to be late for work.'

When she started to get up, Reichen held her back. 'Don't worry about that. I know the woman who runs the place, I'll make your excuses for you. I have it on good authority that she fancies me.'

'Do you now?'

Reichen grunted, baring the points of his fangs with his broad grin. 'Poor dear is mad for me.'

'Mad for an arrogant thing like you?' Helene teased. 'Darling, don't flatter yourself. She may want you only for your decadent body.'

'True enough,' he replied, 'but you won't hear me complaining either way.'

Helene smiled, not resisting in the least as he pulled her down onto his lap for a deep, hungered kiss.

By nightfall, Lex was fully recovered from the agony Renata had dealt him. His rage – his festering hatred for her – remained.

He cursed her over and over in his mind as he leaned against a rotting wall of a rat-infested crack house in Montreal's worst slum, watching as a young human male tied off his arm with an old leather belt. The loose tail caught between a smattering of broken, decayed teeth, the junkie stuck the needle of a filthy syringe into the field of scabs and bruises that tracked along his emaciated arm. He moaned as the heroin entered his bloodstream.

'Ah, fuck, man,' he rasped around a shaky sigh as he released his tourniquet and fell back against a putrid mattress on the floor. He ran his tattooed hands over his pale, pimply face and greasy brown hair. 'Ah, Christ . . . that right there's some prime shit, baby.'

'Yes,' Lex said, his voice airless in the dank, urine-soaked darkness.

He'd spared no expense on the drugs; money was of little concern to him. No doubt the lowlife junkie he'd picked up selling his body on the street had never had such an expensive high. Lex was willing to bet the young man's personal services had never fetched such a rich sum either. He'd all but leapt into the car when Lex pulled over and flashed a hundred dollars and a bag of heroin in front of his face.

Lex cocked his head and watched as the human savored his fix. They were alone in the squalid room of the abandoned apartment building. The place had been overrun with vagrants and addicts when they'd first arrived, but it took Lex only a few minutes – and an irresistible mental command, courtesy of his second-generation Breed lineage – to drive the humans out so he could conduct his business in private.

Still reclining on the floor, the junkie stripped out of his sleeveless T-shirt then began to unbutton his loose-fitting, grime-stained blue jeans. He crudely fondled himself as he worked the fly open, bleary eyes rolling in his skull, searching listlessly through the dark.

'So, you want me to suck your dick or what, man?'

'No,' Lex said, repulsed by the very idea.

He stepped away from his position across the room and walked slowly toward the junkie. Where to begin with him?

he wondered idly. He had to play this thing out carefully or he'd be back on the street, searching for someone else.

Wasting precious time.

'You like my ass instead, baby?' the human whore slurred. 'If you want to fuck me, you gotta pay double. That's my rule.'

Lex's laugh was low, genuinely amused. 'I'm not interested in fucking you. Bad enough I have to look at you, that I have to smell your revolting stench. Sex is not the reason you're here.'

'Well, what the hell then?' A note of panic edged the stale air, a sudden kick of human adrenaline that Lex's heightened senses easily detected. 'You sure as shit didn't bring me here for a little polite conversation.'

'No,' Lex agreed pleasantly.

'Okay. So, what the fuck do I look like to you, asshole?'

Lex smiled. 'Bait.'

With movements so fast not even the soberest human eye could track them, he reached out and hauled the junkie up off the floor. Lex had a knife in his hand. He stuck it into the human's gaunt belly and ripped a slash across his midsection.

Blood surged out of the wound, hot and wet and fragrant.

'Oh, Jesus!' the human screamed. 'Oh, my fucking God! You stabbed me!'

Lex drew back and let the man fall back limply onto the floor. It was all he could do to keep himself from lunging after him in a blind thirst.

Lex's physical transformation was swift, brought on by the sudden presence of fresh, flowing blood. His vision sharpened with the narrowing of his pupils, an amber glow washing over the room as his eyes changed to that of a predator. His fangs stretched long behind his lips, saliva gushing into his mouth as the urge to feed swelled.

The junkie was sobbing now, sputtering pathetically as he

clutched at the gaping wound in his belly. 'Are you crazy, you fucking asshole? You might have killed me!'

'Not yet,' Lex replied thickly around his fangs.

'I have to get out of here,' the man murmured. 'Gotta get help—'

'Stay,' Lex ordered him, smiling as the feeble human mind wilted under his command.

He had to force himself to keep his distance. Let the situation play out as he intended it to. A gut wound would bleed hard, but death would come slowly. Lex needed him alive for a while, long enough for his scent to travel out onto the street and into the surrounding alleyways.

The human he'd bought tonight was merely chum to be tossed into the water. Lex was looking to attract bigger fish.

He knew as well as any other member of the Breed that nothing drew a vampire faster, or more surely, than the prospect of bleeding human prey. This deep into the underbelly of the city, where even the dregs of human society rushed about in an unspoken state of terror, Lex was counting on the presence of Rogues.

He wasn't disappointed.

The first two came sniffing around the crack house in mere minutes. Rogues were hopeless addicts, as much as the junkie now curled up in a fetal position and weeping quietly on the floor as his life slowly leeched out of him.

Although few of the Breed lost themselves to Bloodlust – the permanent, insatiable thirst for blood – the ones who did rarely, if ever, came back from it. They lived in the shadows, savage, rootless monsters whose only purpose in living was to feed their hunger.

Lex slid back into the corner of the room as the two predators crept inside. They immediately fell upon the human, tearing at him with fangs that never receded, eyes burning with the color and heat of fire.

Another Rogue found the room. This one was larger than the others, more brutal as he threw himself into the carnage and began to feed. A scuffle broke out among the feral vampires. The three of them turned on each other like snarling, rabid dogs. Fists pounding, fingers tearing, fangs ripping through flesh and bone, each powerful male fought viciously to win his prey.

Lex watched transfixed. Giddy from the violence, and drunk from the scent of so much spilled blood, human and Breed.

He watched, and he waited.

The Rogues would fight one another to the death, like the base animals they were. Only one of them would prove the strongest in the end.

And that was the one Lex needed.

After a whole day of waiting for nightfall, now he had another two hours to kill before he could catch his ride back to Boston.

Nikolai seriously considered skipping the airport rendezvous and heading out on foot instead, but even with his Breed stamina and hyperspeed, he would hardly clear the state of Vermont before sunrise drove him into hiding again. And frankly, the idea of bunking down in some low-country barn with a bunch of agitated livestock didn't exactly have him dying to strap on a pair of Nikes and hit the open road.

So, he would wait.

Damn it.

He and patience had never been the closest of friends. He'd been just about batshit with boredom by the time the sun had finally set and he was able to get out of the mausoleum shelter.

He supposed it was that same boredom that led him into the humid tenderloin of Montreal, where he hoped to find something diverting to do while he cooled his heels. He didn't much care how he used the time, but he'd deliberately sought out the one area of the city where the odds of finding a reason to burn off steam with his knuckles or his weapons were better than good.

In this particular block of rat-infested alleys and low-rent slums, his immediate choices were limited to crackheads, traffickers – be they dealers in narcotics or skin – and vacant-eyed streetwalkers of both genders. More than one idiot eyeballed him as he strode the block in no particular direction. Someone was even stupid enough to flash the business end of a blade at him as he passed, but Niko just paused and gave the toothless scumbag a dimpled, fang-tipped grin of invitation and the threat was gone as quickly as it had appeared.

Although he wasn't opposed to confrontation in any form, fighting humans was a bit beneath him. He preferred more of a challenge. What he really itched to find right now was a Rogue. Last summer, Boston had been knee-deep in blood-addicted vampires. The fighting had been hard and heavy – with at least one tragic loss on the Order's side – but Nikolai and the rest of the warriors had made it their mission to sweep the city clean.

Other metropolitan areas still lost the occasional civilian to Bloodlust, and Niko would have bet his left nut that Montreal was no different. But aside from the pimps, pushers, and prostitutes, this stretch of brick and asphalt was feeling about as dead as the crypt where he'd been forced to spend the day.

'Hey, baby.' The female smiled at him from a shadowed doorway as he walked past. 'You lookin' for something specific, or just window-shoppin'?'

Nikolai grunted, but he paused. 'I'm a specific kind of guy.'

'Well, maybe I got what you need.' She grinned at him and hopped off her perch on the concrete stoop. 'Matter of fact, I'm sure I got just exactly what you need, sugar.'

She wasn't a beauty, with her brittle, teased-up brassy hair, dull eyes, and sallow skin, but then again Nikolai didn't expect he was going to be spending much time looking at her face. She smelled clean, if deodorant soap and hairspray could be considered clean-smelling scents. To Niko's acute senses, the woman reeked of cosmetics and perfumes, with an undercurrent of recent narcotic use that seeped from her pores.

'Whattaya say?' she asked, sidling up to him now. 'You wanna go someplace for a little while? If you got twenty bucks, I'll give you half an hour.'

Nikolai stared at the pulse point ticking in the woman's neck. It had been several days since he'd last fed. And he did have two hours of do-nothing ahead of him . . .

'Yeah,' he said, giving her a nod. 'Let's take a walk.'

She took his hand and led him around the corner of the building and down an empty alley.

Nikolai didn't waste any time. As soon as they were secluded from potential onlookers, he took her head in his hands and bared her neck for his bite. Her startled cry was squashed the instant he sank his fangs into her carotid and began to drink.

The woman's blood was unremarkable – the usual copper heaviness of human red cells, but laced with a bittersweet tang of the speedball she'd had before stepping out for her night's work. Nikolai gulped down several mouthfuls, feeling the blood's energy course through his body in a low vibration. It wasn't unusual for a Breed male to get aroused by the act of feeding. The response was purely physical, an awakening of cells and muscles.

That his cock was fully erect now and straining for relief didn't surprise him at all. It was the fact that his head was swimming with thoughts of a certain raven-haired female – a female he had no intention of seeing ever again – that made Niko rear back in alarm.

'Mmm, don't stop,' his human companion moaned, pulling his mouth back to the wound at her neck. She too was feeling the effects of the feeding, enthralled as all humans became when held under the bite of the Breed. 'Don't stop, baby.'

Nikolai's vision was swamped with amber fire as he clamped

back down on her throat. He knew she wasn't Renata, but as his hands skimmed up the woman's bare legs and under the short denim skirt she wore, he pictured himself caressing Renata's long, beautiful thighs. He imagined it was Renata's blood that fed him. Renata's body that responded so eagerly to his touch.

It was Renata's fevered gasps that drove him as he ripped at the cheap thong panties with one hand and worked to free himself with the other.

He needed to be inside her.

He needed –

Holy hell.

A light breeze eddied through the alleyway, carrying with it the stench of vampires gone Rogue. And there was spilled blood too. Human blood. A damned lot of it, mixed with the vile odor of bleeding Rogues.

Nikolai froze with his hand still on his fly, shocked stupid in one blinding instant.

'Jesus Christ.'

What the fuck was going on?

He yanked the woman's skirt back down and swept his tongue over her neck wound, sealing up his bite.

'I said, don't st—'

Niko didn't give her a chance to finish the thought. With a glance of his palm over her brow, he scrubbed her mind of the entire thing. 'Get out of here,' he told her.

He was already jogging up the alley by the time she shook out of her daze and started moving. He followed his nose to a dilapidated building not far from where he'd been. The stench emanated from inside, a couple floors off the street.

Nikolai climbed the lightless stairwell to the second floor. His eyes were practically watering from the overwhelming stink of death that rolled out from under a closed door. His hand on the gun holstered at his hip, Niko approached the place.

There was no sound on the other side of the battered, graffiti-tagged door. Only death, human and Breed. Niko turned the loose knob and braced himself for what he would find.

It had been a massacre.

An apparent junkie lay in a supine sprawl amid discarded syringes and other trash that littered the blood-soaked floor and a fouled mattress. The body was so ruined it was hardly recognizable as human, let alone a distinguishable gender. The other two bodies were savaged as well, but definitely Breed – without question, both of them Rogues judging by the size and stench of them alone.

Nikolai could guess what might have happened here: a lethal struggle over prey. This fight was fresh, maybe only minutes old. And the two dead suckheads wouldn't have been able to shred each other so thoroughly before one or the other went down.

There had been at least one more Rogue involved in this scuffle.

If Niko was lucky, the victor might still be in the area, licking his wounds. He hoped so, because he'd love to give the diseased bastard a taste of his 9mm's custom rounds. Nothing said 'Have a nice day' like a Rogue's corrupted blood system going into allergic meltdown from a dose of poisonous titanium.

Nikolai went to the boarded-up window and tossed the crudely nailed panels aside. If he was looking for action, he'd just found it in spades. Below, on the street, stood an enormous Rogue. He was bloodied and battered, looking like ten kinds of hell.

But holy shit . . . he wasn't alone.

Alexei Yakut was with him.

Incredibly, Lex and the Rogue walked toward a waiting sedan and got in.

'What the fuck are you up to?' Niko murmured under his breath as the car roared up the street.

He was about to leap out the open window and follow on foot when a shrill scream sounded behind him. A woman had wandered into the carnage and now gaped at him in terror, an accusing, shaky finger pointed in his direction. She screamed again, loud enough to wake every crackhead and dealer in the neighborhood.

Nikolai eyed the witness and the bloody evidence of a struggle that looked anything but human.

'Damn it,' he growled, glancing over his shoulder in time to see Lex's car disappear around the corner. 'It's all right,' he told the shrieking banshee as he left the window and approached her. 'You didn't see a thing.'

He wiped her memory and shoved her out of the room. Then he took out a titanium blade and stuck it into the remains of one of the dead Rogues.

As the body began to sizzle and dissolve, Niko set about cleaning up the rest of the mess that Lex and his unlikely associate had left behind.

⇥ CHAPTER TWELVE ⇤

Renata stood at the counter of the lodge's galley kitchen, a knife gripped loosely in her hand. 'What kind of jelly do you want tonight – grape or strawberry?'

'Grape,' Mira replied. 'No, wait – I want strawberry this time.'

She was perched on the edge of the wood countertop next to Renata, her legs swinging idly. Dressed in a purple T-shirt, faded blue jeans, and scuffed sneakers, Mira might have seemed like any other normal suburban little girl waiting on her dinner. But normal little girls weren't made to eat the same thing, practically day in and day out. Normal little girls had families to love and care for them. They lived in nice houses on pretty, tree-lined streets, with bright kitchens and stocked pantries and mothers who knew how to cook endless wonderful meals.

At least, that's what Renata imagined when she thought of the ideal picture of normal. She didn't know from any kind of personal experience. As a child of the streets before Yakut found her and brought her to the lodge, Mira didn't know what normal was either. But it was that wholesome, normal kind of life that Renata wished for the child, as futile a wish as it seemed, standing in Sergei Yakut's dingy kitchen, next to a beat-up range that probably wouldn't work even if it did have a gas line running to it.

Since Renata and Mira were the only ones at the lodge

who ate food, Yakut had left it up to Renata to see that she and the child were regularly fed. Renata didn't particularly care what she had for sustenance – food was food, a necessity of function, nothing more – but she hated not being able to treat Mira to something nice once in a while.

'Someday you and I are going to go out and have ourselves a real dinner, one with five entirely different courses. Plus dessert,' she added, slathering the strawberry jam over the slice of white bread. 'Maybe we'll have two desserts apiece.'

Mira smiled under the short black veil that fell to the tip of her little nose. 'Do you think they'll be chocolate desserts?'

'Definitely chocolate. Here you go,' she said, handing the plate to her. 'PB&J, heavy on the J, and no crusts.'

Renata leaned back against the counter as Mira bit into the sandwich and ate like it was as delicious as any five-course meal she could imagine. 'Don't forget to drink your apple juice.'

'M-kay.'

Renata stabbed the plastic straw into the juice box and placed it next to Mira. Then she started putting things away, wiping down the counter. Every muscle tensed when she heard Lex's voice in the other room.

He'd been gone since dusk. Renata hadn't really missed him, but she had wondered what he'd been up to in the time since he'd left. The answer to that question came in the form of a drunken female cackle – several drunken females, by the sound of the laughter and squealing going on in the main area of the lodge.

Lex often brought human women home to serve as his blood Hosts and general entertainment. Sometimes he'd keep them for days at a time. Occasionally he'd share his spoils with the other guards, all of them using the women however they saw fit before scrubbing their memories and dumping them back into their lives. It sickened Renata to be under the same roof while Lex was in a party mood, but no more than it infuriated her that Mira had to be exposed – even peripherally – to his games as well.

'What's going on out there, Rennie?' she asked.

'Finish your sandwich,' Renata told her when Mira stopped eating to listen to the ruckus in the other room. 'Stay here. I'll be right back.'

Renata walked out of the galley and down the hallway toward the disruption.

'Drink up, ladies!' Lex shouted, dropping a box of liquor bottles on the leather sofa.

He wouldn't be consuming the alcohol, nor the other party favors he'd procured. A couple of clear, rolled-up plastic bags, each fat with what was likely cocaine, were tossed out onto the table. The sound system came on, a bass beat throbbing behind crude hip-hop lyrics.

Lex grabbed the curvy brunette with the giddy cackle and brought her under his arm. 'I told you we were going to have us some fun tonight! Come here and show me some proper gratitude.'

He certainly was in a rare, good mood. And no wonder. He'd come back with quite a haul: five young females dressed in tall heels, skimpy tops, and micro-short skirts. At first, Renata guessed them to be prostitutes, but on closer look she decided they were too clean, too fresh under their heavy makeup to be part of the street life. They were probably just naive club girls, unaware that the persuasive, attractive man who picked them up was actually something out of a nightmare.

'Come in and meet my friends,' Lex told the giggling group of women as he motioned the other Breed males around to view his evening's catch. There was a moment of palpable apprehension as the four muscle-bound, heavily armed guards leered hungrily at their human appetizers. Lex pushed three of the women toward the eager vampires. 'Don't be shy, ladies. This is a party, after all. Go say hello.'

Renata noticed he was keeping a tight hold on the two prettiest girls. Typical of Lex, he had obviously reserved the best for himself. Renata was about to turn around and go back to Mira in the kitchen – to try to ignore the bloody orgy that was about to begin – but before she took two steps away, Sergei Yakut came thundering out of his private quarters.

'Alexei.' Fury rolled off the elder vampire in waves of heat. He glared at Lex, his eyes flashing amber. 'You've been gone for hours. Where were you?'

'I've been in the city, Father.' He attempted a magnanimous smile, as if to say his time away from his duties hadn't been entirely about serving his own selfish needs. 'Look what I brought you.'

Lex pulled one of the females away from the guards and held her out for Yakut's inspection. Yakut didn't even spare a glance for the prize Lex offered. He stared only at the two women Lex was keeping for himself.

The Gen One grunted. 'You would scrape shit off your boot heels and tell me it's gold?'

'Never,' Lex replied. 'Father, I would never so much as consider—'

'Good. These two will do,' he said, indicating Lex's females.

As irate as he had to be, as humiliated as he must have felt by the public jab to his pride, Lex didn't say a word. He dropped his gaze and waited in silence as Yakut collected his two female companions and strode with them toward his private quarters.

'I expect not to be disturbed,' Yakut ordered darkly. 'Not for any reason.'

Lex gave a nod of restrained obeisance. 'Yes, Father. Of course. Whatever you wish.'

*   *   *

Nikolai heard music and loud voices before he was even five hundred feet out from the lodge. He stole in close, moving through the woods like a ghost, past Lex's car parked around back, the hood still warm from the drive out of the city.

Niko wasn't sure what he was going to find. He wasn't expecting a damned party, but that's what seemed to be going on inside the main house. The place was lit up like a Christmas tree, light pouring out of the windows of the great room where someone was apparently entertaining a number of females. Hard-core rap vibrated all the way into the earth beneath Nikolai's boots as he drew up to the side of the building and peered inside.

Lex was there, all right. He and the rest of Yakut's body-guards, gathered together in the rustic hall. Three young women danced on the pelt rugs in just their panties, all of them clearly intoxicated, based on the amount of liquor and narcotics spread out on the table nearby. The four Breed guards howled and cheered them on, the vampires probably just seconds away from pouncing on the unsuspecting females.

Lex, meanwhile, sat in a pensive slouch on the leather sofa, his dark eyes fixed on the women even though his thoughts seemed to be miles away. There was no outward sign of the Rogue Lex had been cozying up to in the city. No sign of Sergei Yakut either, and the fact that his entire security detail was tied up with this convenient little peep show made Niko's warrior instincts switch to instant red alert.

'What the hell are you up to?' Niko mouthed under his breath.

But he knew the answer even before he started moving for the rear of the lodge, where Yakut kept his private chambers. Where a subtle yet persistent odor confirmed Niko's suspicions with the worst kind of dread.

Goddamn.

The Rogue was here.

Nikolai smelled freshly spilled blood too, basic human stock, the scent of it almost overwhelming the closer he got to Yakut's quarters. Blood and sex, to be exact, as if the Gen One had been gorging himself on both for some time.

A sudden scream rent the night.

Female. A sound of total terror, coming from within Yakut's chambers.

Then, muffled gunfire.

Pop, pop, pop!

Nikolai flew through a rear door of the lodge, hardly surprised to find it unlocked to the outside and flapping open. He crashed into Yakut's room, his semiauto pistol gripped in hand and ready to unload its chamber full of titanium high-test rounds.

The scene that greeted him was total carnage.

On the bed was Sergei Yakut, sprawled naked atop a female who was pinned beneath his lifeless body, her throat torn open where the vampire had been feeding on her just a second before. She wasn't moving, and there was no telling the color of the woman's skin or hair because most of her was currently saturated in blood – her own and Yakut's.

Half of the Gen One's face was missing. Sergei Yakut's head was little more than shattered bone, tissue, and gore from the trio of bullets that had been shot point-blank into the back of his skull. He was dead, and the Rogue who killed him was too gripped by Bloodlust to realize Nikolai's presence. The suckhead had put down the gun he'd used to kill Yakut and was currently getting busy with another naked female who'd been trapped in the corner of the room. Her eyes were rolled back in her head and she wasn't moving. Shit, she wasn't breathing either, although the Rogue kept drinking from her, savaging her neck with his huge fangs.

Niko moved in behind the suckhead and put the muzzle of his Beretta against the big, shaggy head. He squeezed the trigger – two dead-on, titanium-laced blasts into the bastard's brain. The Rogue dropped to the floor, writhing and spasming from the hit. The titanium kicked in fast, and the dying vampire let loose with a howl so loud and otherworldly it shook like thunder in the old wooden rafters of the lodge.

Renata flew out of the kitchen with her pistol drawn. Her battle senses had gone as taut as piano wire at the low, distant crack of gunshots – and the inhuman howl that followed – coming from elsewhere in the lodge.

Music was still blaring in the great room. Lex's visitors were no longer clothed and raucous from the continued free-flowing drugs and alcohol. The women were all over the guards and one another as well, and from the rapt look in the Breed males' hungering eyes, they wouldn't have noticed if a bomb went off in the other room.

'Idiots,' Renata accused under her breath. 'Didn't any of you hear that?'

Lex looked up, concern darkening his expression, but she wasn't really waiting for an answer from him. She ran toward the hallway and Yakut's private chambers. The hall was dark, the air thick. Everything too silent back here. Too still.

Death hung like a shroud, almost choking her as she neared the open door of the vampire's quarters.

Sergei Yakut was no longer alive; Renata felt that truth in her bones. Gunpowder, blood, and an overwhelming, sickly sweet scent of rot and decay warned her that she was about to walk into something awful. Though nothing could have truly prepared her for what she saw as she pivoted around the doorjamb, gun raised and gripped in both hands. Ready to kill whoever stood in its path.

The sight of so much death, so much blood and gore, took her aback. It was everywhere: the bed, the floor, the walls.

And it was on Sergei Yakut's apparent killer too.

Nikolai stood in the center of the carnage, his face and dark shirt splattered scarlet. In his hand was a large semi-automatic pistol, the nose of the blunt black barrel still smoking from its recent discharge.

'You?' The word slipped past her lips, shock and disbelief like a ball of ice in her gut. She glanced at Yakut's body – his obliterated remains – sprawled across the bed on top of a lifeless female. 'My God,' she whispered, stunned to see him here at the lodge again, but even more shocked by the rest of what she was seeing. 'You . . . you killed him.'

'No.' The warrior shook his head somberly. 'Not me, Renata. There was a Rogue in here with Yakut.' He indicated a large mass of smoldering cinders on the floor – the source of the offending stench. 'I killed the Rogue, but I was too late to save Yakut. I'm sorry—'

'Put down your weapon,' she told him, uninterested in apologies. She didn't need them. Renata felt some pity for Yakut's violent end, a sense of stunned incredulity that he was actually dead. But no sorrow. None of that absolved Nikolai of his apparent guilt. She steadied her aim on him and cautiously stepped farther into the room. 'Put your gun down. Now.'

He kept his grip firm on the 9mm pistol. 'I can't do that, Renata. I won't, not so long as Lex is still breathing.'

She frowned, confused. 'What about Lex?'

'This murder was his doing, not mine. He brought the Rogue here. He brought the women to distract Yakut and the guards, so the Rogue could get close enough to kill.'

Renata listened but kept her gun locked on target. Lex was a snake, sure, but a murderer? Would he actually take steps to kill his own father?

Just then, Lex and the other guards approached from up the hall.

'What's going on? Is something wrong in—'

Lex fell silent as he reached the open doorway to his father's chambers. In her peripheral vision Renata saw him look from Yakut's body on the bed to Nikolai. He staggered back a half-pace, not so much as breathing. Then he exploded, total rage. 'You son of a bitch! You goddamned murdering son of a bitch!'

Lex lunged, but it was a halfhearted attempt, one he abandoned completely as Nikolai's pistol swung in his direction. The warrior didn't flinch, not his gaze nor a single muscle. He was utterly calm as he stared at Lex down the barrel of his weapon, even while Renata's gun and those of the other guards were trained on him. 'I saw you in the city tonight, Lex. I was there. The crackhouse. The bait you laid out to attract Rogue vampires. The suckhead you brought back with you here tonight . . . I saw it all.'

Lex scoffed. 'Fuck you and your lies! You saw no such thing.'

'What did you have to promise that Rogue in exchange for your father's head? Money doesn't matter to blood addicts, so whose life did you offer up as the price – Renata's? Maybe that tender little child instead?'

Renata's chest went tight at the thought. She dared a quick glance at Lex and found him sneering coldly at the warrior, giving a slow shake of his head.

'You'd say anything right now to save your own neck. It won't work. Not when you yourself threatened my father's life not even twenty-four hours ago.' Lex turned to look at Renata. 'You heard him say as much, didn't you?'

Reluctantly she nodded, recalling how Nikolai had given Sergei Yakut a very public warning that someone needed to shut him down.

Now Nikolai was back and Yakut was dead.

Mother Mary, she thought, glancing once more to the lifeless body of the vampire who'd kept her practically a prisoner for the past two years. He was dead.

'My father wasn't in any kind of danger at all until the Order came into the picture,' Lex was saying. 'One failed attempt on his life, now this . . . this bloodbath. You were the one who lay in wait to make your move. You and the Rogue you brought with you tonight, waiting for the chance to strike. I can only guess that you came here looking to kill my father from the start.'

'No,' Nikolai said, a flash of amber lighting his wintry blue eyes. 'The one who needs killing is you, Lex.'

In a split-second reaction, just as she saw the tendons in his arm flex as his finger began to depress the trigger of his gun, Renata hit Nikolai with a hard mental blast. As little affection as she felt for Alexei, she could not stand more death tonight. Nikolai roared, spine arching, face contorting with pain.

More effective than bullets, the blast took him down to his knees in an instant. The other guards stormed into the room and grabbed his gun and the rest of his weapons. The barrels of four pistols were trained on the warrior's head, awaiting kill orders. One of the guards cocked the hammer back, eager for more bloodshed even though the room was ripe with death already.

'Stand down,' Renata told them. She looked to Lex, whose face was tight with anger, his eyes avid and glittering, his sharp fangs visible between his parted lips. 'Tell them to stand down, Lex. Killing him now will do nothing but make all of us murderers in cold blood too.'

Incredibly, it was Nikolai who began to chuckle. He lifted his head, an obvious effort while the blast still held him down. 'He has to kill me, Renata, because he can't risk a witness. Isn't that right, Lex? Can't have somebody walking around who knows your dirty secret.'

Lex drew his own pistol now and strolled right up to Nikolai to put the nose of the gun up against the warrior's forehead. He snarled, his arm quivering with the ferocity of his rage.

Renata went stock-still, horrified that he might actually pull the trigger. She was torn, part of her wanting to believe what Nikolai had said – that he was innocent – and afraid to believe him. What he said about Lex simply could not be true.

'Lex,' she said, the only sound in the room. 'Lex . . . do not do this.'

She was less than a breath away from hitting him with some of what she gave Nikolai when the gun slowly lowered.

Lex growled, finally easing off. 'I wish a slower death on this bastard than I am capable of giving him. Take him to the main hall and restrain him,' he told the guards. 'Then someone get in here and look after my father's body. One of you scrub those females in the other room and dump them off the property. I want this bloody mess cleaned up immediately.'

Lex turned a dark look on Renata as the guards began dragging Nikolai out of the room. 'If he tries anything at all, unleash all you've got and lay the son of a bitch flat.'

⇥ CHAPTER THIRTEEN ⇤

'*Pardonnez-moi,* Monsieur Fabien. There is a telephone call for you, sir. From a Monsieur Alexei Yakut.'

Edgar Fabien gave a dismissive wave to the Breed male who served as his personal secretary and continued to admire the crisp cut of his custom-tailored slacks in the wardrobe mirror. He was being fitted for a new suit, and, at the moment, nothing Alexei Yakut had to say to him was important enough to warrant an interruption.

'Tell him I'm in a meeting and cannot be disturbed.'

'Begging your pardon, sir, but I have already informed him that you were unavailable. He says it's an urgent matter. One that requires your immediate personal attention.'

Fabien's reflection glowered back at him from under his pale, manicured brows. He didn't attempt to hide the outward signs of his rising irritation, which showed in the amber glint of his eyes and in the sudden, churning colors of the *dermaglyphs* that swirled and arced over his bare chest and shoulders.

'Enough,' he snapped at the expert tailor sent over from Givenchy's downtown store. The human backed off at once, collecting his pins and measuring tape and obediently slinking away at his master's command. He belonged to Fabien – one of many Minions the second-generation Breed vampire employed around the city. 'Get out of here, both of you.'

Fabien stepped off the wardrobe dais and stalked over to

his desk phone. He waited until both servants had left the room and the door was closed behind them.

With a snarl, he picked up the receiver and punched the blinking button that would connect him to Alexei Yakut's holding call. 'Yes,' he hissed coldly. 'What is this urgent matter of yours that simply could not wait?'

'My father is dead.'

Fabien rocked back on his heels, truly taken off guard by the news. He exhaled a sigh meant to sound of boredom. 'How convenient for you, Alexei. Shall I offer my congratulations along with my condolences?'

Sergei Yakut's heir apparent ignored the jab. 'There was an intruder at the lodge tonight. Somehow he managed to sneak into the place. He killed my father in his bed, in cold blood. I heard the disturbance and tried to intervene, but . . . well. Unfortunately, I was too late to save him. I am grief-stricken, of course—'

Fabien grunted. 'Of course.'

'—but I knew that you would want to be notified of the crime. And I knew that you and the Enforcement Agency would want to come out here immediately to arrest my father's assailant.'

Every cell in Fabien's body stilled. 'What are you saying – that you have someone in custody? Who?'

A low chuckle on the other end of the line. 'I see I finally have your attention, Fabien. What would you say if I told you that I have a member of the Order subdued and waiting for you here at the lodge? I'm sure there are some individuals who would be of the mind that one less warrior around to contend with, the better.'

'You're not actually trying to convince me that this warrior is responsible for killing Sergei Yakut, are you?'

'I'm telling you that my father is dead and I am in command of his domain now. I'm telling you that I have a member of the Order in my keeping, and I am willing to hand him over to you. A gift, if you will.'

Edgar Fabien was quiet for a long moment, considering the sizable prize Alexei Yakut was presenting him. The Order and its vigilante members had few allies within the Enforcement Agency. Fewer still within the private circle to which Fabien belonged. 'And what are you expecting in return for this . . . gift?'

'I've already told you, when we met before. I want in. I want a piece of whatever action it is that you're dealing. A big piece, you understand?' He chuckled, so very full of himself. 'You need me on your side, Fabien. I should think that's obvious to you now.'

The last thing Edgar Fabien or any of his associates needed on their side was a grasping pissant like Alexei Yakut. He was a loose cannon, one that would have to be dealt with carefully. If Fabien had his druthers, he'd opt for swift extermination, but there was someone else who ultimately would need to make that call.

As for the captive member of the Order? Now, that was intriguing. That was a boon well worth considering, and the many appealing possibilities it presented made Fabien's four-hundred-year-old heart beat a little faster.

'I will have to make a few . . . arrangements,' he said. 'It may take me an hour or so to line up resources and make the drive out to the lodge to retrieve the prisoner.'

'One hour,' Alexei Yakut agreed eagerly. 'Don't keep me waiting any longer than that.'

Fabien bit back his acid reply and ended the call with a terse 'I will see you then.'

He sat down on the edge of his desk and looked out at the nighttime skyline twinkling in the distance beyond his Darkhaven estate. Then he walked to his safe and twisted the combination lock, turned the crank handle to open the secured storage box.

Inside was a cell phone reserved for emergency calls only. He hit a programmed number and waited for the encrypted signal to connect.

When the airless voice on the other end answered, Fabien said, 'We have a situation.'

Heavy chains circled his bare torso, binding him to a rough-hewn wooden chair. Nikolai felt similar restraints on his hands, which were caught behind him, and his feet, which were bound at the ankles and held hard against the chair legs.

He'd taken a hell of a beating, and not just from the debilitating mind blast he'd gotten courtesy of Renata. Thanks to that crippling blow, he had been in and out of consciousness for some time, struggling just to lift his eyelids even now. Of course, part of the problem there was that his face was bruised and battered, his eyes swollen, lips cracked open and bitter with the taste of his own blood. He'd been too weak to put up much of a fight when Lex and his guards had worked him over like a punching bag as they stripped him down to his skivvies and hauled him into the lodge's great room to await his fate.

Nikolai didn't know how long he'd been sitting there. Long enough that his hands felt numb from lack of circulation. Long enough to have noticed when Renata had come through the room a while ago, protectively ushering Mira away from the whole ugly scene. He had watched her from under a hank of his sweat-soaked hair, seeing the pain and tension in her face as she'd shot a baleful glance in his direction.

Her reverb was probably hitting her pretty hard by now, he guessed. Niko told himself that the twinge he felt was just another muscle screaming from abuse; he couldn't possibly be stupid enough to feel any kind of sympathy for the female's suffering. He couldn't possibly be stupid enough to care what she thought of him – that she might actually think he'd done what Lex accused him of – but damn it, he did care. His frustration at not being able to talk to Renata only amplified his physical pain and fury.

Across the room from him, the four guards were examining his weapons and the handmade hollowpoint titanium rounds that were one of Nikolai's personal creations. They had all of his gear laid out on a trestle table, well out of his reach. Niko's cell phone – his link to the Order – lay in shards on the floor. Lex had taken great pleasure in smashing it under his boot heel before he left Nikolai to the supervision of his guards.

One of the beefy Breed males said something that made the other three laugh before he pivoted around with Niko's semiauto and pointed it in his direction. Nikolai didn't flinch. In fact, he barely breathed, watching from within the puffy slit of his left eye, every muscle slumped as if he were still unconscious and unaware of his surroundings.

'Whattaya say we wake him up?' joked the guard with the gun in his hand. He swaggered toward Niko, temptingly within arm's reach, if Niko's arms hadn't been heavily secured behind him. The nose of the 9mm lowered slowly, down past his chest, then past his abdomen too. 'I say we castrate this murdering piece of shit. Blow his balls off and let the Enforcement Agency take him away in pieces.'

'Kiril, stop being a jackass,' one of the others warned. 'Lex said we couldn't touch him.'

'Lex is a pussy.' Polished black steel grated with a cold *snick* as Kiril chambered a round. 'In two seconds, this warrior's going to be nothing but a pussy too.'

Nikolai held himself very still as the gun pressed snugly against his groin. Part of his patience was born of genuine fear, as he was rather fond of his manly bits and had no wish to lose them. But overriding even that was the understanding that his opportunities to turn this situation in his favor were few and fleeting. He had shaken off most of the internal effects of Renata's talent, but he couldn't be sure of his physical strength unless he tried it.

And if he tried it now and failed . . . well, he didn't want to contemplate the odds of walking away with his manhood intact if he tried to break out of his bonds and succeeded only in upsetting trigger-happy Kiril.

A hard palm cuffed the side of his skull. 'You in there, warrior? I got something for you. Time to wake up.'

Eyes closed to conceal their change from blue to amber, Nikolai let his head loll bonelessly with the blow. But inside of him, fury was beginning to kindle in his belly. He had to hold it at bay. Couldn't let Kiril or the others see the change in his *dermaglyphs* and risk telegraphing the fact that he was very much awake and aware and totally pissed off.

'Wake up,' Kiril growled.

He started to lift Niko's chin, but then a noise outside the lodge drew his attention away. Gravel spraying and crunching underneath the tires of approaching vehicles. A fleet of them, by the sound of it.

'The Agency is here,' one of the other guards announced.

Kiril backed away from Nikolai, but he took his time disarming the pistol. Outside, the vehicles were slowing down, coming to a halt. Doors opened. Boots hit the gravel drive as the Darkhavens' policing agents poured out. Nikolai counted more than half a dozen pairs of feet moving toward the lodge.

Shit.

If he didn't get himself out of this disaster pretty damn quick, he was going to wake up in the hands of the Enforcement Agency. And for a member of the Order, a group the Agency had long wished extinct, arrest by them would make Lex and his guards' treatment seem like a trip to a spa. If he fell into the Agency's hands now – particularly as an accused killer of a Gen One – Niko knew without question he was as good as dead.

Lex greeted the new arrivals like he was holding court for visiting dignitaries. 'This way,' he called from somewhere outside the lodge. 'I have the bastard contained and waiting for you in the hall.'

'*He* has the bastard contained,' Kiril muttered sourly. 'I doubt Lex could contain his own ass if he was using both hands.'

The other guards chuckled cautiously.

'Come on,' Kiril said. 'Let's get the warrior on his feet so the Agency can take him out of here.'

Hope surged in Niko's chest. If they freed him of the restraints, he might have a slim chance of escaping. Very slim, considering the approaching pound of boots and firepower headed in his direction from outside the lodge, but slim was a hell of a lot better than none.

He kept up his lifeless slump in the chair, even as Kiril squatted in front of him and unlocked the chains around his ankles. Impatience gnawed at him. Nikolai's every impulse was to bring his knee up and crack the guard under the jaw.

He had to clamp his molars down onto his tongue to keep himself unmoving, breathing as shallowly as he could, waiting for the better opportunity when the guard then went around the back of him and picked up the lock binding the chains on his torso and wrists. A twist of the key. A crisp *clack* of carbide steel as the lock fell open.

Nikolai flexed his fingers, took a deep, unconstricted breath.

He opened his eyes. Grinned at Kiril's comrades the instant before he brought his arms up and around and grabbed onto Kiril's big head in both hands.

In fluid motion, he gave a violent twist and vaulted up off the chair. The chains fell away and Nikolai was on his feet with the loud *snap* of Kiril's breaking neck.

'Holy Christ!' shouted one of the remaining guards.

Someone fired a wild shot. The other two scrabbled for their weapons.

Niko yanked Kiril's gun out of its holster and returned fire, dropping one guard with a bullet to the head.

The commotion brought shouts of alarm from the hallway outside. Boots started pounding. A small army of Enforcement Agents storming in to take control of the situation.

Damn it.

Not much time left to make a break for it before he would be staring down the barrels of no less than half a dozen guns – a few seconds at most.

Nikolai hauled the dead bulk of Kiril's body around in front of him and held it there like a shield. The corpse took a couple of quick hits as Niko started moving backward, toward the window on the other side of the long room.

In the open doorway now, a crowd of black-clad Agents in SWAT gear, all of them bristling with some fairly serious-looking semiauto firepower.

'Freeze, asshole!'

Niko shot a look over his shoulder at the window a few feet behind him. It was his best, only option. Surrendering now and going out peacefully with his Agency executioners was an alternative he refused to consider.

With a roar, Niko grabbed two fistfuls of Kiril's deadweight and swung the body into the glass. He held on as the window shattered around him, using the forward momentum of the vampire's corpse to carry him off his feet and through the makeshift hole.

He heard a shouted command behind him – an order for one of the Agents to open fire.

He felt cool night air on his face, in his sweat-dampened hair.

Then, before he could so much as register the smallest taste of freedom –

Pow! Pow! Pow!

His bare back lit up as though it were on fire. His bones and muscles went limp, melting away inside him as a surge of bile and acid scorched the back of his throat. Nikolai's vision swam toward a sudden, consuming darkness. He felt the earth come up fast beneath him as he and dead Kiril tumbled out onto the ground beneath the window.

Then he felt no more.

CHAPTER FOURTEEN

Lex stood with Edgar Fabien under the eaves of the main lodge, watching as the Enforcement Agents shoved the warrior's body into the back of an unmarked black van.

'How long will the sedatives hold him?' Lex asked, disappointed to have learned that the weapon Fabien had ordered to open fire on Nikolai contained tranquilizer darts instead of bullets.

'I don't expect the prisoner will wake up until long after he is securely housed at the Terrabonne containment facility.'

Lex glanced over at the Darkhaven leader. 'A con-tainment facility? I thought those places were used for processing and rehabilitating blood addicts – some kind of Enforcement Agency holding tank for Rogue vampires.'

Fabien's smile was tight. 'No need to trouble yourself with the details, Alexei. You did the right thing in contacting me about the warrior. Obviously, an individual as dangerous as he has proven to be warrants special consideration. I will personally see to it that he is handled in the proper manner. I'm sure you have enough on your mind during this time of unimaginable, tragic loss.'

Lex grunted. 'There is still the matter of our . . . agree-ment.'

'Yes,' Fabien replied, letting the word trail out slowly between his thin lips. 'You've surprised me, Alexei, I must admit that. There are some introductions I would like to make on your behalf. Very important introductions. Naturally this will require the utmost discretion.'

'Yes, of course.' Lex could hardly contain his eagerness, his greed to know more – to know everything there was to know – right here and now. 'Who do I need to meet? I can be at your place first thing tomorrow night—'

Fabien's condescending chuckle grated. 'No, no. I'm not talking about anything as public as that. This would require a special meeting. A secret meeting, with a few of my associates. *Our* associates,' he amended with a conspiratorial look.

A private audience with Edgar Fabien and his peers. Lex was practically salivating at the very idea. 'Where? And when?'

'Three nights from now. I will send my car to pick you up and bring you to the location as my personal guest.'

'I look forward to it,' Lex said.

He offered his hand to the Darkhaven male – his powerful new ally – but Fabien's gaze had strayed past Lex's shoulder to the broken window of the lodge's great room. Those shrewd eyes narrowed, and Fabien's head cocked to the side.

'You have a child out here?' he asked, something dark gleaming in his raptorlike gaze.

Lex turned, just in time to see Mira attempting to duck out of sight, her short black veil swinging with the quick movement. 'The brat served my father, or so he liked to think,' he said dismissively. 'Ignore her. She is nothing.'

Fabien's pale brows rose slightly. 'Is she a Breedmate?'

'Yes,' Lex said. 'An orphan my father picked up some months ago.'

Fabien made a low noise in the back of his throat, somewhere between a grunt and a purr. 'What is the girl's talent?'

Now it was Fabien who seemed unable to hide his avid interest. He was still watching the open window, craning his neck and searching as though willing Mira to appear there again.

Lex considered that eager look for a moment, then said, 'Would you like to see what she can do?'

Fabien's glittering gaze was answer enough. Lex led the way back into the lodge and found Mira creeping down the hallway toward her bedroom. He went up and grabbed her by the arm, wheeling her around to face the Darkhaven leader. She whimpered a little at his rough handling, but Lex ignored the brat's complaining. He pulled off her veil and pushed her in front of Edgar Fabien.

'Open your eyes,' he demanded. When she didn't immediately comply, Lex persuaded her with a rap of his knuckles against the back of her small blond head. 'Open them, Mira.'

He knew she had because in the next moment, Edgar Fabien's expression went from one of moderate inquisitiveness to outright wonder and amazement. He stared, transfixed, his jaw slack.

Then he smiled. A broad, awestruck grin. 'My God,' he breathed, unable to tear his gaze away from Mira's witchy eyes.

'What do you see?' Lex asked.

It took Fabien some time before he answered. 'Is it . . . could this possibly be my future I am looking at? My destiny?'

Lex pulled Mira away from him now, not missing Fabien's reflexive grab at the girl, as though he wasn't quite ready to release her yet. 'Mira's eyes do indeed reflect future events,' he said, placing the short veil back over her head. 'She is quite a remarkable child.'

'A minute ago you said she was nothing,' Fabien reminded him. Narrowed, assessing eyes traveled over the girl. 'What would you be willing to take for her?'

Lex saw Mira's head snap in his direction, but his attention was fixed solidly on the transaction suddenly laid out in front of him. 'Two million,' he said, tossing the figure out casually, as if it were a trivial sum. 'Two million dollars and she is yours.'

'Done,' Fabien said. 'Phone my secretary with a bank account number and the funds will be there within the hour.'

Mira reached out and grabbed Lex's arm. 'But I don't want to go anywhere with him. I don't want to leave Rennie—'

'There, there, now, sweetheart,' Fabien cooed. He stroked his palm over the top of her head. 'Go to sleep, child. No more fussing. Sleep now.'

Mira fell back, caught in the vampire's trance. Fabien snatched her into his arms and cradled her like a baby. 'A pleasure doing business with you, Alexei.'

Lex nodded. 'And with you,' he replied, following the Darkhaven leader out of the lodge and waiting as he and the girl disappeared into a dark sedan that idled in the drive.

As the fleet of vehicles rolled out, Lex considered the evening's surprising turn of events. His father was dead. Lex was free from blame and poised to take control of all that he had deserved for so long. He would soon be ushered into Edgar Fabien's elite circle of power, and he was suddenly two million dollars wealthier.

Not bad for a night's work.

Renata turned her head to the side on her pillow and cracked one eye open, a small test to see if the reverb had finally passed. Her skull felt like it had been hollowed out and stuffed with wet cotton, but that was a major improvement over the hammer-and-anvil agony that had been her companion for the past few hours.

A tiny pinprick of daylight shone in through a small weevil hole in the pine shutter. It was morning. Outside her room, the lodge was quiet. So quiet that for a second she wondered if she'd just woken up from a horrible dream.

But in her heart, she knew it was all real. Sergei Yakut was dead, killed in a bloody assault in his own bed. All the grisly, gore-soaked images playing through her mind had actually happened. And most disturbing of all, it was Nikolai who stood accused and was arrested for the murder.

Regret over that gnawed at Renata's conscience. With the benefit of a clear head and being some hours removed from the blood and chaos of the moment, she had to wonder if she might have been too hasty to doubt him. Maybe they all had been too hasty to condemn him – Lex in particular.

Suspicion that Lex might have had some role in his father's death – as Nikolai had insisted – put a knot of unease in her stomach.

And then there was poor Mira, far too young to be exposed to so much violence and danger. A mercenary part of her wondered if they both might be better off now. Yakut's death had released Renata of his hold on her. Mira was free too. Maybe this was the chance they both needed – a chance to get somewhere far away from the lodge and its many horrors.

Oh, God. Dare she even wish it?

Renata sat up, swung her legs over the side of the bed. Hope buoyed her, swelling large in her chest.

They could leave. Without Yakut to track her down, without him alive and able to use his link to her by blood, she was finally free. She could take Mira and leave this place, once and for all.

'Mother Mary,' she whispered, clasping her hands together in a desperate prayer. 'Please, give us this chance. Let me have this chance – for the sake of that innocent child.'

Renata leaned up near the wall she shared with Mira's bedroom. She rapped her knuckles lightly on the wood panels, waiting to hear the girl's answering knock.

Only silence.

She knocked again. 'Mira, are you awake, kiddo?'

No answer at all. Only a lengthening quiet that felt like a death knell.

Renata was still wearing her clothes from last night, a sleep-wrinkled long-sleeve black T-shirt and dark denim jeans. She threw on a pair of lug-sole ankle boots and hurried out into the hallway. Mira's door was just a few steps down . . . and it stood ajar.

'Mira?' she called, walking inside and taking a quick look around.

The bed was unmade and rumpled from where the child had been at one point during the night, but there was no sign of her. Renata pivoted and raced to the bathroom they shared at the other end of the hall.

'Mira? Are you in there, mouse?' She opened the door and found the small room empty. Where could she have gone? Renata spun around and headed back up the paneled corridor toward the main living area of the lodge, a terrible panic beginning to rise up her throat. 'Mira!'

Lex and a couple of guards were seated around the table in the great room as Renata ran in from the hallway. He spared her only the briefest glance then went back to talking with the other males.

'Where is she?' Renata demanded. 'What have you done with Mira? I swear to God, Lex, if you've hurt her—'

He pinned her with a scathing look. 'Where's your respect, female? I have just come back in from releasing my father's body to the sun. This is a day of mourning. I'll not hear a word of your bleating until I'm damned good and ready.'

'To hell with you, and your false mourning,' Renata seethed, charging toward him. It was nearly impossible to keep from hitting him with a blast of her mind's power, but the two guards who rose on either side of Lex, drawing their weapons on her, helped to keep her anger in check. 'Tell me what you did, Lex. Where is she?'

'I sold her.' The reply was so casual, he might have been discussing an old pair of shoes.

'You . . . you did what?' Renata's lungs squeezed, losing so much air she could hardly draw another breath. 'You can't be serious! Sold her to who – those men who came for Nikolai?'

Lex smiled, gave her a vague shrug of admission.

'You bastard! You disgusting pig!' The total, ugly reality of all that Lex had done crashed down on her. Not only what he'd done to Mira, but to his own father, and, as she saw with awful clarity now, what he'd done to Nikolai too. 'My God. Everything he said about you was the truth, wasn't it? You were the one responsible for Sergei's death, not Nikolai. It was you who brought in the Rogue. You planned the whole thing—'

'Be careful with your accusations, female.' Lex's voice was a brittle snarl. 'I am the one in command here now. Make no mistake, your life belongs to me. Piss me off and I can have you erased from existence as easily as I sent that warrior to his death.'

Oh, God . . . no. Shock blew through her chest in a chill ache. 'He is dead?'

'He will be soon enough,' Lex said. 'Or wishing he was, once the good doctors in Terrabonne have their fun with him.'

'What are you talking about? What doctors? I thought you had him arrested.'

Lex chuckled. 'The warrior is on his way to a containment facility run by the Enforcement Agency. Safe to say that no one will hear from him ever again.'

Contempt boiled up in Renata for all that she was hearing, and for her own role in seeing Nikolai wrongfully charged. Now both he and Mira were gone, and Lex stood there grinning with smug vanity for the deception he'd orchestrated. 'You disgust me. You're a fucking monster, Lex. You are a sickening coward.'

She took a step toward him and Lex gave the guards a jerk of his chin. They blocked her, two huge vampires glowering at her. Daring her to make a reckless move.

Renata eyed them, seeing in those hard gazes the years of animosity that this group of Breed males felt for her – animosity coming most intensely from Lex himself. They hated her. Hated her strength, and it was clear that any one of them would welcome the opportunity to put a bullet in her head.

'Get her out of my sight,' Lex ordered. 'Take the bitch to her room and lock her in for the rest of the day. She can provide our night's entertainment.'

Renata didn't let the guards within arm's reach of her. As they moved to grab her, she swept them each with a sharp mental jolt. They shouted and leapt away, recoiling from the pain.

But no sooner had they dropped back did Lex spring on her, fully transformed and spitting with fury. Hard fingers curled into her shoulders. His body weight slammed her backward, up off her feet. He was furious, pushing her like she was nothing but feathers. His strength and speed propelled her with him across the floor and into the shuttered window on the far wall.

Solid, unmovable logs crashed against her spine and thighs. Renata's head cracked back against the thick shutters with the impact. Her breath left her on a broken gasp. When she opened her eyes, Lex's face loomed right up against hers, his thin pupils seething outrage from within the center of his fiery amber irises. He brought one hand up and caught her jaw in a bruising grasp. Forced her head to the side. His fangs were enormous, sharp as daggers and bared dangerously near her throat.

'That was a very stupid thing to do,' he growled, letting those pointed teeth graze her skin as he spoke. 'I should bleed you out for that. In fact, I think I will—'

Renata summoned every ounce of power she had and turned it loose on him, blasting Lex's mind in a long, ruthless wave of anguish.

'Aaagh!' His scream rang out like a banshee's wail.

And still Renata kept blasting him. Pouring pain into his head until he released her and crumbled to the floor in a boneless sprawl.

'Se-seize her!' he sputtered to his guards, who were recovering now from the smaller strikes Renata had dealt them.

One of them raised his gun on her. She blasted him, then gave the second guard another dose as well.

Damn it, she had to get out of there. Couldn't risk using any more of her power when she'd pay dearly for every strike once her reverb hit. And she wouldn't have long before the crippling wave roared up on her.

Renata spun around, broken glass crunching under her boots from last night's chaos. She felt a small breeze cutting through the locked shutters. Realization dawned: There was no window behind her, only freedom. She took hold of the sturdy wood panels and gave a hard yank. The hinges groaned but didn't quite give way.

'Kill her, you fucking imbeciles!' Lex gasped from behind her. 'Shoot the bitch!'

No, Renata thought, desperate as she pulled on the stubborn wood.

She couldn't let him stop her. She had to get out of there. She had to find Mira, take her somewhere safe. She'd promised her, after all. She'd made a promise to that child and God help her, she would not fail.

With a cry, Renata put all her muscle and weight into tearing down the shutters. Finally they loosened. Adrenaline coursing through her, she ripped them free completely and threw the shutters aside.

Sunlight poured over her. Blinding, brilliant, it washed into the great room of the lodge. Lex and the other vampires shrieked, hissing as they scrambled to shield their sensitive eyes and move out of the scorching path of the light.

Renata climbed out and hit the ground running. Lex's car sat on the gravel drive, doors unlocked, keys dangling from the ignition. She hopped in, turned over the engine, and gunned it into the certain – but temporary – safety of daylight.

≼ CHAPTER FIFTEEN ≽

The most recent round of torture had ended a couple of hours ago, but Nikolai's body tensed in reflex when he heard the soft *click* of the electronic lock on the door of his room. He didn't have to guess where he was – the clinical white walls and the fleet of medical apparatus flanking his wheeled bed was clue enough to tell him that he'd been taken to one of the Enforcement Agency's containment facilities.

The industrial-grade steel restraints clamped tight at his wrists, chest, and ankles told him that his current personal accommodations were courtesy of the Rogue treatment and rehabilitation wing of the facility. Which, in case there had been any question before, meant that he was as good as dead. Like the Breed equivalent of a Roach Motel, once you strolled through these doors, you never came back.

Not that his captors intended to let him enjoy his stay for any length of time. Nikolai got the distinct impression that their patience with him was near its end. They'd beaten him nearly unconscious after the tranqs wore off, working him over to get his confession to having killed Sergei Yakut. When that didn't get them anywhere, they started in with tasers and other creative electronics, all the while keeping him drugged enough that he could feel every jolt and prod yet too sedated to fight back.

The worst of his tormentors was the Breed male coming into the room now. Niko had heard one of the Enforcement Agents call him Fabien, spoken with enough deference to indicate the vampire ranked fairly high up on the chain of command. Tall and lanky, with narrow features and small, darting eyes under his slicked-back fair hair, Fabien had a nasty sadistic streak barely hidden behind the veneer of his elegant suit and pleasant civilian demeanor. The fact that he had come in alone this time couldn't be a good sign.

'How was your rest?' he asked Niko with a polite smile. 'Perhaps you're ready to chat with me now. Just the two of us this time, what do you say?'

'Fuck you,' Nikolai growled through his extended fangs. 'I didn't kill Yakut. I told you what happened. You arrested the wrong guy, asshole.'

Fabien chuckled as he walked to the side of the bed and stared down at him. 'There was no mistake, warrior. And I personally could give a damn whether or not you were the one who blew that Gen One's brains all over his walls. I have other, more important questions to ask you. Questions you *will* answer, if your life means anything to you at all.'

That this male evidently knew he was a member of the Order put a dangerous new spin on Nikolai's incarceration. As did the evil glimmer in those shrewd raptorlike eyes.

'What exactly does the Order know about the other Gen One assassinations?'

Nikolai glared up at him, silent, jaw set tight.

'Do you really think you can do anything to stop them? Do you think the Order is so powerful that it can keep the wheel from turning when it's been in motion secretly for years already?' The Breed male's lips spread into a caricature of a smile. 'We will exterminate you one by one, just as we are doing with the last remaining members of the first generation. Everything is in place, and has been for a long time. The revolution, you see, has already begun.'

Rage coiled in Nikolai's gut as he realized just what he was hearing. 'You son of a bitch. You're with Dragos.'

'Ah . . . now you begin to understand,' Fabien said pleasantly.

'You're a fucking traitor to your own race, that's what I understand.'

The facade of civil behavior fell away like a mask. 'I want you to tell me about the Order's current missions. Who are your allies? What do you know about the assassinations? What are the Order's plans where Dragos is concerned?'

Nikolai sneered. 'Blow me. Tell your boss he can blow me too.'

Fabien's cruel eyes narrowed. 'You have tested my patience long enough.'

He got up and walked to the door. A curt wave of his hand brought the guard on duty inside. 'Yes, sir?'

'It is time.'

'Yes, sir.'

The guard nodded and disappeared, only to return a moment later. He and a facility attendant wheeled in a woman strapped to a narrow bed. She'd been sedated as well, and wore only a thin, sleeveless hospital gown. Lying beside her was a tourniquet, a package of thick needles, and a coiled IV tube.

What the hell was this about?

But he knew. He knew as soon as the attendant lifted the human's limp arm and fixed the tourniquet around the area of her brachial artery. The needle and siphoning tube were next.

Nikolai tried to ignore the clinical process taking place beside him, but even the subtlest scent of blood made his senses fire up like holiday lights. Saliva surged into his mouth. His fangs stretched longer in anticipation of feeding.

He didn't want to hunger – not like this, not when he was certain Fabien intended to use it against him now. He tried to ignore his thirst but it was already rising, responding to the visceral urge to feed.

Fabien and the other two vampires in the room were not immune either. The attendant worked expediently, the guard keeping his distance near the door while Fabien watched the blood Host being readied for the feeding. Once everything was in place, Fabien dismissed the attendant and sent the guard back to his post outside.

'Hungry, are we?' he asked Niko when the others had gone. He held the feeding tube in one hand, the fingers of his other hand poised on the valve that would begin the flow of blood from the woman's arm. 'You know, this is the only way to feed a Rogue vampire in containment. Blood intake must be closely monitored, controlled by trained attendants. Too little and he starves; too much and his addiction becomes stronger. Bloodlust is a terrible thing, don't you agree?'

Niko snarled, wanting so badly to leap up off the bed and strangle Fabien. He struggled to do just that, but it was a futile effort. The combination of sedatives and steel restraints held him down. 'I'll kill you,' he muttered, breathless from exertion. 'I promise you, I will fucking kill you.'

'No,' Fabien said. 'It is you who's going to die. Unless you start talking now, I'm going to put this tube down your throat and open the valve. I won't shut it off until you indicate that you're ready to cooperate.'

Jesus Christ. He was threatening to overdose him. No Breed vampire could handle that much blood at once. It would mean almost certain Bloodlust. He would turn Rogue, a one-way ticket to misery, madness, and death.

'Would you like to talk now, or shall we begin?'

He wasn't idiot enough to think Fabien or his cronies would release him, even if he did cough up details about the Order's tactics and current missions. Hell, he could have a rock-solid guarantee of walking away free, but he'd be damned if he'd betray his brethren just to save his own neck.

So, this was it, then. He'd often wondered how he would check out. Figured he'd go down in a blaze of glory, a hail of bullets and shrapnel, hopefully taking a dozen suckheads with him. He never guessed it would be something as pitiful as this. The only honor in it was the fact that he would die keeping the Order's secrets.

'Are you ready to tell me what I want to know?' Fabien asked.

'Fuck off,' Niko ground out, more pissed than ever. 'You and Dragos both can go straight to hell.'

Fabien's gaze sparked with rage. He forced Nikolai's mouth open and shoved the feeding tube deep into his throat. His esophagus constricted, but even his gag reflex was weak due to the sedatives coursing through his body.

There was a soft *click* as the valve on the human's arm was opened.

Blood gushed into the back of Nikolai's mouth. He choked on it, tried to close his throat and refuse it, but there was too much – an endless flow that pumped swiftly from the blood Host's tapped artery.

Niko had no choice but to swallow.

He gulped down the first mouthful. Then another.

And still more.

Andreas Reichen was in his Darkhaven office reviewing accounts and downloading the morning's e-mail when he noticed the message waiting in his in-box from Helene. The subject was a simple handful of words that made his pulse kick with interest: *found a name for you.*

He clicked open the e-mail and read her brief note.

After some determined investigative work, Helene had gotten the name of the vampire her missing club girl had been seeing recently.

Wilhelm Roth.

Reichen read it twice, every molecule in his bloodstream growing colder as the name sank into his brain.

Helene's e-mail indicated that she was still digging for more information and would report back as soon as she had anything further.

Jesus.

She couldn't know the true nature of the viper she'd uncovered, but Reichen knew plenty.

Wilhelm Roth, the leader of the Hamburg Darkhaven and one of the most powerful individuals in Breed society. Wilhelm Roth, a gangster of the first degree, and someone whom Reichen knew very well, or had at one time.

Wilhelm Roth, who was mated to a former lover of Reichen's – the woman who'd taken a piece of Reichen's heart when she left him to be with the wealthy, second-generation Breed male who could give her all the things Reichen could not.

If Helene's vanished employee had been associated with Roth, it was certain the girl was dead by now. And Helene . . . good Christ. She was already too close to the bastard just by having learned his name. If she got any closer by continuing to look for information on him . . . ?

Reichen picked up the phone and dialed her cell. No answer. He tried her flat in the city, cursing when the call went into voicemail. It was much too early for her to be at the club, but he dialed it anyway, damning the daylight that kept him trapped in his Darkhaven and unable to drive over to speak with her in person.

When all his options failed, Reichen fired back a response via e-mail.

Do nothing more where Roth is concerned. He is dangerous. Contact me as soon as you receive this message. Helene, please . . . be careful.

A medical equipment truck came to a halt at the gated entrance of an unassuming, two-story brick building some forty-five minutes outside the heart of Montreal. The driver leaned out his window and typed a short sequence into an electronic keypad located on the security kiosk outside. After a moment or two, the gate opened and the truck rolled inside.

It must be delivery day; this was the second supply vehicle Renata had observed entering or leaving the nondescript location since she'd arrived a short time ago. She had spent most of the day in the city, hiding out in Lex's car while she recovered from the worst of her reverb from the morning. Now it was late afternoon. She wouldn't have long – just a few short hours before dusk fell and the night grew thick with predators. Not long at all before she became the hunted.

She had to make the most of that time, which is why she found herself staked out down the road from the isolated, camera-monitored gate of a peculiar building in the town of Terrabonne. It had no windows, no signage out front. Although she couldn't be certain, her gut instinct was telling her that the squat slab of concrete and brick at the end of a private access road was the place Lex had mentioned – the containment facility where Nikolai had been taken.

She prayed it was, because at the moment, the warrior was the only thing close to an ally she had, and if she wanted to find Mira – if she stood any chance of retrieving the child from the vampire who had her now – she knew that she couldn't do it alone. But that meant finding Nikolai first, and praying she found him alive.

And if he was dead? Or if he was alive but refused to help her? Or decided to kill her outright for her role in his wrongful arrest?

Well, Renata didn't want to consider where any of those potentials would leave her. Worse, where they would leave an innocent child who depended on Renata to keep her safe.

So, she waited and she watched, calculating a way past the

security gate. Another supply truck rolled up to the entrance. It came to a stop and Renata seized the opportunity.

Jumping out of Lex's car and running low to the ground, she raced up along the back of the vehicle. While the driver punched in his access code, she hopped up on the rear bumper. The trailer doors were locked, but she slipped her fingers around the handles and held on as the gate clattered open and the truck lurched through.

The driver swung around to the back of the building, following a stretch of asphalt that led to a pair of shipping and receiving bays. Renata climbed up to the roof of the trailer and hung on tight as the truck turned around and began to back into an empty dock. As it neared the building, a motion sensor clicked and the receiving door lifted. There was no one waiting as daylight filled the hangarlike opening, but then if the place was held by the Breed, anyone manning this area would be turning crispy after just a few minutes on the job.

Once the truck backed inside completely, the big door started to descend. There was a second of darkness between the closing of the bay and the electronic flutter of the overhead fluorescent lights coming on. Renata scrambled down and leapt off the rear bumper just as the driver got out of the truck. And now, coming out of a steel door on the other side of the space, was a muscular man in a dark military-style uniform.

The same kind of uniform as the ones worn by the Enforcement Agents Lex had called to arrest Nikolai last night. Complete with a semiautomatic pistol holstered at his hip.

'Hey, how's it going?' the driver called out to the guard.

Renata crept around the side of the truck before the vampire or the human could spot her. She waited, listening to the jangle of the lock being freed. When the guard got closer, she sent him a little hello of her own, a mental jolt that made him rock back on his heels. Another small blast had him staggering. He clutched his temples in his hands and gasped a vivid curse.

The human driver turned to look after him. 'Whoa. You okay there, buddy?'

The brief inattention was all the opportunity Renata needed. She dashed silently across the wide bay and slipped inside the access door the guard had left unsecured.

She ducked past an empty office containing a workstation with monitors displaying the gated entrance. Beyond that, a narrow hallway offered two possibilities: a bend that appeared to lead toward the front of the building or, farther down the hall, a stairwell to the second floor.

Renata opted for the stairs. She hurried toward them, past the spoke that branched off to the side. Another guard was in that stretch of hallway.

Damn it.

He saw her rush by. His boots thundered closer.

'Stop!' he shouted, coming around the corner of the corridor. 'This is a restricted area—'

Renata pivoted and took him down with a hard mental blast. As he writhed on the floor, she gunned it into the stairwell and raced up the flight to the floor above.

For what wasn't the first time, she berated herself for having left the lodge without any weapons. She couldn't keep burning off her power before she even knew if Nikolai was here. She was only operating near half strength as it was; to fully recover from unloading on Lex that morning, she probably needed to shore up for the rest of the day. Unfortunately, not an option.

She peered through the reinforced glass of the stairwell door, taking in the clinical layout of the place. A handful of Breed males in white lab coats strolled past on their way to one of the many rooms that branched off the main corridor.

Too many for her to take on by herself, even if she was running on all cylinders.

And then there was the small matter of the armed Enforcement Agent posted at the far end of the hallway.

Renata leaned against the interior wall of the stairwell, tipping her head back and quietly exhaling a curse. She'd made it in this far, but what the hell made her think she could penetrate a secured facility like this and actually survive?

Desperation was the answer to that question. A determination that refused to accept that this might be as far as she could go. She had no choice but forward. Into the fire, if that's what it took.

Fire, she thought, her gaze turning back to the corridor outside the stairwell. Mounted on the wall across from her was a red emergency alarm.

Maybe there was a chance, after all . . .

Renata crept out of the stairwell and pulled the lever down. A pulsing bell split the air, sending the place into instant chaos. She slipped into the nearest patient's room and watched as attendants and clinicians raced around in confusion. When it seemed they were all occupied with the false emergency, Renata stepped out into the empty corridor to begin her room-to-room search for Nikolai.

It wasn't difficult to decide where he might be. Only one room had an armed Enforcement Agent assigned to it. That guard was still there, manning his post despite the alarm that had sent the rest of the floor's attendants scattering.

Renata glanced at the gun riding the guard's hip and hoped like hell she wasn't making a huge mistake.

'Hey,' she said, approaching him at an easy gait. She smiled brightly despite the fact that in that same instant he was scowling and reaching for his weapon. 'Can't you hear that alarm? Time for you to take a break.'

She hit him with a sudden, sizable blast. As the big male

crumbled to the floor, she ran to peer inside the room behind him.

A blond vampire lay strapped to a bed, naked, convulsing and straining against the metal bonds that held him down. The Breed skin markings that swirled and arced over his chest and down his thick biceps and thighs were livid with pulsating color, seeming almost alive the way the saturations mutated from shades of crimson and deep purple to darkest black. His face was hardly human, completely transformed by the presence of his fangs and the glowing coals of his eyes.

Could it be Nikolai? At first, Renata wasn't sure. But then he lifted his head and those feral amber eyes locked on to her. She saw a flash of recognition in them, and a misery that was palpable even from a distance.

Her heart twisted, burning with regret.

Good Lord, what had they done to him?

Renata grabbed the bulk of the unconscious guard and dragged him with her into the room. Nikolai bucked on the bed, snarling incomprehensibly, words that sounded close to madness.

'Nikolai,' she said, going to his bedside. 'Can you hear me? It's me, Renata. I'm going to take you out of here.'

If he understood, she couldn't be certain. He growled and fought his bonds, fingers flexing and fisting, every muscle taut.

Renata bent down to strip a set of keys from the guard's belt. She took his pistol too, and swore when she realized it was merely a tranq gun loaded with less than half a dozen rounds.

'I guess beggars can't be choosy,' she muttered, stuffing the weapon into the waistband of her jeans.

She went back to Nikolai and started unlocking his restraints. When she freed his hand, she was stunned to feel it clamp down around her own.

'Leave,' he snarled viciously.

'Yeah, that's what we're working on here,' Renata replied. 'Let go so I can unlock the rest of these damned things.'

He sucked in a breath, a low hiss that made the hairs at her nape prickle to attention. 'You . . . leave . . . not me.'

'What?' Frowning, she pulled her hand free and leaned over him to loosen the other restraint. 'Don't try to talk. We don't have much time.'

He gripped her so hard she thought her wrist would snap. '*Leave. Me. Here.*'

'I can't do that. I need your help.'

Those wild amber eyes seemed to stare right through her, hot and deadly. But his punishing grasp eased. He fell back onto the bed as another convulsion racked him.

'Almost done,' Renata assured him, working quickly to unlock the last of his bonds. 'Come on. I'll help you up.'

She had to pull him to his feet, and even then he didn't seem steady enough to stay upright, let alone make the hard dash their escape was going to call for. Renata gave him her shoulder. 'Lean, Nikolai,' she ordered him. 'I'll do most of the work. Now let's get the hell out of here.'

He growled something indecipherable as she wedged herself under his bulk and started walking. Renata rushed for the stairwell. The steps were difficult for Nikolai, but they managed to make it down them all with only a few falters.

'Stay here,' she told him when they reached the bottom.

She sat him down on the last step and dashed out to clear their path to the shipping and receiving bay. The office at the end of the hall was still empty. Beyond the access door, however, the driver was still talking with the guard on duty, both of them anxious due to the bleat of fire alarms pealing all around them.

Renata strolled out with the tranquilizer gun drawn. The vampire saw her coming. Faster than she could react, he had drawn his pistol and fired off a shot. Renata hit him with a mental blast, but not before she felt a ripping heat slam into her left shoulder. She smelled blood, felt the hot trickle of it leaking down her arm.

Damn it – she was hit.

Okay, now she was really pissed off. Renata blasted the vampire again and he staggered to one knee, dropping his weapon. The human driver screamed and dove behind the truck for cover as Renata strode forward and shot the vampire with two tranq rounds. He went down with barely a whimper. Renata walked around to find the driver cowering by the wheel.

'Oh, Jesus!' he cried as she came to stand before him. He put his hands up, face slack with fear. 'Oh, Jesus! Please don't kill me!'

'I won't,' Renata answered, then shot him in the thigh with the tranq.

With both males down, she ran back to get Nikolai. Ignoring the screaming pain in her shoulder, she hurried him into the receiving bay and shoved him into the back of the supply truck where he'd be safe from daylight outside.

'Find something to hold onto,' she told him. 'Things are going to get bumpy now.'

She didn't give him a chance to say anything. Working quickly, she slammed the doors and threw the latch, sealing him inside. Then she jumped into the idling cab and threw the vehicle into gear.

As she crashed the truck through the receiving bay's door and sped up the drive toward escape, she had to wonder if she'd just saved Nikolai's life or condemned them both.

ᴥ CHAPTER SIXTEEN ᴥ

His head was beating like a drum. The constant, rhythmic pounding filled his ears, so deafening it dragged him toward consciousness after what seemed like an endless, fitful sleep. His body ached. Was he lying on the floor somewhere? He felt cold metal underneath his naked body, the heavy bulk of cardboard shipping crates jabbing into his spine and shoulder. A sheet of plastic covered him like a makeshift blanket.

He tried to lift his head but hardly had the strength. His skin felt livid, pulsating from head to toe. Every inch of him felt wrung out, stretched tight, hot with fever. His mouth was dry, his throat parched and raw.

He thirsted.

That need was all he could focus on, the only coherent thought swimming through his banging skull.

Blood.

Christ, he starved for it.

He could taste the hunger – the black, consuming madness – in every shallow breath that sifted through his teeth. His fangs filled his mouth. His gums throbbed where the huge canines descended, as though his fangs had been there for hours. Some distant, sober part of his logic noted the misfire on that calculation; a Breed vampire's fangs normally displayed only in moments of heightened physical response, whether reacting to prey or passion or pure animal rage.

The drum still banging away in his head only made the throb of his fangs deepen. It was the pounding that woke him. The pounding that would not let him sleep now.

Something was wrong with him, he thought, even as he peeled his burning eyes open and took in the too-sharp, amber-washed details of his surroundings.

Small, confined space. Lightless. A box filled with more boxes.

And a woman.

All else faded once his gaze found her. Dressed in a long-sleeved black shirt and dark jeans, she lay in a fetal ball across from him, arms and legs tucked hard into the curve of her torso. A lot of her chin-length inky hair had fallen over the side of her face, concealing her features.

He knew her . . . or felt that he should.

A less cognizant part of him knew only that she was warm and healthy, defenseless. The air was tinged with the merest trace of sandalwood and rain. Her blood scent, some dim instinct roused to tell him. He knew it – and her – with a certainty that seemed etched in his own marrow. His dry mouth was suddenly wet in anticipation of feeding. Need coupled with opportunity lent him a strength he didn't have a moment ago.

Quietly he levered himself up off the floor and moved into a low crouch. Sitting on his haunches, he cocked his head, watching the female sleep. He crept closer, a predatory crawl that brought him right on top of her. The amber glow of his irises bathed her in golden light as he let his starving gaze roam over her body.

And that ceaseless drumming was louder here, the vibration so clear he could feel it in the soles of his bare feet. It banged in his head, commanding all of his attention. Drawing him closer, then closer still.

It was her pulse. Staring down at her, he could see the soft tick of her heartbeat fluttering at the side of her neck. Steady, strong.

The very spot he meant to catch between his fangs.

A low rumble – a growl emanating from his own throat – rolled through the stillness of the place.

The female stirred under him.

Her eyelids flipped open, startled, then went wider. 'Nikolai.'

At first the name hardly registered to him. The fog in his mind was so thick, his thirst so total, he knew nothing else but the urge to feed. It was more than an urge – it was insatiable compulsion. Certain damnation.

Bloodlust.

The word traveled through his hunger-swamped mind like a phantom. He heard it, knew instinctively to fear it. But before he could fully grasp what the word meant, it was ghosting away from him, back to the shadows.

'Nikolai,' the woman said again. 'How long have you been awake?'

Her voice was familiar to him somehow, a peculiar comfort to him, but he couldn't quite place her. Nothing seemed to make sense to him. All that made sense was that tempting thud of her carotid and the deep hunger that compelled him to reach out and take what he needed.

'You're safe here,' she told him. 'We're in the back of the supply truck I took from the containment facility. I had to stop and rest for a while, but I'm good to go now. It's going to be dark soon. We should keep moving before we're spotted.'

As she spoke, images flashed through his memory. The containment facility. Pain. Torture. Questions. A Breed male called Fabien. A male he wanted to kill. And this brave woman . . . she was there too. Incredibly, she had helped him to escape.

Renata.

Yes. He knew her name after all. He didn't know why she

had come for him, or why she would try to save him. Didn't matter.

She was too late.

'They forced me,' he croaked, his voice sounding detached from his body, rough as gravel. 'Too much blood. They forced me to drink it . . .'

She stared at him. 'What do you mean, they forced you?'

'Tried to . . . to push me into overdose. Addiction.'

'Blood addiction?'

He gave a vague nod and coughed, pain racking his chest. 'Too much blood . . . it brings on Bloodlust. They asked me questions . . . wanted me to betray the Order. I refused, so they . . . punished me.'

'Lex said they would kill you,' she murmured. 'Nikolai, I'm sorry.'

She lifted her hand as though she might touch him.

'Don't,' he growled, snatching her by the wrist.

She gasped, tried to pull free. He didn't let her go. Her warm skin seared his fingertips and palm, everywhere he touched her. He could feel the movement of her bones and lean muscles, the racing of her blood as it coursed through the veins of her arm.

It would be so easy to bring that tender wrist up to his mouth.

So tempting to pin her beneath him and drink himself straight into damnation.

He knew the precise moment that she went from surprise to apprehension. Her pulse kicked. Her skin tightened in his grasp.

'Let go of me, Nikolai.'

He held on, the beast in him wondering whether to start on her wrist or her neck. His mouth watered, fangs aching to pierce her tender flesh. And he hungered for her in another way too. There was no hiding his rigid need. He knew it was the Bloodlust driving him, but that didn't make him any less dangerous.

'Let go,' she said again, and when he finally released her, she scooted back, putting some distance between them. There wasn't far for her to go. Stacked boxes hemmed her in from behind, beyond that the wall of the truck's interior. The way she moved, halting and careful, made the predator in him sense weakness.

Was she in some kind of pain? If so, her eyes didn't reflect it. Their pale color seemed steely as she stared at him, defiant.

He glanced down and his feral eyes lit on the gleaming barrel of a pistol.

'Do it,' he murmured.

She shook her head. 'I don't want to hurt you. I need your help, Nikolai.'

Too late for that, he thought. She had pulled him out of purgatory at the hands of his captors, but he'd already gotten a taste of hell. The only way out was to starve the addiction, deny it from taking full hold. He didn't know if he was strong enough to fight his thirst.

He wouldn't be, so long as Renata was near him.

'Do it . . . please. Don't know how much longer I can hold out . . .'

'Niko—'

The beast in him exploded. With a roar, he bared his fangs and lunged for her.

The shot rang out that next instant, a stunning clap of thunder that finally, gratefully, silenced his misery.

Renata sat back on her heels, the tranq gun still gripped in her hands. Her heart was racing, part of her stomach still lodged in her throat after Nikolai had sprung on her with his huge fangs bared. Now he lay in a sprawl on the floor, motionless except for his shallow, labored breathing. Aside from his churning skin markings, with his eyes shut and his fangs hidden behind his closed mouth, there was little way to tell that he was the same violent creature who might have torn out her jugular.

Shit.

What the hell was she doing here? What the hell was she thinking, allying herself with a vampire, imagining she might actually be able to trust one of their kind? She knew first-hand how treacherous they were – how lethal they could turn in just an instant. She might have been killed just now. There was a moment when she really thought she would be.

But Nikolai had tried to warn her. He didn't want to harm her; she'd seen that torment in his eyes, heard it in his broken voice in that instant before he would have leapt on her. He *was* different from the others like him. He had honor, something she'd assumed was lacking in the Breed as a whole, given that her examples were limited to Sergei Yakut, Lex, and those who served them.

Nikolai couldn't have known her weapon didn't hold bullets, and yet he'd forced her to take him down. Begged her for it. She had been through some pretty rough things in her life, but Renata didn't know that kind of torment and suffering. She was quite sure she hoped she never would.

The wound in her shoulder burned like hell. It was bleeding again, worse, after this tense physical confrontation. At least the bullet had passed through cleanly. The nasty hole it left behind was going to need medical attention, although she didn't see a hospital in her near future. She also didn't think it wise to stay near Nikolai now, especially while she was bleeding and the only thing keeping him away from her carotid was that single dose of sedatives.

The tranq gun was empty.

Night was falling, she was nursing a bleeding gunshot wound and the added bonus of her lingering reverb. And staying in the stolen truck was like hiding out with a large bull's-eye target on their backs.

She needed to ditch the vehicle. Then she needed to find someplace safe where she could patch herself up well enough for her to push on. Nikolai was an added problem. She wasn't ready to give up on him, but he was no use to her in his current condition. If he could manage to shake the terrible after-effects of his torture, then maybe. And if not . . . ?

If not, then she had just wasted more precious time than she cared to consider.

Moving gingerly, Renata climbed out the back of the trailer and latched the doors behind her. The sun had set, and dusk was coming fast. In the distance, the lights of Montreal glowed.

Mira was somewhere in that city.

Helpless, alone . . . afraid.

Renata climbed into the truck and started the engine. She drove back toward the city, uncertain where she was heading until she eventually found herself on familiar ground. She never thought she'd be back. Certainly never like this.

The old city neighborhood hadn't changed much in the two years she'd been gone. Cramped tenements and modest post–World War II bungalows lined the twilit street. A few of the youths coming out of the convenience store on the corner glanced at the medical supply truck as Renata drove past.

She didn't recognize any of them, nor any of the shiftless, vacant-eyed adults who made this stretch of concrete their home. But Renata wasn't looking for familiar faces out here. There was just one person she prayed was still around. One person who could be trusted to help her, with few questions asked.

As she rolled up on a squat yellow bungalow with its trellis of pink roses blooming out front, a queer tightness balled in her chest. Jack was still here; Anna's beloved roses, well tended and thriving, were evidence enough of that. And so was the small ironwork sign that Jack had made himself to hang beside the front door, proclaiming the cheery house *Anna's Place.*

Renata slowed the truck to a stop at the curb and cut the engine, staring at the youth halfway house she'd been to so many times but never actually entered. Lights were on inside, throwing off a welcoming, golden glow. It must have been near suppertime because through the large picture window in front she could see that two teenagers – Jack's clients, though he preferred to call them his 'kids' – were setting the table for the evening meal.

'Damn it,' she muttered under her breath, closing her eyes and resting her forehead on the steering wheel.

This wasn't right. She shouldn't be here. Not now, after all this time. Not with the problems she was facing. And definitely not with the problem she was currently carrying in the back of the truck.

No, she had to deal with this on her own. Start the engine, wheel the truck around, and take her chances on the street. Hell, she was no stranger to that. But Nikolai was in bad shape, and she wasn't exactly at the top of her game either. She didn't know how much longer she could drive before –

'Evenin'.' The friendly, unmistakable Texas drawl came from directly beside her at the open driver's side window. She didn't see him walk up, but now there was no avoiding him. 'Can I help ya with . . . any . . . thing . . .'

Jack's voice trailed off as Renata lifted her head and turned to face him. He was a little grayer than she remembered, his short, military-style buzzcut looking thinner, his cheeks and jowls a bit rounder than when she'd last seen him. But he was still a jovial bear of a man, more than six feet tall and built like a tank despite the fact that he was easily pushing seventy.

Renata hoped her smile seemed better than the wince it was. 'Hi, Jack.'

He stared at her – gaped, actually. 'Well, I'll be damned,' he said, slowly shaking his head. 'It's been a long time, Renata. I hoped you'd found a good life somewhere . . . When you quit coming around a couple of years ago, I worried that maybe—' He stopped himself from completing the thought, gave her a big old grin instead. 'Well, hell, it don't matter what I worried about because here you are.'

'I can't stay,' she blurted, her fingers gripping the key in the ignition, ready to give it a twist. 'I shouldn't have come.'

Jack frowned. 'Two years after I see you last, you show up out of the blue just to tell me you can't stay?'

'I'm sorry,' she murmured. 'I have to go.'

He put his hands on the open truck window, as if he meant to physically hold her there. She glanced at the tan, weathered hands that had helped so many kids out of trouble on Montreal's streets – the same hands that had served his home country in war some four decades past, and which now nurtured and protected that trellis of pink roses as though they were more precious to him than gold.

'What's going on, Renata? You know you can talk to me, you can trust me. Are you okay?'

'Yeah,' she said. 'Yeah, I'm fine, really. Just passing through.'

The look in his eyes said he didn't buy that for a second. 'Someone else in trouble?'

She shook her head. 'Why would you think that?'

'Because that's the only way you ever came around here before. Never for yourself, no matter how badly you personally might have needed a hand up.'

'This is different. This isn't anything you should be involved in.' She started the truck. 'Please, Jack . . . just forget you even saw me here tonight, okay? I'm sorry. I have to go.'

No sooner had she grabbed the shifter to put the truck into gear than Jack's strong hand come to rest on her shoulder. It wasn't a hard touch, but even the smallest pressure on her wound made her practically jump out of her skin. She sucked in her breath as the pain lanced through her.

'You're injured,' he said, those wiry gray brows crashing together.

'It's nothing.'

'Nothing, my ass.' He opened the door and climbed up on the runningboard to get a better look at her. When he saw the blood, he muttered a ripe curse. 'What happened? Were you stabbed? Some gangbanger try to roll you for your truck, or your cargo? You have a chance to call the cops yet? Jesus, this looks like a gunshot wound, and you've been bleeding for some time now—'

'I'm fine,' she insisted. 'It's not my truck, and none of this is what you think.'

'Then you can tell me all about it while I take you to the hospital.' He crowded her in the cab, gesturing for her to make room. 'Move over. I'll drive.'

'Jack.' She put her hand on his thick, leathery forearm. 'I can't go to the hospital, or the police. And I'm not alone in here. There's someone in the back of the truck and he's in bad shape too. I can't leave him.'

He stared at her, uncertain. 'You do something against the law, Renata?'

Her exhaled laugh was weak, full of things she couldn't say. Things he couldn't know and sure as hell wouldn't believe even if she told him. 'I wish it was only the law I had to deal with. I'm in danger, Jack. I can't tell you more than that. I don't want to get you involved.'

'You need help. That's all the info I need.' His face was serious now, and beyond the wrinkles and thinning, graying hair, she saw a glimpse of the unshakable Marine he'd been all those years ago. 'Come inside and I'll get you and your friend someplace to rest awhile. Get something for your shoulder too. Come on, there's plenty of room in the house.

Let me help you – for once, Renata, let someone help you.'

She wanted that so badly, in a place buried so deep within her it ached. But bringing Nikolai into someplace public was too great a risk, to him and to anyone who might see him. 'Do you have somewhere other than the house? Somewhere quiet, with less traffic in and out. It doesn't have to be much.'

'There's a small apartment over the garage out back. I've been using it for storage mostly since Anna's been gone, but you're welcome to it.' Jack hopped out of the truck and offered his hand to help her climb down. 'Let's get you and your friend inside so I can have a look at that wound.'

Renata stepped down onto the pavement. What about moving Nikolai? She was certain he was still sleeping off the tranquilizer, which would help conceal what he truly was, but there was no way she could hope that Jack wouldn't find the naked, bloodied and beaten, unconscious male just the slightest bit unusual. 'My, um, my friend is really sick. He's in bad shape, and I don't think he'll be able to walk on his own.'

'I've carried more than one man out of the jungle on my back,' Jack said. 'My shoulders may be a little bent now, but they're broad enough. I'll take care of him.'

As they walked together around to the back, Renata added, 'There's one more thing, Jack. The truck. It needs to disappear. Doesn't matter where, but the sooner the better.'

He gave her a brief nod. 'Consider it done.'

CHAPTER SEVENTEEN

As Nikolai came awake, he wondered why he wasn't dead. He felt like hell, eyes slow to open in the dark, muscles sluggish as he took a mental inventory of his current condition. He remembered blood and agony, arrest and torture at the hands of a bastard called Fabien. He remembered running – or, rather, someone else running while he stumbled and struggled just to stay upright.

He remembered darkness all around him, cold metal beneath him, drums pounding relentlessly in his head. And he distinctly remembered a pistol being pointed in his direction. A pistol that went off by his own command.

Renata.

She been the one holding that gun. Aiming it at him to prevent him from attacking her like some kind of monster. Why hadn't she killed him like he'd wanted? For that matter, why had she come looking for him at the containment facility in the first place? Didn't she realize she might have been killed right along with him?

He wanted to be pissed off that she would do something that reckless, but a more reasonable part of him was just damned grateful to be breathing. Even if breathing was about all he was capable of doing at the moment.

He groaned and rolled over, expecting to feel the hard floor of the truck under his body. Instead he felt a soft mattress, a fluffy pillow cradling his head. A light cotton blanket covered his nakedness.

What the hell? Where was he now?

He vaulted up to a sitting position and was rewarded with a violent lurch of his gut. 'Ah, fuck,' he murmured, sick and light-headed.

'Are you all right?' Renata was here with him. He didn't see her at first, but now she was getting up from the tattered chair where she'd been sitting a moment ago. She padded over to the bed. 'How are you feeling?'

'Like shit,' he said, his tongue thick, mouth desert dry.

He winced as a small bedside lamp clicked on. 'You look better. A lot better, actually. Your eyes are back to normal and your fangs have receded.'

'Where are we?'

'Someplace safe.'

He looked around at the eclectic jumble of the room: mismatched furniture, storage bins stacked against one of the walls, a small collection of artist's canvases in various stages of completion leaning between two file cabinets, a small closet of a bathroom with floral-patterned towels and a quaint claw-footed tub. But it was the shutterless window arranged directly across the room from the bed that really clued him in. It was deep night on the other side of the glass right now, but by morning the room would be flooded with UV light.

'This is a human residence.' He didn't mean for it to sound like an accusation, especially when it was his own damned fault he was in this situation. 'Where the hell are we, Renata? What's going on here?'

'You were in bad shape. It wasn't safe for us to keep traveling in the supply truck when the Enforcement Agency and possibly Lex as well would be looking for it as soon as the sun set—'

'Where are we?' he demanded.

'A halfway house for street kids – it's called Anna's Place. I know the man who runs it. Or I knew him, that is . . . from before.' Some flicker of emotion swept over her face. 'Jack is a good man, trustworthy. We're safe here.'

'He's human.'

'Yes.'

Just fucking lovely. 'And does he know what I am? Did he see me . . . like I was?'

'No. I kept you covered as best I could with the plastic tarp from the truck. Jack helped bring you up here, but you were still sleeping off the tranquilizer I shot you with. I told him you were out of it because you were sick.'

Tranqs. Well, at least that answered the question of why he wasn't dead.

'He didn't see your fangs or your eyes, and when he asked about your *glyphs*, I told him they were tattoos.' She gestured to a shirt and black warm-ups folded on the bedside table. 'He brought you some clothes. After he gets back from ditching the truck for us, he's going to look for a pair of shoes that might fit you. There's a toiletries kit in the bathroom – part of his welcome wagon for new arrivals at the house. He only had one fresh toothbrush to spare, so I hope you don't mind sharing.'

'Jesus,' Niko hissed. This was only getting worse. 'I have to get out of here.'

He threw off the blanket and grabbed the clothing from the little table. He was none too steady on his feet as he tried to step into the nylon pants. He fell back, his bare ass planted on the bed. His head was spinning. 'Damn it. I need to report in with the Order. Think your good buddy Jack has a computer or a cell phone I could borrow?'

'It's two o'clock in the morning,' Renata pointed out. 'Everyone in the house is sleeping. Besides, I'm not even sure you're well enough to make it down the garage stairs. You need to rest a while longer.'

'Fuck that. What I need is to get back to Boston ASAP.' Still seated on the bed, he slipped on the warm-ups and hiked them over his hips, tugging the drawstring tight to cinch the extra-large waistband. 'I've lost too much time already. Gonna need someone to come up here and haul my lame ass back in—'

Renata's hand came down on his, surprising him with the contact. 'Nikolai. Something's happened to Mira.'

Her voice was as sober as he'd ever heard it. She was worried – bone-deep worried – and for the first time, he noticed the smallest fissure in the otherwise unbreakable, icy facade she presented to any and all around her.

'Mira is in danger,' she said. 'They took her with them when they came to arrest you at the lodge. Lex sent her off with a vampire named Fabien. He . . . he sold her to him.'

'Fabien.' Niko shut his eyes, exhaled a curse. 'Then she is probably already dead.'

He wasn't expecting Renata's choked cry. The raw sound of it made him feel like a callous jackass for speaking his grim thoughts aloud. For all of Renata's strength and tough independence, she had a very tender spot reserved for that innocent, remarkable child.

'She can't be dead.' Her voice took on a wooden edge, but her eyes were wild, desperate. 'I promised her, do you understand? I told her I would never let anyone hurt her. I meant that. I would kill to keep her safe, Nikolai. I would die for her.'

He listened, and, God help him, he knew her pain better than she could ever guess. As a boy, he had made a similar pact with his younger brother – Christ, so long ago – and it had nearly destroyed him to have failed.

'That's why you came after me at the containment facility,' he said, understanding now. 'You risked your neck to break me out of there because you think I can help you find her?'

She didn't say anything, just held his gaze in a silence that seemed to stretch out forever. 'I have to get her back, Nikolai. And I don't think . . . I'm just not sure I can do it on my own.'

Part of him wanted to tell her that the fate of one lost little girl was not his problem. Not after what that bastard Fabien had just put him through at the containment facility. And not when the Order had its hands full with other, more critical missions. Life and death on a massive scale, true do-or-die, save-the-world kind of shit.

But when he opened his mouth to tell her so, he found he didn't have the heart to say that out loud to Renata now.

'How's your shoulder?' he asked her, indicating the wound that had been bleeding a few hours ago in the truck and driving his already weak control nearly to the edge. On the surface, it looked better now, bandaged in clean white gauze and smelling faintly of antiseptic.

'Jack patched me up,' she said. 'He was a medic for the Marines when he served in Vietnam.'

Niko saw the tenderness in her expression when she spoke of the human, and he wondered why he should feel even the slightest twinge of jealousy, particularly when that human male's military service aged him well into his AARP years. 'So, he's a Marine, eh? How'd he end up working in a Montreal youth shelter?'

Renata smiled a bit sadly. 'Jack fell in love with a local girl named Anna. They got married, bought this house together and lived here for more than forty years . . . until Anna died. She was killed in a robbery. The homeless kid who stabbed her for her purse did it while he was high on heroin. He was looking for money for his next fix, but he only got about five dollars in change.'

'Jesus,' Niko exhaled. 'I hope the piece of shit didn't get away with it.'

Renata shook her head. 'He was arrested and charged, but

he hanged himself in jail while awaiting trial. Jack once told me when he heard that news, that's when he decided to do something to help prevent another death like Anna's, or another kid from being lost to the streets. He opened his house – Anna's Place – to anyone who needed shelter, and gave the kids warm meals and a place to belong.'

'Sounds like Jack's a generous man,' Niko said. 'A hell of a lot more forgiving than I could be.'

He had the strongest urge to touch her, to just let his fingers come to rest on her skin. He wanted to know more about her, more about her life before she got mixed up with Sergei Yakut. He had the feeling things didn't come easy for her. If Jack had helped to smooth her path, then Nikolai had nothing but respect for the man.

And if she could trust the human, so would he. He hoped like hell Jack was all Renata believed him to be. It would be a hell of a thing if he proved otherwise.

'Let me have a look at your shoulder,' he said, happy to change the subject.

When he moved toward her, Renata hesitated. 'You sure you can handle that? Because I'm fresh out of tranq rounds, and it hardly seems sporting to mind blast a vampire in your feeble condition.'

A joke? He chuckled, caught off guard by her humor, especially when things were looking more than a little grim for both of them. 'Come here and let me see Jack's handiwork.'

She leaned forward to give him better access to her shoulder. Niko moved aside the soft cotton blanket she was wrapped in, letting the edge of the fabric slide down her arm. As carefully as he lifted the bandage and inspected the cleaned, sutured wound beneath it, he still felt Renata flinch with discomfort. She held herself perfectly still as he gingerly checked both sides of her shoulder. The bleeding had slowed to a trickle, but even that thin rivulet of scarlet hit him hard. He was out of the woods as far as Bloodlust went, but he was still Breed, and Renata's sweet sandalwood-and-rain blood scent was intoxicating, especially up close.

'Overall, it looks decent,' he murmured, forcing himself to pull away. He replaced the bandages and sat back on the edge of the bed. 'The exit wound is still pretty livid.'

'Jack says I'm lucky that the bullet went straight through and didn't hit any bones.'

Niko grunted. She was lucky to have been blood-bonded to a Gen One male. Sergei Yakut may have been a vicious, good-for-nothing bastard, but the presence of his nearly pure Breed blood in her system should hasten her healing like nothing else. In fact, he was surprised to see her looking so tired. Then again, it had been quite a long night so far by any standards.

Based on the dark circles smudged under her eyes, she hadn't slept at all. She hadn't eaten either. A tray of food sat untouched on the metal card table nearby.

He wondered if it was grief over Yakut's death that added to her fatigue. She was clearly concerned for Mira, but by all rights, and as hard as it was for him to accept the idea, she was also a female who'd recently lost her mate. And here she was, nursing a gunshot wound on top of all that simply because she'd decided to seek his help.

'Why don't you rest for a while,' Nikolai suggested. 'Take the bed. Get some sleep. It's my turn to be on watch.'

She didn't argue, much to his surprise. He got up and held the blanket for her as she climbed in and struggled to position herself around her shoulder wound.

'The window,' she murmured, pointing at it. 'I was going to cover it for you.'

'I'll take care of that.'

She fell asleep in less than a minute's time. Niko watched her for a moment, and then, when he was certain she wouldn't feel it, he gave in to his urge to touch her. Just a brief caress of her cheek, his fingers trailing into the black silk of her hair.

It was wrong to desire her, he knew that.

In his condition, at what was just about the worst of possible circumstances, it was probably stupid as hell for him to crave Renata the way he did – the way he had nearly from the instant he first laid eyes on her.

But in that moment, had she lifted her lids and found him there beside her, nothing would have kept him from pulling her into his arms.

A pair of halogen high-beams pierced the blanket of fog that spilled down onto the valley road from Vermont's densely forested Green Mountains. In the backseat, the chauffeured vehicle's passenger stared impatiently at the dark landscape, his Breed eyes throwing off amber reflections in the opaque glass. He was pissed off, and after speaking with Edgar Fabien, his contact in Montreal, he had ample reason to be upset. The only glimmer of promise had been the fact that amid all the recent fuckups and disasters narrowly averted, somehow, Sergei Yakut was dead and, in the process, Fabien had managed to net a member of the Order.

Unfortunately, that small victory had been short-lived. Just a few hours ago, Fabien had sheepishly reported that the Breed warrior had escaped the containment facility and was currently at large with the female who'd apparently aided him. If Fabien's hands weren't already full with the other important business he'd been assigned, the Montreal Darkhaven leader might be getting an unexpected visit tonight as well. He could deal with Fabien later.

Annoyed by this mandatory detour through cow country, what infuriated him the most by far was the recent malfunction of his best, most effective instrument.

Failure simply could not be tolerated. One mistake was one

too many, and, like a watchdog that suddenly turns on its owner, there was only one viable solution for the problem awaiting him up this particular stretch of rural backcountry road: termination.

The vehicle slowed and made a right off the asphalt, onto a bumpy dirt one-laner. A rambling Colonial-era stone fence and half a dozen tall oaks and maples lined the drive that led up to an old white farmhouse with a wide, wraparound porch. The car came to a stop in front of a big red barn around the back of the house. The driver – a Minion – got out, walked around to the rear passenger door, and opened it for his vampire Master.

'Sire,' the human mind slave said with a deferential bow of his head.

The Breed male inside the car climbed out, sniffing derisively at the taint of livestock in the so-called fresh night air. His senses were no less offended as he turned his head toward the house and saw the dim light of a table lamp glowing in one of the rooms, the inane yammering of a television game show drifting out of the open windows.

'Wait here,' he instructed his driver. 'This won't take long.'

Stones crunching under his polished leather loafers, he walked over the gravel to the covered porch steps leading to the farmhouse's back door. It was locked, for all that it mattered. He willed the bolt open and strode inside the blue-and-white gingham-trimmed eyesore of a kitchen. As the door creaked closed behind him, a middle-aged human male holding a shotgun came in from the hallway.

'Master,' he gasped, setting the rifle down on the counter-top. 'Forgive me. I wasn't aware that you, ah . . . that you w-were coming.' The Minion stammered, anxious, and evidently wise enough to know that this was no social call. 'H-how may I serve you?'

'Where is the Hunter?'

'The cellar, sire.'

'Take me to him.'

'Of course.' The Minion scrambled past and opened the back door, holding it wide. When his master had exited, he dashed around to lead the way to the coffinlike entrance of the cellar along the side of the house. 'I don't know what could have gone wrong with him, Master. He's never failed to carry out an assignment before.'

True enough, although that only made the current failure of such a perfect specimen all the more inexcusable. 'I'm not interested in the past.'

'No, no. Of course not, sire. My apologies.'

There was a clumsy struggle with the key and lock, the latter having been installed in order to keep the curious out, rather than as a measure to keep the cellar's deadly occupant inside. Locks were unnecessary when there was another, more effective method in place to ensure that he wasn't tempted to stray.

'This way,' said the Minion, opening the steel doors to reveal a lightless pit that opened into the earth below the old house.

A flight of wooden stairs descended into the dank, musty darkness. The Minion moved ahead, tugging a string attached to a bare bulb to help light the way. The vampire behind him saw well enough without it, as did the one housed down here in the empty, windowless space.

The cellar contained no furniture. No diversions. No personal effects. By deliberate design, it contained no comforts whatsoever. It was filled with precisely nothing – a reminder to its occupant that he too was nothing beyond that which he was summoned from here to do. His very existence was merely to serve, to follow orders.

To act without mercy or mistake.

To give no quarter, nor expect any in return.

As they walked into the center of the cellar, the huge Breed male seated quietly on the bare earth floor looked up. He was naked, elbows resting on his updrawn knees, his head shaved bald. He had no name, no identity at all except the one that was given to him when he was born: Hunter. The fitted black electronic collar around his neck had also been with him all his life.

In truth, it *was* his life, for if he should ever resist instruction, or tamper with the monitoring device in any way, a digital sensor would trip and the UV weapon contained within the collar would detonate.

The big male stood up as his Minion handler gestured for him to rise. He was impressive, a Gen One standing six and a half feet, all lean muscle and formidable strength. His body was covered in a web of *dermaglyphs* from neck to ankle, skin markings inherited through blood, passed down from father to son within the Breed.

That he and this vampire shared similar patterns was to be expected; after all, they were born of the same Ancient paternal line. Both of them had the blood of the same alien warrior swimming in their veins – one of the original fathers of the vampire race on earth. They were kin, although only one of them knew that. The one who had been patiently biding his time, living behind countless masks and deceptions while carefully arranging his pieces on a massive and complex board. Manipulating fate until the time was right for him to finally, rightfully, rise to his place of power over both Breed and humankind alike.

That time was coming.

Coming soon, he could feel it in his bones.

And he would abide no missteps in the ascent to his throne.

Eyes as golden as a falcon's met and held his gaze in the dim light of the cellar. He didn't appreciate the pride he saw there – the trace of defiance in one who had been raised to serve.

'Explain to me why you failed to carry out your objective,' he demanded. 'You were sent to Montreal with a clear mission. Why were you unable to execute it?'

'There was a witness' came the cool reply.

'That's never stopped you before. Why now?'

Those unflinching golden eyes showed no emotion whatsoever, but there was challenge in the subtle lift of the Hunter's square jaw. 'It was a child, a young female.'

'A child, you say.' He shrugged, unmoved. 'Even easier to eliminate, don't you think?'

The Hunter said nothing, just stared at him as if awaiting judgment. As if he expected to be condemned and could give a damn.

'You were not trained to question your orders or to back away from obstacles. You were bred for one thing – as were the others like you.'

The stern chin came up another inch, questioning. Mistrusting. 'What others?'

He chuckled low under his breath. 'You didn't actually think you were unique, did you? Far from it. Yes, there are others. An army of others – soldiers, assassins . . . expendable pawns I've created over a period of several decades, all of them born and raised to serve me. Others, like you, who live only because I will it.' He glanced pointedly at the collar that ringed the vampire's neck. 'You, like the others, live only so long as I will it.'

'Master,' interrupted the Minion handler. 'I'm certain this was a one-time error. When you send him out next time, there will be no problems, I assure—'

'I've heard enough,' he snapped, slanting a look at the human who by association had also failed him. 'There will be no next time. And you are of no use to me anymore.'

In a flash of motion, he wheeled on the Minion and sank his fangs into the side of the man's throat. He didn't drink, just punctured the carotid and released him, watching with complete disregard as he collapsed on the earthen floor of the cellar, bleeding profusely. The presence of so much pumping blood was almost too much to bear. It was hard to waste it, but he was more interested in proving a point.

He glanced at the Gen One vampire beside him – grinning as the male's *glyphs* began to pulse with the deep colors of hunger, his golden eyes now fully amber. His fangs filled his mouth, and it was obvious that every instinct within him was screaming for him to lunge on the sputtering prey and feed before the blood and the human were both dead.

Except he didn't move. He stood there, defiant still, refusing to give in to even that most natural, savage side of himself.

Killing him would be easy enough; just a code typed into his cell phone and that rigid, unentitled pride would be blown to bits. But it would be far more enjoyable to break him first. So much the better if breaking him could serve as an example to Fabien and anyone else who might be stupid enough to disappoint him.

'Outside,' he commanded the servant assassin. 'I'm not finished with you yet.'

CHAPTER EIGHTEEN

Renata stood at the pedestal sink in the bathroom, spat the last of her toothpaste down the drain, then rinsed with several handfuls of cool water. She'd gotten up much later than she intended. Nikolai said she had looked like she needed the rest, so he'd let her sleep until almost ten in the morning. She could have slept another ten days and she'd probably still be tired.

She felt awful. Achy all over, weak-limbed. Unsteady on her feet. Her body's internal thermostat couldn't seem to decide between freezing cold and overheated, leaving her racked with alternating shivers and waves of perspiration beading on her brow and the back of her neck.

With her right hand braced on the sink, she put her other under the running faucet, thinking to clamp her cool, wet fingers around the furnace that burned at her nape. One slight shift of her left arm and she hissed in pain.

Her shoulder felt like it was on fire.

She winced as she carefully unbuttoned the top of a big oxford shirt she was borrowing from Jack. Slowly she shrugged out of the left sleeve so she could remove the bandage and inspect her wound. The tape stung as she peeled it away from her tender, aggravated skin. Coagulating blood and antiseptic ointment coated the thick pad of gauze, but the wound underneath was still swollen and seeping.

She didn't need a doctor to tell her that this wasn't good

news. Blood and thick yellow fluid drained from the angry red circle surrounding the bullet's open point of entry. Not good at all. Nor did she need a thermometer to confirm that she was probably spiking a fairly high fever due to the onset of infection.

'Shit,' she whispered at her haggard, sallow face in the mirror. 'I don't have time for this, damn it.'

An abrupt knock on the bathroom door made her jump.

'Hey.' Nikolai knocked again, two quick raps. 'Everything okay in there?'

'Yeah. Yeah, it's all good.' Her voice scraped like sandpaper in her throat, little better than a hard rasp of sound. 'I'm just brushing my teeth.'

'You sure you're all right?'

'I'm fine.' Renata wadded up the soiled bandage and tossed it into the trash bin next to the sink. 'I'll be out in a few minutes.'

The answering pause didn't give her the impression he was going anywhere. She cranked the water to a higher volume and waited, unmoving, her eyes on the closed door.

'Renata . . . your wound,' Nikolai said through the wood panel. There was a gravity to his tone. 'It's not healed yet? It should have stopped bleeding by now . . .'

Although she hadn't wanted him to know what was going on, there was no use denying it now. All of his kind had impossibly acute senses, especially when it came to detecting spilled blood.

Renata cleared her throat. 'It's nothing, no big deal. Just needs new dressing and a fresh bandage.'

'I'm coming in,' he said, and gave the doorknob a twist. It held, locked from the push-button mechanism on the inside. 'Renata. Let me in.'

'I said, I'm fine. I'll be out in just a—'

She didn't have a chance to finish. Using what could only

have been the power of his Breed mind, Nikolai sprang the lock and opened the door wide.

Renata might have cursed him out for barging in like he owned the place, but she was too busy trying to yank the long, loose sleeve of the shirt up to cover herself. She didn't care so much if he saw the inflamed state of her gunshot wound; it was the other marks that she wanted to make disappear.

The permanent ones that had been burned into the skin of her back.

She managed to get the soft cotton cloth around her, but all the shifting and tugging made her shoulder scream and her gut turn inside out as the pain brought on a hefty wave of nausea.

Panting now, awash in a cold sweat, she plopped herself down on the closed toilet lid and tried to act like she wasn't about to lose her stomach all over the tiny black-and-white tiles under her feet.

'For crissake.' Nikolai, bare-chested, his borrowed warm-ups hanging low on his trim hips, took one look at her and dropped into a squat in front of her. 'You're far from okay in here.'

She flinched as he reached for the sagging open collar of the shirt. 'Don't.'

'I'm just going to check your wound. Something's not right. It should be healing by now.' He moved the fabric away from her shoulder and scowled. 'Shit. This doesn't look good at all. How does the point of exit look?'

He stood up and leaned over her, his fingers careful as he slid more of the shirt out of his way. Even though she was burning up, she could feel the heat of his body as he hovered so near to her in the small space. 'Ah, fuck . . . this side is worse than the front. Let's get you out of this shirt so I can see exactly what we're dealing with.'

Renata froze, her entire system seizing up. 'No. I can't.'

'Sure you can. I'll help you.' When she didn't budge, just sat there holding the front of the big shirt in her tight fist, Nikolai grinned. 'If you think you have to be modest with me, you don't. Hell, you've already seen me naked so it's only fair, right?'

She didn't laugh. She couldn't. It was hard to hold his gaze, hard to believe the concern that was starting to darken his wintry blue eyes as he waited for her answer. She didn't want to see revulsion there, nor, even worse, pity. 'Will you just . . . go away now? Please? Let me take care of this myself.'

'Your wound is infected. You're running a fever because of it.'

'I know.'

Nikolai's face went sober with some emotion she couldn't discern. 'When was the last time you fed?'

She shrugged. 'Jack brought me some food last night, but I wasn't hungry.'

'Not food, Renata. I'm talking about blood. When was the last time you fed from Yakut?'

'You mean drink his blood?' She couldn't mask her revulsion. 'Never. Why would you ask that? Why would you think it?'

'He drank from you. I saw him feeding at your vein in his quarters at the lodge. I guess I assumed it was a mutual arrangement.'

Renata hated to think about that, let alone be reminded that Nikolai had witnessed her degradation. 'Sergei used me for blood whenever he felt the need. Or whenever he wanted to make a point.'

'But he never gave you his blood in exchange?'

Renata shook her head.

'No wonder you're not healing faster,' Nikolai murmured. He gave a slight shake of his head. 'When I saw him drinking from you . . . I thought you were mated to him. I assumed you were blood-bonded to each other. I thought maybe you cared for him.'

'You thought I loved him,' Renata said, realizing where he was heading. 'It wasn't that. Not even close.'

She exhaled a sharp breath that grated in her throat. Nikolai wasn't pushing her for answers, and maybe precisely because of that, she wanted him to understand that what she felt for the vampire she had served was anything but affection. 'Two years ago, Sergei Yakut plucked me off a downtown street and brought me to his lodge along with several other kids he'd collected that night. We didn't know who he was, or where we were going, or why. We didn't know anything, because he put us all in some kind of trance that didn't lift until we found ourselves locked up together inside a large, dark cage.'

'The one inside the barn on his property,' Nikolai said, his face grim. 'Jesus Christ. He brought you in as live game for his blood club?'

'I don't think any of us realized that monsters truly existed until Yakut, Lex, and a few others came out to open the cage. They showed us the woods, told us to run.' She swallowed past the bitterness rising in her throat. 'The slaughter began as soon as the first of us broke for the forest.'

In her mind, Renata relived the horror in excruciating detail. She could still hear the screams of the victims as they fled, and the terrible howls of the predators who hunted them with such savage zeal. She could still smell the summery tang of pine and loamy moss, nature's scents smothered all too soon by that of blood and death. She could still see the vast darkness surrounding her in the unfamiliar terrain, unseen branches that smacked her cheeks and tore at her clothes as she tried to navigate her escape.

'None of you stood a chance,' Nikolai murmured. 'They told you to run only to toy with you. To give themselves the illusion that blood clubs have anything to do with sport.'

'I know that now.' Renata could still taste the futility of all that running. Terror had taken shape out of the black night in the form of glowing amber eyes and bared, bloodied fangs like nothing she'd ever dreamed in her worst nightmare. 'One of them caught up to me. He came out of nowhere and began to circle me, readying for the attack. I'd never been more afraid. I was scared and angry and something inside me just . . . snapped. I felt a power coursing through me, something stronger than the adrenaline that was flooding my body.'

Nikolai nodded. 'You didn't know about the ability you possessed.'

'I didn't know about a lot of things until that night. Everything had turned inside out. I just wanted to survive – the only thing I knew how to do. So when I felt that energy flowing through me, some visceral instinct told me to turn it loose on my attacker. I pushed it outward with my mind and the vampire staggered back as if I'd physically struck him. I threw more at him, and still more, until he was down on the ground screaming and his eyes were bleeding and his entire body was convulsing in pain.' Renata paused, wondering if the Breed warrior staring at her in silence was judging her for her total lack of remorse over what she'd done. She wasn't about to apologize or make excuses. 'I wanted him to suffer, Nikolai. I wanted to kill him, and I did.'

'What other choice did you have?' he said, reaching out and very tenderly brushing his fingertips along the line of her cheek. 'What about Yakut? Where was he during all of this?'

'Not far behind. I had started running again when he stepped into my path and headed me off. I tried to take him down too, but he withstood it. I sent everything I had at him, to the point of exhaustion, but it wasn't enough. He was too strong.'

'Because he was Gen One.'

Renata gave an acknowledging tilt of her head. 'He explained it to me later, after that initial bout of reverb had knocked me unconscious for three full days and I woke to find myself pressed into service as a personal bodyguard to a vampire.'

'You never tried to leave?'

'In the beginning, I tried. More than once. It never took him long to locate me.' She tapped her index finger against the vein at the side of her neck. 'Hard to get very far when your own blood is better than GPS for your pursuer. He used my blood as insurance of my loyalty. It was a shackle I couldn't break. I was never going to be free of it.'

'You're free now, Renata.'

'Yeah, I suppose I am,' she said, the answer sounding as hollow as it felt. 'But what about Mira?'

Nikolai stared at her for a long moment, saying nothing. She didn't want to see the doubt in his eyes, no more than she wanted empty assurances that there was anything either one of them could do for Mira now that she was in enemy hands. All the worse when she was currently weakened by her wound.

Nikolai pivoted to the claw-footed white tub and gave the twin handles a crank. As water rushed into the basin, he turned back to her where she sat. 'A cool bath should bring your temperature down. Come on, I'll help you clean up.'

'No, I can manage on my own—'

He gave her a no-arguments lift of his brow. 'The shirt, Renata. Let me help you out of it so I can have a better look at what's going on with that wound.'

Obviously, he wasn't about to give it up. Renata sat very still as Nikolai unfastened the last few buttons on the tent-sized oxford and gently eased it off her. The cotton fell in a soft crush on her lap and around her hips. Despite that she was wearing a bra, modesty ingrained in her from her early years in the church orphanage made her lift her hands up to shield her breasts from his eyes.

But he wasn't looking at her in a sexual way just then. All his focus was on her shoulder right now. He was gentle, careful, his fingers probing lightly around the area. He followed the curve of her shoulder over and around to where the bullet had left her flesh. 'Does it hurt when I touch you here?'

Even though his touch was barely a skimming contact, pain radiated through her. She winced, sucking in her breath.

'Sorry. There's a lot of redness and swelling near the exit wound,' he said, his deep voice vibrating in her bones while his touch moved lightly on her. 'It doesn't look great, but I think if we flush it out and . . .'

As his voice trailed off, she knew what he was seeing now. Not the raw gunshot wound, but two other blemishes on the otherwise smooth skin of her back. She felt those marks sear as hotly as they had the night they'd been put there.

'Holy hell.' Nikolai's breath left him in a slow sigh. 'What happened to you? Are these burn marks? Jesus . . . are they brands?'

Renata closed her eyes. Part of her wanted nothing more than to shrink away and vanish into the tile, but she forced herself to remain still, her spine rigidly erect. 'They are nothing.'

'Bullshit.' He stood before her and lifted her chin on the edge of his hand. She let her gaze drift up to meet his and found his pale eyes sharp with intensity. There was no pity in those eyes, only a cold outrage that took her aback. 'Tell me. Who did this to you – was it Yakut?'

She shrugged. 'Just one of his more creative ways of reminding me that it's not a good idea to piss him off.'

'That son of a bitch,' Nikolai fumed. 'He had his death

coming. Just for this – for everything he did to you – the bastard damn well had it coming.'

Renata blinked, surprised to hear such fury, such fierce protectiveness, coming from him. Particularly when Nikolai was one of the Breed and she was, as was made clear to her often enough the past two years, merely human. Existing only because she was useful. 'You're not like him at all,' she murmured. 'I thought you would be, but you're nothing like him or Lex or the others. You're . . . I don't know . . . different.'

'Different?' Although the intensity hadn't left his eyes, Nikolai's mouth quirked at the corner. 'Was that almost a compliment, or just your fever talking?'

She smiled despite her state of general misery. 'Both, I think.'

'Well, different I can handle. Let's cool you down before you start throwing around the n-word.'

'The n-word?' she asked, watching as he took the bottle of liquid hand soap from the sink and squirted some into the running bath.

'Nice,' he said, and tossed her a wry look over his thick shoulder.

'You're not comfortable with nice?'

'It's never been one of my specialties.'

His grin was crooked and more than a little charming as it made his lean cheeks dimple on both sides. Looking at him like this, it wasn't hard to imagine he was a male of many specialties, not all of them the bullets-and-blades variety. She knew firsthand that he had a very nice, very skilled mouth. As much as she wanted to deny it, a part of her was still burning from their kiss back at the lodge, and the heat she felt had nothing to do with her fever.

'Get undressed,' Nikolai told her, and for one addled second she wondered if he'd been able to read her thoughts. He ran his hand back and forth through the sudsy water in the tub, then shook it out. 'It feels about right. Go on, climb in.'

Renata watched him set the soap bottle back down on the sink, then start a search of the vanity cabinet below, taking out a folded washcloth and a large towel. While his back was to her and he was distracted searching the toiletries pack for soap and shampoo, Renata quickly slipped out of her bra and panties then stepped into the bathtub.

The cool water was bliss. She sank down with a sigh, her fatigued body instantly soothed. As she carefully settled in and submerged herself up to her breasts in the soapy bath, Nikolai ran a washcloth under cold water at the sink.

He folded it and pressed it gently against her brow. 'That feel all right?'

She nodded, closing her eyes as he held the compress to her forehead. The urge to lean back against the tub was tempting, but when she tried to, that brief moment of pressure on her shoulder made her recoil, hissing in pain.

'Here,' Nikolai said, putting the palm of his free hand at the center of her back. 'Just relax. I'll hold you up.'

Renata slowly let her weight come to rest on his strong hand. She couldn't remember the last time anyone had taken care of her. Not like this. God, had there ever been a time? Her eyes drifted closed in silent gratitude. With Nikolai's strong hands on her tired body, a strange, utterly foreign sensation of safety spread over her, as comforting as a blanket.

'Better?' he asked.

'Mm-hmm. It's nice,' she said, then opened one eye just a slit and glanced at up him. 'N-word. Sorry.'

He grunted as he took the cold compress away from her brow. He was looking at her with a seriousness that made her heart kick a little in her chest. 'You want to tell me about those marks on your back?'

'No.' Renata's breath seized up at the thought of baring

even more to him than she had already. She wasn't ready for that. Not with him, not like this. It was a humiliation she could hardly stand to think about, let alone put into words.

He didn't say anything to break the silence that stretched out between them. He dipped the washcloth into the water and brought some of the sudsy lather to her good shoulder. The coolness flowed over her, rivulets running over the swell of her breast and down her arm. Nikolai swabbed her neck and breastbone, then carefully made his way over to the wound on her left side.

'Is this all right?' he asked, his voice a low tremor.

Renata nodded her head, unable to speak when his touch felt so tender and welcome. She let him wash her, her gaze drifting to the beautiful pattern of color on his bare chest and arms. His *dermaglyphs* weren't as numerous or as thickly tangled as Yakut's had been. Nikolai's Breed markings were an artful twining of swirls and flourishes and flamelike shapes that danced across his smooth golden skin.

Curious, and before she realized what she was doing, Renata reached out to trace one of the arching designs that tracked down his thick biceps. She heard his slight intake of breath, the sudden halt of his lungs as her fingers played lightly over his skin, the deep rumble of his growl.

When he looked at her, his brows were low over his eyes. His pupils thinned sharply, and the blue of his irises began to flicker with amber sparks. Renata pulled her hand back, an apology at the very tip of her tongue.

She didn't get the chance to say a word.

Moving faster than she could track him, and with a predator's smooth grace, Nikolai closed the scant few inches that separated them. In the next instant his mouth was brushing sweetly against hers. His lips were so soft, so warm and coaxing. All it took was one tempting slide of his tongue along the seam of her mouth and Renata eagerly, hungrily, let him in.

She felt a new heat kindling to life within her, something stronger than the pain of her wound, which faded to insignificance under the pleasure of Nikolai's kiss. He brought his hand up out of the water behind her and cradled her in a careful embrace, his mouth never leaving hers.

Renata melted into him, too weary to consider all the reasons it would be a mistake to let this continue any further. She wanted it to continue – wanted it so badly she was shaking. She couldn't feel anything but Nikolai's strong hands caressing her, heard only the pound of her own heart and his, the heavy beats matched in tempo. She tasted only the heat of his seductive mouth claiming her . . . and knew only that she wanted more.

A knock sounded from outside the garage apartment.

Nikolai growled against her mouth and drew back. 'Someone's at the door.'

'That'll be Jack,' Renata said, breathless, her pulse still throbbing. 'I'll go see what he wants.'

She tried to shift in the tub to get out and felt her shoulder light up with pain.

'The hell you will,' Nikolai told her, already standing up. 'You're staying put. I'll handle Jack.'

Nikolai was a large male by any standards, but he seemed enormous now, his clear blue eyes crackling with burnished amber and the *dermaglyph* markings on his muscular arms and torso alive with color. He was apparently large elsewhere too, a fact that was hardly concealed by the loose-fitting nylon pants.

When the knock sounded again outside, he cursed, the tips of his fangs gleaming. 'Does anyone besides Jack know we're here?'

Renata shook her head. 'I asked him not to say anything to anyone. We can trust him.'

'I guess it's as good a time as any to find that out, eh?'

'Nikolai,' she said as he grabbed the shirt she'd been wearing and shrugged into the long sleeves. 'About Jack . . . he's a good man. A decent man. I don't want anything to happen to him.'

He smirked. 'Don't worry. I'll try to be nice.'

CHAPTER NINETEEN

'Nice,' Niko exhaled through a tight grimace. He was feeling anything but nice as he closed the bathroom door and walked into the main room of the apartment.

Being alone with Renata while she sat nude in the tub, touching her – kissing her, for crissake – had shifted all of his systems into overdrive. But as torqued as he was, his raging hard-on was the least of those concerns as he approached the door where Jack was knocking again from outside. It was one thing to pretend there wasn't a tent pole erected in his pants, quite another to hope no one would notice that his eyes were burning as bright as hot coals and that his extended canines would put a rottweiler to shame.

At least the loose shirt covered his *glyphs*. Niko didn't have to see his body to know that his skin markings were alive and pulsing with the deep colors of arousal. Awfully hard to try to explain them away as tattoos now.

Nikolai stared at the door and willed himself to chill out, cool down. He had to extinguish the fire in his irises, and that meant powering down the lust that Renata's touch had stirred in him. He focused on slowing his pulse, a hell of a struggle when his cock was in command of his blood flow.

'Hello?' came the drawled greeting from outside. Jack knocked again, the dark shadow of his head bobbing on the other side of the curtained window of the door. He seemed conscious of keeping his voice at a discreet level. 'Renata, that you, darlin'? You awake in there?'

Shit. No choice but to let him in. Nikolai growled low under his breath as he reached out to flip the dead bolt. He'd assured Renata that he would go easy on the old guy, but things could go south as soon as he opened the damned door. And if the human gave off so much as a whiff of suspicion, he was going to find himself on the short list for a mind scrub.

Niko freed the lock and twisted the doorknob. He backed off from the wedge of daylight that poured in through the opening and positioned himself behind the door as it swung open.

'Renata? All right if I come in for a minute?' A scuffed brown cowboy boot stepped over the threshold. 'Thought I'd better look in on you this morning before I get busy around the house with the kids.'

As the human in worn-out Levi's and a white cotton undershirt entered, Nikolai splayed his hand on the door and eased it shut to seal out the morning sunshine. He sized up the aged man in a glance, taking in the craggy face, shrewd eyes, and silvered, military-style buzzcut. He was a big man, a little soft around the middle, a little bowed around the knees, but his tattooed arms were tan and still firm with enough muscle to indicate that while he might be old, it didn't mean he was afraid of hard work.

'You must be Jack,' Nikolai said, careful to speak in a way that kept his fangs under wraps behind his lip.

'That's right.' A small nod as Niko was subjected to a similar measuring look. 'And you're Renata's friend . . . She, ah, didn't get around to telling me your name last night.'

Apparently the amber glow was gone from Niko's blue irises, since he doubted Jack would be reaching out to shake his hand right now if the old guy was staring into a pair of other-worldly eyes that threw off sparks like a furnace.

'I'm Nick,' he said, sticking close enough to the truth for now. He gave the former soldier's hand a brief shake. 'Thanks for helping us out.' ·

Jack nodded. 'You're looking a lot better this morning, Nick. Glad to see you're up and around. How's Renata doing?'

'Okay. She's in the bathroom washing up.'

He didn't see any reason to bring up the infection. No sense getting well-meaning Jack so worried that he started talking about doctors or trips to the hospital. Although based on what Nikolai had seen of Renata's wound, if her healing process didn't get a serious boost – and get one soon – there would be no alternative but a visit to the nearest ER.

'I'm not gonna ask how it is she ended up with a bullet hole in her shoulder,' Jack said, watching Nikolai closely. 'From the shape the both of you were in last night, and the fact I had to adios an apparently stolen medical supply truck, I'd be tempted to guess whatever trouble's chasing you is drug-related. But I know Renata's smarter than that. I don't believe for a minute she'd let herself get mixed up in something like drugs. She didn't want to tell me about any of it, and I promised her I wouldn't press. I'm a man of my word.'

Niko held the old man's stare. 'I'm sure she appreciates that. We both do.'

'Yeah,' Jack drawled, steely eyes narrowing. 'But I am curious about something. She's been MIA for the past couple of years . . . you got anything to do with that?'

It wasn't phrased as an overt accusation, but it was obvious that the old man had been concerned about Renata and also had the sense that her long absence hadn't necessarily been good for her. Man, if he only knew what she'd been through. The gunshot wound she was sporting now was just the icing on what had been a very nasty cake.

Nikolai shook his head. 'I've only known Renata for a few days, but I can tell you that you're right about her being too smart to fall into problems with drugs. That's not what this is about, Jack. But she is in danger. The only reason I'm standing here is because she risked her neck to pull me out of a shitload of trouble yesterday.'

'That sounds like Renata,' Jack said, his expression lost somewhere between pride and concern.

'Unfortunately, because she stepped in to help me, now there's a target on both our backs.'

Jack grunted as he listened, wiry brows knitting together. 'She tell you how we know each other?'

'Some of it,' Niko said. 'I know that she trusts and respects you. I assume you've been here to help her a time or two before now.'

'Tried, more like it. Renata never wanted help from me or from anyone else. Not for herself, anyway. But there were a lot of other kids she brought to my house for help. She couldn't stand to see a child in pain. Hell, she wasn't much more than a kid herself the first time she came around. Always kept to herself for the most part, a real loner. She doesn't have any family, you know.'

Nikolai shook his head. 'No, I didn't know that.'

'The Sisters of Benevolent Mercy raised her the first twelve years of her life. Her mother gave her up to the church orphanage when Renata was just a baby. She never knew either of her parents. By the time Renata was fifteen, she was already on her own, having left the nuns to live on the streets.'

Jack walked over to a metal file cabinet that stood with some of the other stuff stored in the apartment. He fished a set of keys out of his jeans pocket and stuck one of them into the lock on the front of the piece. 'Yessir, Renata was a tough little customer, even in the beginning. Skinny, wary, she looked like someone who would hardly stand up to a stiff breeze, but that girl had a spine of solid steel. Didn't take bullshit from anyone.'

'Not much has changed there,' Nikolai said, watching the old man pop open the bottom drawer. 'I've never met a woman like Renata.'

Jack looked over at him and smiled. 'She's special, all right. Stubborn too. A few months before the last time I saw her, she showed up with a face full of bruises. Apparently some drunk rolled out of a bar and got the idea that he wanted some company for the night. He saw Renata and tried to shove her into his car. She fought him, but he got a few hard punches in before she was able to get away.'

Nikolai cursed under his breath. 'Son of a bitch should have been gutted for laying a hand on a defenseless female.'

'That was my thinking too,' Jack said, deadly serious, the protective soldier once more. He eased down into a squat and withdrew a polished wooden case from the file cabinet. 'I taught her a few self-defense moves – basic stuff. Offered to send her to some classes on my dime, but of course she refused. A few weeks passed and she was back again, helping another kid with nowhere left to turn. I told her I had something for her – a gift I had made special for her. Swear to God, if you'd seen her face, you'd think she would rather have bolted into oncoming traffic than have to accept any kindness from someone.'

Nikolai didn't have to work to imagine that look. He'd seen it once or twice himself since he'd met Renata. 'What was your gift for her?'

The old man shrugged. 'Nothing much, really. I had an old set of daggers I picked up in Nam. I took them to an artist fella I knew who worked with metals and had him customize the handles for me. He hand-tooled each of the four grips with a few of the strengths I saw in Renata. I told her they were the qualities that made her unique and would see her through any situation.'

'Faith, honor, courage, and sacrifice,' Nikolai said, recalling the words he'd seen on the blades Renata seemed to treasure so much.

'She told you about the blades?'

Niko shrugged. 'I've seen her use them. They mean a lot to her, Jack.'

'I didn't know,' he replied. 'I was surprised that she accepted them in the first place, but I didn't think she'd still keep them after all this time.' He blinked quickly, then busied himself with the box he'd pulled out of the file cabinet. He opened the lid and Niko caught the glint of dark metal resting inside the felt-lined case. Jack cleared his throat. 'Listen, like I said before, I'm not going to press for details about what the two of you are involved in. It's clear enough that you're in some pretty big trouble. You can stay here as long as you need to, and when you're ready to go, just know that you don't have to leave here empty-handed.'

He set the open box down on the floor in front of him and gave it a little push in Nikolai's direction. Inside were two pristine semiautomatic pistols and a box of rounds.

'They're yours if you want them, no questions asked.'

Niko picked up one of the .45s and inspected it with an appreciative eye. It was a beautiful, well-tended Colt M1911. Probably military-issued weapons from his service time in Vietnam. 'Thank you, Jack.'

The old human warrior gave him a brief nod. 'Just take care of her. Keep her safe.'

Nikolai held that steady stare. 'I will.'

'Okay,' Jack murmured. 'Okay, then.'

As he started to get up, someone shouted his name from outside in driveway. A second later, footsteps were pounding up the wooden stairs to the garage apartment.

Niko shot Jack a sharp look. 'Does anyone know we're in here?'

'Nope. Anyway, that's just Curtis, one of my newer kids.

He's fixing my dinosaur of a computer. Damn virus attack again.' Jack went over to the door. 'He thinks I'm looking for a boot disk in here. I'll get rid of him. Meantime, if you think of anything else you two might need, you just ask.'

'How about a phone?' Niko asked, replacing the pistol next to its mate.

Jack reached into his front pocket and pulled out a cell phone. He tossed it to Nikolai. 'It should have a few hours of battery time. It's all yours.'

'Thanks.'

'I'll check in with you again later.' Jack grabbed the door-knob and Nikolai backed into the shadows, as much a reflex because of the daylight outside as it was an effort to stay out of sight from the unwanted visitor who'd arrived at the top of the stairs. 'Well, I was mistaken, Curtis. I checked everywhere and there's no disk in any of my boxes up here.'

Niko saw the other human's head trying to peer around the edge of the door as Jack closed it firmly behind him. There was a clopping shuffle of feet on the steps as Jack escorted the other human away.

Once he was certain they were gone, Nikolai dialed a remote access number that was maintained by the Order's Boston headquarters. He typed in Jack's cell phone number and a code that would identify him to Gideon, then waited for the callback.

Midday in a compound that housed a bunch of vampires was generally a dead zone of inactivity, but none of the seven warriors gathered in the weapons room of the Order's subter-ranean headquarters seemed to notice the time, not even the handful of them blessed enough to have loving Breedmates warming their beds. Since regrouping at the compound before daybreak, the warriors had kept themselves busy reviewing current mission statuses and laying out objectives for the night to come. Hashing out Order business for hours on end was nothing new, but this time there had been none of the usual good-natured smacktalk or joking squabbles over who was grabbing up the best assignments.

Now, a few yards away, at the area used for target practice, a quintet of pistols were being fired one after the other, paper bull's-eyes at the other end shredded into minuscule confetti. The compound's shooting range was used more for entertainment than necessity, since all of the warriors had dead-on aim. Even so, that never stopped any of them from testing one another and busting asses just to keep things lively.

There was none of that today. Only the steady hail of all that thundering noise. The racket was oddly comforting, if only because it helped mask the silence, and the fact that the entire compound was vibrating with a low-level current of unrest. For the past thirty-six hours, the mood there had been sober, draped in a collective, if unspoken, dread.

One of their own was missing.

Nikolai had always tended to be something of a maverick, but that didn't mean the male was unreliable. If he said he was going to do something – or be somewhere – you could damn well count on him to follow through. Every time, no exceptions.

And now, when he should have been back from Montreal a full day and a half ago as planned, Niko was off-grid and out of contact.

Not good, Lucan thought, sensing he wasn't alone in that sentiment as he looked at the other warriors who also waited for word of Nikolai and dreaded what it eventually might be.

As a Gen One Breed and the founder of the Order in the Middle Ages, Lucan was the de facto leader of this cadre of modern-day vampire knights. His word was law in this compound. In times of crisis – for better or worse – it was his response that set the tone for the other warriors. He was well conditioned not to show worry or doubt, a skill that came naturally to that part of him that was virtually immortal, a powerful predator who'd been walking this Earth for some nine hundred years.

But the part of him that was human – the part of him who had come to appreciate life all the more for having met his Breedmate, Gabrielle, just a summer ago – could not pretend that the potential loss of one more soldier in this private war within the vampire nation would be anything but catastrophic. To say nothing of the fact that the warriors of the Order, both the ones who had been with him from the start and the newer members who'd joined the fight in the past year, had become like family to him. So much had changed in that time. Now there were several females living in the compound too, and for one of the warriors and his mate – Dante and Tess – a baby several months on the way.

The stakes were higher than ever for the Order now, one evil defeated only to see another, even more powerful, rise in its place. In just a year's time, the warriors' primary mission had gone from hunting down Rogues in an effort to keep the peace, to pursuing a dangerous enemy who'd been hiding in plain sight for many long decades. An enemy who had been patiently constructing his strategy while concealing a deadly secret and waiting for the opportunity to unleash it. If he were to succeed, it wouldn't be just the Breed populations in peril, but all of humankind as well.

It didn't take much for Lucan to recall the savagery of the Old Times, when the night was ruled by a handful of blood-thirsty creatures from another world, creatures who dealt in wide-scale terror and death. They fed like locusts and wreaked destruction like the deadliest marauders. Lucan had made it his life's mission to eradicate the beasts from existence, even though it had meant slaying the Ancient who was his own father.

The Order had declared war, had wielded swords and ridden into battle to take them all out . . . or so they'd believed. The idea that one had survived put a deep chill in Lucan's immortal bones.

He looked at the warriors who served alongside him and couldn't help feeling some of his age. He couldn't help feeling that they had all been handed a test last year – perhaps their first true test since the Order's formation – and the worst of it was still to come.

Lost in dark thoughts as he paced the back of the weapons room, Lucan didn't realize the training area's doors were sliding open until Gideon came rushing through them. The blond vampire's vintage Chucks skidded to a squeaking halt on the white marble in front of Lucan.

'Niko's back on grid,' he announced, visibly relieved. 'His ID just came up on a cell phone with a Montreal exchange.'

'About fucking time,' Lucan said, the snarled reply betraying none of his concern. 'You got him on the line?'

Gideon nodded. 'He's on hold back in the tech lab. I thought you'd want to talk to him personally.'

'Damn straight I do.'

The gunfire at the range came to an abrupt stop as one of the other warriors, the Order's only other Gen One member, Tegan, jogged back and delivered the news of Niko's contact to the five males shooting at targets. The warriors at the range – Dante and Rio, longtime members; Chase, who'd left the Enforcement Agency to join the Order last summer; and the two newest recruits, Kade and Brock, both brought in by Niko – put down their weapons and strode forward behind Tegan, all of them a knot of muscle and grim purpose.

Rio, one of the warriors who was tightest with Nikolai, was the first to speak. His scarred face was taut with concern. 'What happened to him up there?'

'He's only given me the *Reader's Digest* version so far,' Gideon said. 'But it's all sorts of fucked up, starting with Sergei Yakut's murder two nights ago.'

'Holy hell,' Brock muttered, raking his dark fingers over his skull-trimmed black hair. 'This Gen One assassination shit is getting way out of hand.'

'Well,' Gideon added, 'that's not exactly the worst of it. Niko was arrested for the killing and taken into Enforcement Agency custody.'

'Ah, shit,' Kade replied, his pale silver eyes narrowing. 'You don't suppose he—'

'No way,' Dante said without a second's hesitation. 'I doubt he shed a tear for blood-clubbing scum like Yakut, but there's no way Nikolai had a hand in his death.'

Gideon shook his head. 'Nope. And it wasn't the work of an assassin, either. Niko says Yakut's own son brought in a Rogue to kill his father. Unfortunately for Nikolai, Yakut's son has some kind of alliance with the Enforcement Agency. They hauled Niko in and threw him into a containment facility.'

'What the fuck?' This time it was Sterling Chase who spoke up. Being a former Agent himself, he was as aware as any of the warriors in the room how unpleasant a visit to one of those Agency-managed Rogue holding tanks could be. 'Since he's conscious enough to phone in, I assume he's not still being held there.'

'He escaped somehow,' Gideon said, 'but I don't have all the details yet. I can tell you that there's a female involved, a Breedmate who was a member of Yakut's household. She's with Niko now.'

Lucan didn't comment on that troublesome newsflash, although his dark expression probably spoke plainly enough for him. 'Where are they?'

'In the city somewhere,' Gideon replied. 'Niko wasn't sure of the exact location, but he says they're secure for now. Are you ready for the real kicker?'

Lucan arched a brow. 'For fuck's sake. There's more?'

'Afraid so. The guy who tossed Niko's ass in the containment facility and personally oversaw his torture? Apparently during one of his chattier moments, the son of a bitch admitted a connection to Dragos.'

⇥ CHAPTER TWENTY ⇤

Nikolai was in the middle of a cell phone conversation when Renata came out of the bathroom from her long, much-needed soak. She'd evidently fallen asleep in the tub at some point because the last thing she remembered was hearing Jack's voice in the garage apartment after Nikolai had gone out to meet him, and there was no sign of him now. She stepped into the room, her hair damp at the ends and clinging to her neck, her body wrapped in the towel Nikolai had set out for her.

She was groggy and achy, still overly warm, but the cool-water bath had been just what she'd needed. Nikolai's kiss hadn't been half bad either.

Speaking in low, confidential tones, he glanced over at her from where he sat straddling a folding chair near the card table in the center of the room, his pale blue eyes doing a quick but thorough head-to-toe scan of her body. There was an unmistakable heat in that brief gaze, but he was all business on the phone with what she could only assume was the Order back in Boston. Renata listened as he provided an efficient run-through of the circumstances of Yakut's murder, Lex and Fabien's apparent alliance, Mira's disappearance, and the containment facility escape that had brought Nikolai and Renata to Jack's place for temporary shelter.

From the sound of it, the male on the other end of the line –

Lucan, she'd heard Nikolai call him – was concerned for their safety and glad they were both in one piece, although not at all pleased to hear that they were holed up at the mercy of a human. Nor did Lucan seem enthused about the fact that Nikolai was talking about helping Renata locate Mira. She could hear the deep voice on the other end of the line growl something about 'Breedmate's problems' and 'current mission objectives' as though the two were mutually exclusive.

The cursed response when Nikolai added that Renata was nursing a gunshot wound was audible all the way across the room.

'She's tough,' he said, glancing her way now, 'but she took a pretty hard hit in the shoulder and it's not looking too healthy. It might be a good idea to arrange a pickup, take her into the Order's protection until everything shakes down up here.'

Renata glared her disapproval and gave a shake of her head. Big mistake. Even that slight jostle made her vision swim, and it was all she could do to position her backside at the edge of the bed before her legs gave out beneath her. She dropped down onto the mattress, fighting off a vicious wave of cold sweats.

She tried to hide her misery from Nikolai, but the look he gave her said it was no use pretending she wasn't in bad shape.

'Has Gideon turned up anything on Fabien yet?' he asked, getting up to pace the floor. He listened for a minute, then exhaled a low sigh. 'Fuck. Can't say I'm surprised about that. He had the arrogant stink of a politician all over him, so I had a feeling the bastard was well connected. What else do we have?'

Renata held her breath in the silence that stretched out. She could see that the news on the other end of the line wasn't good.

Nikolai blew out a long sigh and ran his hand through his

hair. 'How long does Gideon think it will take him to dig into those restricted files and turn up an address? Shit, Lucan, I'm not sure we should wait that long, considering – yeah, I hear you. Maybe while Gideon's hacking on that end I should go pay Alexei Yakut a visit. I'd bet my left nut that Lex knows where to find Fabien. Hell, I wouldn't doubt it if Lex has been there a time or two himself. I'd be glad to squeeze the information out of him, then go deal with Fabien personally.'

Nikolai listened for a moment before grunting a low curse. 'Yeah, sure, I know . . . much as I'd like a little payback from the son of a bitch, you're right. We can't afford the risk of scaring Fabien to ground before we've got a solid lead on his ties to Dragos.'

Renata glanced up in time to catch Nikolai's grim look. She waited for him to add that nothing was more critical than ensuring Mira's safety and tracking down the vampire who was holding her. She waited, but those words never left Nikolai's lips.

'Yeah,' he murmured. 'Have him call when he finds something. I'm going to head out tonight and do some recon on this end too. If I turn up anything useful, I'll be in touch.'

He ended the call and set the cell phone down on the card table. Renata stared at him as he walked over to the bed and dropped into a crouch in front of her.

'How are you feeling?'

He reached up like he was going to check her shoulder – or maybe simply caress her – but Renata flinched away from him. She couldn't sit there and act as if she wasn't feeling more than a little bit confused and pissed off right now. Betrayed, even, as ridiculous as it was to think she could have counted on him in the first place.

'Did the cool water help your fever at all?' he asked, his brows furrowed. 'You're still looking kind of pale and wobbly. Here, let me have a look—'

'I don't need your concern,' she bit out. 'And I don't need your help either. Forget that I asked you. Just . . . forget every-thing. I wouldn't want my problems to interfere with any of your current mission objectives.'

His scowl deepened. 'What are you talking about?'

'I have my priorities, and you clearly have yours. Sounded to me like your buddy Lucan is calling the shots for you now.'

'Lucan is one of my brothers-in-arms. He's also the leader of the Order, so yeah, he's earned the right to call the shots when it comes to Order business.' Nikolai stood up, crossing his arms over his chest. 'Something big is going down, Renata. Yakut's murder was only a small part of it, and he wasn't the first. There've been several other Gen One assassinations that have taken place in the States and abroad. Someone's been quietly taking out the oldest, most powerful members of the Breed.'

'What for?' She looked up at him, curious against her will.

'We're not sure. But we believe it all ties back to one indi-vidual, a very dangerous second-generation Breed male named Dragos. The Order flushed him out of hiding a few weeks ago, but he managed to get away from us. Now he's gone underground again. Son of a bitch has been lying real low. Any lead we can grab to get close to him is critical. He has to be stopped.'

'Sergei Yakut killed dozens of human beings – just for sport,' Renata pointed out. 'Why didn't you and the rest of the Order put a stop to him?'

'Until recently, we didn't know where to find him, let alone know about his extracurricular activities. Even if we had, he was Gen One, and as much as we hated it, the Order wouldn't have been able to move on him without a lot of bureaucratic bullshit standing in our way.'

Renata's thoughts grew dark, spinning back across the time she'd spent under Yakut's control. 'There were times when

Sergei drank from me . . . when he used me for blood, that I saw something monstrous in him. I mean, I know what he was – what all of your kind is – but once in while, I would look in his eyes and I swear there was no humanity in him. All I could see in his gaze was something truly evil.'

'He was Gen One,' Nikolai said as though that should explain it. 'Only half of their genes are human. The other half are something . . . else.'

'Vampire,' she murmured.

'Otherworlder,' Nikolai corrected.

He stared at her as he said it and Renata had the abrupt impulse to laugh. But she couldn't, not when his expression was so completely serious. 'Lex loves to boast that he is grandson to a conquering king from another world. I always assumed he was full of shit. Are you telling me what he said is actually true?'

Nikolai scoffed. 'A conqueror, yes, but not a king. The eight Ancients who arrived here thousands of years ago and fathered their young on human women were bloodthirsty savages, rapists . . . deadly creatures that decimated entire communities. Most of them were wiped out by the Order in the Middle Ages. Lucan led the charge against them after his mother was killed by the creature who fathered him.'

Renata just listened now, too astonished to ask all the questions churning in her head.

'As it turns out,' Nikolai added, 'one of the Ancients survived the Order's war on them. He'd been placed in hiding by one of his sons – a Gen One vampire named Dragos. We have good reason to believe the Ancient is still alive today and that Dragos's last surviving son, his namesake and the bastard we intend to shut down, is just waiting for his chance to unleash him on the world.'

'Two years ago I was sure that vampires didn't really exist. Sergei Yakut changed my mind. He proved to me that vampires not only existed, but they were scarier and more dangerous than anything I'd seen in books or movies. Now you're saying there's something even worse than him out there?'

'I'm not trying to scare you, Renata. I just think you should have the facts. All of them. I'm trusting you with that.'

'Why?'

'Because I want you to understand,' he said, the words too gentle.

As if he were apologizing to her in some way.

Renata lifted her chin, a coldness settling in her chest. 'You want me to understand . . . what? That the life of one missing child means nothing in light of all this?'

He cursed softly under his breath. 'No, Renata—'

'It's okay. I get it now, Nikolai.' She couldn't keep the bitterness from her voice, not even when she was still struggling to absorb all of the staggering things she'd just heard. 'Hey, no big deal. After all, you never actually agreed to anything with me and I'm used to being let down. Life's a bitch, right? It's just good to know where we both stand before we let this thing go any further.'

'What's going on here, Renata?' He stared at her, his gaze too penetrating, as if he could see right through her. 'Is this really about Mira? Or are you upset because of what's been happening between us?'

Us. The word stuck in her brain like a foreign object. It felt so unfamiliar, so dangerous. Far too intimate. There had never been an 'us' for Renata. She'd always depended only herself, asking nothing of anyone. It was safer that way. Safer now too.

She'd broken her own rule when she went after Nikolai to enlist his help in finding Mira. Look what it had gotten her: a festering gunshot wound, crucial time lost, and not a single step closer to locating Mira. In fact, now that word was certainly out about her abetting Nikolai in his escape from Fabien's custody, she stood little hope of getting close to the vampire on her own. If Mira was in danger before, Renata might have just made things worse for the little girl.

'I have to get out of here,' she said woodenly. 'I've lost too much time already. I couldn't bear it if anything happens to that child because of me.'

Worry and frustration made her push off from the bed. She stood up – too quickly.

Before she could take two steps away from Nikolai, her knees turned to jelly. Her vision went dark for a second and suddenly she was sinking, pitching forward. She felt strong arms cushion her, Nikolai's voice quiet beside her ear as he scooped her up and lifted her onto the bed.

'Stop fighting, Renata,' he said as she came out of her faint and blinked up at him. Poised over her, he smoothed the backs of his fingers along the side of her face. So tender, so calming. 'You don't need to run. You don't need to fight . . . not with me. You're safe with me, Renata.'

She wanted to close her eyes and shut out his gentle words. She was so afraid to believe him, to trust. And she felt so guilty accepting his comfort knowing that a child could be suffering, probably crying for her in the dark and wondering why Renata had broken her promise.

'Mira's all that matters to me,' she whispered. 'I need to know that she's safe, and that she always will be.'

Nikolai gave a solemn nod. 'I know how much she means to you. And I know how hard it is for you to ask for help from someone. Jesus Christ, Renata . . . you willingly risked your life to break me out of that containment facility. I'll never be able to repay you for what you did.'

She turned her head on the pillow, unable to hold his piercing gaze. 'Don't worry, you're under no obligation to me. You don't owe me a thing, Nikolai.'

Warm fingers glided along her jaw. He cupped her chin in

his palm and gently guided her face back to him. 'I owe you my life. Where I come from, that's no small thing.'

Renata's breath stilled as he looked into her eyes. She hated herself for the hope that was kindling in her heart – hope that she truly wasn't alone right now. Hope that this warrior would assure her that everything was going to work out, and that no matter what kind of monster had Mira, they would find her, and she was going to be all right.

'I'm not going to let anything happen to Mira,' he said, forcing her to hold his intense gaze. 'You have my word on that. I'm not going to let anything happen to you either, which is why I'm going to get you medical care for your shoulder as soon as the sun sets tonight.'

'What?' She tried to raise up and winced from the sharp stab of pain. 'I'll be fine. I don't need a doctor—'

'You're not fine, Renata. You're getting worse by the hour.' His expression was grave as he looked from the searing wound in her shoulder back to her eyes. 'You can't continue like this.'

'I'll survive,' she insisted. 'I'm not about to quit now, when Mira's life is on the line.'

'Your life is on the line too. Do you understand?' He shook his head and muttered something dark and nasty under his breath. 'You could die if this wound doesn't get treated. I won't let that happen, so that means you have a date with the nearest emergency room tonight.'

'What about blood?' She watched as every muscle in Nikolai's body seemed to tense up the moment the words left her lips.

'What about it?' he asked, his voice wooden, unreadable.

'You asked me earlier if I'd ever taken Sergei's blood. Would I be healed now if I had?'

He lifted his shoulder in a vague shrug, but the tension in his big body remained. When he lifted his gaze to hers, there were flashes of amber burning into the wintry blue of his irises. His pupils were thinning by fractions as he stared at her.

'Would I be healed now if you gave me your blood, Nikolai?'

'Are you asking me for it?'

'If I were, would you give it to me?'

He exhaled sharply, and when his lips parted to draw another breath, Renata saw the sharp points of his fangs. 'It's not as simple a question as you might think,' he replied, a rough edge to his voice. 'You will be bonded to me. The same way Yakut was linked to you through your blood, you will be linked to me. You'll feel me in your blood. You will be aware of me always, and it can't be undone, Renata – not even if you drink from another Breed male down the line. Our bond will trump any others. It can't be broken, not until one of us is dead.'

This was no small thing; she understood that. Hell, she could hardly believe she was considering it at all. But deep down, crazy as it might be, she trusted Nikolai. And she truly didn't care about the cost to herself. 'If we do this, will I be well enough to walk out of here tonight and search for Mira?'

His jaw was clamped tight enough to make a muscle jerk in his cheek. He stared at her, his features going more feral by the moment. Bit by bit, the blue of his eyes was engulfed by a fiery glow.

When it didn't seem like he would answer her, Renata reached out and laid her hand firmly on his arm. 'Will your blood heal me, Nikolai?'

'Yes,' he said, the word sounding strangled in his throat.

'Then I want to do this.'

As he held her gaze in an intense silence, she thought about all the times Sergei Yakut had fed from her veins, how degraded and used she'd felt . . . how revolted she'd been by the idea that her blood was nourishing such a cruel, monstrous being. She would never have considered taking any part of him into herself, not even if it had been a matter of her own survival. It would have killed a piece of her soul to willingly put her mouth on Yakut's body. To drink from him? She wasn't even sure that her love for Mira could have overcome something as vile as that.

But Nikolai wasn't a monster. He was honorable and just. He was tender and protective, a male who was feeling more and more a partner to her the farther they traveled down this uncertain road. He was her best ally right now. Her brightest hope of retrieving Mira.

And deeper still, in a place that was all woman, with needs and wants she hardly dared to examine too closely, she craved a taste of Nikolai. She craved that more than she had a right to.

'Are you sure, Renata?'

'If you'll give me your blood, then yes,' she said. 'I want to take it.'

In the long silence that followed, Nikolai sat back from her on the bed. She watched as he unbuttoned the big oxford shirt, waiting for her uncertainty – her apprehension – to worsen. It didn't happen. As Nikolai stripped off the shirt and sat before her bare-chested, his *dermaglyphs* pulsing, every arch and swirl saturated with variegating shades of wine-dark colors, she felt no misgivings at all. When he crawled up toward her and lifted his right arm up to his mouth, baring his huge fangs, then sinking them into his wrist, she felt nothing even close to fear.

And when, in that next moment, he placed the bleeding punctures next to her lips and told her to drink, Renata had no inclination whatsoever to refuse.

The first taste of Nikolai's blood on her tongue was a shock.

She'd expected to be swamped by the bitter taste of copper, but instead she tasted warm, muted spices and a power that spread through her like liquid electricity. She could feel his blood coursing down her throat, into every fiber of her body. Light flowed into her limbs from within, and the ache in her wounded shoulder began to ease as she drew more of Nikolai's healing strength inside her.

'That's it,' he murmured, his fingers stroking her damp hair away from her cheek. 'Ah, Christ, that's it, Renata . . . drink until you feel you've had enough.'

She pulled long and hard from his wrist, with an instinct she never knew she had. It felt right to be drinking from Nikolai like this. It felt more than right . . . it felt incredible. The more she took from him, the more alive she felt. Every nerve ending blinked on as though a switch had been thrown in her core.

And as he continued to caress her, to nourish and heal her, Renata began to feel a new kind of heat building swiftly inside her. She moaned, swept up in the molten wave that washed through her. She writhed, and knew better than to mistake the feeling for anything but what it was . . . desire. A desire that she had been trying to deny since she first met Nikolai, and which now was rising up to consume her.

She couldn't resist suckling at him deeper.

She needed more of him.

She needed all of him, and she needed him now.

CHAPTER TWENTY-ONE

Nikolai braced himself on the edge of the bed, knotting his free hand in the sheet and holding onto it like a tether line as Renata continued to feed. She drank from him like she did everything else: with fearless strength and ferocious conviction. No hedging anxiety in her jade-green eyes, no uncertainty in her firm grasp on his arm. And each pull of her mouth on his open vein, every sure, coaxing sweep of her tongue across his skin, ratcheted him tighter than anything he'd ever felt before.

In all things she set her mind to, Renata was a force to be reckoned with. She was unlike any female Niko had ever known – in many ways, as much a warrior as any of the Breed males who'd served alongside him in the Order. She had a warrior's heart and a warrior's honor, and an unshakable resolve that demanded his total respect. Renata had saved his life, and for that he owed her. But holy hell . . . what was happening between them here had nothing to do with duty or obligation.

He was starting to care for her – more than he was comfortable admitting, even to himself.

He wanted her too. Christ, did he ever. His need was made all the worse for the erotic suction of her mouth as it worked on his vein, her lithe body undulating in heated reaction to his otherworldly blood feeding her uninitiated cells.

Renata moaned, a throaty purr of arousal as she moved

closer to him on the mattress, each grinding movement of her body loosening the towel that covered her. She didn't seem to notice, or care at all that Nikolai's amber gaze was traveling the entire nearly naked length of her. Her shoulder wound was looking better already. The swelling and redness was receding, and the too-sallow color of the rest of her skin was looking more healthy by the minute. Renata was getting stronger, more vibrant and demanding, one fever being replaced by another.

He probably should have told her that aside from its nourishment and healing properties, Breed blood was also a potent aphrodisiac. He figured he could handle whatever might happen, but damn . . . nothing would have prepared him for Renata's molten response.

Crawling up against him now, still suckling at him, she reached over with one hand and freed his clenched fist from the tangled sheet. She guided his fingers under the folds of the bath towel to her breasts. He couldn't resist running the pad of his thumb over the tight nipple of one, then the other. Her breath sped up as he caressed her warm, tender skin, the hard flutter of her heart beating against his hand as she impatiently guided him lower . . . over the soft plane of her abdomen to the silky juncture of her thighs.

She was drenched and hot, the cleft of her sex like warm, wet satin as he slid one finger along her core. She clenched her thighs around him, holding him there as if he had any thought at all to leave. She took another draw from his wrist, the pull so thorough he felt it all the way to his balls. Squeezing his eyes shut, he dropped his head back and hissed a slow, wordless groan, the tendons in his neck going as taut as cables. His cock was rock-solid and standing at full attention between his legs. Another minute of this torment and he was going to lose it right there in his borrowed pair of warm-ups.

'Ah, fuck,' he snarled, pulling his hand away from the sweet temptation of her aroused body. He slowly lowered his chin to look at her. When his eyelids lifted, the heat from his transformed irises bathed Renata in an ember-bright glow. She was gloriously naked, sitting there in front of him like a dark goddess, her lips fastened to his wrist, her pale eyes dusky as she stared up at him, unabashed.

'No more,' he muttered, his voice rough, the words thickened by the presence of his fangs. He was gasping for breath, every nerve ending electrified. 'We have to stop . . . Jesus Christ . . . we'd better stop now.'

She moaned in protest but, very gently, Nikolai withdrew his wrist from Renata's feeding grasp and brought the twin punctures to his lips. A sweep of his tongue over the wounds sealed them closed.

With hooded, hungry eyes, she watched him lick the place where her mouth had been, her own tongue darting out to wet her lips. 'What's happening to me?' she asked, running her hands across her breasts, her spine stretching and arching with feline grace. 'What did you . . . do to me? My God . . . I'm burning up.'

'It's the blood bond,' he said, hardly able to form a complete sentence for the way his senses were throbbing with awareness – and need – of this woman. 'I should have warned you . . . I'm sorry.'

He started to move away but she grabbed his hand and held it. Gave a nearly imperceptible shake of her head. Her chest rose and fell with each pump of her lungs, and the heavy-lidded gaze she fixed on him looked anything but offended. Knowing that he shouldn't take advantage of the situation, Nikolai reached up and stroked the pink blush that filled her cheek.

Renata moaned as his touch lingered, turning her face into his palm. 'Is it . . . is it always like this when you let a woman drink from you?'

He shook his head. 'I don't know. You're the first.'

She glanced up at him, a small frown creasing her brow. He could see the surprise register behind the blood-induced lust that filled her gaze. A quiet cry slipped past her lips and then she was moving toward him without any hesitation, her hands coming up to frame his face.

She kissed him, long and hard and deep.

'Touch me, Nikolai,' she murmured against his mouth.

It was as much a demand as the urgent press of her lips on his, her tongue pushing past his teeth. Niko ran his hands all over her naked skin, meeting her kiss thrust for thrust, his body as hungry as hers was, and he couldn't blame his ferocious need on the natural response of a blood bond. His hunger for Renata was something else completely, although just as consuming.

Greedily, he reached back down to the haven of her sex. This time, he couldn't play at touching her, not when her scent was intoxicating him as much as the heated silk of her core was driving him mad. He stroked her wet folds, cleaving them with his fingers and spreading her open to him like a flower. She arched up to meet him as he penetrated her with first one finger, then another. He filled her, reveling in the tight clench of her body, the subtle ripples of her tight inner muscles as he stroked and teased her toward climax.

He was so engrossed in her pleasure that he hardly noticed her hands were moving until he felt her tugging at the drawstring of his pants. He hissed when she slipped underneath the waistband and found his stiff cock. She palmed the head of him, slicking her fingers with the drop of fluid that beaded there, then torturing him with a slow, steady stroke of her hand down the length of his shaft.

'You want me too,' she said, not quite a question when the answer was overflowing her hand.

'Oh, yes,' Niko answered anyway. 'Hell yes . . . I want you, Renata.'

She smiled hungrily and pushed him down onto his back on the bed. She inched his pants down off his hips, but they only made it as far as his knees. With his thick erection jutting up like a proud soldier, Nikolai watched enthralled as Renata climbed over and straddled him. He knew better than to expect any bit of coyness or hesitation. She was bold and unstoppable, and he'd never been more glad of anything in his life. Her eyes locked unflinchingly on his, Renata sank down onto his cock in a long, slow slide.

Good Christ, she felt incredible on him. So hot and tight, so damn wet.

He told himself it was only the aftershock of the blood bond making her this wanton, that she would be reacting this way to any Breed male who fed her. It was just a physical reaction, like tinder igniting when held too close to a flame. Her awareness of him right now was probably subconscious at best – she had an itch and he was the scratch she needed, plain and simple. Fine by him. It didn't need to be anything more complicated, and he wasn't idiot enough to want it to be. This sex between them right now wasn't personal, and Niko told himself he was good with that.

He told himself a lot of bullshit things as he laid his head back with a groan and let Renata take all that she needed from him.

Renata had never felt more alive. Nikolai's blood was a fire in her senses, every nuance of the moment buffeting her with vivid awareness. The wound in her shoulder gave her no pain now; her need for Nikolai was all she knew.

He held her hips as she impaled herself on his sex, her mind lost to all but the heat of him filling her, the masculine beauty of his big body moving in a shared rhythm beneath her. Through the swamping haze of her desire, she admired the corded muscles of his arms and chest, a symphony of strength, flexing and contracting, power made all the more stunning by the artful colors and patterns of his changeable *dermaglyphs.*

Even his fangs, which by rights should have terrified her, took on a lethal beauty now. The sharp tips of them gleamed with every sawing breath he dragged through his teeth. The blood she'd taken from him must have made her a little bit crazy, because some dim part of her wanted those lethal canines pressed up close against her neck, piercing her flesh as she rode him.

She could still taste his blood on her tongue, sweet and wild and dark, an electric tingle that spread all through her and lit her up from within.

She craved more of that power, more of him . . .

All of him.

Renata dug her fingers into his thick biceps and drove deeper, harder, chasing that dangerous need his blood had unleashed in her. He took every desperate thrust of her hips, holding her steady as a shattering orgasm slammed into her. She cried out as the pleasure washed over her, a scream of release that she couldn't have contained even if her life depended on it. The intensity was far too much to bear. She trembled from it, awed by the force of her passion for him – a passion she had been afraid to feel for so long.

She didn't fear Nikolai.

She wanted him.

Trusted him.

'Are you okay?' he asked her, little more than a growl as he continued to rock with her. 'Are you in any pain now?'

She shook her head, unable to speak when every nerve ending in her body was still taut with need and vibrating with sensation.

'Good,' he murmured, and slipped his hand around the back of her neck to draw her down for a kiss. His mouth was hot on hers, his fangs grazing her lips and tongue. He felt so good . . . tasted so good.

The fire that had banked somewhat with her release kindled back to furious life. She moaned as the need rose up again, moving her hips in time with the hunger that pulsed in her core. Nikolai didn't let her want for long. He pistoned along with her, increasing their tempo until she was breaking apart again, drifting on wave after wave of pleasure. Then he took over completely, filling her and withdrawing, every stroke seeming to touch someplace deeper within her, then deeper still. He came on a hoarse shout, his spine arching beneath her, his pelvis bucking her with the force of his release. Renata's climax joined his a moment later, a prolonged disintegration that left her shaking and liquid in his arms.

And still she wanted more.

She wanted more, even after the next orgasm and the next. Even after she and Nikolai both were sweating and spent, she hungered for still more.

Edgar Fabien felt six pairs of shrewd, measuring eyes root on him as his secretary whispered an urgent message into his ear. An interruption at this hour – in the midst of such important company as these specially invited Breed dignitaries who'd come into Montreal from the United States and abroad – practically screamed bad news. And it was, though Fabien allowed no such outward indication.

The assembled males had been privately assessing one another as they'd arrived one by one this evening, all of them summoned to Edgar Fabien's Darkhaven residence to await transport to an exclusive gathering to take place elsewhere. To preserve their anonymity, the group had been instructed to don black hooded masks at all times. They had been forbidden to ask personal questions of one another, or to discuss their individual dealings with the Breed male who had called this meeting and laid down the terms of its covert attendance. Dragos had made it clear that now more than ever he would be watching for weakness, or for the slightest reason to deem Fabien or his other lieutenants standing in this very room unworthy of the glorious future he was planning to unveil at the formal gathering.

As the secretary whispered the rest of his message, Fabien was glad for the dark hood that concealed his reaction from the others. He kept his stance relaxed, every muscle loose and at ease, as he was informed that one of his Minions from the city was waiting outside with unanticipated, but critical, news that could not be delayed. News about a Breed male and an injured woman in his company, who, from the description, could be none other than the pair who'd escaped the containment facility.

'Will you all excuse me?' Fabien said, his smile tight beneath his disguise. 'I've a small matter to attend to outside. I won't be a moment.'

A few dark heads inclined as Fabien pivoted to stroll out of the room.

Once the reception room door was closed and he and his secretary had walked several yards down the long hallway, Fabien tore off his hood. 'Where is he?'

'Awaiting you in the front vestibule, sir.'

Fabien stormed off in that direction, wringing the black hood in his hands. As he reached the door, his secretary rushed up ahead to hold it open for him. The Minion was leaning against the wall, engrossed in chewing his fingernails down the quick, his unkempt, overlong bangs hanging into his eyes. When he looked up and saw his Master enter, the human's disgusting sloth was replaced with a hound's eagerness to please.

'I have brought you some news, Master.'

Fabien grunted. 'So I've heard. Speak, Curtis. Tell me what you saw.'

The Minion explained how earlier in the day he'd gone to ask a question of his human employer – a homeless shelter operator who'd hired Curtis to work on his computers – and unexpectedly discovered that the vampire warrior was hiding in the shelter's garage apartment. Curtis hadn't been able to get a close look, but had gotten near enough to tell that the huge male was Breed. It wasn't until just a short while ago that he confirmed his suspicions. Apparently the warrior and the female who was with him had become rather friendly. The pair were too busy in bed to notice when Curtis later sneaked back up to the garage and spied them together through the window.

The Minion had gotten an eyeful, and was able to provide a very detailed physical description of both the warrior Nikolai and the Breedmate Renata.

'You're certain neither of them is aware that you were there?' Fabien asked.

The Minion chuckled. 'No, Master. Trust me, they weren't paying attention to anything but each other.'

Fabien nodded and glanced at his watch. It would be dusk within the hour. He'd already assigned a team of Enforcement Agents to head out on another cleanup task for him tonight. Perhaps he should send a second unit into the city with Curtis. Bad enough that the warrior had managed to escape him at the containment facility. The news hadn't gone over well when Fabien had informed Dragos of the problem, but the bungle would be cushioned somewhat if he could assure him that the warrior had been dealt with – swiftly and permanently.

Yes, Fabien thought, as he reached into his suit coat pocket for his cell phone and dialed the Enforcement Agency detail who reported to him.

Tonight he would clean the slate of a couple recent mistakes, and when he presented himself to Dragos at the gathering, he would do so bearing fortuitous news and a charming little gift that his new commander was certain to enjoy.

⇥ CHAPTER TWENTY-TWO ⇤

D o you think he'll hurt her?'
Renata's voice was quiet, breaking the prolonged silence
in the humid apartment. She was seated across from Nikolai
at the card table, wearing an extra-large gray T-shirt and her
own jeans, laundered and returned earlier in the day, courtesy of Jack. Her shoulder wound was looking a hell of a lot
better, and every time Niko had asked, she insisted she wasn't
feeling much pain. He figured his blood would carry her for
a few hours at least. They'd been out of bed for a while now,
both of them bathed and dressed, and carefully avoiding the
subject of all that had happened between them today.

Instead, Nikolai kept himself busy cleaning and prepping
Jack's twin Colt .45s, while he and Renata put plans together
for their trek out to Yakut's lodge shortly. Although Niko
doubted Lex would willingly cough up information on his
alliance with Edgar Fabien, he had a feeling a few strategi-
cally placed rounds would loosen the bastard's tongue.

He hoped so, because without a solid lead on the Darkhaven
leader's probable location, the odds of finding Mira unscathed
by Fabien's twisted proclivities were diminishing by the second.

'Do you think he will . . . do anything to her?'

Niko looked over and saw the dread in Renata's eyes.
'Fabien's not a good man. I honestly don't know what he
intends for her.'

She glanced down at that, her slim dark brows drawn

together. 'You didn't tell me everything your friends back in Boston learned about him.'

Shit. He should have known Renata would call him on this. He'd deliberately skimmed over the worst of what Gideon had told him, figuring the sordid details wouldn't help them locate Mira any faster and would only make Renata worry more. But he respected her too much to lie to her.

'No, I didn't tell you everything,' he admitted. 'Do you really want to know all of it?'

'I think I need to know.' She met his gaze again, her pale green eyes sober, as steady as a warrior girded for battle. 'What did the Order find out about him?'

'He's second-generation Breed, easily several hundred years old,' Niko said, starting with the least of Fabien's offenses. 'He's been the leader of the Montreal Darkhaven for the past century and a half, and he's also got far-reaching ties into the upper tiers of the Enforcement Agency, which means he's politically connected too.'

Renata scoffed quietly. 'That's a resume, Nikolai. You know what I'm asking. Give it to me straight.'

'All right.' He nodded, not bothering to hide his admiration. Or his concern. 'Even though he's got a lot of friends in high places, Edgar Fabien's not what you'd call a model citizen. Apparently he's got some fairly sick kinks that have caused him a bit of trouble over the years.'

'Kinks,' Renata said, all but spitting the word.

'His tastes tend to run on the sadistic side, and he . . . well, he's been known to enjoy the company of children from time to time. Particularly young girls.'

'Jesus Christ,' Renata exclaimed in a tight rush of her breath. She closed her eyes and turned her face aside, all of her going very still, as though it took some work to keep from breaking down. When she finally looked back at Niko, there was a murderous glint in her unblinking jade-green gaze. 'I'll kill him. I swear it, Nikolai. I will fucking kill him if he's done anything to her.'

'We're gonna get him,' he assured her. 'We're going to find him, and we're going to get Mira back.'

'I can't fail her, Nikolai.'

'Hey,' he said, reaching out to cover her hand with his. '*We* won't fail her. Got it? I'm with you on this. We're gonna get her back.'

She looked at him in silence for a long moment. Then, very slowly, she flipped her hand over and linked her fingers through his. 'She's going to be safe . . . right?'

A trace of uncertainty, one of the first times he'd heard it in her voice. He wanted to erase the doubt for her, and the worry, but all he could offer was his promise. 'We're going to get her back, Renata. You've got my word on that.'

'Okay,' she said. Then, more resolutely, 'Okay, Nikolai. Thank you.'

'You're really something, you know that?' She started to shake her head in denial, but Niko gave her hand a gentle squeeze, keeping her centered. 'You're strong, Renata. Stronger than you know. Mira's lucky to have you on her side. Hell, so am I.'

Her answering smile was faint and slightly sad. 'I hope you're right.'

'I'm hardly ever wrong,' he said, grinning at her and barely resisting the urge to lean across the little table and kiss her. But that would only lead to one thing – something that his libido was already imagining in explicit detail.

'So, how long are you going to fondle those Colts before you let me have a look at one?'

Niko leaned back in the metal folding chair and chuckled. 'Take your pick. You sure you know how to handle—'

He didn't have a chance to finish the thought. Renata reached out for the gun nearest to her and a full magazine of rounds. She had the weapon loaded, locked, and ready for action in three seconds flat. Niko had never seen anything sexier in his life.

'Impressive.'

She set the pistol down on the table and arched one slim dark brow at him. 'You want help with yours now too?'

He started to laugh, but swallowed the sound before it left his mouth.

They weren't alone.

Renata followed his gaze upward, to where Nikolai could swear he heard a muted thud. It came again, then a small creak of the garage roof.

'We've got company,' he whispered to her.

Renata gave him a nod, already getting up from her chair. She slid the loaded .45 to him across the table and moved in swift, efficient silence to begin loading the other.

No sooner had Nikolai picked up the gun than the garage apartment door burst inward, kicked off its hinges. A huge vampire in the black SWAT gear of the Enforcement Agency rushed inside, the laser sights of his silenced automatic rifle locked on Renata.

'Son of a bitch!' Niko shouted. 'Renata, shoot him!'

For an awful second, she didn't move. Nikolai thought she had frozen up in shock, but then the Agent let out a howl of pain and dropped his weapon to clutch at his temples. He went down on his knees, but there were two more armed males right behind him. They leapt over the shrieking obstacle and opened fire in the small space. Renata took cover behind one of the metal file cabinets, firing on the Agent in the lead. Niko targeted the second newcomer, but his shot went wild as the small window above the bed shattered and yet another Enforcement Agent dropped into the fray, armed to the gills.

'Nikolai – behind you!' Renata called.

She hit this latest arrival with a debilitating blast of her mind's power, and the bastard crumpled to the floor, writhing and convulsing before Niko stilled him with a couple of rounds to the head.

Renata crippled one of the others with a shot to the knee, then took him out completely with a dead-aim bullet between the eyes. Nikolai killed another, and realized belatedly that he'd completely lost sight of the first male who'd come through the door. The son of a bitch was no longer whimpering where Renata had dropped him.

To Niko's horror, the huge vampire had Renata in his hands, lifting her off the ground and throwing her into the nearest wall. The Breed male's strength was immense, like all of their kind. Renata crashed against the solid surface, then fell hard to the floor. She lay there unmoving, obviously too dazed to retaliate.

Nikolai's roar of fury rattled the feeble table and chairs. His vision went nuclear with the sudden flood of amber into his eyes, and his fangs punched hard from his gums, stretching long and sharp in his anger. He sprang on the other vampire from behind, grabbing the big head in his hands and twisting savagely. The crunch of splitting bone and shredding tendons wasn't enough for him. As the lifeless Agent slumped over, Niko kicked his body away from Renata and pumped his skull full of lead.

'Renata,' he said, hunkering down in front of her and pulling her into his arms. 'Can you hear me? Are you okay?'

She moaned, but managed a shaky nod. Her eyes opened, then went wide as she stared past him to the ruined doorway. Niko swung his head around and locked gazes with a human male he'd seen once before – the human who'd tried to get a look at Nikolai when Jack had come up to the apartment that morning. Jack had called him Curtis, said the kid was doing some work for him in the house.

As Niko looked into that emotionless face that showed no

reaction whatsoever to Niko's glowing eyes and bared fangs, he knew what he was seeing now . . .

'Minion,' he growled. He released Renata gently as he got back to his feet. 'Stay put. I'll handle him.'

The Minion knew he'd made a grave mistake showing his face after the melee he'd probably instigated. He pivoted toward the night outside and started running down the stairs two at a time.

Nikolai grunted, seeing red as he bolted out of the apartment in pursuit. He vaulted over the railing of the second-story staircase, going airborne as the Minion's feet were just getting their taste of pavement. Nikolai landed right on top of him, tackling him down to the black asphalt of the driveway.

'Who made you?' he demanded, knocking the human's face against the rough pavement. 'Who's your Master, goddamn you! Is it Fabien?'

The Minion didn't answer, but Niko knew the truth anyway. He flipped him over and slammed his spine down hard. 'Where is he? Tell me where to find Fabien. Talk, you son of a bitch, or I'll gut you right here and now.'

Distantly, Nikolai heard the bang of a screen door. Footsteps running through the grass.

Then Renata's voice rang out from above him in the wrecked doorway of the garage apartment. 'Jack, no! Go back inside!'

Nikolai glanced over his shoulder just in time to see the old man's horrifed expression. Jack's eyes held his in utter disbelief, his grizzled jaw going slack. 'Jesus Christ,' he murmured, his feet slowing to a halt. 'What the . . . hell . . .'

And then, beneath him, Niko felt the Minion squirm.

He registered the brief glint of a blade only a half-second before the human mind slave slashed open his own throat.

Renata flew down the wooden stairs in heartsick panic. 'Jack, please! Go back in the house now!'

But he merely stood there, frozen in place as if he couldn't hear her, couldn't see her. Couldn't process anything that was happening around him in these past few minutes of complete and utter chaos. Jack was a mute, unmoving statue in the driveway.

And Nikolai . . .

Dear God, Nikolai looked like the stuff of anyone's worst nightmare. Blood-soaked, immense, his face a terrifying mask of lethal fangs and fierce, glowing eyes. When he got up off the body of the dead Minion and wheeled around to face Jack, he couldn't have seemed more predatory and inhuman, his breath sawing through his teeth, his massive chest and shoulders heaving from the combat.

'Sweet Mary, Mother of God,' Jack murmured, crossing himself as Nikolai took a couple of steps away from the Minion's corpse. Belatedly he glanced over and saw Renata racing toward him across the driveway. 'Renata, get out of here!'

Renata ran to put herself between the two males – Nikolai at her back, Jack gaping at her like she had just stepped into the middle of an active mine field.

'Oh, Jesus . . . Renata, honey . . . what are you doing?'

'It's okay, Jack,' she told him, calmly holding her hands up in front of her. 'Everything's okay, I promise you. Nikolai won't hurt you. He won't hurt either one of us.'

The old man's face scrunched in confusion. But then he stared past her to Nikolai and the dimmest spark of recognition flickered across his features. His pallor was ghostly white against the night all around him, and his legs looked like they might give out beneath him. 'It is you . . . but how? Just what the hell are you?'

'It's not safe for you to know that,' Renata interjected. 'It would be too dangerous, for us as well—'

'It's too late.' Nikolai's voice was a low growl close behind her. 'He's already seen too much here. We need to contain this situation, and we don't have a lot of time before more humans get curious and make things worse.'

Renata nodded. 'I know.'

Nikolai's hand came to rest gently on her good shoulder. 'That means Jack too. I can't let him walk away with his memory of this intact. Everything has to be scrubbed – starting with our arrival last night. He can't remember that you and I were ever here.'

She winced, but she couldn't argue. 'Do I have a minute to say good-bye?'

'A minute,' Nikolai said. 'But that's about all we can risk.'

'What the hell's going on here?' Jack mumbled, some of his shell shock dissipating and the retired warrior in him coming online. 'Renata . . . just what the hell kind of trouble are you in, girl?'

She offered him a weak smile as she moved forward and pulled him into a hug. 'Jack, I want to thank you – for helping us last night, but even more, for just being you.' She drew away from him to look into his kind old eyes. 'You may not realize this, but you were my anchor so many times. Whenever I lost my faith in humanity, your kindness restored it. You've been a true friend, and I love you for that. I always will.'

'Renata, I need you to tell me what's going on. This man you're with . . . this *creature*. For crissake, am I losing my mind, or is he some kind of—'

'He's my friend,' she said, meaning it so sincerely even she was taken aback by her conviction. 'Nikolai is my friend. That's all you need to know.'

'We have to go now, Renata.'

Nikolai's voice was calm, all business. She nodded, and when she glanced over at him, she saw that he was back to his normal state now. Jack sputtered in confusion, but Nikolai merely reached out to take the human's hand.

'Thank you for all you've done, Jack. You're a good man.' Nikolai didn't wait for a reply. With his free hand, he lifted his palm to Jack's forehead and pressed it there for a long moment. 'Go back into the house and go to bed. When you wake up in the morning, you'll forget we were here at all. You will discover there was a break-in upstairs in the apartment – Curtis was mixed up with some bad people, the robbery got out of hand, and he was killed.'

Jack said nothing, but he nodded his agreement.

'You won't see us when you open your eyes,' Nikolai told him. 'You won't see any of the blood or glass. You're going to turn around, head back into your house, and climb into bed where you'll stay for the rest of the night.'

Again Jack bobbed his head in compliance. Nikolai removed his hand from the old man's brow. Jack's eyes blinked open, calm and unfazed. He looked at Renata, but it was an empty stare that seemed to pass right through her. She stood there, watching in sadness as her old, dear friend pivoted around in silence and began a slow trek back to the house.

'You all right?' Nikolai asked her, placing his arm around her waist as they waited in the driveway for Jack to disappear.

'Yeah, I'm okay,' she said quietly, letting herself lean into his strong embrace. 'Let's clean up this mess and get out of here.'

⇥ CHAPTER TWENTY-THREE ⇤

A bout damn time he got here,' Alexei Yakut complained to himself as he watched a pair of headlight beams rico-chet off the trees outside the main lodge. Irritated to have been kept waiting this past half hour, Lex moved away from the window in his father's former quarters – quarters that now belonged to him, like everything else his dead father had left behind.

The black vehicle prowling up the drive was huge, obvi-ously an SUV. Lex rolled his eyes in disgust. He'd expected a male of Edgar Fabien's status to travel in something more elegant than a Humvee loaner taken right out of the Enforcement Agency fleet. Lex's own standards demanded much more than such a utilitarian mode of transport, especially for an event as important as the one he would be attending with Fabien. For fuck's sake, they might as well be arriving at the gathering in a pickup truck for all the statement they would make in that inelegant Agency vehicle.

If he was in charge of things – *when* he was in charge, Lex mentally amended – he would arrive nowhere without a proper motorcade befitting his elite rank.

He strode out of his chambers in an impatient huff, adjusting the line of his suit coat as his polished alligator-hide loafers tapped softly across the wide plank beams of the floor. He knew he looked good – which was the point – but he was far more accustomed to his longtime service uniform of boots and leather. He was an adaptive individual; he didn't think it would take much to get used to his new identity.

In the great room outside, the lodge's two remaining guards sat at a table playing cards. One of them glanced up as Lex entered, the subtle lift of his hand not quite fast enough to hide his amused smirk.

'That necktie looks like it's cutting off your air, Lex,' joked the other guard, chuckling at his own humor. 'Better loosen that shit up before you pass out.'

Lex glared as he ran his finger along the rim of the too-tight collar of his five-hundred-dollar shirt. 'Blow it out your ass, cretin. And open the fucking door. My ride is here.'

As the guard lumbered over to carry out the command, Lex wondered how long he should keep the two boneheads around. Sure, they'd served beside him in his father's employ every day for the better part of a decade, but a male like Lex deserved respect. Maybe he would teach both of them that lesson when he arrived back in a couple nights from the weekend gathering.

Lex forced a welcoming smile for Fabien as the guard opened the door . . . except it wasn't Edgar Fabien standing there to greet him. It was a uniformed Enforcement Agent, with three more behind him.

'Where's Fabien?' Lex demanded.

The tall Agent at the front gave Lex a slight bow of his head. 'We'll be rendezvousing with Mr Fabien at a separate location, Mr Yakut. Do you need assistance with anything before we escort you to the vehicle?'

Lex grunted, his ego soothed somewhat by the Agent's deferential tone. 'I have a couple of bags in the other room,' he said with a dismissive wave in the direction of his quarters. 'One of your men can fetch them for me.'

Another nod of obeisance from the one in front. 'I will see to your things personally. After you, sir.'

'This way,' Lex said, permitting the escort detail into the lodge as he strolled ahead of their leader to his quarters down the hall. Once inside, he paused near the bed to point out the things he wanted to take. 'Grab the garment bag and that leather duffel on the floor over there.'

When the Agent didn't move to pick up the bags, just stood there beside him, Lex turned an indignant glare on him. 'Well? What the hell are you waiting for, idiot?'

The answering look he got was flat as a blade, and equally cold.

And then Lex understood the chill, because in that next instant, he heard the stacatto *pop* of several muted gunshots in the other room and his blood ran to ice in his veins.

The Enforcment Agent standing next to him smiled a pleasant smile.

'Mr Fabien asked me to personally deliver a message from him, Mr Yakut.'

Renata looked tired as Nikolai walked up to her from the field where they'd dumped the bodies of the dead Enforcement Agents. In a few hours, dawn would obliterate all traces of the vampires, not that anyone aside from the local wildlife would notice this far off the nearest road and this far out of the city.

'I threw their uniforms and gear in the back of the vehicle,' Renata told him as he approached. 'The extra weapons are behind the front seats. Keys are in the ignition.'

Niko nodded. After cleaning up all evidence of the Breed assault on the garage apartment, he and Renata had commandeered the Agency's SUV, which their attackers had been helpful enough to leave parked along a side street near Jack's place.

'You hanging in there?' he asked, seeing the fatigue in her eyes. 'We can wait here and rest awhile if you need to.'

She shook her head. 'I want to keep moving. We're only a few miles from the lodge.'

'Yeah,' Niko said. 'And I'm not expecting Lex to roll out a red carpet for us when we get there. Things could get ugly real fast. It's been a couple of hours since you mind-blasted those Agents. How long before your reverb sets in?'

'Probably not long,' she admitted, glancing down at the moonlit grass at their feet.

Niko lifted her chin and couldn't keep from stroking the delicate line of her cheek. 'All the more reason to hang out here for a while.'

She drew away from him, stubborn with determination. 'All the more reason to keep going before the reverb hits. I'll rest after we have Mira.' She pivoted around and started walking to the vehicle. 'Who's driving – you or me?'

'Hey,' he said, catching her hand before she could get very far. He walked up to her and wrapped his arm around the small of her back, easing her into his embrace.

God, she was so beautiful. Any idiot could appreciate the fragile, feminine perfection of her face: the pale, almond-shaped eyes that glittered like moonstones beneath the inky fringe of her lashes; the impish nose and lush, sexy mouth; the milky skin that looked like flawless velvet against the ebony gloss of her hair. Renata's physical beauty was stunning, but it was her courage – her unshakable honor – that really did Niko in.

Somehow, in the short time they'd been forced together, Renata had become a true partner to him. He valued her, trusted her, as much as he did any of his brethren in the Order.

'Hey,' he repeated, quieter now, staring into her brave, beautiful face and awed all over again by this extraordinary woman who was proving to be such a vital ally to him. 'We made a pretty good team back there, didn't we.'

'I was scared as hell, Nikolai,' she confessed softly. 'They came at us so quickly. I should have reacted faster. I should have—'

'You were amazing.' He smoothed an errant wisp of hair from her face and hooked it behind her ear. 'You *are* amazing, Renata, and I'm damned glad to know that I've got you at my back.'

She gave him a small, almost shy smile. 'Same here.'

Maybe it wasn't the ideal time for him to want to kiss her, standing in a godforsaken stretch of backcountry, a trail of blood and death behind them and more of the same sure to be waiting down the line before this journey was over. But all Nikolai wanted to do right now – what he needed, here and now, this very moment – was to feel Renata's lips pressed against his.

He gave in to the urge, leaning in and taking her mouth in a tender, unhurried kiss. Her arms went around him, tentatively at first, but her hands were warm and giving as she stroked his back and held him to her, even after their kiss had ended and she laid her cheek against his chest.

When she spoke, her voice was barely above a whisper. 'Are we going to find her, Nikolai?'

He pressed his lips to the top of her head. 'Yes, we are.'

'Do you think she's okay?' His hesitation was brief, but long enough that it brought Renata out of his arms. She frowned, her eyes dimming with hurt. 'Oh, my God . . . you don't believe she is. I can feel your doubt, Nikolai. You think something's happened to Mira.'

'It's the blood bond you feel,' he said, not even close to a denial of what Renata had read so accurately in him.

She was backing away now, her feet shuffling in the dark grass as she moved toward the SUV. Her face had taken on a stricken look. 'We have to go now. We have to find Lex and force him to tell us where she is!'

'Renata, I still think you should wait here awhile and rest. If the reverb hits you—'

'Fuck the reverb!' she cried, tossing her head in mounting panic. 'I'm going to Yakut's place. You can either ride along or stay behind, but I'm leaving right fucking now.'

He could have stopped her.

If he'd wanted to, he could have been on her faster than she could track him, physically preventing her from taking another step toward the vehicle. He could have tranced her with a simple brush of his hand over her face and forced her to wait out the pain that would probably wipe her out completely not long after they reached the lodge.

He could have held her back in any number of ways, but instead he circled around to the driver's side of the black Humvee before she got there and blocked her entry with his body.

'I'll drive,' he said, giving her no chance to argue. 'You're shotgun.'

Renata stared at him for a second, then walked over and climbed into the passenger seat.

They found their way back to the road and drove the short distance to Yakut's wooded property in silence. Niko cut the lights as they approached at a slow roll. He was about to suggest they bail out and move in on the lodge by foot when he noticed something was off about the place.

'Is it always this quiet?'

'Never,' Renata said, shooting him a grave look. She reached behind the seats to pick up some of the Agency weapons. She looped the strap of an automatic rifle over her head, then handed Nikolai one for himself. 'Lex only had two guards left, but it doesn't look like anyone is here at all.'

And even from this distance, Niko detected the scent of spilled blood. Breed blood, coming from more than one source.

'Wait here while I go check things out.'

She gave him an insubordinate scoff that he might have predicted was coming.

They both climbed out of the vehicle and moved in tandem toward the dark main house. The front door was wide open. Fresh tire tracks were laid out in the gravel drive, wide, deep-set tracks like the kind an oversized SUV would leave behind.

Niko had a feeling the Enforcement Agency had been here too.

The lodge was utterly silent, reeking with the stench of recent vampire deaths. He didn't need to turn on the lights to see the carnage. His keen vision spotted the two dead males just inside, both shot point-blank in the head with several rounds.

He guided Renata around the corpses, following his nose to the back of the place, to Yakut's private quarters. He knew what he was going to find in here as well. Even still, he stepped into the room and let out a furious curse.

Lex was dead.

And with him, so was their best hope of locating Edgar Fabien tonight.

⇥ CHAPTER TWENTY-FOUR ⇤

Renata's breath seized up at the sound of Nikolai's muttered curse. She reached for the light switch near the open door of Yakut's bedroom. Slowly flipped it on.

She couldn't speak as she stared down at Lex's lifeless body, his eyes vacant and clouded over with death, three large bullet holes bored into the front of his head. She wanted to scream. God in heaven, she wanted to drop to her knees, fist her hands in her hair, and howl to the rafters – not with grief or shock, but complete and thorough rage.

But her lungs were constricted in her breast.

Her limbs were weighted down, arms and legs too heavy to move.

What hope she'd been harboring – as small as it was – that they might come here and get a solid lead on Mira's location seeped out of her, as surely as Lex's blood had seeped into the floorboards of his father's room.

'Renata, we'll find another way,' Nikolai said from somewhere near her. He bent down over the body and removed a cell phone from the pocket of Lex's suit coat, flipped it open and pressed some of the keys. 'We've got Lex's call history now. One of these numbers might be Fabien's. I'll contact Gideon and have him chase them down. We're gonna have something on Fabien very soon. We'll get him, Renata.'

She couldn't answer; she had no words. Turning slowly, she walked out of the room, hardly conscious that her feet were moving. She drifted through the dark lodge, past the bodies lying in the great room and down a hallway . . . unsure where she was heading, yet unsurprised when she found herself standing in the center of the tiny room where Mira had slept.

The small bed was just as she'd left it, as if waiting for its occupant's return. Over on the squat little nightstand was a wildflower Mira had picked earlier in the week, on one of the rare times Sergei Yakut had permitted the child to venture outside. Mira's flower was wilted now, the fragile white petals drooping and lifeless, green stem as limp as a piece of string.

'Oh, my sweet mouse,' Renata whispered into the darkened, empty room. 'I'm sorry . . . I'm so sorry I'm not there for you right now . . . '

'Renata.' Nikolai stood in the hallway outside the room. 'Renata, don't do this to yourself. You are not to blame. And this isn't over, not yet.'

His deep voice was soothing, a comfort just to hear him, and to know that he was there with her. She needed that comfort, but because she didn't deserve it, Renata refused to run into his arms as she so desperately wanted to do. She stayed where she was, rigid and unmoving. Wishing she could reverse all her failings.

She couldn't bear to remain in the lodge for another minute. There were too many dark memories here.

Too much death all around her.

Renata let the dead flower fall out of her fingers and onto the bed. She pivoted around toward the doorway. 'I have to get out of this place,' she murmured, guilt and anguish twisting in her chest. 'I can't . . . I'm suffocating in here . . . can't . . . breathe.'

She didn't wait for him to reply – couldn't wait in there, not one more second. Pushing past him, she ran out of Mira's vacant room. She didn't stop running until her feet had carried her out the back of the main house and into the surrounding forest. And still her lungs squeezed as though they were caught in a vise.

In the back of her skull, she could feel a headache blooming. Her skin wasn't aching yet, but she was bone weary and she knew it wouldn't be long before reverb took her down. At least her shoulder was feeling decent. The gunshot wound was still there, still a dull throb deep in her muscles, but Nikolai's blood had worked some kind of magic on the infection.

Renata felt strong enough that when she glanced over and saw the locked barn – the outbuilding where she and so many others had been brought as bait for Yakut's sick blood sport – she didn't think twice about stalking over to it and pulling the Enforcement Agency rifle around from where it had shifted to her back. She shot the heavy lock until it broke off and fell to the ground. Then she flung open the door and let loose with more shots inside, peppering the large holding pen, the walls and rafters – all of it – with an obliterating hail of bullets.

She didn't let up on the trigger until the magazine was empty and her throat was raw from her screams. Her shoulders heaved, chest sawing like a bellows.

'I should have been here,' she said, hearing Nikolai come up behind her outside. 'When Lex turned her over to Fabien, I should have stopped him. I should have been there for Mira. Instead I was in bed, too weak with reverb . . . useless.'

He made a small noise, a wordless dismissal of her guilt. 'You couldn't have known she was in danger. You couldn't have prevented any of what occurred, Renata.'

'I should never have left the lodge!' she cried, self-contempt searing her like acid. 'I ran away, when I should have stayed here the whole time and worked on getting Lex to tell me where she was.'

'You didn't run away. You went to look for help from me. If you hadn't done that, I would be dead.' His footsteps moved closer, coming up gently behind her. 'If you had stayed here all this time, Renata, then you would have been killed tonight along with Lex and the other guards. What happened here was a coldly planned execution, and it's got Fabien's name all over it.'

He was right. She knew he was right, on all points. But it didn't make her hurt any less.

Renata stared, unseeing, into the gunpowder-choked chasm of the barn. 'We have to go back to the city and start searching for her. Door to door, if we have to.'

'I know what you're feeling,' Nikolai said. He touched her nape and she forced herself to step away from his tenderness. 'Goddamn it, Renata, don't you think that if I thought kicking down doors from here to Old Port was going to get us closer to Fabien, I'd be right on board with you? But that's not gonna buy us a thing. Especially not with daybreak just a few hours away and riding hard on our heels.'

She shook her head. 'I don't need to worry about daylight. I can go back into the city by myself—'

'Like hell you will.' His hands were gruff as he turned her around to face him. His eyes glittered with sparks of amber, and an emotion that looked remarkably like fear, even in the darkness. 'You're not going anywhere near Fabien without me.' He stroked her brow, his fierce eyes burning into her. 'We're in this together, Renata. You know that, right? You know that you can trust me?'

She stared into Nikolai's face and felt a well of emotion begin to rise up within her, felt it rise over her like a swamping wave she couldn't hold back if she tried. Tears stung her eyes, then filled them. Before she could stop the flood, she was weeping as though a dam had burst inside her and all the hurts she'd ever felt – all the pain and emptiness of her entire existence – came rushing out of her in great, heaving sobs.

Nikolai wrapped his strong arms around her and held her

close. He didn't try to make her tears stop. He didn't feed her soft lies to make her feel better, or give her false promises to cushion her despair.

He just held her.

Held her, and let her feel that she was understood. That she was not alone, and that maybe, in some small way, she might be worthy of being loved.

He picked her up, lifting her into his arms, and began to carry her away from the bullet-riddled barn. 'Let's find you someplace to rest for a while,' he said, his soothing voice rumbling in his chest, vibrating against her as she clung to him.

'I can't go back into the lodge, Nikolai. I won't stay in there.'

'I know,' he murmured, bringing her deeper into the woods. 'I have another idea.'

He set her down in a leaf-strewn alcove between two towering pines. Renata didn't know what to expect, but she never would have imagined what she witnessed in those next moments.

Nikolai knelt down near her and spread his arms wide, his chin lowered, his immense, muscled body held in a study of quiet concentration. Renata felt the energy around them crackle. She smelled rich, fertile earth, like the forest after a rainstorm. A warm breeze tickled her nape as Nikolai touched his fingertips to the ground on either side of him.

There was a quiet rustle of movement in the grass nearby – a whisper of life. Renata saw something snake up from beneath Nikolai's hands and couldn't keep from gasping in awestruck wonder when she realized what she was seeing.

Tiny vines, shooting through the soil, running toward the twin pines on either side of her.

'Oh, my God,' she murmured, rapt with amazement. 'Nikolai . . . what's happening here?'

'It's all right,' he said, watching the vines – commanding them, hard as it was to believe.

The tendrils spiraled around the tree trunks and climbed higher, filling in with leaves that multiplied exponentially as she watched. Well over her head some eight feet, the vines leapt across the space between the pines. They twisted together, then sent off shooting lengths of vegetation, creating a living canopy that stretched all the way to the ground where Renata and Nikolai sat.

'You're doing this?' she asked, incredulous.

He gave her a nod but kept his focus on his creation, more and more leaves unfolding on the vines. Thick walls of fragrant shelter formed a haven around them, the lush greenery interspersed with the same tiny white flowers that Renata had found in Mira's room.

'Okay . . . how are you doing this?'

The rustle of growing plant life slowed and Nikolai turned a nonchalant look on her. 'My mother's gift, passed down to her two sons.'

'Who's your mom, Mother Nature?' Renata said, laughing, delighted in spite of the knowledge that the beautiful flowers and vines were just a temporary veil. Outside, all of the ugliness and violence remained.

Nikolai smiled and shook his head. 'My mother was a Breedmate, like you. Your talent is the power of your mind. This was her talent.'

'It's incredible.' Renata ran her hand over the cool leaves and delicate petals. 'God, Nikolai, your ability is . . . I want to say amazing, but that doesn't even come close.'

He shrugged. 'I've never had much use for it. Give me a clip full of hollowpoints or a few blocks of C-4 any day. Then I'll show you amazing.'

He was making light of it, but she sensed that his glibness shielded something darker. 'What about your brother?'

'What about him?'

'You said he can do this too?'

'He could, yes,' Nikolai said, the words sounding a bit hollow. 'Dmitri was younger than me. He's dead. It happened a long time ago, back in Russia.'

Renata winced. 'I'm sorry.'

He nodded, plucked a leaf from the mass of vegetation, and tore it into pieces. 'He was just a kid – a good kid. He was a couple of decades younger than me. Used to follow me around like a goddamn puppy, wanting to do everything I was doing. I didn't have a lot of time for him. I liked to live on the edge – shit, I guess I still do. Anyway, Dmitri got it into his head that he needed to impress me.' He exhaled a raw, strangled curse. 'Stupid fucking kid. He would have done anything to make me notice him, you know? To hear me say that I approved, that I was proud of him.'

Renata watched him in the dark, seeing in him the same guilt she felt when she thought about Mira. She saw the same dread in him, the same inward condemnation that a child was in grave peril – might even be dead already – all because someone they trusted had failed them.

Nikolai knew that torment. He had lived it himself.

'What happened to Dmitri?' Renata asked him gently. She didn't want to tear open old hurts, but she needed to know. And she could see from the weight that had settled over him that Nikolai had carried his pain for too long. 'You can tell me, Nikolai. What happened to your brother?'

'He wasn't like me,' he said, the words contemplative, as if bogged down by their history. 'Dmitri was smart, a crack student. He loved his books and philosophy, loved peeling the layers off things, figuring out how everything around him worked so he could put them back together again. He was brilliant, truly gifted, but he wanted to be like me.'

'And what were you like back then?'

'Wild,' he said, saying it more like an epithet than a boast. 'I'm the first to admit it. I've always been a little reckless, not really caring where I ended up tomorrow so long as I was having a good time today. Dmitri liked contemplation; I like adrenaline. He enjoyed putting things together; I like blowing them up.'

'Is that why you joined the Order, for the adrenaline rush of fighting?'

'That's partly why, yeah.' He rested his elbows on his knees and stared at the ground. 'After Dmitri's murder, I had to get away. I blamed myself for what happened. My parents blamed me too. I left the country and came to the States. Hooked up with Lucan and the others in Boston not long after that.'

She didn't miss the fact that he'd said his brother was killed, not merely dead. 'What happened, Nikolai?'

He blew out a long sigh. 'I had an ongoing mutual hatred with a Darkhaven asshole out of the Ukraine. We got into pretty serious hand-to-hand with each other from time to time, out of boredom mostly. Except one night Dmitri hears this dickhead in a tavern talking shit about me and decides to call him on it. Dmitri drew a blade and cut the guy in front of his pals. It was a lucky hit – D sucked with weapons. Anyway, he pissed the bastard off and two minutes later, my brother is lying in a pool of his own blood, his head cleaved off his neck.'

'Oh, my God.' Renata sucked in a sharp breath, feeling sick in her heart. 'I'm so sorry, Nikolai.'

'Me too.' He shrugged. 'Afterward, I went out and tracked Dmitri's killer down. I took his head and brought it to my parents as an apology. They turned me away, said it should have been me who was dead, not D. Couldn't fault them for that. Hell, they were right, after all. So I split and never looked back.'

'I'm sorry, Nikolai.'

She didn't know what else to say. She had little experience offering comfort, and even if she did, she wasn't sure he would want it or need it. Like a man suddenly uncomfortable in his own skin, Nikolai grew quiet for a long moment.

He cleared his throat, then he ran a hand over his scalp and rose to his feet. 'I should go out and have another look around the lodge. Will you be all right out here for a few minutes?'

'Yeah. I'm fine.'

He stared at her, searching her face. She didn't know what she wanted him to say to her, but the look in his eyes seemed shuttered. 'How are you doing? No sign of reverb yet?'

Renata shrugged. 'A little, but not too bad.'

'And your shoulder?'

'Good,' she said, flexing her left arm to show him she wasn't in any pain. 'It feels a lot better now.'

A longer, more awkward silence stretched between them, as if neither one knew whether to bridge it or do the easier thing and let it lengthen. It wasn't until Nikolai started to part some of the thick vines to leave that Renata reached out to touch him.

'Nikolai . . . I, um . . . I've been meaning to thank you,' she said, conscious of the fact that although he had paused, she kept her hand on his arm. 'I need to thank you . . . for giving me your blood earlier today.'

He turned toward her, gave a mild shake of his head. 'Gratitude is nice, but I don't need it. If our situations were reversed, I know you would have done the same thing for me.'

She would have; Renata could say that without the slightest doubt. This man who had been a stranger to her not quite a week ago – this warrior who also happened to be a vampire – was now her most trusted, intimate friend. If she was being honest with herself, she had to acknowledge that Nikolai was far more than that, and had been even before he shared his blood with her. Even before the sex that still made her toes curl just to think about it.

'I'm not sure how to do this . . .' Renata looked up at him, struggling with the words but needing to say them. 'I'm not used to counting on anyone. I don't know how to be with someone like this. It's nothing I've ever had before, and I just . . . I feel like everything I thought I knew, all the things that once helped me survive, are deserting me. I'm adrift . . . I'm terrified.'

Nikolai stroked her cheek, then wrapped her in his embrace. 'You're safe,' he said tenderly beside her ear. 'I've got you, and I'm going to keep you safe.'

She didn't realize how badly she needed to hear those words until Nikolai spoke them to her. She didn't know how badly she could want his arms around her or how deeply she could crave his kiss until Nikolai pulled her closer and brushed his mouth across hers. Renata kissed him with abandon, letting herself drift into the moment because Nikolai was with her, holding her, giving her safe harbor.

His kiss growing more passionate, he eased her down onto her back on the cushioned earth of their shelter. Renata reveled in the feel of his weight atop her, his warm, sure hands caressing her. He delved under her loose T-shirt, smoothing his fingers over her belly and up to her breasts.

He gave her lip a small, teasing stroke of his fangs as he drew back from kissing her. His eyes glowed like embers under the heavy fall of his lids. She didn't need to see his transformed face to know that he wanted her. The very hard evidence of that pressed insistently against her hip. She ran her hands up his spine and he groaned, his pelvis kicking with a reflexive thrust.

Her name was a throaty moan as he trailed his mouth past her chin and down the length of her neck. He pushed her shirt up and Renata arched her back to greet his lips as he descended on her bare breasts and the smooth plane of her stomach. She was lost in the pleasure of his kiss. Aching for the feel of his skin against hers.

With deft fingers, he unfastened her jeans and slid them down her thighs. His mouth followed his progress, searing her from hip to ankle as he pulled her legs free and pushed her clothing aside. She cried out as he then bent between her thighs and suckled her, his tongue and fangs bringing on a rush of exquisite torment.

'Oh, God,' she gasped, hips rising up off the ground as he buried his mouth in her sex.

She didn't know how he managed it so quickly, but a moment later he was naked too. He loomed over her, something more than human, more than simply male, and everything female in Renata trembled with desire. She opened her legs to him, greedy to feel him inside her, filling the emptiness with his strength and heat.

'Please,' she moaned, panting with need.

He didn't make her ask him twice.

Moving to cover her, Nikolai wedged his knees between her legs and spread her wide beneath him. The head of his cock nudged into the slick cleft of her body, then plunged, long and slow and deep.

His growl as he sank down into her was fierce, a roll of thunder that echoed in her bones and in her blood. He pumped slowly, taking his time at first, even though it was clear that patience was torture. Renata could feel the intensity of his hunger for her, the depth of his pleasure as her body sheathed him, head to balls.

'You feel so good,' he murmured, sucking in a hiss as he withdrew then filled her again, deeper than before. He thrust hard, shuddering with the effort. 'Jesus, Renata . . . you feel so fucking good.'

She linked her ankles around his backside as he fell into a

more urgent tempo. 'Harder,' she whispered, wanting to feel him pound away her fears, a hammer to smash through all her guilt and pain and emptiness. 'Oh, God, Nikolai . . . fuck me harder.'

His answering snarl sounded as eager as it was wild. Slipping his arm beneath her, he tilted her to meet his strokes, driving into her with all the fury she so desperately needed. He swept down on her mouth for a fevered kiss, catching her cry as her climax roared up on her like a storm. Renata quaked and shuddered, clawing at him as he continued to pump, every muscle in his back and shoulders going as hard as granite.

'Ah, Christ,' he ground out between his teeth and fangs, his hips banging against her fast and furious, a reckless rhythm that felt so good. So right.

His coarse shout of release was echoed by her own as Renata came again, clinging to him as she lost herself to this delicious new sense of abandon.

She truly was adrift, but in this moment she felt no fear. She was safe with this wild, reckless man – she truly believed that. She trusted Nikolai with her body and with her life. As she lay there with him in an intimate tangle, it wasn't so difficult to imagine that she could trust him with her heart as well.

That she might, in fact, be falling in love with him.

The knocking was insistent – a frantic beat on the solid oak door of Andreas Reichen's Darkhaven in Berlin.

'Andreas, please! Are you there? It's Helene. I must see you!'

At just after 4 A.M., only a short while before the sun would first peek over the horizon, only a few stragglers in the household remained awake. The rest of Reichen's kin – nearly a dozen in all, young Breed males and mated couples with small children, some of them newborn infants – had already gone to bed for the day.

'Andreas? Anyone?' Another panicked series of knocks,

followed by a terrified-sounding cry. 'Hello! Someone, please . . . let me in!'

Inside the mansion, a young male came out of the kitchen where he'd been warming a cup of milk for his Breedmate who awaited him upstairs in the nursery, where she was tending their fussy baby son. He knew the human female who was at the door. Most of the Darkhaven knew her, and Andreas had made it clear that Helene was always welcome in his home. That she had come unannounced at such a late hour, and while Andreas was away on private business for two nights, was unusual.

Even more unusual was the fact that the typically in-control businesswoman was so obviously afraid.

Awash with concern for what may have happened to Andreas's human companion, the Darkhaven male set down the cup of steaming milk and raced across the marble floor of the vestibule, his bathrobe flying behind him like a sail.

'I'm coming,' he called, raising his voice to be heard over Helene's ceaseless knocking and tear-choked pleas for help on the other side of the door. His fingers flew over the keypad of the mansion's security system. 'One moment! I'll be right there, Helene. Everything's going to be fine.'

When the electronic light blinked to indicate the sensors were disabled, he threw the dead bolts and opened the door.

'Oh, thank God!' Helene rushed toward him, her makeup in ruins, wet black trails running down her cheeks. She was pale and trembling, her usually shrewd eyes seeming somehow vacant as she made a quick visual search of the foyer. 'Andreas . . . where is he?'

'Gone to Hamburg on private business until tomorrow night. But you are welcome here.' He stepped back to give her space to enter the mansion. 'Come in, Helene. Andreas wouldn't want me to turn you away.'

'No,' she said somewhat dully. 'I know he would never turn me away.'

She came into the foyer and seemed instantly calmer.

'They knew he would never turn me away . . .'

It was at that moment the young Darkhaven male noticed that Helene was not alone. Behind her, rushing in now before he could do so much as cry out in alarm, was a team of heavily armed Enforcement Agents dressed from head to toe in black.

He swung his head around to look at Helene in disbelief. In abject horror.

'Why?' he asked, but the answer was there in her empty eyes.

Someone had gotten a hold of her. Someone very powerful. Someone who had turned Helene into a Minion.

The thought no sooner registered before the first shot hit him. He heard more rounds being fired, heard the screams of his family as the Darkhaven awoke to terror.

But then another bullet slammed into his skull, and his world and everything in it went silent and black.

⊰ CHAPTER TWENTY-FIVE ⊱

Nikolai sat inside the shade of the vine shelter and watched a single nimbus of sunlight shine through the leaves and into Renata's dark hair while she slept. Ultraviolet light was toxic to his kind – lethal after about half an hour's sustained exposure – but he couldn't work up the desire to patch the small hole in the vegetation and snuff out the errant ray. Instead, for the past several minutes, he'd been sitting next to Renata and watching, admittedly, much too intrigued, as the light soaked into her ebony hair, infusing the silky strands with a dozen different shades of copper, bronze, and burgundy.

What the hell was wrong with him?

He was sitting there staring at her hair, for crissake. Not just staring, but staring with total rapt fascination. To Niko, that seemed to indicate one of two equally disturbing facts: Either he should seriously consider looking into night courses with Vidal Sassoon, or he was a complete goner when it came to this female.

Goner as in gone for good, ruined for any other.

Somewhere, somehow, he had let himself fall in love with her.

Which explained why he couldn't keep his hands – and other parts – off her. It also explained why he'd spent the entire night, with the exception of his quick trip into the lodge before daybreak – lying beside Renata, holding her in his arms.

And if he'd needed any explanation for why his chest had felt so constricted and heavy when she broke down crying last night, or why he'd felt compelled to share with her his guilt over the loss of Dmitri all those years ago, he supposed that being in love with her would do it.

As much as he had wanted to convince her that she was safe with him, Nikolai felt safe with her too. He trusted her whole-heartedly. Would kill to protect her, would die for her without a second's doubt if it came down to it. She may not have been a part of his life for very long now, but he was hard-pressed to imagine not having her in it.

Ah, fuck.

He really had fallen in love with Renata.

'Just fucking brilliant,' he muttered, then winced when she stirred at the sound of his voice.

She opened her eyes, smiled when she saw him sitting there. 'Hi.'

'Morning,' he said, casually reaching above her head to knit the vines closed and seal out the last of the sunlight.

He found her slow, catlike stretch even more fascinating than her hair. She was wearing the cotton oxford he'd ruined last night, half the buttons scattered on the ground of the shelter. The big shirt was split open down the front, barely covering her nakedness. No complaints from him.

'How are you feeling?'

She seemed to consider it for a second, then glanced over at him with a frown. 'I feel really good. I mean, last night was . . . ' She actually blushed, a sweet pink color filling her cheeks. 'Last night was incredible, but I thought for sure I'd be laid out flat with reverb by now. I don't understand . . . it never hit me at all. I mean, I had a little bit of pain, but based on what happened during the attack at Jack's place, I should have been in agony most of the night.'

'Has that ever happened before?'

She shook her head. 'Never. Every time I use my ability, the reverb follows.'

'But not last night.'

'Not last night,' she said. 'I've never felt better.'

Niko might have made a lame joke about the miraculous effects of his sexual prowess, but he knew it was a different kind of magic that had pulled Renata through her reverb. 'You drank my blood yesterday. That's what's different.'

'You think your blood not only helped my shoulder but also helped with this? Is that even possible?'

'It's definitely a possibility. A Breedmate who regularly drinks a vampire's blood becomes much stronger than she would be without it. Aging slows to a snail's pace. Her body's cells, muscles, and entire metabolism reach peak fitness and health. And yeah, a lot of times a Breed male's blood will impact her psychic ability too.'

'That's why Sergei never had me drink from him,' Renata said, her mind already speeding ahead toward the same conclusion Niko had reached. 'He made no secret that he liked the fact that my power was limited to small bursts. The couple of times I tried to hit him with it, I could never hold it on him long enough to take him down, and in the end the effort always cost me dearly once the reverb set in.'

'Sergei Yakut was Gen One,' Niko reminded her. 'His blood in your system might have made you practically unstoppable.'

Renata scoffed quietly. 'Just one more shackle he kept on me. He must have known I would have killed him if I had even the smallest hope that I might succeed.' She fell silent for a minute, idly plucked at a blade of grass on the floor of the makeshift shelter. 'I did try to kill him . . . the day Mira and I fled the lodge together. That was the day he put the hot andiron to my back. He did other things to me that day too.'

Nikolai didn't have to ask what more she had endured. The scars from the brands that had been seared onto her back were heinous enough, but to think Yakut's punishment went even further . . . Niko's blood roiled with outrage. He put his hand over hers. 'Jesus, Renata. I'm sorry.'

She glanced up at him, a steady green gaze that wasn't seeking sympathy. 'His only mercy was that he didn't force Mira to watch everything that was done to me. But Sergei told me that if she or I tried to escape again, or if I ever turned my mind's power on him even a little, it would be Mira who'd pay in the same ways I had. He promised worse for her, and I knew he meant it . . . so I stayed. I stayed, and I obeyed him, and every hour of every day I hoped for some miracle that would erase Sergei Yakut from my life.' She paused, reaching up to caress his face. 'Then you came and every-thing changed. I guess in many ways, you are my miracle.'

Nikolai captured her hand and placed a kiss in the heart of her palm. 'We're both fortunate.'

'I'm glad Sergei is dead,' she confessed softly.

'He should have suffered more,' Niko said, not even trying to curb the dark edge of his voice. 'But he's gone.'

Renata nodded. 'And now Lex is dead too. Yakut's guards. All of them.'

'By this hour of the morning, he and the others in the lodge are nothing but ash,' Niko said as he reached up to hook some of her glossy black hair behind her ear. 'After you fell asleep last night I went back in and opened all the shutters for the sunlight to do its thing. I also called Boston to give them the numbers in Lex's cell phone. Gideon's going to call us with details once he's run traces on them.'

Another nod, her voice soft with hope. 'Okay.'

'While I was in there, I also brought you something I thought you might be missing.'

He leaned over to the stash of weapons and other assorted supplies he'd retrieved and picked up the silk-and-velvet package that belonged to Renata.

'My blades,' she gasped, joy brightening her face as she took the package from his hands. She untied the ribbons that secured it and unrolled the length of velvet that encased the four custom-engraved daggers. 'Jack gave these to me . . .'

'I know. He told me that he had them made for you as a gift. He said he wasn't sure you'd kept them.'

'I've cherished them,' she murmured, tracing the hand-tooled hilts with her fingertip.

'I told him that you still had them. He was glad to hear how much they mean to you.'

Her tender gaze bathed him in gratitude. 'Nikolai . . . thank you. For doing that for Jack, and for giving these back to me. Thank you.'

She came toward him and kissed him. The brief press of her lips slowly melted into something deeper. Nikolai cupped her face in his hands, smoothing his thumbs over the softness of her jaw, the delicate angle of her cheekbones. She parted her lips as his tongue swept along their seam, then moaned sweetly as he delved inside.

His fangs stretched into sharp points as lust ran through him like fire. Between his legs, his sex was a column of granite, rising instantly to the thought of having Renata beneath him. When her hand trailed down past the waistband of his pants to touch him, his greedy cock leapt, surging even harder under the heat of her palm as she stroked him.

'What time is it?' she murmured against his fevered mouth.

He grunted, too engrossed in the torment of her petting to immediately process the question. Through the rough sawing of his breath, he managed to rasp, 'It's early. Probably some-time around nine.'

'Well, damn, I guess that is pretty early,' she murmured, moving her mouth away from his and kissing a trail of heat along his throat, playing over the knob of his Adam's apple. 'You can't be out in the sunlight, right?'

'Nope.'

'Hmm.' Her moist lips descended, onto his bare chest. He leaned back onto his elbows as she followed one of his *glyphs* with the tip of her pink tongue, tracing the arcs and the tapering swirls around his nipple and across the plane of his stomach. When she spoke, her voice vibrated all the way into his bones. 'So, I guess that means we're stuck here for a while, huh?'

'Yeah.' The word was more gasp than sound. Her kiss trav-eled lower now, past his navel, still following the lines of his *dermaglyphs,* heading for the part of him that was straining, throbbing with the need to feel those moist hot lips clamped around him.

'Stuck here until nightfall, I suppose.'

'Uh-huh.' She took one end of the waistband's drawstring ties between her teeth and gave it a hard tug. The knot fell loose, and she pulled the warm-ups down, just enough to bare the eager head of his cock. She licked him, watching his face as she swirled her devilish tongue around the fat plum of his flesh, suckling at the drop of slick fluid that beaded there.

'Ah, Christ . . .'

'So,' she murmured, her breath skating across his wet skin, tormenting him even more. 'What are we going to do in here all day while we wait for nightfall?'

Niko chuckled. 'Baby, I can think of a hundred things I'd like to do with you.'

She smiled up at him in challenge. 'Only a hundred?'

Before he could fire back a smartass reply, she wrapped her lips around his cock and took him deep into her mouth. As Niko's body went nuclear with pleasure, he found himself praying that the day and his time alone with this incredible woman – his woman – could stretch on forever.

◄ CHAPTER TWENTY-SIX ►

Renata walked into the back door of the lodge and paused just over the threshold. She had left Nikolai in the shelter, deciding that her need for the bathroom, a hot shower, and a change of clothes that actually fit her was greater than her reluctance to step foot ever again in Sergei Yakut's domain.

Now she hesitated. The early afternoon sun was a warm presence at her back, encouraging her along, but inside the lodge was dim and cold. Shadows played over the toppled furniture and stretched across the rough planks of the floor. She drifted in, and walked toward the place where Lex had fallen.

His body was gone, the blood too. Nothing but the smallest trace of ash left behind – just as Nikolai had promised. The shutters on the bedroom window were thrown wide open, but the sun had since moved past. A fresh breeze carried the scent of pine pitch and crisp forest air into the dank stillness of the place. Renata breathed it deeply into her lungs, letting the fragrance of the new day purge her memories of all the death and blood and violence that had cloaked the lodge last night.

Today, in this new light, so much seemed different to her. She herself seemed different, and she knew the reason why. *She was in love.*

For the first time in a very long time, perhaps in all her life, she knew a sense of true hope. It nestled in her heart – a belief that her future held something more than just bare survival, that she might at some point measure happiness in years, not rare, fleeting moments. Being with Nikolai, whether in his arms or standing by his side, made her believe so many things were possible.

Renata walked into the great room, bolstered by the fact that this would be the last time she'd need to look at the place. This was good-bye.

When she and Nikolai left here to continue their search for Mira, this lodge, the terrible barn and holding pen out back, Sergei Yakut, Lex, and everything else that scarred the past two years of her life would be history. She would leave all of it here, the ugliness and pain banished from any part of her future.

This part of her life was over.

She strode into the small bathroom she'd shared with Mira, at peace with herself and her surroundings as she turned on the hot water for the shower. As a humid steam began to roll out from the curtain, she unfastened the few buttons left on Jack's borrowed oxford shirt and stood there for a moment, naked, contemplating her future with new eyes. She didn't know what awaited once night fell and a dangerous new leg of this journey began, but she was ready to face it head-on.

With Nikolai beside her – with hope and love burning as bright as a flame in her heart – she was prepared to take on anything.

Like a battle-bound knight seeking anointing and blessing, Renata stepped under the hot spray of the shower. She closed her eyes in a solemn prayer as the cleansing water poured over her.

Nikolai stayed in the shade of the vine shelter as Renata's footsteps approached from outside.

'Knock, knock,' she called to him through the leaves.

'Coming in now, so watch the daylight. Wouldn't want you going crispy on me.'

She parted some of the thick greenery and slipped inside, mouthing a quick apology when she noticed he had Lex's cell phone at his ear. Niko had called the Order soon after she'd gone out to the lodge to clean up. The news out of Boston was a mix of good and bad, along with an extra helping of seriously fucked up.

The good? One of the numbers on Lex's phone was, in fact, Edgar Fabien's. Using that bit of intel, Gideon had been able to hack into Fabien's records in the International Identification Database. Now the Order had the addresses for the Darkhaven leader's Montreal residence, his country house, as well as data on all his other property holdings, both business and personal. Gideon had access to Fabien's cell phone numbers, license plate tags, computer files, even the son of a bitch's electronic surveillance equipment at the Montreal Darkhaven.

And that's where the bad had come in.

Edgar Fabien wasn't home. Gideon's hacking had turned up a video feed from early last night showing a group of seven Breed males – one of them presumably Fabien – leaving the Darkhaven in the company of Enforcement Agency armed escorts. It had been hard to tell who Fabien's visitors were, as their tailored suits all looked alike and their faces had been completely obscured by dark hoods.

As for the seriously fucked up part, the group of vampires had left with a child in tow. A young girl who evidently hadn't gone along peacefully. Gideon's description of the petite blond female left no question whatsoever that it was Mira.

'You still with me?' Gideon asked on the other end of the line.

'Yeah, still here.'

'Lucan wants Fabien brought into Boston for questioning. That means we need him alive, my man.'

Niko exhaled a curse. 'First we have to find the bastard.'

'Yeah, well, I'm all over that. I ran GPS tracers on all of Fabien's cell phones. Got a lock on a location about an hour north of Yakut's place – one of the properties on record for Edgar Fabien. It's got to be him.'

'You're sure?'

'Sure enough that we've already sent backup your way. Tegan, Rio, Brock, and Kade are heading north to rendezvous with you as we speak.'

'Backup on the way?' Niko asked, eyeing a sliver of UV light that was peeking through the leaves of the shelter. The Order had protective daylight gear for emergency situations, but not even a late-generation vampire wearing head-to-toe anti-UV clothing would be able to withstand the kind of sunlight that would hit him in the driver's seat of a nearly seven-hour road trip. 'Jesus, you can't be serious. Who pulled the short straw for that mission?'

Gideon chuckled. 'Headstrong females, my man. In case you haven't noticed, we've been overrun with them as of late.'

'Yeah, I've noticed.' Niko couldn't help glancing over at Renata, who was checking some of the weapons they'd collected from Lex and the others. 'What's the situation, then?'

'Dylan is driving the guys up in the Rover with Elise riding shotgun. Their ETA in your area is close to nine o'clock, just after sundown. Since Fabien has a number of unknown associates with him, we're gonna need to get in and out of there gracefully, without unnecessary casualties.' Gideon paused. 'Listen, I know you're concerned about the kid. Her safety is important, no question, but this is big, Niko. If Fabien can lead us anywhere close to Dragos, we have to make sure we bag him tonight. That's mission number one, straight from Lucan.'

'Yeah,' Nikolai said. He knew the mission. He also knew that he could not let Renata down, or Mira for that matter. 'Shit . . . okay, Gideon. I hear you.'

'I'll call you if Fabien moves between now and sundown. Meantime, I'm working on a rendezvous point for you to meet up with the guys tonight to put an infiltration plan in motion. I should have something in an hour or two. Call you then.'

'Right. Later.'

Nikolai closed the phone and set it down beside him.

'Was Gideon able to get anything out of those phone numbers?' Renata asked, watching him carefully. 'Do we have any leads on Fabien's Darkhaven?'

Niko nodded. 'We've got his address—'

'Thank God,' she breathed. Relief gave way swiftly to determination, as fierce as he'd ever seen it in her. 'Where is he? Is his Darkhaven in the city proper, or on the outskirts somewhere? I can make a covert run over there right now to get the lay of the land. Hell, the way I'm feeling – no reverb, my shoulder on the mend – maybe I should walk straight up to his front door and hit him with a blast—'

'Renata.' Niko put his hand over hers and shook his head. 'Fabien's on the move. He's not in the city anymore.'

'Then where?'

He could have told her about the GPS signal Gideon was tracking. He could have told her that Fabien had Mira in his custody and that the girl was likely only an hour north of where they were sitting right now. But he also knew that if he told Renata that – if he gave her anything close to certainty on the whereabouts of the child who meant so much to her – there would be no stopping her from taking off on her own right now to find her.

Niko's pledge to the Order was his duty – his life-sworn honor – but Renata? This female was his heart. He couldn't jeopardize his brethren's mission any more than he could allow the woman he loved to walk headlong into danger without him there to see her through. Neanderthal thinking, maybe, especially given that Renata was one woman who knew how to handle herself in just about any situation. She was well trained and capable, definitely courageous, but damn it . . . she meant too much to him to take that kind of risk. Flat out, not an option.

'We're waiting for solid intel on where Fabien has gone,' he said, the lie bitter on his tongue, regardless of his good intentions. 'In the meantime, the Order is sending in reinforcements. We'll be meeting up with them tonight.'

Renata listened, clearly trusting him at his word. 'Does the Order have any idea whether Mira might be with Fabien wherever he is now?'

'We're working on it.' Nikolai found it difficult to hold her unblinking pale green gaze. 'When we find Fabien, we'll find Mira. She's going to be okay. I promised you that, remember?'

When he thought she might just nod her head or glance away, Renata instead reached out to cup his face in her palm. 'Thank you . . . for standing by me through all of this. I don't know how I will ever be able to repay you, Nikolai.'

He brought his hand up to hers and placed a tender kiss in her palm. He was going to say something glib, one of the usual empty quips he used so often whenever things around him got too real with emotion or too raw with honesty. He had his methods down pat: Deflect with humor. Disarm with nonchalance. Cut and run like hell at the first inkling of his own vulnerability.

But all those old, reliable weapons he'd honed to razor sharpness failed him now.

He stroked his thumb across the back of Renata's hand and let himself get lost in the verdant haven of her eyes.

'I'm not very good at this,' he murmured. 'I want to tell you something . . . shit, I'm gonna fuck it up probably, but I want you to know that I care about you. I do . . . a hell of a lot, Renata.'

She stared at him, going so still and silent he wasn't even sure she was breathing.

'I care,' he blurted out, frustrated at himself for fumbling through the words that he wanted to be perfect for her. 'I don't know how it happened, or what it will even mean to you – if anything – but I need to say it anyway, because this is real. It's real, and I've never felt this way before. Not about anyone.'

Her mouth softened into the smallest smile as he rambled clumsily, trying to find a way to tell her the depth of what was in his heart. Trying and failing miserably.

'What I'm trying to say is . . . ' He shook his head, feeling like a blithering ass, but Renata's soft touch on his face soothed him. Her clear gaze brought him back, front and center, grounding him. 'What I'm trying to tell you is, I'm falling for you . . . falling really hard. I wasn't looking for this to happen. I didn't think I'd ever truly want it, but . . . ah, Christ, Renata . . . when I look in your eyes, one word leaps into my mind every single time: *Forever.*'

She exhaled slowly and her little smile spread into beaming joy.

Niko ran his hands over her soft skin, into her damp hair. 'I'm in love with you, Renata. I know I'm not a poet – shit, not even close. I don't have all the fancy words I wish I could say to you . . . but I want you to know that what I'm feeling for you is real. I love you.'

She laughed softly. 'What makes you think I'd want poetry or fancy words? You just said exactly what I want to hear, Nikolai.' She slid her hand around to the back of his neck and pulled him toward her for a long, passionate kiss. 'I love you too,' she whispered against his mouth. 'I'm scared as hell to admit that, but it's true. I love you, Nikolai.'

He swept his lips over hers and held her close, wishing he didn't ever have to let go. But dusk would be coming before long, and there was still one thing he needed to do. 'You have to do something for me.'

Renata nestled against him. 'Anything.'

'I don't know what's going to happen tonight, but I need to know that you'll be going into this as strong as you can be. I want you to take some more of my blood.'

She rose out of his embrace and playfully arched a brow at him. 'Are you sure you're not just trying to get into my pants again?'

Niko chuckled, a jolt of heat arrowing right into his groin at the very idea. 'I wouldn't turn it down. But I'm serious . . . I want you to drink from me again now. Will you do that for me?'

'Yes. Of course.'

He smoothed a dark tendril from her forehead. 'There's one more thing, Renata. When we move in on Fabien tonight, it would kill me if anything . . . well, I just can't risk getting separated from you. I'm gonna need to know that you're all right at all times, or my focus is going to be for shit. I need to have a link to you. I know how you felt about Yakut using your blood as a tether on you, and I promise you that's not what I—'

'Yes, Nikolai,' she said, interrupting him with a gentle stroke of her fingers over his mouth. 'Yes . . . you can drink from me.'

His answering curse was low with relief. 'It's forever,' he reminded her firmly. 'You need to understand that. Like the blood bond you have to me now, if I drink from you, we can't ever undo it.'

'I do understand,' she said, no hesitation at all. She moved closer to him and kissed him, long and deep. 'I understand the bond would be forever . . . and I'm still saying yes.'

Niko groaned, fire lighting in his veins. His fangs stretched, and his sex rose to instant attention, all of him eager to claim Renata as his own. He kissed her, his heart slamming hard against his rib cage when she slipped her tongue past his lips to toy with the sharp points of his fangs.

'I want you naked for this,' he said, unable to curb the edge of command that was leaking into his voice. He was partly human, but there was another part of him – a wilder part – that knew less patience than he would like.

Niko watched with blazing amber eyes as Renata quickly obeyed him, stripping out of her clothes and lying back on the shaded grass floor of the shelter, thighs falling open, presenting herself to him without a speck of inhibition.

'Oh, yeah,' Niko growled. 'That's much better.'

He was rampant with need for her. Tearing off his own clothes and tossing them aside, he climbed up over her hips and straddled her. His cock thrust outward, kicking as she petted it with teasing, feather-light strokes. He held her smoldering gaze as he brought his wrist up to his mouth and bit into his flesh.

'Let me taste you again,' she said, rising up to meet his vein as he carried the bleeding punctures to her mouth. Crimson drops splashed down onto her breasts, so vivid against her creamy skin. She moaned, closing her eyes as she suckled him, savored him.

Niko watched her drink, watched her body begin to writhe with arousal. With his free hand, he caressed her, unable to resist running his fingers through the blood that had spilled on her. The sight of his blood marking her skin was as erotic as anything he'd ever seen. His touch ventured farther down, into the molten core of her that was so ready for him. Her thighs clamped around his wrist, holding him against her as the first orgasm rocketed through her.

Nikolai growled with pure male adoration as he fed his

female from his body and felt hers clamoring to have him. He let her drink for several long minutes, until her body was on fire beneath him again.

He too was on fire.

Gently he took his wrist from her mouth and sealed the punctures closed with a sweep of his tongue. Renata was still arching and writhing, still moaning for him, as he braced himself over her and plunged home. She cried out as he filled her, her fingernails scoring his shoulders in delicious pain.

Nikolai made love to her as slowly as he could – as slowly as his fevered body would permit him. She came again, clenching around him and wringing a furious release from him as well. It hardly slowed him down. He was still hard inside her, still hungry for this woman . . . his woman.

With a trembling hand, Nikolai smoothed the stray ebony locks from the side of Renata's beautiful throat. 'Are you sure?' he asked her, his voice hardly recognizable to himself, it was so raw and desperate. 'Renata . . . I want you to be certain.'

'Yes.' She arched up to greet his thrust, her steady gaze beseeching. 'Yes.'

With a feral snarl curling up from his throat, Nikolai bared his fangs and descended on her.

The sweet taste of Renata's blood surging into his mouth leveled him as totally as a roundhouse kick to the gut. Ah, Christ . . . now he knew. How many times had he busted the other warriors' asses about being mated and finding one female who would make them blind to any other? Easily hundreds of times. Thousands, probably.

What a clueless ass he'd been.

Now he knew. Renata owned him, even before he'd given himself to her with his bite. He was on his knees before this female, and he'd gladly stay there for the rest of his life.

Niko drank deeper, drowning in the pleasure of the bond they were forging through their mingled blood and through the heated rhythm of their joined bodies. His teeth still holding her beneath him as he took his last taste of her, Nikolai came again, harder this time, a staggering release that slammed into him like a freight train. He held on to her, shuddering with intense satisfaction. Although he could have sipped from her vein all night, Nikolai forced himself to move away, sealing her wounds with a loving sweep of his tongue.

He stared down at her, his gaze bright on her skin. 'I love you,' he rasped, needing her to hear it and to believe it. He wanted her to remember it later tonight, after they reached Fabien's location up north and Nikolai explained to her why he'd felt the need to lie to her today. He kissed her chin, her cheek, her brow. 'I love you, Renata.'

She smiled up at him drowsily. 'Mmm . . . I really like the sound of that.'

'Then I'll have to make sure you hear it a lot.'

'Okay,' she murmured, her fingers playing in the sweat-dampened hair at his nape. 'That was incredible, by the way. Is it always going to be that good?'

He groaned. 'I have a feeling it might only get better.'

She laughed, and the vibration made his sex rouse to life again. 'If you keep this up, I'm going to have to go back inside and take another shower.'

He gave her a meaningful grind of his pelvis, driving his erection deeper. 'Oh, I can keep it up. Don't worry, that's never going to be a problem when you're around.'

'You'd better be careful, or I might hold you to that.'

Niko chuckled despite his heavy mood. 'Sweetheart, you can hold me any way you like.'

He kissed her again, and growled with delight as she wrapped her legs around him and rolled him onto his back to begin a slow, torturous ride.

CHAPTER TWENTY-SEVEN

There had been a time in Andreas Reichen's almost three hundred years of walking this Earth when death had rained down upon him like a deluge. Once, when a senseless, brutal wave of slaughter had visited his otherwise peaceful domain.

Back then, in the humid summer of 1809, it had been a pack of Rogue vampires that had forced their way inside this very Darkhaven to rape and kill several of his kin. The attack had been a random thing, the mansion and its residents merely unfortunate enough to be standing in the path of the blood-addicted gang of Rogues. They'd battered their way past the unprotected doors and windows, feeding and killing too many innocents . . . yet there had been survivors. The Rogues had wreaked their terror and moved on like the pestilence they were, eventually being hunted and destroyed by a member of the Order who'd come to Reichen's aid.

The carnage back then had been unbearable, but it hadn't been complete.

What faced Reichen upon his return home this evening had been a calculated attack. Not a brute-force entry, but treachery. An enemy welcomed inside like a friend. And the slaughter that had occurred here this time – probably in the small hours of morning, just before the sun rose – had been a total annihilation.

No one had been spared.

Not even the youngest souls in the residence.

With an awful silence permeating the air like a disease, Reichen walked through the blood and destruction as one of the dead himself. His footsteps tracked sticky scarlet stains across the marble of the vestibule and foyer, past his young nephew, who'd been so pleased to name Reichen godparent to his infant son just weeks ago. The ginger-haired new father sprawled by the door had been the first to die, Reichen guessed, unable to look at the lifeless face that stared unseeing to the bullet-riddled staircase leading to the Darkhaven's sleeping quarters on the upper floors.

More death waited in the hallway outside the library, where another male had been cut down in midstep. Still more lives extinguished near the stairwell to the cellar, one of Reichen's cousins and his Breedmate, both of them dead while trying to escape the gunfire.

He didn't see the body of the boy until he almost stumbled over it – a tow-haired vampire child who'd evidently attempted to hide in one of the cabinets of the sideboard in the dining room. His assailants had dragged him out and shot him like a dog on the antique Persian rug.

'Good Christ,' Reichen choked, sagging to his knees and lifting the boy's limp hand to his mouth to stifle his hoarse cry. 'For the love of God . . . why? Why them and not me!'

'He said you would know why.'

Reichen closed his eyes at the wooden sound of Helene's voice. She spoke too slowly, the syllables too flat . . . toneless.

Heartless.

He didn't need to turn around to face her to know that her eyes would seem oddly dull to him now. Dull because all of her warmth – all of her humanity – had been recently bled out of her.

She was no longer his lover, nor his friend. She was Minion.

'Who turned you?' he asked, letting go of the dead boy's hand. 'Who do you belong to now?'

'You should know, Andreas. You sent me to him, after all.'

Son of a bitch.

Reichen's jaw clenched, molars nearly cracking from the pressure. 'Wilhelm Roth. He sent you here to do this to me. He used you to destroy me.'

That Helene said nothing only made the realization cut all the deeper. As wrenching as it would be to look into his former lover's eyes and see a soulless shell of the woman he'd cared for, Reichen had to see for himself.

He stood up and slowly turned around. 'Oh, Christ. Helene . . .'

Dried blood splattered her face and clothing – almost every square inch of her, covered in the blood of his dearest friends and relatives. She must have been right there in the center of the entire slaughter, an unfeeling, unaffected witness to it all.

She said nothing as she stared at him, her head cocked a bit to the side. Her once-bright and clever eyes were now as vacant and cold as a shark's. Down at her side, she held a large butcher knife from the kitchen in her hand. The wide blade glittered in the lamplight of the dining room's crystal chandelier.

'I'm sorry,' he murmured, his heart twisted in a vise. 'I didn't know . . . When you e-mailed and left me the message with Roth's name, I tried to warn you. I tried to reach you . . .'

He let the words trail off, knowing that explanations didn't matter. Not now.

'Helene, just know that I am sorry.' He swallowed the bile that rose in the back of his throat. 'Just know that I truly did care for you. I loved y—'

With a banshee shriek, the Minion lunged for him.

Reichen felt the sharp edge of the blade cut across his chest and arm, a deep, punishing slice. Ignoring the pain, ignoring the sudden inhaled scent of his own blood, he grabbed the flailing arm of Roth's mind slave and wrenched it behind her. She screamed, bucking and fighting as he brought his left arm down and locked both of her limbs tight at her sides. She cursed and shouted, calling him vile names, spitting in fury.

'Shh,' Reichen whispered beside her ear. 'Shh now . . . be quiet.'

Like a feral animal, Helene kept squirming, kept shrieking for him to let her loose.

No, he corrected himself. *Not Helene.* This was no longer the woman he knew. She was gone, lost to him the moment she brought Wilhelm Roth's death squad into this Darkhaven. In truth, for so many reasons, she was never his to claim. But God help her, she hadn't deserved this end. None of the fallen here deserved such horror.

'It's all right now,' he murmured, bringing his right hand up to stroke her cold, bloodstained cheek. 'It's all over now, darling.'

A scream tore out of her throat as she yanked her face out of his grasp. 'Bastard! Let me go!'

'Yes,' he said. He wrested the butcher knife from her grasp. 'It is finished now. I'm going to let you go.'

With sorrow choking him, Reichen turned the handle around in his fingers and held the point to her breast.

'Forgive me, Helene . . .'

Holding her tight against him, he plunged the blade deep into her chest. She made no sound as she died, just exhaled a long, slow sigh as she deflated in his arms and hung there, limp as a rag doll. As gently as he could, Reichen eased her body to the floor. The knife dropped out of his hand and fell beside her, coated with the bright crimson of their mingled blood.

Reichen took one long, unflinching look at the wreckage that had been his home. Now that it was over, he wanted to memorize every bloodstain, every life that had been cut short because of his inattention. His failure. He needed to remember, because in a short while none of this would exist.

He couldn't let any of it remain, not like this.

Nor would he would let these deaths go unmet.

Reichen pivoted and strode away from the carnage. His boots echoed hollowly on the wood floor in the hall, his steps the only sound in what had become a grisly mass tomb. By the time he reached the front lawn of the estate, his chest was no longer tight but cold.

As cold as stone.

As cold as the vengeance he intended to visit on Wilhelm Roth and all those associated with him.

Reichen paused outside on the moonlit grass. He faced the mansion and, for a moment, simply watched it in its perfect, eerie quietude. Then he whispered a prayer, old words that felt rusty on his tongue for their neglect.

Not that prayers would do him any good now. He was forsaken, now more than ever. Truly alone.

Reichen dipped his head to his chest, summoning his terrible talent. It swelled within him, a heat that swiftly intensified, balling into a molten, churning orb in his gut.

He let it grow. He let it turn and gain strength until his insides felt seared by its fury.

And still he held it back.

He kept it inside him until the fireball banged against his rib cage, smoke and cinder drifting up to burn the back of his throat. Until the fireball consumed him, illuminating his entire body with a white-hot glow. He staggered on his heels, fighting to keep it building until he knew it would wreak total, instant destruction.

Finally, with a grief-filled roar, Reichen turned loose the power within him.

Heat shot out of his body, tumbling and spinning as it sped

forward, a sphere of pure explosive energy. Like a missile deployed on a laser-sighted target, the orb rocketed into the open door of the Darkhaven mansion. A second later, it detonated, a thing of awesome, hellish beauty.

Reichen was knocked back with the sonic blast of the explosion.

He lay in the grass, watching with detached satisfaction as the flames and sparks and smoke devoured even the tiniest pieces of what had been his life.

≼ CHAPTER TWENTY-EIGHT ≽

'W'e're loaded up and ready to roll, Renata. Do you need more time before we head out?'

Standing in the gravel drive in front of the lodge, Renata turned as Nikolai approached her from behind. 'No. I don't need any more time here. I'm ready to leave this place.'

He wrapped his arms around her, cocooning her in his strength. 'I just talked with Gideon. Tegan, Rio, and the others are making good progress. They should be at our rendezvous point within the hour.'

'Okay. Good.'

Renata leaned into his embrace, glad for his sheltering warmth . . . and his love. Nikolai had kept her near him in their vine haven until the sun had set, soothing her fears with his body, transporting her away from the ugly reality of what had originally brought them together – and what might lay in wait for them tonight, when they finally had the opportunity to confront Edgar Fabien.

The truth was, she was worried about what they might find. Bone-deep worried, and even though Nikolai hadn't said anything to suggest that he had his doubts too, she could tell that his mind was heavy with thoughts he seemed determined to hide from her.

'You can tell me, you know.' She drew out of his arms and faced him. 'If you have a bad feeling about tonight . . . you can tell me.'

Something flickered across his expression, but he didn't speak it. He shook his head. Placed a chaste kiss to her brow. 'I don't know what we might be walking into with Fabien. But I can tell you that no matter what, I'm going to be right there with you, okay? We're gonna get through this.'

'And once we have Fabien, we're going to go get Mira,' she said, searching his eyes. 'Right?'

'Yeah,' he said, his unflinching, steely gaze holding her steady. 'Yes, I promise. I gave you my word on that. I'm not going to let you down.'

He brought her to him once more, catching her in a grasp that seemed unwilling to let go. Renata held him too, listening to the strong, rhythmic pound of his heartbeat beneath her ear . . . and wondering why her own pulse seemed to be clanging a warning in her veins like a death knell.

In a remote hundred-acre parcel of no-man's land a couple hours north of Montreal, the woodland evening shuddered with the buzzsaw whine of an outboard motor speeding a boat across a mostly uninhabited lake. The land and lake, like the transportation provided for Dragos to reach this place, belonged to Edgar Fabien.

Although Fabien had been a disappointment recently, Dragos supposed the Darkhaven leader deserved some measure of credit for the two-prong approach to this important gathering. While the rest of the attendees arrived last night by car, this evening a speedboat had been dispatched to carry Dragos to the site's small dock out back, after a seaplane had brought him from the city to another inland body of water also on Fabien's property. Following the setback suffered a few weeks ago during Dragos's run-in with the Order, he had become far more cautious about how he traveled in the open, among other things. He'd come too far to take chances. Risked too damned much to throw it away on carelessness or the incompetence of others.

He cast a contemptuous eye toward the other passenger seated in the boat with him. The Hunter's face was impassive in the milky glow of the moon overhead, his huge body held perfectly still as the driver turned the wheel and the cigarette boat's prow cut through the water to angle toward the lone dock up ahead on the shore.

The Hunter probably knew that he was heading toward his own death. He'd failed in his mission to kill the Gen One in Montreal, and that called for steep punishment. He would be dealt with tonight, and if Dragos could use that punishment as an additional display of his power before the lieutenants who were gathered to greet him now, so much the better.

The boat's engine downshifted as they came up on the unlit, unassuming wooden dock where Edgar Fabien waited to greet them. Gas fumes rolled up off the water, nauseatingly sweet. Fabien's deep bow and fawning welcome had a similar effect.

'Sire, it is the honor of a lifetime to welcome you to my domain.'

'Indeed,' Dragos drawled as he stepped off the craft onto the dark wood planks of the dock. He gestured for the Hunter to follow him, and did not miss Fabien's reaction when he glimpsed the size and immensity of the Gen One serving at Dragos's command. 'Is everyone assembled inside?'

'Yes, sire.' Fabien came out of his bow and rushed to walk at Dragos's side. 'I have good news. The warrior who escaped containment has been eliminated. Both he and the female who aided him. One of my Minions rooted the pair out, and last night I sent a team of my best agents to clean up the problem.'

'You're certain the warrior is dead?'

Fabien's smug smile grated. 'I would stake my own life on it. I sent trained professionals to the task. I trust their skill implicitly.'

Dragos grunted, unimpressed. 'What a comfort it must be to know that kind of trust in your subordinates.'

Fabien's confidence faltered at the jab, and he cleared his throat awkwardly. 'Sire . . . another moment, if you would.'

Dragos dismissed the Hunter from his presence with a curt wave. 'Go up to the house and wait for me. Speak to no one.'

As the Gen One killer strode ahead, Dragos paused to turn an impatient look on Fabien.

'My lord, I'd hoped – that is, I thought a gift might be in order,' he stammered. 'To celebrate this important event.'

'A gift?' Before he could ask what Fabien thought Dragos could possibly need from him, Fabien snapped his fingers and an Enforcement Agent emerged from the shadows of the surrounding trees, guiding a young child in front of him. The girl seemed lost in the dark, her blond hair glowing like cornsilk, her tiny face dipped down. 'What is the meaning of this?'

'A young Breedmate, sire. My gift to you.'

Dragos stared at the waif, on the whole unimpressed. Breedmates were a rare enough occurrence among human populations, that much was true, but he preferred his stock to be of fertile, childbearing age. This girl would not be ripe for several more years, which no doubt was what intrigued Fabien the most about her.

'You can keep her,' Dragos said, resuming his trek toward the gathering. 'Have your man drive the boat back across the lake while we're meeting. I will radio him when he is needed again.'

'Go,' Fabien ordered in response, then he was right back at Dragos's side, as eager as a hound begging for scraps. 'Sire, about the child . . . really, you must see for yourself. She is gifted with an extraordinary talent that I am certain you will appreciate. She is an oracle, my lord. I've witnessed it for myself.'

Against his will, curiosity pricked to attention. His steps slowed, then stopped. 'Bring her.'

When he pivoted around, Fabien's eager grin spread even wider. 'Yes, sire.'

The child was ushered to him once more, her footsteps resisting, stubborn heels digging into the old pine needles and sand that littered the small slope up from the dock. She tried to fight off the vampire guard who held her, but it was useless effort. He simply shoved her forward until she was standing directly in front of Dragos. She kept her chin wrenched down, her eyes cast to the ground at her feet.

'Lift your head,' Fabien commanded her, hardly waiting for her to comply before he took her skull in both his hands and forced her to look up. 'Now, open your eyes. Do it!'

Dragos didn't know quite what to expect. He wasn't at all prepared for the startling paleness of her gaze. The girl's irises were as clear as glass – flawless mirrors that instantly mesmerized him. He was vaguely aware of Fabien's hissed excitement, but all of Dragos's attention was rooted on the child and the incredible glimmer of her eyes.

And then he saw it . . . a flicker of movement in the placid reflection. He saw a form moving through thick shadows – a body he thought he recognized as his own. The image became clearer the longer he stared, rapt and eager to see more of the gift Fabien had described.

It *was* him.

It was his lair as well. Even veiled in dark mist, the images reflecting back at him were intimately familiar. He saw the subterranean laboratory, the holding cells . . . the UV light cage that contained his greatest weapon in the war he'd been preparing for all these many centuries. It was all there, shown to him through this Breedmate child's eyes.

But then, a moment of stunning alarm.

His pristine lab, so rigidly secured and orderly, was in ruins.

The holding cells had been thrown open. And the UV light cage . . . it was empty.

'Impossible,' he murmured, struck with a grim, furious awe.

He blinked hard, several times, wanting to dislodge the vision from his head. When he opened his eyes again, he saw something new in the child's damnable eyes . . . something even more unfathomable.

He saw himself, begging for his life. Weeping, broken.

Pitiful.

Defeated.

'Is this some kind of fucking joke?' His voice shook – both with anger and with something too weak for him to acknowledge. He tore his gaze away from the girl and fixed it on Fabien. 'What the hell is the meaning of this?'

'Your future, sire.' Fabien's face had gone quite pale. His mouth worked for a moment without sound, then he finally sputtered, 'The child . . . you see, she is an oracle. She showed me standing here, at this very gathering, presenting you with a vision of your future that pleased you immensely. When I saw that, I knew I had to save her for you, my lord. I had to offer her to you, no matter what it cost.'

Dragos's blood was lava scorching his veins. He should kill the idiot here and now, just because of this insult. 'You obviously misread what you saw.'

'No!' Fabien cried, grabbing hold of the girl and wheeling her around. He gave her a hard shake. 'Show me again! Prove to him that I am not mistaken, damn you!'

Dragos watched as still as stone while Fabien peered into her eyes. The Darkhaven leader's horrified gasp told him all he needed to know. He reeled back, as white as a sheet. As stricken as if he'd just witnessed his own murder.

'I don't understand,' Fabien muttered. 'It's all changed. You have to believe me, sire! I don't know how she's changed the vision, but the little witch is lying now. She has to be!'

'Get her out of my sight,' Dragos growled to the Enforcement Agency guard who held her. 'I'll take her with me when I leave, but until then, I don't want to see hide nor hair of her.'

The guard gave a nod and removed the child, practically dragging her up to the house.

'Sire, I beg you,' Fabien pleaded. 'Forgive me for this . . . unfortunate mistake.'

'I will deal with you later,' Dragos said, not bothering to couch the threat that rode undercurrent of his words.

He resumed his progress toward the gathering, more determined than ever to make his authority – his unmatched power – understood to all.

≼ CHAPTER TWENTY-NINE ≽

It was fully dark when Niko and Renata arrived at the coordinates Gideon had supplied for Edgar Fabien's property up north. The Darkhaven leader evidently owned a sizable chunk of wooded land, far enough out of Montreal that the surrounding area remained widely undeveloped: acre after acre of huge conifers and evergreens, not a living soul in sight except for the occasional deer or moose that bolted at the first scent of the heavily armed vampire creeping through their unspoiled sanctuary.

Nikolai had been running solo reconaissance on the area for the past few minutes. A two-story house made of logs and stone was tucked into a thick corner of the forest. A narrow, unpaved drive, barely wide enough for one vehicle, cut a meandering path through the trees to the front of the house. Niko skirted that driveway from the cover of the woods, taking note of the two SWAT-garbed Enforcement Agents posted near the halfway mark and the three large black Humvees parked in single-file formation just outside the front door of the place. Three more vampire guards, M16 rifles at the ready, covered the entrance. The east and west sides were each also under watch by an armed sentry.

Although he didn't figure they'd leave the back of the place vulnerable to infiltration, Niko moved around that way to get the lay of the land. He heard the soft lap of water even before he saw the quiet lake and the empty dock at the shore some

three hundred yards behind the hous[e]
place another Enforcement Agency duo

Damn it.

Getting into the site to nab Fabien wasn't
Unless he and the Order dropped in from
wanted to pull Dragos's associate out of ther
going to have to mow down a few Agency gu[a] [i]n the
process. And that wasn't even factoring in the unknown group
of Breed males who had accompanied the Montreal
Darkhaven leader here last night. Yanking Fabien tonight
without a lot of civilian casualties might be verging on the
impossible. Double that estimate when the problem of
rescuing Mira was added to the mix. So, basically the net
of his recon was that shit was likely to get very messy in
here, no two ways about it.

And then there was the situation with Renata.

One of the hardest things Nikolai had ever done was spend
the entire day with her, knowing that he had deceived her.
He wanted to tell her – after they'd made love, after she'd
honored him with the gift of her blood and the completed
bond that now joined them eternally. He'd wanted to tell her
a dozen times over, in a dozen different moments, but selfishly,
he held the truth back from her for her own protection. He
still held on to the hope that she would understand his caution
– that she might even be grateful that he made her wait to
learn of Mira's location until he and the other warriors had
a chance to iron out a solid evac strategy.

Yeah, he was going to keep telling himself that, because he
didn't want to consider any other alternatives.

Shaking off the regret that dogged his steps and the dread
that kept threatening to crawl up the back of his neck, Nikolai
moved to a better vantage point in the cover of the woods. He
peered through the brushy pine branches, watching several of
the house's occupants as they passed a window on the ground

He took a quick headcount of the hooded Breed males as they strode as a group toward another area of the place. Five, six, seven . . . and then another, this one without the black head covering.

Oh, Christ.

Nikolai knew him. He'd seen the son of a bitch up close and personal only a few weeks prior, when a mission for the Order had sent Niko to meet with one of the highest-ranking officials in the Enforcement Agency. At the time, the male was going by a long-standing alias – one of two false names the Order had uncovered not long afterward. Now they knew the bastard by his true name, the one his traitorous Gen One father before him had carried as well.

Dragos.

Holy . . . shit.

For weeks the Order had been searching exhaustively for even the most minute lead on Dragos, all without success. Now here he was, plunked down right in front of them like a fish in a barrel. Motherfucker was here. And goddamn it, he was going down – *tonight.*

Niko eased back into the thicket, then hauled ass in a southerly direction, where he'd left Renata with their purloined Agency SUV. He couldn't wait to call Tegan and Rio and give them this good news.

Edgar Fabien's confusion and distress over the debacle of his botched gift for Dragos haunted him like a wraith as he and the others followed their newly arrived leader into the conference room of the northern retreat. He knew it was dangerous, generally deadly, to displease Dragos, something he'd avoided very well until recently. But he also knew – as he assumed the rest of the Breed males gathered here for this meeting did – that Dragos had brought them all together tonight for a specific purpose. This was to be a historic night. A reward, Dragos had promised, for their years of covert partnership and loyalty toward a common goal.

After so much time and effort spent currying Dragos's favor these past decades, Fabien only prayed he hadn't thrown it away in that one unfortunate instant down near the dock.

'Be seated,' Dragos instructed them as they filed in and he took his place at the front of the meeting room. He watched as Fabien and the six others, all still concealed behind their black hoods, filled the chairs that were gathered around the slab of polished granite that served as the conference table. 'Each of us assembled here in this room shares a common interest – that being the current and future state of our race.'

Fabien nodded in agreement beneath his hood, as did several others at the table.

'We share a common resentment for the corruption of our bloodlines by the stain of humanity and for the craven way those in power within the Breed have chosen to govern us with regard to the inferior mankind. Since the first seeds of the race were sown on this planet, vampirekind has degenerated into a fat, complacent disgrace. With each new generation born, our bloodlines grow more and more diluted with humanity. Our leaders prefer us to skulk in hiding from the *Homo sapiens* world, all of them fearful of being found out, and masking that cowardice with laws and policies put in place supposedly to protect the secret of our very existence. We have been weakened by fear and secrecy. It is high time that changed, and a new, powerful leadership is required.'

Now the nods became more vigorous, the murmured agreements more fervent.

Dragos began a leisurely pace at the front of the room, his hands clasped loosely at his back. 'Not everyone shares our desire to reverse the past failings and restore the Breed to a position of power. Not everyone sees the future that we do.

Some would say the price is too steep, the risks too great. A thousand excuses for why the Breed should maintain its status quo and not take the bold steps required to seize the kind of future to which we are entitled.'

'Hear, hear,' Fabien interjected, greed for that future licking at him like a flame.

'I am pleased that those of you in this room understand the fact that bold steps must be taken,' Dragos said. 'Each of you individually has played a part in advancing our vision to its next level. And you have done it all without question, without knowledge of one another . . . until now. Our own time of secrecy is over. Please,' he said, 'remove your hoods, and let us begin the newest phase of our alliance.'

Fabien reached up for the black cloth that covered his head, uncertainty making his fingers hesitate. He paused until a couple of the other attendees had pulled their hoods off before he found the courage to remove his own.

For a moment, none of the Breed males said a word. Glances passed around the table, some smug with recognition of known peers, others wary of the strangers who had now, with this admission of willful treason, become their most intimate allies. Fabien knew several of the half dozen faces who stared back at him – all of them high-ranking Darkhaven or Enforcement Agency officials, some from the United States and others from abroad.

'We are a council of eight,' Dragos announced. 'Just like the Ancients who arrived here so long ago. We are, all of us, second-generation sons to those powerful otherworlders. Soon, once the last Gen One vampire is eliminated, we will be among the eldest and most powerful of our race. Each of you has helped with that effort, either by providing the locations of the remaining members of our first generation or by supplying the cause with Breedmates to carry the seeds of our revolution.'

'What about the Order?' asked one of the European atten-dees, his German accent sharp as a razor blade. 'There are two Gen One warriors we've yet to contend with.'

'And we will,' Dragos said smoothly. 'I will be planning direct assaults on the Order very soon. After their recent strike against me, it will be my personal pleasure to bury their oper-ation and see the warriors – and their mates – meet their demise.'

An Enforcement Agency director from the West Coast of the United States leaned back in his chair and arched his dark brows. 'Lucan and his warriors have survived other attacks before. The Order has been in existence since the Middle Ages. They won't go down without a fight – a very hard, bloody one.'

Dragos chuckled. 'Oh, they will bleed. And if I have my way, they'll beg for mercy and be given none. Not from the powerful army I'll have at my command.'

'When will we begin building this army?' someone else in the group asked.

Dragos's smile went broad with malice. 'We began fifty years ago. In truth, this revolution began even longer ago than that. Much longer.'

All eyes were trained on him as he strode over to a laptop computer he'd instructed Fabien to have ready in the room. As he typed a command on the keyboard, the conference room's large flat-panel monitor rose up from the floor. Dragos entered more instructions and soon that dark monitor blinked on, displaying what appeared to be a research laboratory.

'A satellite link to one of my strongholds,' he explained, using the touchpad to remote-control the camera on the other end of the connection. 'It is here that I've been putting the pieces in place.' The camera's eye roamed toward a wall of coded, cryogenic drums, then past a fleet of microscopes, computers, and DNA storage beakers lined up on rows of tables. In the midst of all this scientific equipment were several Minions dressed in masks and white lab coats.

'It looks like a genetics lab,' said the German.

'So it is,' Dragos replied.

'What kind of experiments are you conducting?'

'All kinds.' Dragos went back to the keyboard and typed in another string of commands. The laboratory camera went dark, only to be replaced with another view, this one a panoramic angle of a long corridor lined with prison cells. Although from the camera's position it was difficult to make out anything but the most rudimentary shapes, it was obvious that the cells contained women, some of them heavy with child.

'Breedmates,' Fabien breathed. 'There must be twenty or more of them in there.'

'They don't always survive the procedures and testing, so the numbers tend to fluctuate,' Dragos said in a conversational tone. 'But we have had our successes with the breeding process. These females and the ones who went before them are giving birth to the greatest army this world will ever know. An army of Gen One killers who are at my complete command.'

A hush as thick as a winter cloak fell over the gathering.

'Gen One?' asked the director from the West Coast. 'That can't be possible. You would need one of the Ancients in order to produce a first-generation Breed vampire. All of those other-worlders were exterminated by the Order some seven hundred years ago. Lucan himself declared war on all of the Ancients and saw to it that none survived.'

'Did he?' Dragos grinned, baring just the tips of his fangs. 'I think . . . not.'

With a few more keystrokes, he brought up still another camera view on the satellite connection. This time the focus homed in on a large, heavily secured room, which had in its center a cylindrical cell constructed of light beams. The ultraviolet rays emitting from that cage of tight vertical bars was nearly blinding, even onscreen.

And contained inside that UV cell crouched a hairless, naked creature who would stand likely seven feet tall. His nude body was immense, every inch of him covered in *dermaglyphs*. He looked up as the camera lens zoomed in on him from somewhere across the room. Amber eyes, pupils all but devoured by the fire blazing out of the sockets, narrowed with lethal awareness. The creature came out of its crouch and lunged to attack, only to be thrown back by the searing heat of the UV bars that held it prisoner. It opened its mouth and let out a furious roar that didn't need to be heard in order to be understood.

'My God,' more than one of the attendees gasped.

Dragos turned a deadly sober look on the group. 'Behold . . . our revolution.'

Lex's cell phone vibrated on the center console of the SUV. Renata picked it up and glanced at the digital display: *Unknown Caller*.

Shit.

She couldn't be sure if the call was actually for Lex or if it was for Nikolai, since he'd been using the phone to call back and forth with the Order. She didn't know how long he'd be out running reconnaissance, and she was about to lose her mind cooling her heels waiting for him. She needed to be doing something. At least feeling that they would be making some good progress toward finding Mira soon . . .

The cell phone kept buzzing in her hand. She hit the *Talk* button but didn't say anything. Just opened the line and let the caller reveal himself first.

'Hello? Niko – you there, amigo?' The deep voice rolled with a Spanish-tinged accent, as warm and smooth as caramel. 'It's Rio, my man—'

'He's not here,' Renata said. 'We're in position at the site north of the city, waiting for you guys to arrive. Nikolai's out on recon. He shouldn't be long.'

'Good,' said the warrior. 'We're almost there, ETA about forty-five minutes on the outside. You must be Renata.'

'Yes.'

'Gotta thank you for saving our boy's ass up there. What you did was . . . well, he's lucky to have you working on his side. We all are.' She could hear the genuine concern and gratitude in the vampire's voice, and she found herself very curious to meet the other warriors whom Nikolai called friends. 'Everything okay on that end? How about you? You doing all right, hanging in there?'

'I'm good. Just anxious to get this done tonight.'

'Understood,' Rio replied. 'Niko told us about the little girl – Mira. I'm sorry for what you've gone through, knowing that a sick individual like Fabien is holding her. I know it couldn't have been easy for you waiting around all day to rendezvous with us either.'

'No, it hasn't been. I just feel so helpless,' she confessed. 'I hate the feeling.'

'I am sorry about that. We're not going to let anything happen to her tonight when we go in there, Renata. I'm sure Nikolai explained to you that getting our hands on Edgar Fabien is critical to the Order, but we're going to do our best so that the child comes out of this situation just fine—'

A sudden chill permeated her chest as Rio's words sank in. 'What did you say?'

'She's going to be fine.'

'No . . . that you wouldn't let anything happen to her tonight . . . in there . . . '

On the other end of the line, a long beat of silence ticked by. '*Ah, Cristo.* Niko didn't tell you about the video feed we have from Fabien's Darkhaven last night?'

The chill in her got colder now, ice spreading from her chest to her limbs. 'A video feed . . . from last night,' she replied numbly. 'What was on it? Did you see Mira? Oh, God. Has Fabien done something with her? Tell me.'

'Madre de Dios,' he said on a long exhale. 'If Niko did not . . . I'm not sure it's my place to tell you now—'

'Tell me, goddamn it.'

She heard a rumble of rapid conversation in the background before Rio finally relented. 'The child is with Fabien and several others we haven't yet identified. We picked up the intel from a security surveillance feed at Fabien's Darkhaven. They left last night and we tracked them to the property where you are now.'

'Last night,' Renata murmured. 'Fabien's been holding Mira here . . . *since last night*. And what about Nikolai . . . Are you telling me that he knew this? When did he hear about this? When!'

'I have to ask you to just hang in there for a little while longer,' Rio said. 'Everything's going to be all right . . . '

Renata knew the warrior was still talking, still issuing reassurances to her, but his voice faded away from her consciousness as bone-deep anger and fear – a hurt so profound she thought it might shred her into pieces – engulfed her. She closed the phone, cutting off the call and dropping the device onto the floor at her feet.

Mira was here since last night, with Fabien.

All this time.

And Nikolai knew that.

He knew it, and he kept it from her. She could have been here hours ago – in the daylight hours – doing something, anything, to see Mira to safety. Instead, Nikolai had deliberately withheld the truth from her, and, as a result, she had done nothing.

Not totally nothing, she admitted, stricken with guilt for the pleasure she'd enjoyed with him while Mira was only about an hour out of her reach.

'Oh, God,' she whispered, feeling sick at the thought.

She was vaguely aware of footsteps approaching the vehicle, her senses lighting up before her mind could process the sound. The blood bond she now shared with Nikolai told her it was him well before his dark form appeared at the window. He opened the SUV door and climbed inside like hell was on his heels.

'It's Dragos,' he said, searching the console, dashboard, and seat for the cell phone. 'Holy shit, I don't fucking believe it, but it was him. I just saw the son of a bitch inside the house with Fabien and the others. Dragos is here – right in our grasp. Where the hell is that phone?'

Renata stared at him, seeing a stranger as he leaned forward and reached for the cell phone where it lay near her feet on the floor of the vehicle. She hardly heard what he was saying. Hardly cared now.

'You lied to me.'

He came back up, Lex's phone gripped in his hand. The adrenaline crackle that had been lighting his eyes dimmed a bit when he met her gaze. 'What?'

'I trusted you. You told me I could trust you – that I could count on you – and I did. I believed you, and you betrayed me.' She swallowed past the terrible lump in her throat and forced herself to spit the words out. 'Mira is here. She's been here with Fabien since last night. You knew that . . . *you kept it from me.*'

He went quiet, but he didn't even attempt to deny what she was saying. He looked at the phone in his hand as if he just now realized how it was that she had discovered his deception.

'I could have been here, Nikolai. Hours ago, I could have been here, doing something to get Mira out of that monster's hands!'

'Which is exactly why I didn't tell you,' he said gently.

She scoffed, heartbroken. *'You betrayed me.'*

'I did it to protect you. Because I love—'

'No,' she said, shaking her head to keep from being played for a fool again. 'No. Don't say that to me. How can you say that when you used those very words to keep me distracted – to make me believe that you actually cared about me while you and your buddies in the Order made plans of your own around me?'

'It's not like that at all. Nothing that happened between us today – nothing I said to you – had anything to do with the Order. Today was about you and me . . . it was about us.'

'Bullshit!' He reached for her and she drew back, out of his grasp. She opened the door and got out of the SUV. He was out of the vehicle and around to her side, blocking her with his body, all of it happening so fast she couldn't even begin to track his movements. 'Get away from me, Nikolai.'

'Where are you going?' he asked gently.

'I can't sit here any longer and do nothing.' She took a step around him but he was right there again. The gentleness in him was fading fast, replaced by a firmness that said he would keep her there in shackles if he thought he needed to.

'I can't let you do this, Renata.'

'That's not your choice to make,' she fired back, trembling with fear and outrage. 'Damn it, that was never your choice to make for me!'

He growled a curse and lunged for her.

Renata hardly knew what she had done until he froze in midstep, clutching the sides of his head in his hands. He hissed, his eyes throwing off amber sparks as he pinned her in a shocked, furious gaze. 'Renata. Do not—'

She blasted him again, all of her fear for Mira and her pain at his betrayal pouring out of her in a punishing stream of mental heat. Nikolai crashed down onto his knees, groaning and writhing from the jolt of pain she'd unleashed on him.

Renata bolted away from him, into the forest, before she allowed herself to be deterred by the regret already swelling up in her.

⇥ CHAPTER THIRTY ⇤

The house was under heavily armed, guarded watch on all sides. Impossible to breach without being noticed by at least one of the Enforcement Agents staked out like the vampire equivalent of an antiterrorist SWAT team. Every one of them carried a shoot-first-ask-questions-later attitude, from their dark-visored black helmets and combat gear, to the bone-shredding automatic rifles they held at the ready.

Thanks to the agents who'd raided Jack's place the other night, Renata and Nikolai had come away with transportation, uniforms, and weapons. She didn't think she would be lucky enough to fake her way into the building, but on first glance, garbed as they were, the agents on watch might think her one of their own.

She put on the helmet she'd taken with her from the SUV and dropped the tinted visor. Adopting as much of a soldier's swagger as she could manage, Renata stepped out of the woods and approached the vampire guarding the west side of the house.

The agent spotted her immediately. 'Henri? What the fuck are you doing out there?'

Renata shrugged, lifted her good arm in a *hell if I know* gesture. She couldn't risk speaking to him – no more than she could risk using her gun to mow this obstacle down. If she let off a bunch of rounds, she would have the whole security detail on her ass. No, she had to keep her cool and just continue walking toward him with the hope that he wouldn't open fire out of raised suspicion alone.

'What's the matter with you, idiot?'

Renata shrugged again. Getting closer.

Her fingers itched to let her blades fly – he made an easy target standing as still as a stump – but the slightest whiff of spilled blood would call every vampire in the vicinity to attention. Renata knew she had to get close enough to reach him with her mind. Her only option was to hit him with a swift, solid blast.

'You fucking ingrate, Henri, get back to your post,' the agent growled. He reached for a small communication device clipped to his belt. 'I'm calling Fabien to report you. If you want to piss him off, go ahead, but I don't want any part of—'

Using all the power at her command, Renata unleashed a savage bolt of energy from her mind and sent it crashing into the vampire standing before her. His words choked off with a grunt and he went down like a stone. She kept blasting him until he was silent. When she was certain he was dead, she bent down and liberated him of both his weapon and his comm device.

Renata opened the side entrance door a bare sliver and did a quick glance of the area just inside. It was clear. She slipped inside, heart hammering in her chest, breath steaming against the closed visor of her helmet.

For all her fury at Nikolai for not telling her that Mira was here with Fabien, now she knew only gratitude that the Order had visual proof of the child's location. It was too late to second-guess how she'd left things with Nikolai. Too late to worry that maybe she should have waited for him and his brothers-in-arms to be there to back her up. Part of her knew that she'd been unfair, but she'd gone too far to take it back.

She'd made an impulsive, emotional decision based on

wounded feelings. It was a decision that might cost her the friendship she had with Nikolai – maybe even his love – but as much as she regretted that already, she couldn't undo it now. Nikolai might never forgive her for jeopardizing his mission; she would understand if he couldn't.

Now she could only pray that Mira didn't end up paying the price.

Niko roused to the nagging buzz of a cell phone going off next to his head. He was on the ground next to the vehicle. No idea how long he'd been there. The cell phone vibrated again, jiggling in the grass and old leaves that littered the forest floor. It took nearly all his effort to move his hand up to grab the damned thing. Clumsily he flipped it open. Tried to say something, but only managed a dry croak.

'Yeah,' he said once more, forcing his limbs to drag himself up off the ground into a seated slump against the front wheel of the SUV.

'Niko?' Rio's voice came through the receiver, heavy with concern. 'You sound like shit, amigo. Talk to me. What's going on?'

'Renata,' he said, holding his banging head in his hands. 'Pissed off . . .'

Rio cursed. 'Yeah, I gathered that. My fault, man. I didn't realize she wasn't clued in about the girl being moved last night—'

'She's gone,' Niko said. When he thought of that, all his senses started coming back online like a switch on a backup generator had been thrown inside him. 'Ah, fuck, Rio . . . I pissed her off and now she's gone in after Mira on her own.'

'Madre de Dios.'

On the other end of the line, he heard Rio give Tegan and the others a quick rundown of the situation. 'That's not the worst, my man,' Nikolai added, ignoring the shooting pain in his head as he got up from the ground and made a staggering run for the back of the SUV. 'This gathering of Fabien's? It's bigger than we realized . . . Dragos is up here too.'

'Are you sure about that?'

'I saw the bastard with my own eyes. He's here.' Nikolai was grabbing automatic weapons out of the back as fast as his sluggish arms could move. He draped his body with the rifles, stuffed a pistol in the back of his stolen Enforcement Agency uniform and another one in an ankle holster. 'The house is surrounded by guards, so when you get here, come in on foot and split up.'

'Niko, what are you doing?'

He didn't reply to that; didn't think his old friend was going to like his answer. Instead, he pulled extra magazines and clips from the vehicle and loaded up with as much ammo as he could carry. 'You've got two men at the halfway point on the drive and three at the front of the place. Take them out first and you'll have the cleanest way in.'

'Nikolai.' Rio's voice was low with warning. 'Amigo, whatever you're thinking right now . . . don't.'

'She's in there, Rio. Inside with Dragos and Fabien, and God knows who else . . . and she's alone. I'm going in after her.'

Rio bit out something nasty in Spanish. 'Stay put. We're not even ten minutes away from you and we're hauling ass, my man.'

Niko closed up the back of the SUV. 'I'm gonna rig some kind of perimeter diversion—'

'Goddamn it, Nikolai, if this female wants to kill herself, it's not your problem. We'll help her however we can, but—'

'She's my mate, Rio.' Nikolai blew out a ripe curse. 'We're blood-bonded . . . and I love her. I love her more than life itself.'

The warrior's answering sigh sounded heavy with understanding, and defeat. 'I suppose there's no point in telling you that you're defying Lucan's direct orders if you go in there right now. If Dragos is on site, that makes this shit even more critical and you know it. We need you to stay put and wait for backup.'

'Can't do that,' Nikolai replied.

He closed the phone and tossed it into the open driver's-side window. Then he headed out to go find his woman.

⊰ CHAPTER THIRTY-ONE ⊱

Dragos permitted himself to revel in the awe of his under-lings as they gaped at the Ancient trapped in its UV prison cell onscreen. From the wonder on their faces – the rapt incredulity – one would think he'd managed to catch lightning in a bottle. In truth, what he had achieved these past long decades was something even greater than that.

The seven Breed males gathered with him in the room now looked upon him like a god, and rightfully so. He was the architect of a revolution that would turn the entire planet on its head. Tonight they were witnessing history, and the start of a future he had personally designed.

'How can this be?' someone murmured. 'If that truly is one of the Ancients who fathered our race, how did he survive the war with the Order?'

Dragos smiled as he walked closer to the screen. 'My father was an original member of the Order . . . but he was, first and foremost, this creature's son. During the bloodshed perpetrated by the Order when Lucan declared war on the Ancients, my father and his alien sire made a pact. In exchange for shared power in the future, my father would hide him away until the hysteria died down. Unfortunately, after making good on his promise, my father did not survive the war. But the Ancient did, as you can see.'

'So, you intend to carry on your father's agreement with that . . . thing?' Fabien asked, his expression drooping like a lapdog who'd just lost his bone to a feral wolf.

'The Ancient is entirely under my control. He is a tool that I make use of whenever and however it suits me and our cause.'

'How so?' asked another of the group.

'Allow me to show you.' Dragos strolled to the door of the conference room. He snapped his fingers at the Hunter who waited outside, then pivoted back to his associates as the big Gen One obediently followed in on his heels. 'Take off your shirt,' he ordered the Hunter.

The huge male complied in silence, baring massive shoulders and a hairless chest covered in a dense, tangled network of *glyphs*. More than one head snapped back to the monitor to compare those hereditary skin markings to the creature contained inside the UV cell.

'They bear similar *dermaglyphs*,' Fabien gasped. 'This male is the Ancient's kin?'

'A Gen One son, bred for the sole purpose of serving the cause,' Dragos said. 'All of the Hunters in my personal army are the strongest, most lethal weapons in the world. They have been specially raised and trained at my direction. They are flawless killers, and they are unfailingly loyal to me.'

'How can you be certain of that?' asked the Darkhaven leader from Hamburg, a shrewd male who would no doubt appreciate the realtime demonstration that Dragos had in mind.

'You notice this Hunter wears a collar. It is a GPS monitoring device, only this collar is also equipped with an ultraviolet laser. Every Hunter wears one, from the time he can walk. I can track his every move, locate him in an instant. And if he displeases me in any way,' Dragos said, casting a meaningful look at the Hunter standing so rigidly stoic beside him, 'all it takes is one simple remote-controlled command and the laser activates, sending a UV light as thin as a razor around the Hunter's neck, severing the head.'

One or two males at the table exchanged uncomfortable looks.

It was the German who spoke up first, his gaze glittering with interest. 'What should happen if the collar is tampered with, or removed?'

Dragos grinned, not at the German, but at the Hunter himself. 'Let's find out, shall we?'

Although her every instinct screamed at her to creep in like a thief on the prowl, Renata strode through the west corridor of her enemies' lair as if she had every right to be there. She heard the low rumble of male conversation coming from one of the large rooms out back. Elsewhere in the house, there was nothing but quiet, until . . .

A child's soft sobs, drifting toward her from a stairwell leading to the second floor.

Mira.

Renata flew up the steps and followed the cries to the end of the hallway. A bedroom door had been locked from outside. She ran her hand along the top of the frame but didn't find a key.

'Damn it,' she whispered, drawing one of her blades from the twin sheaths at her sides.

She wedged the point between the door and jamb just above the lock and gave it a hard lever. The wood cracked, loosening just a bit. Twice more and finally she had enough room to jimmy the thing free. With shaking, eager hands, Renata opened the door.

Mira was in there, thank God.

Her veil was gone, and as soon as she looked up and saw the black-clad figure coming into the room, she scuttled into the corner in absolute terror.

'Mira, it's me,' Renata said, flipping open her dark visor. 'It's okay now, kiddo. I'm here to take you home.'

'Rennie!'

Kneeling down, Renata held out her arms. With a hitching little cry, Mira flew into her embrace.

'Oh, mouse,' Renata whispered, pressing relieved kisses to the top of her blond head. 'I've been so worried about you. I'm sorry I didn't come sooner. Are you all right, sweetheart?'

Mira nodded, her small arms wrapped tightly around Renata's neck. 'I was worried about you too, Rennie. I was afraid I'd never see you again.'

'Me too, kiddo. Me too.' She hated to let go, but they still had to get out of there before Fabien and his cronies caught up to them. Renata stood, lifting Mira up into her arms. 'We have to run now. Hold on to me, okay?'

Renata hadn't even taken two steps with the child before the rapid blasts of automatic gunfire erupted from all directions somewhere outside the house.

Dragos was eager to demonstrate the technological beauty of the Hunter's UV collar when all hell broke loose outside the gathering. He shot a killing look at Edgar Fabien as the group leapt out of their seats in stunned alarm.

'What's going on out there?' he demanded of their host. 'Is this another of your fuckups?'

Fabien's narrow face took on an unhealthy shade of pale. 'I-I don't know, sire. Whatever it is, I'm sure my agents will handle—'

'Fuck your agents!' Dragos roared. He scrabbled for the radio and barked an order for the driver to bring the boat around, then got right up into the face of the Hunter. 'Outside, now. Handle this. Kill anyone in your path.'

The Hunter – his highly trained, flawlessly obedient soldier – just stood there, as immovable as a pillar of stone.

'Get out there. I command you!'

'No.'

'What?' Dragos could not believe his ears. He felt the gazes of his underlings root on him. He could taste their disbelief, their doubt. A silence bloomed, ripe with measured expectation. 'I issued you a direct order, Hunter. Do it, or I will terminate you right here and now.'

With more gunfire ringing just outside the walls of the house, the Hunter had the audacity to look Dragos square in the eye and shake his head. 'Either way, I am dead. If you want me to fight so you can live, disable my collar.'

'How dare you even so much as suggest—'

'You waste time,' he said, apparently unfazed by the chaos rising all around them. 'Release me from this shackle, you arrogant son of a bitch.'

Just then, one of Fabien's feeble watchmen came rushing to the open doorway. 'Sir, we've got incoming shots arriving from the entire perimeter. We can't be sure yet, but there must be a damned army closing in on us from the woods.'

'Oh, Jesus,' Fabien gasped. 'Oh, sweet Christ! We're all going to die!'

Dragos snarled in fury, not confident in the slightest that Fabien's guards could find their own asses, let alone provide adequate cover for the group of high-ranking Breed males who were currently looking to Dragos as their leader to help them make their escape. Waiting for him to call the shots that would either spare them or take them and their budding revolution down in one fell swoop.

'We're finished here,' he growled. 'Everyone out the back door, to the boat. Follow me.'

As the group began to fall in around him, Dragos cast a glower from over his shoulder at the Hunter. Neither male said a word – mutual hatred easy enough to read in their gazes – as Dragos reached into his pocket and retrieved he device that controlled the Hunter's collar and typed in the code that would disable it.

The instant the collar clicked into neutral, the Hunter reached up and tore it off his neck. Then, with a look that was part disbelief, part cold determination, he strode out the door and toward the heart of the disruption outside.

⇥ CHAPTER THIRTY-TWO ⇥

Nikolai smiled to himself as his diversion tactic created sudden mass confusion all over the place. The agents on watch were tearing around in utter panic, more than one taking a hit from the gunfire blasting in from all directions of the forest. Niko summoned a vine from the tangle of branches above his head in the forest and bade the snaking tendril to wrap itself around the trigger of his last absconded M16.

As the vine did its thing as the previous ones had, holding the rifle aloft and applying more and more pressure to the trigger as the coiling green runner grew thicker and more strong, Niko ran for the side entrance of the house.

It wasn't hard to find Renata. Their blood bond was a beacon for him, leading him through the back of the place to an upward flight of stairs. Renata was just coming down them, Mira held tight in her arms. She met his gaze and, for an endless instant, neither of them said a word. Nikolai wanted to tell her how sorry he was. How relieved he was that she had found the child unharmed.

He had a thousand things he wanted to say to Renata in that moment, not the least of which being that he loved her and that he always would.

'Hurry,' he heard himself murmur. 'You need to get out of here now.'

'The gunfire is everywhere,' Renata said, worry etching her features. 'What's going on?'

'Just a diversion. I had to create a window of opportunity to get both of you out of here.'

She looked relieved, but only for a second. 'Fabien and the others . . . I heard men leaving out the back way a couple minutes ago.'

'I'm on it,' Niko said. 'Now go. Don't stop for anything. Take Mira back to the vehicle. The Order should be rolling in any minute.'

'Nikolai.' He paused, holding Renata's steady gaze, hoping to hear forgiveness if not an affirmation that she might still love him after everything that had occurred. She held his gaze, a crease forming between her brows. 'Just . . . be careful.'

He gave her a grim nod, feeling none of his usual high from the adrenaline rush of awaiting combat. Those days seemed ages behind him, back when nothing much mattered to him except the glory of battle and the triumph of winning, however meaningless the contest.

Now everything mattered – especially where Renata was concerned. Her safety and happiness were all that mattered, even if it meant he might not be in the pic-ture.

'Take Mira back to the vehicle,' he told her again. 'Keep your head down and keep yourself safe. We're gonna get you both out of here.'

He waited until Renata ran out, then he bolted for the back door of the house where his enemies had fled.

The speedboat was just pulling up to the dock out back as Dragos and the others hurried down the slope to meet it. From all around them in the forest and up near the house, Fabien's Enforcement Agents scrambled like ants that had just gotten their hill stomped. Gunfire lit up the night, so haphazard it was impossible to tell which rounds came from the frien-dlies and which from the apparent intruders.

All Dragos knew was that he was not sticking around to let the Order or anyone else take him down.

As he and his group began to pile onto the boat, Dragos put himself in the way of Edgar Fabien.

'There's no room on board for you,' he told the Montreal Darkhaven leader. 'You've jeopardized enough with your idiocy. You stay here.'

'But . . . sire, I – please, I can assure you that I will not disappoint you again.'

Dragos smiled, baring the tips of his fangs. 'No, you won't.'

With that, he raised a 9mm pistol and fired a killing shot right between Fabien's beady eyes.

'Away!' he ordered the boat's driver, Edgar Fabien dismissed from his mind completely as the motor roared and the sleek watercraft sped out to the waiting seaplane at the far end of the lake.

He was too fucking late.

Niko took out a couple of agents on his way down to the lake, but by the time he got there, the speedboat making a bat-out-of-hell exit was little more than churning wake on the water. Nikolai fired a few shots after them, but he was only wasting rounds. Edgar Fabien's corpse lay on the wooden dock. Dragos and the others were more than halfway across the lake now.

'Goddamn it.'

Fury and determination powering him, Nikolai started running along the shore, calling on the preternatural speed that all of his kind possessed when they needed it. The boat was fast, but the water was landlocked. At some point Dragos and his cronies would have to disembark and pick up another means of escape. With any luck, he could catch up to them before they totally got away.

He didn't know how far he'd run – easily a mile – when all of a sudden his chest went cold with dread.

Renata.

Something was wrong. Terribly wrong. He could feel her emotion course through him as if it were his own. She, his brave, unflappable Renata, was right now scared to death.

Ah, Christ.

If anything happened to her . . .

No. He couldn't even think it.

All thoughts of Dragos pushed aside, Nikolai wheeled around and kicked his feet into high gear, praying like hell he could reach her in time.

She hadn't seen the huge vampire coming at all.

One minute she was tearing through the dark woods with Mira held fast in her arms, and the next she found herself staring into the unforgiving face and merciless golden eyes of an immense Breed male whose naked torso, shoulders, and arms were camouflaged by a thick pattern of *dermaglyphs.*

He was Gen One; Renata knew it instinctively. Her instincts also told her that this male was more lethal than most, stone cold.

A killer.

Terror rose up on her like a black tide. She knew that if she blasted him, she'd better be certain she could kill him swiftly, or else she and Mira both would be dead in that same instant. She didn't dare attempt it when Mira might be made to suffer if she failed.

Mother Mary, to have come this far – to finally have Mira ensconced in her arms, mere steps away from freedom . . .

'Please,' Renata murmured, desperate to appeal to even his slightest inkling of mercy. 'Not the child. Let her go . . . please.'

His silence was unnerving. Mira tried to lift her head from Renata's shoulder, but Renata gently eased her back down, not wishing her to be frightened by the messenger of death who'd no doubt been dispatched by Edgar Fabien or Dragos himself.

'I'm going to set her down now,' Renata told him, not even sure he comprehended, let alone would comply. 'Just . . . let her go. I'm the one you want, not her. Just me.'

The hawklike golden eyes followed her every movement as Renata carefully extricated Mira from her grasp and slowly placed the girl's feet on the ground. Renata put herself between the killer and the child, praying her death would be enough to satisfy him and his evil master.

'Rennie, what's going on?' Mira asked from behind her legs, her small hands gripping the pantlegs of Renata's Enforcement Agency fatigues as she peered around her. 'Who is that man?'

The vampire let his stony gaze travel down to the source of that tiny voice. He stared. His shaved head cocked slowly to the side. Then he scowled.

'You,' he said, in a voice so deep it rumbled all the way down to Renata's marrow. Something dark passed across his face. 'Let me see her.'

'No,' Renata pleaded, holding Mira behind her and blocking him from her like a shield. 'She's just a child. She's done nothing against you or anyone else. She's innocent.'

He hit Renata with a look so fierce it nearly knocked her back on her heels. 'Let. Me. See. Her. Eyes.'

Before she could refuse again, before she could think of some way to grab Mira up and flee as fast and as far as they could get, Renata felt Mira take a step out from behind her.

'Mira, no—'

Too late to stop what was going to occur, Renata could only stare in dread as Mira walked right out and looked up, way up, into the hard gaze of the deadly Gen One vampire.

'You,' he said again, peering hard into Mira's sweet face.

Renata could tell the moment he began to witness Mira's gift. His golden eyes went stormy, and he stared, rapt, as the child showed him events certain to come to pass. He stepped closer – too close, when his massive arms could lash out and break Mira without a hint of warning.

'Do not—' she blurted, but he was already reaching for Mira.

'It's okay, Rennie,' Mira whispered, standing before him as innocent as a babe who'd wandered into the lion's den.

And that was when Renata realized something extraordinary was about to happen.

'You saved me,' he whispered, his huge hands dwarfing Mira's tiny shoulders. The vampire sank down to his knees, bringing himself to her level. When he spoke, that deep, deadly voice was quiet with awe and confusion. 'You saved my life. I saw it, just now in your eyes. I saw it that night too . . .'

⇥ CHAPTER THIRTY-THREE ⇤

Nikolai's heart froze in his chest, a stricken, fear-filled lump of ice. With gunfire still erupting in the area, he had made it back through the woods, all the way to the place where his bonded blood had told him he'd find his terrified mate.

Renata was there. She stood in the moonlit darkness of the forest, as still as a statue and looking on as an immense Gen One vampire crouched before Mira, holding the child in his punishing hands.

Jesus Christ.

Niko moved in on soundless feet, creeping in closer and trying to find a position that he could shoot from that wouldn't put either Renata or the girl in the crossfire.

Blast him away, Renata.

Take him the fuck down and get the hell out of there.

She didn't open her mind's power on him. She didn't so much as twitch a finger toward any of her weapons, psychic or otherwise. No, to his horror, she didn't even move. She just stood there, in the center of what could very quickly turn into a hellish storm of bloodshed and violence.

Niko's own fear in that moment was fathomless. All he knew was the terror shredding him from within, his bones chilled, a desperation so savage and complete it set his heart banging like a drum in his chest.

He drew twin 9mm pistols from their holsters at his sides

and stalked forward. Although he was moving at a pace only one of the Breed could manage, Renata glanced up. She felt him there, stirring the very air around her, even if her eyes couldn't quite register his speed. Her blood told her that he was near, just as his would always find her.

He was too consumed with rage to fully notice that she was looking up at him in alarm – alarm directed more at him than the enemy vampire who faced her.

Nikolai charged forward as a flash of movement, totally prepared to kill. He drew to a halt just behind the big Gen One, both barrels held up tight against the *glyphs* that tracked up the back of the vampire's shaved skull.

Everything happened in a blink of time, but it played out in maddening slow-motion frames in Nikolai's consciousness.

He cocked the nines, his fingers on the triggers.

Renata's eyes went wide. She shook her head. 'Niko . . . wait . . . don't!'

The Gen One let go of Mira, letting his big hands fall down at his sides. He didn't even react to the guns trained on his head. His chest expanded as he took in a long breath, then let it out on a resigned sigh.

He wasn't going to fight his death.

He didn't care if he died.

And then Mira was screaming, her child's voice pitched high with fear. 'No! Don't hurt him!'

Nikolai watched in stunned disbelief – in total amazement – as Mira lunged forward and threw her arms around the Gen One's broad shoulders.

'Please, don't hurt him!' she cried, staring up at Niko pleadingly as she attempted to protect the hulking vampire with her tiny body.

'Nikolai.' Renata caught his gaze as he looked up, disbelieving, two large pistols still cocked and ready, leveled at the Gen

One's head. 'Nikolai . . . please, it's okay. Just wait a second.'

He frowned in question, but his warrior stance relaxed somewhat. 'Get up,' he ordered the vampire. 'Stand up, and get away from the child.'

The Gen One complied without comment, slowly unfastening Mira's arms from around his neck and setting her away from him as he rose to his feet.

Niko moved around to face him, weapons still held on him as he guided both Renata and Mira to stand behind him. 'Who the hell are you?'

Sober, expressionless eyes stared at the ground. 'I am called Hunter.'

'You're not Enforcement Agency,' Nikolai said cautiously.

'No. I am a Hunter.'

Renata brought Mira close, holding her as the chaos of the ongoing disruption in the woods and at the house slowly died down around them. 'His eyes, Nikolai,' she said, understanding now. 'He is the golden-eyed assassin who tried to kill Sergei Yakut that night. He's the one Mira witnessed at the lodge.'

Nikolai's expression darkened. 'Is this true? You are a hired killer?'

'I was.' The Hunter gave a grim nod and finally lifted his gaze. 'The child saved me. Something . . . changed in me after I saw the vision in her eyes that night. I saw her saving my life, precisely as it happened a moment ago.'

In that next instant, the surrounding forest came alive with armed men moving in on them from all directions. Nikolai had his weapons at the ready, but he made no move to fire on the newcoming threat. Renata's pulse spiked in panic. 'Oh, shit. Niko—'

'It's all right.' He calmed her with a reassuring look and a few gentle words. 'These are the good guys, my friends from the Order.'

She watched in relief as four of Nikolai's fellow warriors

stepped into the area. All of them were formidable in size and attitude, a cadre of muscle and might that seemed to suck all of the air out of the woods by their presence alone.

'How you doing, amigo? Everything okay here?' asked the smooth caramel voice Renata now recognized as belonging to Rio.

Nikolai nodded, his eyes and weapons still trained on the Gen One in their midst. 'I've got this under control, but the situation at the house is all fucked up. Edgar Fabien is dead, and Dragos and the others slipped out the back. They went by boat to the other side of the lake. I tried to track them, but . . .' He glanced at Renata. 'I had to make sure everything was okay on this end first.'

'We heard a small-engine aircraft buzzing overhead as we arrived,' Rio said.

'Shit,' Nikolai hissed. 'That'll be them, no doubt. They're gone. Goddamn it, Dragos was right here and we lost the bastard.'

'Let me help you find him.'

All eyes turned to the vampire still held in Nikolai's crosshairs.

'Why should we trust you?' Nikolai asked, his gaze narrowing. 'Why would you be willing to help us get Dragos?'

'Because he is the one who created me.' There was no warmth in the golden hue of the Gen One assassin's eyes as he responded to the question, only cold hatred. 'He made me what I am. Me, and all the other Hunters bred to kill for him.'

'Oh, my God,' Renata breathed. 'You mean there are more of you?'

The shaved head nodded soberly. 'I don't know how many, or where they are all located, but Dragos told me himself that I am not the only one of my kind. There are others.'

'Why should we believe you?' asked another of the warriors,

this one almost as dark as the night around them, his teeth and fangs gleaming like pearls against his brown skin.

Another warrior stepped in then, his eyes quick and shrewd, as cunning as a wolf's under the ebony spikes of his cropped hair. 'Let Tegan tell us if we can trust him.'

Renata watched in astonishment and not a little dread as the largest of the group – a warrior who'd held back from the rest like a ghost stalking the shadows – took a few steps forward. Immense, with tawny hair peeking out from under the black knit skullcap he wore, he was a broad, towering slab of muscle and dark energy. Easily as big as the Gen One who stood before him, waiting his judgment.

Saying nothing, the warrior called Tegan held out his large hand. The Hunter took it, his eyes as steady as his grasp.

After a long moment, Tegan gave a vague nod. 'He comes with us. Let's secure this site and get the hell out of here.'

Renata felt a heavy weight lift from her as the tension of the moment gave way to a new purpose. The group split up, most of the warriors heading off to take care of things at Fabien's place while Rio and Nikolai walked Renata, Mira, and their unexpected companion back to the Order's waiting vehicle.

Partway there, Nikolai caught Renata's hand in his. 'We'll catch up to you, Rio.'

The warrior nodded. As they moved on, Renata watched in awestruck wonder as Mira slipped her tiny hand into the larger palm of the Hunter.

'My God,' she said to Nikolai. 'What just happened?'

He shook his head, clearly just as much amazed as she was. 'Gonna take me some time to figure it out, I think. But first I want to figure things out between us.'

'Nikolai, I'm sorry—'

He silenced her with a long, sweet kiss, pulling her into his warm arms. 'I screwed up, Renata. I was so afraid of losing you that I drove you away from me with a stupid, reckless lie. I never would have forgiven myself if anything happened to you, or to Mira. You're my heart, Renata. You are my life.' He stroked her cheek, his gaze engulfing her, drinking her in. 'I love you so much . . . I don't want to live a single moment without you at my side.'

She closed her eyes, overwhelmed with emotion. 'I've never wanted anything more,' she whispered, her throat constricted with joy. 'I love you too, Nikolai. But you have to understand, I'm a package deal. Mira's not my child by blood, but she is the child of my heart. I love her like she is my own.'

'I know,' he said soberly. 'You've proven that in spades.'

Renata glanced up at him, unable to contain the hope that was battering around in her breast. 'Do you think you can find room in your life – in your heart – for both of us?'

'What makes you think I haven't done that already?' He kissed her again, tenderly this time. When he looked into her eyes, his own gaze was so filled with love it swept her breath away. 'Let's get out of here now. I want to take my girls home.'

❄ CHAPTER THIRTY-FOUR ❄

BOSTON. THREE NIGHTS LATER.

The Order's compound seemed vastly different to Nikolai as he walked the corridor that led from the tech lab where he'd been meeting with the other warriors. The mission to thwart Dragos had taken a significant hit a few nights ago, but they'd also come away with a very unexpected advantage in their quest to locate him and shut down his operation.

Unfortunately, while Hunter was shaping up to be a valuable asset, the Order had also lost a crucial ally and trusted friend: Andreas Reichen had fallen off the grid completely, and the word out of Berlin was the worst kind of news. No one knew if the German Darkhaven leader had survived the attack on his residence. Based on the reported slaughter of all his kin and the blaze that consumed the entire property, the Order held out little hope for their friend.

Personally, Nikolai thought it would be a small mercy if Reichen had perished in the raid. He didn't know how such a deep loss could ever be overcome. Certainly no man, Breed or otherwise, would be strong enough to walk away unscathed from such a brutal blow to the soul. As a warrior, Nikolai understood combat casualties. Every warrior walked into battle knowing that he or his brethren might not return to base.

But to lose one's family . . .

He didn't even want to consider what that would do to a

man. Instead Nikolai focused on the blessings he had – one of which could be heard speaking softly as he neared the open doorway of his private quarters.

Renata was inside, seated on the sofa in the living room, reading to Mira.

For a moment, as Niko reached the entrance, he leaned against the jamb simply to listen and to feast his eyes on the beautiful woman who was now his mate. He loved that Renata was as comfortable curled up with a book as she was holding a weapon. She had a softness he admired, an intelligence that continually challenged him, and an inner strength that made him strive to be a male worthy of her devotion.

It didn't hurt that she was also hotter than hell, especially when she was staring down the barrel of a big 9mm or training with her beloved blades. Kade and Brock had been almost permanent fixtures in the weapons room the past few days, if only for the chance to spar with Renata or watch her in action. Nikolai could hardly blame them. But if he was tempted to feel the slightest nip of jealousy, all it took was a sly glance from his woman to put him at ease. She loved him, and for that Nikolai counted himself the luckiest damned male on the planet.

'Hi,' she said now, glancing over as she turned the last page of a chapter and paused to greet him.

'Hi, Niko,' Mira chimed in from under the fall of her short veil. 'You just missed a really good part in the story.'

'I did? Maybe I can talk Renata into reading it to me later,' he said, slanting a heated look at his mate as he stepped into the room. He walked over to the sofa and hunkered down in front of Mira. 'I have something for you.'

'Really?' Her tiny face brightened with a smile. 'What is it?'

'Something I asked Gideon to get for you. Take off your veil and I'll show you.'

He didn't miss Renata's protective look as Mira tore the black fabric away from her face. 'What's this about?'

'It's okay,' he said, taking a small plastic case out of the pocket of his jeans. 'You can trust me. You both can trust me.'

Renata relaxed at the reminder, and watched as Nikolai unscrewed the cap from a contact lens container. 'These are special lenses that Gideon thinks will help with your eyes. How would you like it if you never had to wear that veil again?'

Mira nodded enthusiastically. 'Let me see them, Niko!'

'What kind of lenses are they?' Renata asked, cautiously hopeful.

'Opaque irises to shield the mirroring effect of Mira's own eyes. She'll be able to see through them, but no one looking at her will notice anything unusual about her eyes. Her irises will be covered, in the same way the veil covered them. I thought these would be better.'

Renata nodded, smiling warmly at him. 'Much better. Thank you.'

'Can I try them on?' Mira asked, eagerly peering at the small case in Niko's hand. 'Look, Rennie, they're purple!'

'That's your favorite color,' she said, turning a questioning look on Nikolai.

He'd brought himself up to speed on a lot the past few days, taking on a role he never imagined himself in, let alone imagining it would fit so comfortably on him. He was a blood-bonded male with a Breedmate who loved him and a young child to bring up as their own. And he relished the idea of both.

He, the maverick, the reckless one, had a family of his own now. It was mind-boggling to him, not to mention to the rest of the compound. It was the last thing he ever dreamed he'd wanted or needed, and now, just a few days into it, he couldn't picture life any other way.

His heart had never felt so full.

'Let me help you with those,' Renata said, taking the lenses from him and carefully assisting Mira into them. When they were in place for a few long seconds and the child's talent didn't stir, Renata caught a small laugh in her hand. 'Oh, my God. It worked, Nikolai. Just look at her. The lenses work beautifully.'

He glanced into the wide violet pools of Mira's altered eyes and saw . . . nothing. Only the happy, carefree gaze of a child.

Renata threw her arms around him and kissed him. Mira was right behind her, and Niko caught them both in a heart-felt embrace.

'There's more,' he said, hoping they would enjoy the rest of his surprise. He stood up and took each of them by the hand. 'Come with me.'

He led them up the corridor to the elevator that climbed from the subterranean headquarters to the large mansion that sat topside. He could feel Renata's apprehension in her loose grasp and in the spike of adrenaline that edged into her blood-stream.

'Don't worry,' he whispered against her ear. 'You'll enjoy this, I promise.'

At least, he hoped she would. He'd been working on it for the past day and a half, trying to get everything just right. He guided Renata and Mira into the heart of the estate, toward the candlelit warmth of the formal dining room. The aromas of baked bread and roasted meat drifted out to greet them. Niko himself had no appreciation for human food, but the Breedmates living at the compound certainly did, and judging from the looks he was getting from the two females walking along at his side, they did too.

Renata's astonishment shone in her eyes. 'You cooked dinner?'

'Hell, no. Believe me, I'm the last person you'd want in charge of your meals. I pulled some favors from Savannah,

Gabrielle, and the other women. Your stomach is in very good hands.'

'But I was just with all of them earlier today and no one said anything about this.'

'I wanted to surprise you. They wanted to surprise you, too.'

She didn't say anything more, and he couldn't help noticing that Renata's steps had slowed the closer they got to the dining room. Mira, however, was crackling with excitement. As soon as they reached the arched entryway, she broke away from Niko's loose hold and ran into the gathering, chattering a mile a minute as though she'd lived there all her life.

But not Renata.

She was silent, unmoving. She took one look inside at the table full of dishes and fine porcelain settings and drew in a shallow breath. She said nothing as she looked at the faces of the warriors and their Breedmates, every gaze lifted in welcome as she and Nikolai stood at the door.

'Oh, God,' she finally whispered, her voice broken and raw.

Niko followed her as she backed away, turning into the hallway like she wanted to bolt.

Damn it. He'd been so sure she would enjoy a nice dinner with everyone, but obviously he'd been wrong.

When she spoke to him, her voice was choked with emotion. 'Everyone's waiting in there . . . for us?'

'Don't worry about it,' he said, drawing her into his arms. 'I wanted to do something special for you, and I screwed it up. I'm sorry. You don't have to do this—'

'Nikolai.' She looked up at him, her eyes glittering with tears. 'I've never seen anything lovelier than that table in there, with everyone gathered around it.'

He frowned, baffled now. 'Then what's wrong?'

She shook her head, swallowed a strangled laugh. 'Nothing's wrong. That's just it. Nothing is wrong at all. I'm just so happy.

You have made me so completely happy. I'm afraid to hold on to this feeling. I've never known what it was like, and I'm scared to death that it's only a dream.'

'Not a dream,' he said gently, caressing the stray tear from her cheek. 'And you can hold on to me if you feel afraid. I'm going to be here beside you as long as you'll have me.'

'Forever,' she said, beaming up at him.

Nikolai nodded. 'Yes, love. Forever.'

Renata's elated laugh bubbled out of her. She kissed him hard, then nestled up against his side and walked with him under the shelter of his arm, back to join the others. Back to join the rest of their family.

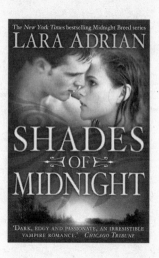

The *New York Times* bestselling Midnight Breed series

LARA ADRIAN

SHADES
OF
MIDNIGHT

'DARK, EDGY AND PASSIONATE, AN IRRESISTIBLE
VAMPIRE ROMANCE.' *CHICAGO TRIBUNE*

A mission to Alaska to investigate a string of savage vampire
attacks sends Breed warrior Kade to the frozen land of his birth,
where he encounters a sexy female bush pilot whose own quest
for answers forces him to confront his darkest secrets, and an
even greater evil that could destroy all he holds dear . . .

Robinson
978-1-84901-282-9
£6.99

www.constablerobinson.com

To order any of the **Lara Adrian** titles simply contact The Book Service (TBS) by phone, email or by post.

Alternatively visit our website at www.constablerobinson.com.

No. of copies	Title	RRP	Total
	Kiss of Midnight	£7.99	
	Kiss of Crimson	£7.99	
	Midnight Awakening	£7.99	
	Midnight Rising	£7.99	
	Veil of Midnight	£7.99	
	Ashes of Midnight	£7.99	
	Shades of Midnight	£7.99	
		Grand total	

FREEPOST RLUL-SJGC-SGKJ, Cash Sales Direct Mail Dept., The Book Service, Colchester Road, Frating, Colchester, CO7 7DW

Tel: +44 (0) 1206 255 800
Fax: +44 (0) 1206 255 930
Email: sales@tbs-ltd.co.uk

UK customers: please allow £1.00 p&p for the first book, plus 50p for the second, and an additional 30p for each book thereafter, up to a maximum charge of £3.00.

Overseas customers (incl. Ireland): please allow £2.00 p&p for the first book, plus £1.00 for the second, plus 50p for each additional book.

NAME (block letters): _____

ADDRESS: _____

_____

_____ POSTCODE: _____

I enclose a cheque/PO (payable to 'TBS Direct') for the amount of £ _

I wish to pay by Switch/Credit Card

Card number: _____

Expiry date: _____ Switch issue number: _____